GRIF'S TOY

Tease and Denial Book One

JOSEPH LANCE TONLET

CREDITS

Edited by Nicole - http://www.angeledits.com
Edited by Lee Jay Stura
Cover Art by Reece Notley
Cover Art by Preston Hultz - http://www.prestonhultz.com

(rev 08.16.16)

ISBN: 0692319689
ISBN-13: 978 0692319680

DEDICATION

To all those extremely twisted, moderately twisted, and perhaps only slightly twisted folks out there with an itch, I hope you find someone who will not only scratch it for you, but who will also love you even more deeply because of it.

Peace,
JLT

CONTENTS

ACKNOWLEDGMENTS

Preston Hultz: PJ is one of my oldest and closest friends. He not only serves as a continual source of encouragement, but also as one of my front-line-editors. He's also an amazing graphic designer. Need a flyer for your organization or group? A print ad? A photo retouched? He's your man. His website and portfolio are here:
http://www.prestonhultz.com

Ann Wright: A dear friend who previews my books and offers invaluable feedback. Thanks for both your friendship and your support!

Donald Gates: Donny was my writing inspiration. It was in his prompting and infections 'can-do' attitude that I finally found the courage to put pen to paper!

JLT's Awesome Beta Team
I honestly couldn't do it without y'all. You have my most sincere gratitude!
The team has gone through numerous incarnations - and I thank everyone who has ever provided any type of feedback - no matter the length or content.

Beth Bellanca
Jen Boltz
Preston Hultz
Ann Wright

CHAPTER 1
BERTRAND AT MISTER A'S

Summer 2014

I WAS IN pain. It was day seven sans orgasm, and I was locked in this beautiful, nearly euphoric state of hyper-arousal. But that euphoria was accompanied by discomfort; my nuts ached to be touched, and my cock felt full like it would burst if it didn't get the release it sought. It wasn't unbearable, and certainly not a pain I hadn't become accustomed to. Earlier in the day, I'd been slightly uncomfortable, but now I hurt. I'd been looking forward to a night out with Wes all week, and perhaps a quiet dinner was just the distraction I needed to take my mind off my uncomfortable state—if only for a little while.

I thought his company would also take my mind off of Tate's Place. We had both been putting in long hours in preparation for making a dream of mine come true; conceiving, from the ground up, and then bringing to life a space where artists—painters, sculptors, photographers—could not only work for free, but also have their supplies provided at no cost. That dream had evolved into Tate's Place. It was a massive undertaking, and we both needed an evening out to relax and refocus on simply being with each other.

We parked several blocks away from the restaurant so we could stroll along Laurel Street and enjoy the mild southern California evening. The scent of jasmine blew past us as we made our way in companionable silence.

When we arrived, Wes held the glass door open, and guided me through with a strong, firm hand at the small of my back. Those little gestures, the ones most people didn't notice, never ceased to fill me with warmth. We walked through the tiled lobby of the Fifth Avenue Financial Centre building toward the elevators. Bertrand's—our favorite restaurant—is located on the twelfth floor and has occupied the rooftop space since the 1960s.

The maître d' was scribbling notes as we approached, but as the elevator door closed behind us, he looked up and a smile immediately graced his familiar face.

"Mr. Griffin and Mr. De Luca, welcome back."

I briefly wondered why, in social settings, my name always preceded his. Was it my wealth? I also wondered if it bothered Wes—or if he even noticed it.

"Good evening, Hamilton," Wes said, as they shook hands. I smiled and tipped my head in salutation. I much preferred Wes take the lead in most social situations. I enjoyed watching Wes' easy confidence as he interacted with folks. His sheer size could be intimidating; however, most people found his handsome, good looks and charm irresistible.

I associated Hamilton as the face of Bertrand's. He was the first person I met when I'd entered the restaurant some four years earlier, and I had never witnessed anyone other than him at the post.

"I have your table prepared," Hamilton was saying as we moved to follow him through the busy but quiet dining room.

I loved Bertrand's. It was one of those darker, sophisticated places with ambient lighting at each of the cloth-covered tables. But rather than the 'stuffy pomp' other on-par places prided themselves on, Bertrand's opted for a 'friendly yet respectful' vibe.

Our table was a high-backed booth set in an even quieter corner. It offered a sense of privacy, but still allowed a full view of the restaurant and its other guests. More importantly, it boasted a stunning view of the beautifully lit San Diego skyline.

During my first visit, I'd mentioned to Hamilton that I thought it was the best table in the house. He'd told me the owner agreed because it was also his favorite—number forty-two. Since then, I'd never sat anywhere else in the restaurant, and now that Wes and I came here as a couple, Hamilton always seated us there.

Hamilton pushed the table back toward us after Wes and I unfolded the starched, white napkins onto our laps.

"Enjoy your evening, gentlemen. If there's anything I can do, please don't hesitate...," he affably intoned as he made his graceful departure.

Wes picked up this evening's menu, glanced at it before placing it aside, and tossed a wink my way. "I love you, Grif," he said, as he leaned in and nuzzled the sensitive spot on my neck just below my ear. As his hand came to rest on my thigh, I relished the familiar excitement which always accompanied Wes' touch. Even the most casual of gestures ignited and fueled my desire for him.

I turned my head and looked into his handsome face. "And I love you, Wes."

His voice was low and husky when he asked, "Chocolate?"

Surprised by the question, particularly in this setting, I paused briefly before swallowing and replying to our coded question with, "Yes, Wes. Chocolate."

I couldn't help but notice the glint in his eye at my response, before he picked the menu back up and studied it.

Several quiet, tense moments passed before he casually said, "Take Stubby out, please." Although his eyes didn't venture off the menu, I'm sure he could tell I heard him by the way my thigh stiffened under his hand.

I flashed a look around to see if anyone had overheard the command. Once I was assured no one had, I turned to him and faintly questioned, "Wes?" I knew there was fear in my voice, but I couldn't keep it at bay.

His dark eyes caught mine. With a sexy grin I knew all too well, he calmly ordered, "Take Stubby out. Spread your legs and give me plenty of access to the little guy. Make yourself comfortable, Grif. It's going to be a long, unpleasant evening for your pint-sized dick…and I'm very much looking forward to it."

I quietly gasped, and my throat grew tight. I couldn't believe he was going to make me do this here…in the presence of forty other guests and half as many staff. As I considered pleading, an embarrassed tear escaped the corner of my eye. *Dammit! Tears would only encourage him.* I vowed the lone tear would be the last one I shed this evening—or at least the last one I shed in the restaurant.

His vivid white smile grew broader as he slid a strong finger across my stubbled face to claim the salty drop. "Bringing you to tears gives me so much pleasure. You are so beautiful."

How could I possibly concede? But, on the other hand, how could I deny him this...or anything? While in Chocolate, we both knew I was his, and my compliance wasn't a question.

He refocused his attention on the menu, fully expecting my obedience. I dropped shaky hands to my lap and slid the zipper of my dress pants down. Glancing around again, I studied the other patrons, certain my crimson cheeks and the hissing of the zipper hadn't gone unnoticed.

No one seemed to notice we were even there, let alone my red face or what Wes had ordered me to do. Ian, our retirement-age and semi-churlish waiter, however, was making his way toward us.

As Wes continued perusing the menu, I turned to him and whispered the single word, "Ian."

Wes placed the menu aside, reached for his water glass and said, "Continue, Grif," as Ian stopped at the table.

"Mr. Marcus, Mr. Weston. Welcome," Ian announced.

He really was good-hearted, but his Parisian lineage often led people who didn't know him to misinterpret his innate lack of small talk for discourteousness, when nothing could be further from the truth. However, his annoying penchant for calling people by their first names—albeit, always preceded with the respectful mister, misses, or miss—never failed to slightly grate on me. No one called me Marcus. *No one.*

I let out a sharp groan as I popped my straining dick free of the confining jockstrap and fitted slacks I was wearing.

Discreetly, I pulled the napkin back over my lap.

"Mr. Marcus, are you okay? You look…flushed, Sir," Ian inquired.

Turning toward me, Wes offered, "Grif's allergies seem to be acting up this evening Ian. I hope we won't disturb the other guests."

Noting the shimmer in my eyes, Ian said, "Not at all, sir. Not at all. May I bring a few extra napkins and something to drink, perhaps?"

"Thank you. A scotch on the rocks would be most appreciated," I managed to respond. Lord knew I could use a strong drink, anything to stop my hands from shaking.

Wes regarded me, before asking, "Do you think that's wise? Mixing alcohol with your allergy medication?" The look in his eye clearly conveyed adult beverages wouldn't be on my menu this evening.

"Perhaps a club soda, sir?" Ian, nodding at Wes' logic, suggested.

I looked up and said, "Club soda with a twist of lime would be perfect. Thank you."

"And for you, Mr. Weston? Your usual Glenlivet 18?" It was less of a question and more of a confirmation as Ian didn't actually wait for a true response before backing away from the table and turning toward the bar.

Wes' hand, which never left my thigh during the brief exchange, moved in circular, teasing motions above my knee. I peeked down to see a small wet spot developing at the center of my napkin. God, I was so hard!

Wes leaned in and whispered, "No alcohol for you this evening, Grif. I want your full attention. I want you to feel all I have planned for you; every painful, embarrassing thing I do to you and your little dick."

I let out a soft mewl.

The growing wet spot hadn't escaped Wes' sharp eye either. He leaned in for a quick kiss and said, "You'll feel like coming before the night is through. Perhaps long before...," his lips slowly brushed my cheek, "...I wouldn't advise doing so without permission. Do you understand?"

I nodded. "Yes, I understand, Wes."

~

I thought back to the last time I'd had an orgasm without first being given direct permission. The night I'd relinquished control over this aspect of our lovemaking had been five and a half months ago.

One evening, after an intense turn in our kitchen, which had me hands-and-knees splayed on the counter, we'd made our way back to the moonlit bedroom, crawled under the cool sheets, and snuggled into each other for a night of peaceful, sated sleep.

Sometime later, with my head resting on the soft brown fur of his chest, he asked, "Grif? Are you asleep, love?"

"No...enjoying the sound of your breathing in my ear...and your smell. I love your smell," I mumbled, half-awake.

He made a sound of contentment, and I felt the rumble beneath my ear. He began gliding his hand along my back in slow, smooth strokes before he shifted so we lay side-by-side, facing each other. His warm breath, tinted with mint toothpaste, blew across my face as he brushed his firm lips along mine and said, "I'd like to ask you for something." His look held nothing but love, but his tone was serious.

"Anything," I said, and ran my palm down his strong

jaw. "You know anything I have is yours."

He smiled, raised his index finger to my lips, gently parted them, and slid the tip beyond my teeth. The touch was tender, yet possessive. Even though I'd just come, desire warmed and filled me once again. I wasn't sleepy any more—and neither was Junior. No one had ever had the effect on me this stunning man did. No one.

He spoke mildly, but in a tone I'd dubbed early on as his *toppy tone*, "Every time we make love, we both come."

I whimpered, nodded my head, and rolled the tip of my tongue across the pad of his thick finger. Stubby was now fully awake.

With a glint in his eye, he said, "But I've got the man-sized dick and you've got…Stubby."

His free hand edged down my pecs, across my flat stomach, and past my straining dick to take hold of my balls.

I nodded again and groaned as he exerted more pressure on my nuts. My tongue, now with a mind of its own, licked and flicked his finger in earnest.

"We both know that's not right, Grif. I have a cock, and you have a toy."

He slipped his finger from my mouth and slid it to one of my nipples. God, I loved the way he knew exactly how to pinch and tweak them to drive me insane.

His lips moved across my face placing soft kisses on my nose, my eyes, and my forehead while the pressure on my balls steadily increased. I panted. The kisses, the tweaking of my nipple, and the pain in my nuts had me ready to beg.

His voice was still soft and in control when he asked, "They shouldn't get the same treatment, my cock and your toy, should they, love? They don't need or deserve the same frequency—the same luxury—of orgasm, do they?"

"Wes," I groaned, "I've never been so turned on in my life."

He flashed his gorgeous, loving smile and teased, "I'm truly glad, love. I mean, if you could see the way you look right now—so fucking tantalizing! But you haven't answered my question."

"Sorry," I breathed, "my nuts...hurts so bad...difficult to think."

"Try for me."

I nodded. "No, Wes, they don't deserve the same amount of pleasure," I managed to hiss. In response, he eased the pressure on my aching balls.

Somehow, I'd been shifted and was lying flat on my back with Wes, still on his side and propped up on an elbow, leaning over the top of me and looking down, like I was something to behold—something to be treasured.

I reached over and rubbed a hand over his defined chest. God, it was such a joy to touch and feel his firm, corded muscles and his dusting of soft brown hair.

"So what I'm asking is if you'll allow me to remedy this imbalance. I'd like to decide what's reasonable—to decide when Stubby receives, or deserves, an orgasm." He gently massaged my nuts and the throbbing dulled to a bearable stinging.

"Of course, you realize your toy isn't even half the size of my cock. That should obviously play a part in frequency, don't you think? My cock, being larger, needs more, deserves more, than your little dick. If you agree and give me this, there'll be a decrease by at least...oh, let's say half...in the number of orgasms I'll allow you to enjoy."

The fucking tears, which had been threatening, broke

9

free and slid down my cheeks. I knew he liked them—more than liked them—and as much as I enjoyed pleasing him, I still fought with self-consciousness when I couldn't control them. As an adult, I rarely cried—rarely felt a deep enough emotion to cry. But, with Wes, a few sentences from him could well such strong feelings, tears were nearly inevitable.

I cupped his cheeks in both hands and asked, "How do you always know exactly what I need? I've never felt so close to anyone, or felt more love for anyone than I do for you." I leaned forward and placed my lips to his. Pulling back I whispered, "Yes, I happily, and with pleasure, give this to you, Wes."

I reached up to swipe the moisture from my face when he said, "Leave them, Grif. I love seeing your tears, both from pain and from pleasure. It makes my cock so stiff. And I know what you need, because I need the exact opposite. We're made for each other—a perfect fit. You bring me such happiness, love."

I couldn't be certain in the dim moonlight, but I thought his eyes may have been shiny as well.

He released my balls and moved his hand upward. Settling on my straining dick, he took the swollen head between his thumb and forefinger and slowly rubbed. "It starts now, love," he said with a perverse smile. "However, there is one thing I'd like to clarify; Junior will be receiving just as much attention and pleasure, probably more, but not the satisfaction or contentment of release."

"Oh God." I whispered. "Yes!"

~

That was five and a half months ago and Wes had been

true to his word; an orgasm was no longer something I took as a given during our lovemaking. In fact, I now shed far more tears than spunk—and fuck, right now I hurt. But, the tremendous amount of psychological pleasure I derive from relinquishing control—only feeling physical pleasure when he decides—furnishes the pain with a sublime and meaningful purpose. His slow, but insistent, caresses to my thigh brought me back to Bertrand's and the incredible man sitting beside me.

I glanced over when he asked, "Where were you, love?"

"Just appreciating a few of the reasons I love you," I replied.

I saw the mischievousness flash across his face as he said, "Reach into my side pocket. There are several items in there. Whatever you pull out first will be…well, just reach in and place whatever you pull out on the table in front of you, please."

My mind began to race as my heartbeat quickened, wondering what else he had in store for this evening. Usually our Chocolate play sessions took place in a far more private setting, and this very public venue had me uneasy and nervous. But, admittedly, it also excited me.

I reached inside the pocket of his sport coat and felt several items within: a small, soft pouch; a flat strap of some sort; and two small, cold intertwined rings. Deciding on the pouch, I pulled it out with a shaky hand. The contents offered a muffled clinking sound as I laid the dark blue, velvet bag on the pristine white table cloth.

"Easy, Grif. Breathe," Wes said, casually shifting in his seat to look at my profile. With a gentle squeeze, he took his hand from my thigh and rested it on the back of my neck.

I closed my eyes, focused on my breathing, and attempted to relax into his reassuring touch. It worked. My hands stilled and the nearly overwhelming apprehension of what the pouch may contain subsided a bit.

"Better?" he asked.

I nodded and opened my eyes to study the pouch.

"Good," his voice soothed. "And how's Stubby doing?"

"He hurts, Wes. I'm so hard, and it feels like forever since...," I trailed off. Pleading for release, although Wes thoroughly enjoyed hearing me beg, was futile. I'd only find relief when he decided it was time—when he allowed it.

With a breathy kiss to my ear, which caused an involuntary shudder to course through me, he said, "Then we're on the right track. I want Junior suffering. I like doing all I can to make him ache with need. And then, of course, more often than not, denying you release." I could feel his lips pull into a smile as he pressed them to my ear.

He knew all too well what this kind of talk did to me; the same way I knew what it did to him. However, I couldn't help but notice he'd purposely positioned himself so his crotch was in shadow, and I wouldn't even have the pleasure of seeing for myself how turned on he was.

"Untie the pouch and empty the contents onto the table."

I undid the simple tie, held the pouch by the bottom, and allowed the contents to lightly clink to the table. In a neat pile before me lay a half dozen small, black-metal clothespins, each no bigger than a few inches long. I squeaked, and my dick jumped.

Before I could even begin to wrap my mind around what this meant, especially in this setting, he said, "Reach back in and remove another item, please. Lay it on the table next to the first."

I nodded again and reached back in, so focused, I missed Ian's approach completely. I only realized he'd returned when our drinks were being taken from his tray and placed on the table. I saw his eyes flick from the pouch and pins on the table to my hand in Wes' pocket. I'd latched onto the strap and froze, unable to move.

Wes, momentarily ignoring Ian, furtively said, "Continue, Grif," as his hand reassuringly stroked the back of my neck.

Ian finished with the task of placing our drinks and straightened. As I placed the strap on the table alongside the pouch, he pleasantly asked, "Will you gentlemen be having appetizers this evening?"

I saw his eyes dart to the strap, and I averted mine. I wouldn't be able to bear it if I saw comprehension light his face.

"Yes, Ian, appetizers sound nice. However, Grif is used to having something small...," he let the statement hang there a few moments before adding, "before dinner. What would you suggest?"

Of course, Wes' comment wasn't lost on me and I could feel my neck flush again under his continued petting. Junior jumped and twitched with pleasure at the public humiliation, even though Ian likely took the comment at face value.

"We have a lovely dish of grilled clams on the half shell with a spicy ginger mignonnette this evening, sir. They're quite superb. I sampled them myself...and they are bite-sized, sir."

"That'll be fine. Thank you, Ian."

Ian backed away, and I inhaled deeply. I hadn't even

realized I'd been holding my breath. I was so hard it hurt, and the wet spot on the napkin had grown to damn near the size of a hockey puck. The napkin was torture itself as well; every time I shifted, its starched, moist surface grazed the head of my over-sensitive dick.

With Ian gone, I lifted and studied the dark brown leather strap. It was a masculine wrist band that had an edge of urbanity, and nearly identical to the one Wes always wore—the one he often used as a cock ring on me—but not nearly as wide. It had weight and firmness, yet the leather—which emitted its distinct and unique fragrance—was soft and supple. I turned it over and stopped when I saw the engraving. "I BELONG TO GRIF" was etched in neat, but graceful, block letters.

"Wes," I said, as I turned my head and searched his eyes.

He stretched his arm out a bit and his well-worn wrist band peeked out from beneath the jacket and shirt cuffs. "I thought it was time to replace this with something a bit more meaningful. Would you mind helping me take it off?"

He held out his wrist, and I removed the band I'd never seen him without—unless it was wrapped around my cock.

"This new one is not only smaller, but it's also adjustable so it will fit nicely around my wrist as well as your toy."

The carnal look he gave me sent a fresh set of shivers crawling down my spine, but it also warmed me to the core. The fact that he'd put so much thought into something he'd constantly be wearing spoke volumes about what was steadily developing between us. And, of course, both made my dick surge even more.

I placed the old band on the table and glanced over at him.

"Thank you, love. Would you put the new one on me,

please?"

As I was fastening it, he said, "I found the private, double meaning of the inscription distinctive in its uniqueness; I do belong to you, Grif—so when it's on me it has that meaning. But this band is also yours—Junior's—so it also has that meaning when you're wearing it. Do you like it?"

I beamed at him. His combination of tough, take-no-prisoners macho guy and loving, sensitive, giving partner never ceased to amaze me. They were both equally him. And both made me long for him like I'd never desired anyone.

"I think it's exceptional, Wes."

He placed another soft kiss at my temple, "I'm glad. Now, I believe there's one more item left in my pocket...would you retrieve it, please?"

"Wes, I'm so close...I hurt...I don't know if I can hold—"

"I know, love, but you'll be good for me, right? Remove the last item and place it on the table."

I reached in, grasped the intertwined rings, pulled them out, and placed them on the table. It took a moment before I realized what they were.

"Captive bead rings?"

"Yes," he answered with a husky voice. "This pair is made for nipples, and I'd like to see you wearing them."

My nipples, already sensitive beyond words, stiffened at the thought, and my breath suddenly became short and shallow. Much to my dismay, the wonderful, warm tingling that had been brewing in my crotch for a week began to spread up my back and down my thighs as I imagined the rings in me—imagined what Wes might do with them once

I was pierced and they were a part of me. I could almost feel him twisting them, almost imagine the exquisite pain he'd subject me to, could almost taste the intense pleasure and satisfaction the rings would offer us both.

The unwanted warmth stretched out across my chest and up my neck signaling what was about to happen. I was going to orgasm without permission. I sought out his gaze as I grasped the edge of the table with both hands in near panic.

"Wes…I can't hold…ohmigod…."

The hand at my neck tightened as his other slipped under my jacket and roughly grasped a nipple, sending breathtaking jolts of pain down to Junior. I tightened my entire body and clamped my eyes shut.

He pinched harder, and I gasped out.

"Don't do it," he growled in warning.

But, as desperately as I fought it, I knew it was too late. I grimaced as, helpless to stop it, spurt after hot spurt poured from Junior, coating the cloth napkin and the front of my trousers.

No!

Once I'd caught my breath, I turned to look at him. The disappointment in myself must have been clear on my face. Over the lump forming in my throat and the unshed tears burning my eyes, I hoarsely said, "I'm so sorry, Wes."

"Hush now," he said reassuringly.

"But I…."

His hand slid from around my neck and rested on the side of my face. Gently thumbing my cheek, he asked, "I know you, Grif, and your deepest desire is to do as I wish, am I right?"

I nodded because we both knew it was true; I'd do anything for him.

"And although you may feel as if you've let me down, nothing could be further from the truth."

I searched his face. I honestly didn't understand. I'd been given clear and express instructions not to orgasm, and I had. How could he not be disappointed?

His thumb still stroked my cheek as he said, "From the look on your face as you came, it's pretty obvious you didn't enjoy the orgasm much at all, did you?"

It wasn't so much a question as it was a statement. And he was right; on those rare occasions when I lost all control and shot without being told I could, the pleasure was almost nonexistent. I wanted to hold it because it hurt—which I unquestionably enjoyed—but more importantly, I wanted to hold it because I wanted to please him.

"You've been uncomfortable and, occasionally, in pretty intense pain, for days," he said as his rich, brown eyes met mine. "You've also been stiff and exposed since we sat down. And, lastly, you've given me an enticing gift of tears this evening. With all that, Grif, how could I find this evening anything other than supremely satisfying?"

God, I loved him so much.

"And besides," he smirked, "when one door closes another always opens."

Um, okay?

After Wes lifted the small pile of items from the table and returned them to his pocket, he leaned in and pressed his lips to mine. His tongue gently pushed its way in, and briefly swiped against mine before retreating. The quick stroke left behind both his captivatingly distinct flavor, and also the slightest hint of scotch.

Still smiling, he said, "I think we should blow this popsicle stand and head home. We'll throw on some sweats, order pizza, and watch the tube. What do you think, love?"

"There's nothing I'd rather do," I returned, with a wide smile.

As I made myself presentable once more, he reached into his breast pocket and pulled out his wallet. After tossing enough cash on the table for an entire dinner and tip, not just drinks and appetizers, he took my hand. With an exultant smirk, he said as we rose to make our exit, "Perhaps during the commercials we'll come up with a suitable punishment for Stubby's little infraction tonight, huh? And maybe, just maybe, if by the end of the evening I feel like you've earned it—and if it pleases me—you'll enjoy a real orgasm."

I was fully erect again before we reached the elevator.

CHAPTER 2
GYM CLASS

Fall 1998

I GRABBED MY backpack and made my way off the stuffy, noisy school bus. My first day attending Cheyenne Mountain Junior High School was behind me, and as I walked up the driveway, I felt an almost overwhelming sense of relief; I'd never been so glad to be home in my life.

Closing the front door behind me, I smelled one of my favorite things—fresh banana bread. Normally I wouldn't have been able to resist the temptation of a detour into the kitchen, but right now, the thought of eating made my stomach roll.

"Mom? Dad?" I called out and hesitantly waited for a response. Relief spread through me as it seemed no one was home—which meant I wouldn't have to make small talk. I made my way down the hall, past Micah's and Meaghan's—the twins—rooms and into mine. Once inside, with the door firmly locked, I stripped and headed for the shower. I'd wanted to do this all day long; I needed to wash the smell off!

Attending junior high school was something I'd been looking forward to all summer. It meant all sorts of new, cool classes like a real art program and playing real sports. I wanted to be on the baseball, football, and soccer teams. It wasn't so much the competition, as much as it was being part of a team and using my body. I get such a high when I'm physically active.

My first period of the day was gym class. I'd planned it that way knowing I'd have the most energy first thing in the morning, and also that I'd be able to skip my morning shower at home.

~

I made my way toward the back of the campus, heading for the Physical Education buildings, and caught glimpses of the mountains now and again. I'd grown up in Colorado Springs and Cheyenne Mountain was a backdrop to everyday life. However, I didn't take it for granted. I loved this part of the Rockies and my family spent lots of time hiking, biking, and camping in the mountains a few miles from our home.

I rounded to the front side of the gymnasium and found a teacher's assistant directing students to wait for the coach inside.

The actual physical activity part of the morning ended up being pretty light. After roll call and assigning our lockers, there wasn't much left of the period. The coach told us to suit up and run a few laps before the end of class.

I found my locker, changed into my gym clothes, and

made my way out to the track. There was a bunch of people hanging around on the field waiting for Coach Armstrong to arrive. I knew a few of them from primary school, but there wasn't anyone who I'd really call a friend, so I stuck mostly to myself.

The next half hour passed quickly as I ran and found a nice pace. I lost myself, as I usually do, in the sound of my footfalls and my deep breathing. I managed to do ten laps before the coach's whistle sounded telling us it was time to hit the showers.

I walked along with a bunch of other guys, wiping the sweat from my face with the front of my shirt, as we all piled into the noisy, slightly tangy smelling locker room.

At thirteen, I'd never had the opportunity to shower with other guys—in fact, I'd never seen another naked male before at all—and I looked forward to the new experience with nervous anticipation. The excitement, unfortunately, was short lived.

I made my way through the maze of half-naked guys and, once at my locker near the end of the row, stripped off my sweaty clothes without so much as a glance around me. I wrapped one of the school's scratchy towels around my waist and headed toward the sound of running water.

Two rows over I found the large, crowded shower bay. As I approached, the athletic smell of the locker room was replaced by the scent of fresh water and shampoo. The sounds of talking and joking grew louder and filled me with a tremendous sense of camaraderie; I'd waited so long to be part of a team. And what a team it was—wet, naked, and male. Wow, I couldn't believe it; so much nudity right there in front of me and all I had to do was look, discreetly of course, and take it all in. The manly, adult-feeling atmosphere had me buzzing with excitement.

A pentagon of poles, arranged in the center of the bay, held four shower heads each. I found an empty one toward the center, twisted it on, and was enjoying the hot, steamy water pounding over my neck and shoulders when I dared my first glance. The tall jock across from me had wavy dark hair—nearly black—and looked to be about sixteen years old. His chest was broad and well defined with a light dusting of fur leading downward.

Unable to resist, I followed the soft trail with my eyes, enjoying his bronze skin and how the water flowed over it, until my gaze finally landed on his crotch. I nearly gasped when I saw his long, thick dick swaying back and forth as he moved a soapy hand over his neck. God, it was *so* big!

I glanced toward the floor and washed my feet before sneaking another peek. Jesus, he was incredible. Feeling the all-too-familiar tingle of excitement in my balls, I decided it was best to avert my gaze, so I turned my back to him. The last thing I wanted was to get a hard-on in the shower bay.

I used the dispenser to gather shampoo and worked up a deep lather while the prickle in my dick subsided.

Facing the opposite direction from the dark jock, not more than five feet in front of me, was a blond. He was at least five inches shorter than the stud behind me and much stockier. Casually, I peeked down at his crotch as he closed his eyes and scrubbed his face. His dick wasn't quite as long as the jock's, but it was still large.

I rinsed off while discreetly scrutinizing the twenty-some-odd dicks around me. It seemed everyone had a huge cock. My mind swam with confusion, and I found myself looking back toward the blond across from me. I'd turned in time to see him check out my crotch and then look away with a strange expression on his face.

I tried to decipher exactly what it was. Sadness? Pity? I

wasn't sure. But I suddenly had the overwhelming urge to get out of there; I'd never felt so exposed in my life.

Flipping off the water, I grabbed my towel, and hustled out of the bay. Back at my locker, I made a halfhearted attempt at drying off and then slipped my jeans over my still damp legs. Only then did I begin to feel like I could breathe normally again.

∼

Leaving my clothes where they fell on my bedroom floor, I headed for the adjoining bathroom. Twisting the shower on, I brushed my teeth as the water warmed. Even though it'd been over eight hours, I could still smell it: the locker room soap and the school's bleached towels. I wanted the odor off of me—out of me—gone!

I stepped into the hot shower and let the familiar scent of my soap and shampoo wash away all the other smells. Safe, in my room and my shower, I let myself really think about what I'd seen that morning. Everyone had a bigger dick than I did. Everyone! And, not only slightly bigger; I wasn't even in the same league.

As the water pounded against me, I remembered an overheard conversation from last summer. At the time, I hadn't given it much thought, but now it took on an entirely different significance.

We'd all sat down at the dining room table for pizza night, and I'd eaten a few slices when I was overcome with sudden stomach cramps. My mom, not overly concerned initially, suggested I lie down on the sofa and rest for a while. However, twenty-five minutes later, when it was clear I wasn't getting any better, I was whisked to the emergency room. By the time we'd arrived, I was in pretty severe pain.

The doctor appeared through the curtain and, after introducing himself to my parents and me, asked them to step outside the curtain, so he could perform his exam. He'd explained he was going to be feeling around my abdomen and I should let him know if any area was more painful than another. He'd lifted up my gown to begin. My parents hadn't been able to persuade me to wear underwear for years—apparently I'd come out of the womb with an aversion to anything which hugged my crotch— so the gown was the only thing I had on. When his exam was complete, he brought the gown back down to cover me up and stepped around to the other side of the curtain.

I heard him speaking with my parents, but the Emergency Room was noisy, not to mention I was in quite a bit of pain, but I did manage to catch snippets of the conversation; "appendix...needs surgery...small for his age...should be larger...don't be too concerned yet."

My hand absentmindedly ran over the wet scar on my lower abdomen as I shut off the water and dried off. Once I'd finished, I closed the bathroom door and stood looking in the full-length mirror on the back of it.

Staring at my reflection, I started a critical appraisal of what I saw: I was tall for a thirteen-year-old, standing at five foot eight already. My fit body had the beginnings of a nice chest, well defined arms, and toned legs from the physical activity I enjoyed.

But there were two major differences between myself and the jock in the shower: hair color and cocks. Where he was dark haired, I was sandy blond, and where his dick was quite large, mine wasn't. But, most frightening of all, was remembering that the jock's dick wasn't really much different from everyone else's in the shower. In fact, the only different one was mine.

～

The next morning, when I should have been in gym class, I sat in the school library with several anatomy books opened in front of me. I'd started out with only one but, not at all liking the answers I was finding, I gathered a couple more. I wanted to find out if what I suspected was true; that I didn't measure up.

After reading everything I could find, which wasn't as much as I would have liked since it was a junior high school library, I finally and reluctantly admitted what I'd realized in the locker room; I was small. Based on the information I was able to find, the average size dick was apparently somewhere around six inches—and I knew I was well below that. However, I also came across the term micropenis, which referred to guys measuring less than two and a half inches—and I was well above that. I sat there, completely unnerved at my undeniable findings.

I was undoubtedly much smaller than average. Instantly, I made a critical decision; I was never going back to gym class!

JOSEPH LANCE TONLET

CHAPTER 3
LOOKOUT POINT

Late Fall 2004

WE DROVE ALONG the quiet residential streets of San Diego with the windows down and enjoyed the evening breeze. Rounding the bend, we got a look at what we'd come to think of as Lookout Point, but in reality, it was called University Heights Park. It was nice to see it empty—as it nearly always was. I briefly wondered why more folks didn't come up here, but then decided I was just grateful they didn't.

I pulled up and killed the engine. The view, which looked out over Mission Valley, Fashion Valley and, on a clear day, Point Loma to the far west, was as captivating as always. This high up, and at the brink of dusk, the city lights flickering on were absolutely amazing. From every angle, it looked like a Christmas village full of twinkling lights.

Beside me sat Tate. One of the best things about our

relatively young friendship was the companionable silence. We could hang out for hours and I'd never feel the nagging need to fill the silence I so often felt with other people. From the first day we'd met a few months ago, we had steadily grown closer, and I now considered him my best friend. It was so easy and comfortable being around him.

"Nice, huh?" I asked, as we both sat and looked out at the beauty from our spot.

Tate nodded and said, "It really is. I love it up here."

I knew he did, probably as much as I did. Tate and I had been coming up here to chill at least a few times a week since we'd discovered it. Sometimes we'd bring beer, like we did tonight, and other times we'd bring takeout. But mostly we just jumped in the car and drove up without much planning ahead. I was driving his car as he'd gotten a head start on a buzz—and because I couldn't stand to be a passenger to Tate's driving.

Up here, in the quiet, we'd mostly sit in silence. But, occasionally, we'd talk about our problems, our college classes, or Tate's girlfriend-of-the-week.

"I heard you on the phone with your advisor this afternoon…everything okay?" Tate asked, as he finished off another beer.

He held the empty can between his legs on the car seat, and it made a slight crunching sound as his legs gripped it a bit too firmly. The noise echoed in the quiet car, and I naturally turned my head while glancing down. I missed the can altogether and instead found myself noticing his crotch—something I realized I'd been doing more and more of since we met. I hastily turned away and stared back out over the valley.

"Yeah, something about this semester's financial aid not

arriving yet. I'm sure it'll all be okay though," I answered with a slight catch in my voice.

I tried to reason out why I'd suddenly started noticing Tate in a sexual way when, at first, I hadn't. I mean sure, I'd noticed he was handsome—who wouldn't—but lately all sorts of sexual fantasies would start popping into my head nearly every time I looked at him. It unnerved me a bit because nothing had really changed in our friendship to prompt these fantasies; he wasn't any different, I wasn't any different. And yet, more and more I found myself thinking about what he'd look like naked—naked and standing over me.

"Grif...," Tate started. But then stopped and pulled out another beer. He seemed to have something on his mind, like he was mulling something over. This was new. Since the first time we'd met, one of the easiest things between us was talking.

"Is something bothering you, Tate?" I asked, as I dug in my back pocket, found my wallet, and pulled a joint from between the folds.

His eyes lit up, and a big grin replaced the pensive one of moments before as he focused on the joint.

He looked out the front windshield for a few seconds, the rather serious expression returning to his handsome face, before continuing, "Nah man. I wouldn't say *bothered*, but I did sorta want to ask you something."

"Sure. Is everything okay? Do you need some cash or something?"

Tate didn't ask for much—and never money. In fact, he rarely talked about money at all. But clearly something important was on his mind.

"Nah, it's all good," he said, turning back to look at me.

I lit the joint, took a long drag, and passed it to him.

He took it with a "Thanks," and held it between his fingers, looking at it—almost fondling it—with a wide smile.

As he took a hit, I couldn't resist sneaking another look at his crotch. As always, the bulge was large and round and, at the moment, it sat at the top of his now outstretched legs. It looked…well, it looked casual, and manly, and sexy, and tempting; exactly as one would imagine the ideal package looking.

I peeked up to find his perceptive gaze fixed on mine. Flooded with embarrassment, I took a long swallow from my bottled water and avoided his eyes.

Shit, I've been caught.

"Good weed, huh?" I said lamely, attempting to smooth over the awkward moment while I screwed the lid back onto my water.

Tate acted like he hadn't heard the comment and instead said in an even tone, "Well…I'd planned on asking you if you were gay tonight…but I don't really see the point now, do you? I think we both know the answer."

The silence was deafening as he waited for me to respond. I felt sick and my face burned. I fumbled with the door handle and scampered out of the car.

I tried to sound casual when I said, "I gotta take a leak…be back in a few."

I made my way down a rough path and eventually found a tree to lean against. I stood there trying to get my breath under control and thinking I couldn't stand losing him; he'd become my best friend—hell, nearly my only friend.

I'd always found it rather complicated to make friends, but that hadn't been the case with Tate; we'd become so close so easily that I had to occasionally remind myself we really hadn't known each other long at all.

I gently slid down the tree, bent my legs to my chest, rested my elbows on my knees, and held my head in my hands. I knew he'd caught me looking. I knew I'd been found out.

Fuck!

I don't know how long I sat there, trying to think of a way to salvage our friendship, but at some point I realized I was no longer alone. I looked up and into Tate's unreadable face.

"Hey," he said softly.

"Hey," I replied in a weak voice, and dropped my gaze back to the ground.

"Look Big Guy, I didn't mean to freak you out back there. It's…well…we're buds, right?"

Unsure, I looked back up. "Are we? Still, I mean?"

He walked the few feet over, leaned against the tree, and slid down to sit next to me.

We sat in silence for a while and watched the lights below. He finally said, "What I wanted to say tonight was…I know you're gay. I mean, I've seen the way you check me out." He glanced over at me and quickly added, "And it's all cool. I mean, you know I'm not, right?"

Fuck, fuck, fuck.

This is exactly why I never—ever—wanted him to know. Every time we watch a game, every time we're at a movie, every time he sees me looking at him now, he'll wonder what I'm thinking.

Things will never be the same.

I was filled with an immediate and deep sadness.

"Tate...," I began.

"No, please let me finish. Okay?"

I nodded.

"I wanted to say," he started hurriedly, as if he had to get the words out before I interrupted again, "I know, Grif. I've known for a bit now." He took a quick breath and continued, "And, I'm straight. But not...narrow...and I know you don't date...so, if you want...well...I'll never turn down a blowjob. In fact, I'm sure it's something I could talk myself into suffering through whenever...."

Shocked, I whipped my head around to look at him. Not only did he have a huge grin on his face but, with his legs stretched out in front of him, I couldn't miss the huge boner he had, too.

I couldn't think. I couldn't breathe. I'd gone from being certain our friendship was over to...umm...being told I could.... What? Give him a blowjob? Whenever I wanted? I had to get up...I had to move...to walk...to think.

"Hey, I think I need a beer," I managed to choke out as I pushed my way up from the tree. Dusting my ass off, I stumbled to the path back up to the car.

A few moments later, I felt him on the trail beside me. He laid a firm hand on my arm and said, "Grif, buddy, I kinda laid a bunch of stuff out there...and your only response is 'I need a beer'?"

Looking down, not able to meet his eyes, and thankful for the growing darkness, I said, "I'm...," then my voice made a weird cracking noise, and I stopped to swallow, "I'm not sure what to say, Tate. I feel as if I should apologize for...for...offending you, or making you feel uncomfortable. But it doesn't seem as if I've done either of those things...so...and you're straight, so.... I'm confused.

I don't know what to say."

He gave me a friendly shove, "Nah, man, it seems like I'm the one who should be apologizing. I'm the one who made you uncomfortable."

I laughed at the absurdity of the situation and continued walking back up the trail. "So I'm apologizing for wanting to…" well, there was no way in hell I was gonna finish that sentence, "…and you're apologizing for offering to let me…" nope, not gonna finish that one either.

We'd reached the car, and I pulled open the door. "How about we grab a few beers, smoke some pot, accept one another's apologies, and let this conversation rest awhile, huh?" God, please let him go for that—please.

He grinned over the roof at me, "Yep, I'm good with that."

I let out a breath and started to slide in, but noticed his continued grin, "So long as we understand each other, Grif; you wanna suck me, and I like blowjobs…nothing more to it than that. No apologies necessary."

Oh Christ, I knew moving in with him had been a spectacularly bad idea. But, I couldn't deny my rigid dick certainly had a differing opinion on the subject.

"No apologies," I agreed, and hoped like hell it would be the end of this particular topic of conversation.

JOSEPH LANCE TONLET

CHAPTER 4
THE FIRST TIME

Winter 2004

I THREW MY bath towel in the hamper and stepped into a pair of baggy, comfortable workout shorts while I thought about the last month. Things, much to my surprise, had been exactly the same between Tate and me as they'd always been—with not a single mention of the crazy, weird, insane conversation up at University Heights Park. In fact, it was like it never even happened; Tate was acting the same as he always had.

But it had happened, and I couldn't stop thinking about it. I couldn't stop thinking about Tate's offer. Was he serious? And even if he was, could I ever do something like that? I mean, sure, I was a virgin, but it's not like I had some hang-up about casual sex. It's not like I thought I was holding out for true love or something.

I'd honestly put the notion of finding a partner and building some sort of idyllic, storybook life together out of my head years ago. Instead, I focused on school, keeping fit, and a few close friendships. And, as much as humanly possible, I purposely avoided even entertaining the prospect of having sex with another guy; I knew such thoughts would only lead to disappointment and I did my best to banish them. But now, I was apparently being offered something I honestly had no idea what to do with.

Distantly, I thought I heard the doorbell and was only brought out of my thoughts when Tate yelled, "Hey, Grif. Pizza's here."

"Be right there. You wanna put the movie in?" I called back.

I made my way down the short hall, which held both of our bedrooms and the shared bath, and into the living room. Tate had the pizza and napkins on the coffee table and was putting the DVD into the player.

"You want beer?" I asked, as I headed into the small, bright kitchen.

I smiled when I noticed Tate had cleaned the refrigerator at some point that day; he was as much of a neat freak as I was.

"Yeah, please. Bring me a couple, would ya? The first one probably won't last long, not with all these jalapeño peppers!"

"You got jalapeños again?"

I couldn't take hot foods, but Tate loved them. I seriously thought his mother had likely served jalapeños with every meal. "It's how we Latinos do everything: hot and spicy," he'd said with a mischievous grin when I'd questioned him about it once.

"Only on one of the pies," he called back around a mouthful of pizza.

I flopped down next to him on the sofa with four Coronas in tow and twisted the cap off one before handing it to him.

"What are we watching?"

Tate had the uncanny knack of picking out the absolute worst movies. But, it was enjoyable nonetheless, as we usually ended up making fun of them and laughing at how awful they were. Not a bad way to spend the evening; my best friend, pizza and beer, and laughing.

"Oh! I think I got a good one this time. I can feel it!" he exclaimed.

I rolled my eyes and reached for the DVD case. *The Dentist*. I'd never heard of it. I flipped over the box, read the synopsis, and found out we were going to be watching a flick about a dentist who takes his wife's infidelity out on his unsuspecting patients.

Groaning, I tossed it back onto the table.

We'd only managed to get through two beers apiece when he laughed and asked, "It's bad, isn't it?" nodding his head toward the TV.

"Oh, it's bad all right. Maybe the worst yet," I said, getting up and making my way into the kitchen to grab us a few more bottles.

As I sat back down on the sofa, I noticed he'd become much more relaxed. He had leaned back into the cushions, his fingers were laced together resting on his stomach, and his legs were outstretched, with his bare feet crossed at the ankles resting on the coffee table.

His eyes were glued to the TV—still watching the terrible movie. I reached over to hand him a beer and caught sight of his ever-present, impressive package. He was wearing a ratty, oversized, t-shirt and dark navy, nylon

JOSEPH LANCE TONLET

track pants that rested against his dick—clearly outlining its contours.

I heard him clear his throat and ask, "Is one of those for me?" and realized I'd been completely lost in the ensnaring sight before me. I glanced up and met the knowing look in his eyes.

"Um, yeah." I responded around the lump in my throat.

"You know, my offer still stands, Grif," he said in a provocative voice I'd never heard him use before.

I couldn't help myself and glanced down again to find his bulge had grown. God, it looked so good, and I desperately wanted to reach out and touch it.

I was suddenly too warm, and my stomach felt totally weird. I couldn't stop my still outstretched hand from shaking and sloshing beer onto the sofa.

"Whoa, Big Guy, let me have that."

I realized he'd taken hold of the shaking bottle and was trying to pry it loose from my tight grip. I let go and turned away in complete embarrassment.

"Sorry," I managed to mumble.

"Hey, dude, I was just letting you know…in case you were interested…," his voice trailed off. I turned back, and he was looking me directly in the eye.

"So you were…you are…serious, aren't you?" I asked, when I could finally form words again.

"Sure. And from the way you look at me, there's no doubt you'd like to. So, why not?" he said with a casualness and ease I certainly wasn't feeling.

Another thing which had made our friendship so enjoyable, aside from his near-freakish cleanliness, was our ability to honestly talk about real things. It was something I

38

found most straight guys didn't really do. Before I even knew the words were coming out of my mouth I said, "I want to."

"Great!" he said eagerly, while placing his thumbs under the waistband of his track pants, ready to slide them down.

"But," I said hesitantly, and he froze with a slight groan.

"I'm not sure this is a good idea. I mean, we're like best friends and all."

I was scared out of my mind and grasping at anything I could to stop this…this…thing which, if I were completely honest, I desperately did not want to stop.

"Dude, you can't just imply a guy's gonna get a blowjob and then pull back! I mean, there's some sort of rule about that…blowjob etiquette or something, isn't there?"

We looked at each other for a moment before we both broke out in laughter. Several minutes later, our eyes watery, I echoed, "Blowjob etiquette?"

"Dude…I had to say something. Big Tate was ready and so was I."

"Wait. You call your…umm…dick *Big Tate*?" I asked, while grinning and rubbing my moist eyes, still feeling the giggle high from moments before.

"Well, yeah. It fits, you know? *Tate* because he's part of me and *Big* because, well…," he stopped and threw me a mischievous wink.

I had something I wanted to say, and with the lightened mood, I felt now was as good a time as any. I wanted to tell him I'd jerked off every night since our talk up at University Heights Park thinking about his offer. I wanted to admit, more than anything, my deep desire to touch and taste him.

Instead, for reasons I could not explain, I blurted out,

"Tate, I don't know what to do. I've never...."

He stilled and looked at me with an odd expression. Then curiosity filled his handsome face.

"Wait, you've never what? Given a blowjob? Or...?"

Here it was, perhaps even bigger than being gay, was the admission of being a twenty year-old virgin. God, he'd think I was such a loser. And he'd be right.

Out of sheer terror, I'd never been with anyone sexually. I couldn't stand to see that look again, like the one so many years ago in that gym shower. I'd never be able to shrug it off again.

How could I admit to anyone that I couldn't bring myself to be naked in front of another person? And, if that fear meant I'd be a virgin for the rest of my life? Well, it was something I'd been trying for years to fool myself into believing I'd be okay with.

"None of it," I finally admitted out loud. Instantly, I regretted my confession.

What had I just said? And why?

I was gently pulled into a one-armed-guy-hug.

"Grif, I had no idea."

"Why would you?"

We sat entwined for several moments before I allowed myself to relax into his shoulder, and his spicy, masculine scent filled my nose. God, he smelled so good.

"Look, I'm not gonna be all girly and romantic and shit. You're a dude."

I tensed against him. Fuck, what was I doing? How could I even allow myself to imagine anyone, let alone a straight guy with a big dick, would understand.

"But, if this is going to be your first time...well, we can

take it slow and…maybe make it a bit special."

"Look, I appreciate that, but you don't have—,"

"Grif, shut up, okay?" he whispered as he tightened the embrace and spoke into the top of my head, blowing my hair with his breath.

"Why don't we agree to do only what you're comfortable with? Only what makes you feel good. How about we start with you just taking your fill of looking? We both know how much you like that—but this time you don't have to worry about being caught. Just enjoy looking, Grif."

He stretched his legs back out, re-crossed his ankles, and pushed his bulge out, putting it more prominently on display. I couldn't believe I was being given permission to look at another guy's dick—without fear of retaliation.

I let out a shallow gasp as I relaxed again and leaned into him, nuzzled the top of my head into the side of his neck, and took in the sight of his crotch with a deep hunger I'd never allowed myself to fully feel.

As I stared down, the bulge grew and lengthened. The outline becoming more and more prominent until the nylon stood tented.

"Tate," I whispered, as my entire body shook. Like I'd suddenly grown cold, but I felt the opposite. I felt heated all over.

"It's okay, Grif. It's all good, Big Guy," he soothed.

I nodded and exhaled deeply. Fuck, on the one hand, I was so incredibly scared, but on the other, this was Tate. There wasn't anyone I trusted and could be myself with more than him.

Tightening his embrace once more, he said, "I think it'd be a good idea to talk about what I do and don't feel comfortable with. You know, so neither of us has any unfulfilled expectations, okay?"

"Sure," I said with a nod—but my stare never left his tented crotch. Jeez, it was *so* big.

"I'm totally cool with you feeling me up anywhere you'd like. And, I'm obviously completely cool with you going down on me," he said with a smile in his now husky voice. "But, Grif…I'm not sure how much I'd be willing to do for you…beyond me holding you like I am now. I mean, when I thought this was only another blowjob…that was something completely different. But, fuck…this is your first time, and it's something you'll always remember. I'd never want you to look back and feel like, *he took advantage of me because he wanted to pop a fucking nut.*"

I lifted my head from his shoulder and turned to face him. His hand slid down my back and came to rest right above my waist. I looked into his dark eyes for a long moment before finally saying, "Tate, I trust you. And, yes, I know you'd like to *pop a fucking nut,* but I also know you. You're a good person. Granted, a male whore, but the most kind-hearted male whore I know."

He chuckled. "I'm not sure, but I think there may be a compliment in there somewhere." His hand made small circles on my back.

Damn, that felt so good. I licked my lips, looked down at his dick again, then back up and asked, "Can I please touch it, Tate?"

"Look, Big Guy, let's get something straight right now," he said. "Unless we have company, or we're in public, you can rub my big dick any fucking time you like. You'll never find anything other than a willing man whore, as you put it, on my end. Although, if we're putting a label on it, I'd prefer *pleasure whore.*"

He brought his hands up, cupped my face, and stroked his thumbs over my cheeks. It was the most intimate gesture I'd ever experienced.

"Now," he said boldly, "why don't you kneel down between my legs, where we both know you'd like to be, and then you can get at what you really want. And, Grif, don't worry; I'll be right here to guide you along in learning all the intricacies of giving a top-notch blowjob. It may take practice—lots of practice," and I heard the mirth in his voice, "but by the time we're done, you're gonna be a pro."

He leaned in, and ever so briefly touched his lips to mine, giving me my first, albeit completely G-rated, kiss. When he pulled back, a playful look covered his face and his eyes were beaming with bad-boy heat.

He spread his legs in invitation, and I slid to the floor between them. I'd never been as exhilarated, or as scared, in my entire life. I laid a hand on each knee and attempted to quell the terror my inexperience induced.

Once in place, I looked up to find his eyes fixed on mine. He was oozing heat, and confidence, and maleness. His gaze briefly flicked from my eyes to his crotch and back again.

All playfulness gone, he quietly directed, "Go ahead, Grif; touch the first dick that doesn't belong to you. Touch my dick."

I licked my lips, my mouth suddenly so dry, and crept my hands up his muscular thighs, resting them on either side of his cock. The added pressure pulled the already taut fabric even tighter against his crotch.

I groaned, "Tate."

"I know, Big Guy. I know," he said. "I imagine it's the same feeling I have when I stare at pussy...mesmerizing, isn't it?"

I nodded in silent agreement. He clenched, straining his dick against the tight fabric even more, and I fucking whimpered.

"Touch it, Grif."

I slid a hand over and took a firm but gentle hold of him through the silky cloth.

"My God, Tate, it's so big, so thick!" I panted and tentatively stroked back and forth.

"Oh, feels good, Grif. Feels so fucking good."

I rested my head in the crook where his leg met his crotch, with my nose nestled in his dark pubes. He lay back, spent, with his eyes closed. Sharp breaths heaved his chest up and down, while thick, white cum covered his flat stomach.

"Are you sure you've never done this before? Because, that was really good. I mean, really, really good." Without lifting his head, he looked down at me with a sated yet mischievous grin. "I'm not saying you won't need more practice. Fuck, lots and lots more practice!"

I laughed and couldn't believe how happy I was, how fulfilled I was, even though I hadn't come and was still stiff as a board. I honestly felt like my heart would explode right out of my chest. Not from any new, post-coital feelings for Tate, but from the experience itself.

It had been fucking awesome. So much better than every fantasy I'd ever had all combined into one. The emotion overwhelmed me, and I buried my face deeper in his crotch.

"Hey, Grif? Whoa, is everything okay, dude?"

Once I'd regained a bit of composure, I looked up at him, and said with a broad grin, "Absolutely perfect, Tate. Thank you. Let me get something to clean you up with. You want another beer?"

"Hmm, a blowjob, a cleanup, and wait service? I may have to bring the next girlfriend in for training by you," he chuckled.

I whopped him on the back of the head as I rounded the couch, then easily dodged his attempted answering blow, and chided with a smile, "Fuck you. Training is extra!"

He laughed and leaned back into the sofa. Throwing his feet up onto the coffee table, he waited for both the cleanup, and the fresh beer.

CHAPTER 5
PENANCE PART ONE

Summer 2014

WES AND I were spending a pleasant evening in the family room—each of us doing our own thing but enjoying being with one another nonetheless. I was studying remodeling bids from various contractors on the building I'd acquired for Tate's Place, while Wes was reviewing electronic security protocols.

He'd long ago concluded his plans for the new space but had since asked to review the security measures of my other businesses, which, I had to admit, were pretty nonexistent. It was quite an undertaking considering the numerous companies and buildings Diaz Inc. encompassed. Not to mention security, electronic or otherwise, was never something I'd given much thought to. It's not like I had a lot of cash or valuables lying around Diaz Inc., or anywhere else for that matter. However, I knew Wes, and therefore understood his innate need to protect. It's what made him exceptional in his chosen career.

I turned off the desk lamp, rubbed my tired eyes, then stood and stretched. Wes glanced up from his position on the sofa while closing his laptop.

"You look a bit worn out, love. How are the bids coming along?"

"Oh, they're fine," I said with a small sigh. "There's just so many. They all start to bleed into one another after a while. Know what I mean?"

"I do," he said with a smile, "and I think we deserve a reward for all of our hard work this evening."

He stood up and made his way to the small liquor cabinet set in one corner of the comfortable room. I listened to the soft clinking of ice being dropped into two glasses and the sound of scotch being poured. I could already taste the smooth, peaty flavor in anticipation.

"I certainly approve of this reward, Mr. De Luca."

"Ah, but there's more," he said with a naughty grin as he opened a drawer and pulled out an unopened pack of cigarettes. Waggling his eyebrows at me, he asked, "One or two wouldn't be so bad, would it?"

Both of us started smoking in our early teens and had struggled with cigarette addiction for years. Before we met, we'd each been doing our best to lead healthier lifestyles on our own—now we were doing it together. It'd been five weeks since our last smoke.

I eyed the pack in his hand with sincere interest. "Oh yes," I said moving toward the French doors which led out to a rough-stoned patio. Wes followed behind me.

Over my shoulder, I asked, "Table or lounges?"

"Lounges. It'd be nice to stretch out."

The mid-fifties, cottage-style house had a great backyard when I'd bought it after graduating from college. It was large, but not overly so, nicely planted, and was surrounded by striking, mature trees. In fact, the backyard had tilted the house's favor and clinched my purchase. I couldn't believe, in the middle of San Diego, such a peaceful and lush oasis could exist.

During the first four months, I had spent every evening out here, studying and getting to know the space, before researching and finally contacting landscape designers for ideas. I wanted a pool which matched the relaxing, natural environment. In the end, I designed an inviting, irregular shaped body of water which had a natural pond feel rather than a man-made pool. It blended into the verdant space seamlessly—like it had always been there.

At the end nearest the patio, a weathered bench overlooked a Koi pond. A bit deeper back, there was a small, meandering, cross-hatched plank pathway leading from one edge of the pond to the other. It served to camouflage the division between pond and swimming waters. And, tucked into the farthest corner of vast foliage, which offered the most privacy, was a small hot tub.

The evening was still warm, but much more bearable than the early afternoon heat.

Wes handed me my drink as he settled onto the oversized lounger next to mine.

"It really is quite tranquil, isn't it?" he asked, looking out over the garden.

I nodded while appreciating the view. "Not to be overly dramatic, but I think it may be my most favorite place on the planet."

I took a sip of the amber liquid and relished the slight

burn and distinctive taste. Wes lit two cigarettes and passed one to me. Our fingers brushed as I accepted it, and I looked into his relaxed brown eyes.

It had taken me a while to say it—hell, to even admit it to myself—as I had given up on the idea of finding someone to love and share my life with, let alone another person who understood me so completely. But here I was, in love with a handsome, sexy, incredibly compassionate man whose strongest desire was to make me happy and build a life together.

I took a few deep drags from the sweet menthol cigarette and my heart swelled with overwhelming joy. Through exhaled smoke, I quietly said, "Love you, Wes."

He looked over and met my sincere gaze, laid his cigarette in the ashtray, and motioned for me to join him. "Come sit with me?"

I stubbed out my cigarette and moved over to stretch out beside him. Snuggling into the crook of his arm, I laid my head on his chest and felt its firmness and warmth. I inhaled and took in his woodsy, masculine scent. God, he always smelled so good.

His hand gently slid up and down my arm as he said into my hair, "And I love you, Grif. I know you feel like you're the lucky one in this relationship, but I'm here to tell you, I'm as lucky as you are, if not more."

I opened my mouth to begin a protest but didn't have a chance as he continued on.

"I get to spend my time with a brilliant artist…who has a fucking banging body. Who is also kind, and caring, and considerate, and intelligent, and just…so damn sexy. I'm thankful every day for you, Grif."

He paused, kissed the top of my head, and seemed to be

contemplating his next words.

"And speaking of aching, I often find it impossibly difficult to believe I've been lucky enough to find all of that in someone who not only understands my desire—my need—to inflict both physical and emotional pain, but someone who appreciates it. Someone who burns with equal desire and gratitude in receiving it, in a way I never believed possible."

He squeezed me tight and resumed kissing the top of my head.

"Make no mistake, Grif, I'm the lucky one."

I ran a hand over the well-defined muscles of his chest—appreciating the strength coiled within them—and nodded my assent.

"Okay, so we're both very, very lucky. We should run out and buy lottery tickets, right?" the playful happiness evident in my voice.

He chuckled and agreed. "Yes. Extremely lucky indeed." Then his voice took on a gruff sound as he said, "And, speaking of lucky, I don't believe Junior has paid penance for his blatant disobedience during our dinner at Bertrand's a few weeks ago."

My hand stopped, and my whole body stiffened in keen anticipation of what might come. "Wes," I murmured—the desire clear and uninhibited in my voice.

With a finger under my chin, he lifted my head and brought our lips together. I loved kissing him and his taste thrilled me. I also loved the unpredictability of his kisses. He was soft at times and demanding at others; lightly brushing, barely bringing our lips together, or completely possessive and brutal.

Drawing an end to the gentle kiss, he asked, "Chocolate,

Grif?"

"Yes, Wes, Chocolate," I whispered eagerly.

Leaning up, hands slightly trembling, as I never quite knew what to expect during these unpredictable sessions, I unbuttoned his shirt and revealed his gorgeous chest. His torso couldn't have fit my ideal more. His brown nipples sat atop well defined, steely pecs; his flat, taut stomach—which I knew he worked hours in the gym to achieve and maintain—begged to be licked. The mysterious, small row of odd symbols tattooed just below and to the right of his navel always caught my attention. And, if that weren't stunning enough all on its own, his pecs were dusted with just the right amount of soft, dark brown hair. It narrowed and tapered down the center of his chest, briefly widening over his stomach, before narrowing again and disappearing under his low waistband. Fucking extraordinary!

With the buttons of his shirt undone, and the fabric pushed aside, I ran my hands lightly over his firm muscles. I'd grown hard at the first mention of chastisement for Junior. My dick jumped and I whispered—nearly implored, "Wes."

"I know, love. I know. It's been awhile. We both need it, don't we?"

I nodded, as my eyes and hands continued down his torso. I stopped, as I occasionally did, and fingered the tattoo. It was odd that we were both marked in nearly the exact same spot; his from a tattoo and mine from the long ago appendectomy.

The tattoo wasn't large—only about four inches wide and perhaps an inch and a half high—but I certainly found it intriguing. I looked up and met his eyes, the question unspoken but understood.

He gently shook his head and said, "Not tonight love."

Over the last several months I'd looked at it from an artist's point of view and commented on its exquisite craftsmanship and asked if it had meaning. The first time, he'd looked away and his only response was a silent nod. Since then, he'd said it was a painful subject and he'd share the details with me later, but never going so far as offering a specific time.

And although I was now far beyond simply curious at its meaning, I understood there had to be a significant story behind it—if only for the fact that it was the solitary question I'd posed which wasn't met with an immediate, straightforward, and honest answer. Confident he'd share its meaning when he was ready, my hands continued their downward journey.

I unfastened the button and slid the zipper of his pants down. The brilliant white briefs he wore stood out distinctly against the light brown of his skin and his big, already straining cock made my mouth water. As I hooked my fingers beneath the waistband, he said firmly, "You may look, but you are not to touch, understood?"

I respectfully answered in the way I knew excited him most. "Yes. I understand, Wes."

Carefully, I pulled back the briefs and simply marveled at the uncovered, bared splendor before me. His dick, so big and thick, lay firmly stretched out and pressed to his flat stomach. The slightly darker head was still partially hidden from full view by his foreskin. His large balls weren't hanging and relaxed, but neither were they pulled up tightly next to his body. And, the entire package was encased in the most amazing, soft, brown hair.

"You're so fucking incredible, Wes," I rasped as I unthinkingly reached a hand up to touch.

I caught myself just as he grinned wickedly and admonished, "Ah, ah...no touching."

I looked up to meet his eyes as one of his hands slowly rubbed his own chest. He let out a soft hiss of pleasure as he dragged his fingers down, slid them across his stomach, and finally rested them on his balls. He rolled them in his palm while his other hand gently grasped his cock near the middle and unhurriedly pulled downward to fully retract the foreskin and unveil the swollen head.

The entire time I could feel his gaze on my face...he was watching me watch him...obviously deriving as much pleasure from denying me as the physical touches to his body provided.

I let out a sound, deep and yearning.

"You like my big, thick dick, don't you, Grif?" he asked gruffly.

He continued to lightly stroke up and down, the foreskin slowly covering and uncovering the head over and over as he moved.

"You want to touch it—I can see it in your eyes. You want to feel its thickness...to have it sit in your hand and feel its weight."

"Yes, Wes. Please, may I?"

Ignoring my request, he continued, "But more than anything, you're a cocksucker. You want to taste it, to feel it filling your mouth and throat, to have your nose buried in my dick hair because you've taken it all the way down to the fucking root, don't you?"

The sight was stunning; him splayed back pleasuring himself and teasing me. I wanted more than anything to do exactly what he knew I wanted; to fucking taste him, to feel him inside my mouth. I was hot beyond words. My breath quickened as I watched and listened.

"Yes, Wes. Please."

He abruptly stopped, pulled me in for a deep, demanding kiss, and then leaned back far enough to look in my eyes and speak against my lips, "Your desire makes me so fucking hot. The way you openly want me…the way you show me that want," he growled. "Need to hurt and humiliate you, Grif. Need to see your handsome face covered with tears."

It had been only two days since I'd been allowed to come but watching and listening to him was more than enough to push me toward the edge.

"Wes, please, more," I pleaded. Knowing he'd understand our phrase and that I couldn't take much more before Junior lost it and shot.

"Okay, love. Okay," he soothed.

He maneuvered us so he was sitting, and laid me back on the lounger.

Even after all these months, I reflexively moved my hand and covered my jean-clad groin. Years of living with the fear of being discovered were difficult to let go.

His dark eyes flicked to my hand and then met mine, "Grif, remove your hand, please."

When I didn't comply, he asked with a patient tone, "Whose little dick is it? Who does it belong to?"

"It's yours, Wes. It belongs to you," I answered in earnest.

"That's right. And I'll do with it exactly what pleases me. Now remove your hand, please."

Even though I was fully clothed, I was still terrified to be laid out and exposed like this. I no longer had a problem being naked in front of him during Vanilla sex. Being naked while making love was something he'd helped me learn to enjoy—beyond words.

But this? This was different from making love; this was Chocolate. I knew what was coming. Junior knew what was coming. We both knew and we both craved it, but the horrible embarrassment, which made the situation what it was, as hot as it was, would never abate itself.

Much louder, Wes instructed with a glare, "Grif, move your fucking hand."

The first of the evening's tears slid down my face as I nodded and said, "Yes, Wes." I laid my hand on the seat cushion next to my trembling leg.

Tracking the tear as it moved across my cheek and down my jaw, he said with a thick voice, "You're so fucking intoxicating."

Leisurely, he popped the buttons of my jeans—one by one. He knew prolonging the inevitable was tormenting me as much as the impending completion was going to.

My entire body began to shake.

"I understand you're scared and you have every reason to want to hide your little dick." The last button undone, "But you can't. Not from me."

He stood, walked to the foot of the lounger and looked down at me. "Lean forward and pull your shirt off."

Once I'd complied, he bent, took hold of the cuffs of my jeans, and slithered them off. I lay there, legs spread and naked except for the jock strap, the only type of underwear I'd worn since living with Tate. I felt completely exposed and I couldn't stop trembling. Wes stood there looking down at me with hunger in his eyes, openly appraising my body.

"God, Grif, you're fucking sexy as hell."

He slowly stroked himself, his eyes never leaving my body, and it was only then that I noticed he was still dressed, his big dick exposed and his chest partially visible through the unbuttoned shirt but otherwise fully covered.

"Keep that position...your legs spread...and gently slide the jock down to your thighs."

Terrified, I squeaked, "Wes, please...."

"Now!" he barked, making it clear there was no room for discussion.

My eyes watered again as I nodded and began to lower the jock down. His unwavering scrutiny felt like fire burning into me. I could feel his desire, like a palpable force between us. He continued to stroke his twitching, thick cock, while beads of moisture gathered on the head.

The sight of him standing there, stroking, looking at me, and knowing in just a few more inches Junior would be exposed, made my balls ache with the need to shoot. I slid the jock the final few inches and felt the evening air hit my dick as I stared into Wes' face.

He stilled and his hand suddenly stopped stroking. I saw a smirk spread across his face as he turned his head to the side and away from me. The unmistakable sound of Wes attempting to suppress a laugh was terrifying. I felt lost. Lost somewhere between that horrific gym shower of so many years ago and the present moment with him.

Blinding—all consuming—fear overtook me, and I instinctively curled up on my side, desperately trying to hide Junior, while body-wracking sobs nearly robbed me of all control.

Almost immediately, I felt the cushion dip beside me, and I was pulled up and wrapped in a tight embrace. His strong hands soothingly stroked my back.

"Shush now," he whispered.

His warm breath on my ear soothed and brought me back to the present moment. He held me for several minutes until I finally calmed and wrapped my arms around his neck as the sobs tapered off into simple tears. I felt safe again.

Once I could get enough breath to speak, I rasped out, "I love you, Wes. Thank you so much. That was...fucking amazing."

"I love you too, Grif. And I'm the one who should be thanking you, babe. You missed it, but I shot a massive fucking load. Felt so good, Grif."

"Yeah?" I asked, with a hint of pride through my tears.

"Yep."

He pulled back slightly, my arms still locked around his neck, and kissed me deeply. I couldn't believe I had this wonderful man in my life—and he was all mine.

His hand slid between us and easily took the entirety of my dick and balls in one palm. He tenderly massaged and whispered in my ear, "Your nuts are so tight...so full."

"Junior...he's aching, Wes."

He flashed that mischievous grin and his hand briefly slipped away from my dick but returned almost immediately. He'd deftly slipped the leather band off his wrist and onto my dick. His thumb found the sensitive spot on my shaft, just below the head, and ever so lightly teased it.

I moaned and tried to buck forward to gain more friction. But a firm hand came to rest on my thigh silently demanding I keep still. Everything in me was saying move, but I stilled.

He locked his intense brown eyes on mine and whispered, "Penance hasn't been paid yet, Grif. I've still got plans—long, painful plans—for you this evening." The teasing at my cock head continued, "And although I'd considered letting you squirt this evening, it has been a few days after all, I've decided there won't be release for Stubby tonight." His superior smugness made Junior twitch. "You'll go to bed stiff and aching, you'll fall asleep wanting to come, and you'll wake up the same way, love. And tell me why, Grif."

I swallowed. I loved that he made me say it...made me acknowledge the power I willingly offered him...and loved that he also made me verbalize the thing which made my dick harder than anything, "Because I have a small dick, Wes." My eyes confidently held his as I continued, "You, and you alone, decide when I'll be granted an orgasm. I will always be thankful when one is allowed."

His kiss was both deep and tender.

I looked down at his thickening cock and gave him a smile. "On the other hand, we both know your big dick deserves more than a single shot this evening. I'd like to help with that."

His eyes were gleeful as his hand left my thigh and cupped my cheek. With a fiendish chuckle, he said, "I'm counting on it, fag."

Oh, I had a feeling it was gonna be a terrible night for me, but an incredible one for Junior.

CHAPTER 6
SIMPLE JUST ASK

Winter 2004

IT WAS OPENING night of *The Bourne Supremacy*. Tate and I were both looking forward to getting away from school and homework, and just losing ourselves in a good movie. The new arrangement regarding movies was now firmly established; Tate would continue to pick our home movies, but I got to chose theatre flicks.

I selected *The Bourne Supremacy* feeling confident it was going to be good. I'd read Robert Ludlum's Bourne series in high school and the first movie, *The Bourne Identity*, was amazing. Popcorn, M&M's, nachos, and Matt Damon. I couldn't wait.

I pulled up to the stop light at Robinson Avenue, a few blocks from our Hillcrest Cinemas destination, and did my best to discreetly glance over to Tate and take him in again before turning back to stare out the windshield at the red light.

He looked damn good tonight dressed in faded black

denim jeans that hung low on his hips and a pale yellow, V-neck sweater, sans an undershirt, which showed off his dark, smooth, Latino skin. His ever-present pendant was visible in the cut of the V-neck. His wavy black hair had been carefully styled to give him the appearance of having just rolled out of bed.

"Tate—," I started, intending to ask him if he thought we should try to find street parking or spring for the cost of parking in the garage, when he interrupted.

"All you have to do is ask."

I turned to find him smiling at me. But, there was something behind it…mischief, perhaps?

I thought I knew what he was referring to and managed to croak out a simple, "Huh?"

"You've been wondering when, maybe even if, it'll happen again. It's been almost a week, and frankly, with the way you've been staring at my dick, I'm not sure how you've managed to last this long without bringing it up."

I felt myself blushing what I'm sure was a deep red. Although it hadn't been what I was going to ask at all, I had to admit, at least to myself, I had thought about little else the past six days—and nights.

He grinned and said lightly, "I should have said something when I realized you were having such a difficult time. But, to be honest, it sorta thrills me knowing you want it so bad but aren't able to bring yourself to ask." He glanced at the stoplight, "The light's green, Grif."

I registered the traffic light and moved the car forward. My hands were shaking. I noticed an open parking spot, just on the other side of the intersection, and pulled in. Once I'd gotten the car parked and turned off, I leaned my forehead against the steering wheel and tried to get my out of control breathing in check.

I felt his cool touch on the back of my burning neck.

"It's okay, Grif," he said with slight amusement in his voice. "You know, the walls in our apartment aren't very thick. Combine that with your squeaky bed and...well, I can hear just about everything...including when you say my name."

"Oh my God, Tate. I'm so...embarrassed." And I was. The last thing I wanted him to know was how much I wanted to do it again. I don't know exactly why I didn't want him to know, but I didn't.

"Dude, don't be. Like I said, I like knowing I have that sort of...effect on you. And, if we're being completely honest here, it makes my dick thick."

I felt him shift in his seat and looked over at him. The bulge in his jeans was undeniable. Of course he caught me staring at it—again—and he shrugged. "Told you. Now reach over, give me a nice feel, and then drive us back home so I can fuck your face."

"Oh jeez, Tate!" I groaned and reached a shaking hand over.

∼

"I'm...gonna stop and check the mail," I said, as we pulled back into our parking spot in the apartment complex.

I knew I was stalling—and he knew I was stalling—but I was so damn nervous. I mean we'd skipped the movie and come back home for the sole purpose of sex. Who does that? I knew I was acting like a total dork, but I needed a few minutes to pull my shit together.

With a knowing wink he pushed the car door open, "Yeah, mail's important stuff." Once the door was closed, he leaned back in and said, "I'll go up and get ready."

He bounded up the steps with an easy, sexy confidence.

Sure, I thought, he can be confident; he doesn't have anything to worry about. But then it occurred to me, I wasn't going to be taking off my clothes, he wasn't going to see me naked, I was just going to…. Okay, thinking about that last part wasn't helping at all.

I made my way to the mailbox, then up to the apartment and let myself in. Leaning my back against the closed and locked door—yep, it was definitely locked, I'd checked it twice—I tried to breathe normally.

The apartment was quiet, and I wondered where Tate was while I flipped through the top couple of envelopes in my hand. More shit from the financial aid department—man, how I despised that department—and surprise, surprise another official looking one from the Superior Court of California addressed to *Javier Tatem Diaz*; more traffic violations to add to his collection, I was sure.

I was brought back to the present by muted sounds coming from the living room. I walked down the short entry hall, stopped dead in my tracks, dropped the mail to the floor, and let out a very unmanly squeak. The sofa's back faced the entry into the living room and there, leaning up against it, was Tate. Stripped down, completely naked, dick pointing skyward, with an easy grin plastered on his handsome face.

"Um…," I stammered, as I quickly lowered to my knees to retrieve the scattered envelopes. I foolishly thought focusing on a task would allow me to compose myself and develop some sort of plan.

I saw him moving toward me out of the corner of my eye, and my hand started that damn shaking thing again. Fuck! He stopped and stood only a few feet in front of me.

"I thought I'd make it easier for you, since you seem to be having such a difficult time asking for what you want."

His tone was playful, but I keenly felt the shame at the

truth in his words. I wasn't some teenager; I could ask for what I wanted. Hell, all he could say at this point was no. So why couldn't I bring myself to say the words?

I'd gathered the fallen mail and remained kneeling, only able to bring myself to look at his feet. And damn, even his feet were attractive.

"Perhaps it'll make things easier if you said out loud what you want, Grif. I know I'll like hearing it."

His tone had lost the playfulness and was somehow darker, more serious and heavy.

I looked up at him, taking a quick inventory of his body as I did, and landed on his dark eyes. I'd never had anyone look at me the way he was. But, then again, I'd never been in a situation even remotely like this one before either.

Just say what you want, I told myself, but I couldn't do it and ended up glancing away—blushing even deeper.

"Okay, if you can't say it to me, Grif, how are you ever gonna say it to...," and he trailed off, apparently sensing my growing discomfort.

Softer he said, "How about you just look at me and tell me what you see? Would that be easier?"

I knew he wanted something from me, and I felt like I sorta knew what it was. Yeah, he was going to enjoy the blowjob if I ever made it that far, but he obviously liked hearing I wanted him. Could hearing me verbalize my desire be just as important, just as much of a turn-on for him, as the blowjob itself?

And hell, if that's all he wanted in return, well, I was damn sure gonna do my best to give it to him. I mean, it wasn't like he was asking for anything but the truth.

I nodded, turned back to meet his eyes, and audibly swallowed before I found my words.

"I see intense, shimmering black eyes flecked with dark brown and gold. A strong brow, cheekbones, and jaw. You haven't shaved since last night and there's sexy stubble covering your chin and the sides of your face."

I paused and swallowed again. I could do this. It wasn't so bad. It was really only saying out loud what I'd been thinking since I first laid eyes on him three months ago.

I looked at his lips which were parted in a smile. "Full, masculine lips and the whitest teeth I've ever seen. But maybe they just seem whiter against your skin color. It's…it's this amazing shade of dark brown." As if on cue, he grinned broader revealing even more teeth and an irresistible smile.

"Black, shiny, slightly curly hair…which looks really thick and like it'd be soft to the touch."

I moved downward to his torso.

"Surprisingly broad shoulders for someone of your height with nicely defined arms and chest. And dark brown nipples that I want to…," I swallowed again, took a deep breath, and continued, "that I want to run my tongue across."

I continued down.

"Considering how much food you can put away, an impressively flat stomach and sexy four-pack." I actually chuckled a bit. Okay, this really wasn't so bad.

"And since we're moving into territory I've actually touched, I can say the light fur starting at your bellybutton, leading down to…."

When my eyes landed on his dick, my breath caught and stopped. There was a glistening string of pre-cum barely beginning to hang from the head of his dick and it was mesmerizing. Okay, I guess he really did like this. I could hardly think. The idea of catching his drip with the tip of my tongue made my head swim.

"Tate…it's extraordinary," I softly moaned.

He growled, a deep, rumbling sound, and firmly took

hold of both sides of my head tilting it up so our eyes met. "Grif, I know this is only your second time, but I'm gonna fuck your mouth—callous and quick—then squirt all over your face. Now open."

I eagerly nodded and did as I was told. I opened wide, and he slid in.

"Oh, fuck. So warm and wet. Nice!"

He wasted no time and began thrusting in a shallow yet purposeful rhythm. God, the feeling as his head slid over my tongue—it was sensational. I felt so full. And he smelled like the scent I'd come to know as him, only more intense.

"Oh, Grif...so good. Gonna be fast and then later I'll lay out on the bed and let you take your time with me, okay, dude? I'll let you explore all you want—take all the time you want. It'll be for you, but this one's for me!"

The grip around my head tightened and the thrusts grew much deeper. I remembered reading something somewhere about relaxing and swallowing. I tried, and suddenly felt his bush rub against my nose...he was all the way in...I'd never felt anything so fucking wonderful in my life. I groaned and it must have done something, made him feel something, because he lost rhythm and his thrusts became more stiff and erratic.

"Oh. My. God!" he loudly moaned.

His dick was slamming in and out of my mouth and throat, saliva ran down my chin, and I strained my eyes up to find him watching his dick fuck my face. "Yeah, fag, suck my fucking big dick!"

Abruptly, he pulled out and started stroking himself, "Look up at me, Grif...I want to see you when I coat your face with my spunk!"

A few more strokes and he yelled, "Oh fuck yeah...gonna shoot, dude!" I felt warm jets hit my cheek, chin, and neck. God, he was so masculine and captivating as he shot. So much pleasure spread across his face. And I had done that to him. I'd given him that pleasure.

He'd closed his eyes but, as his breathing calmed, he opened them and looked down at me. "Oh shit, dude. Stay there, let me get something to clean you up with."

Distantly, I heard the drawer where we kept the dish towels open and close and then water running. But I didn't really register any of it. I was floating.

God, the whole experience had been amazing; the feeling of his big cock sliding in and out of me, his possessive grip keeping my head in place, and when he'd called me a fag…God, why did it make me so fucking hard?

Footsteps and then he was squatting down in front of me. "Here ya go, Grif," he said, handing me a damp towel.

"Thanks," I replied hazily.

"Um. Grif…I'm sorry about calling you a…."

I opened my eyes and saw he was staring at the spot on the floor between us.

"No, Tate. It was good. All of it. Really good."

"You don't have to say that, dude. I can see you didn't enjoy it…you didn't even pop a bone."

Before I even realized what I was saying, I blurted, "Are you kidding, I'm hard as a fucking rock."

He looked down at my crotch and I could see he was perplexed, "You are?"

Oh fuck! What had I said? I quickly moved my hand to cover my crotch and block his view.

"Wait, you're hard?"

Then I saw understanding pass over his face and something else; the same something I'd seen on that fucking jock's face back in junior high. It was the same something that had haunted me for so many years.

"Oh," he said simply and looked away again.

I was going to be sick and everything in me screamed to move—to put distance between us. I scrambled to my feet, raced down the hall to my room, and closed the door.

I heard him calling after me, "Wait. Grif. Aw, fuck."

～

Soft knocking followed a bit later, and an even softer voice asking, "Grif? Can I come in, dude?"

I was lying on my bed, back to the door, and remembering. Remembering the look on Tate's face as understanding dawned. I couldn't believe what I had admitted. I promised myself years ago I'd never see that look again, and then I went and put myself right back in the same place. Fucking stupid, stupid, stupid. Man, he'd never see me the same again. He'd always look at me as some sort of freak—or whatever-the-fuck he thought. I had some savings, not much, but maybe it'd be enough to get my own place. I couldn't stay here. I just couldn't.

There was more knocking. "Grif? Come on, man. Can't we…you know…talk or something?"

"No," I answered sullenly. I knew he was trying and I also knew I was acting like a toddler, but I didn't give a shit. I didn't want to talk. Hell, talking was the last thing I wanted to do.

I heard the unmistakable sound of the knob being turned and the door hesitantly creaking open.

I sighed tiredly, "Tate. I don't want to—,"

"Look, I'm…fuck…I'm really sorry. I didn't mean to…. Aw, shit." He was quiet for several beats and then, with a grin in his voice, "Man, it's no wonder you love my big…,"

Angrily, I whirled to face him and nearly shouted, "Okay, we'll talk about this fucking once and only once.

You hear me? Just this fucking once!"

I jumped off the bed, closed the few feet between us—he actually took a step back and bumped into the closed door—and then I was right in his face. "Yeah, I'm fucking small. Is that what you want to hear? Is it, Tate?" I shouted. "And yeah, I liked sucking your big dick, okay?" He blinked quickly as a tiny bit of my spit hit his cheek. "But you will *never* have the opportunity to look at me that way again, do you understand? I won't fucking have it." My anger was suddenly replaced by deep sadness. I looked down and caught sight of his pendant and found it easier to focus on it...to talk to it...instead of him. "I'll find my own place as soon as I can afford it. I can't stay here."

I turned to step away and felt a hand grab my bicep. Before I even knew what I was doing, I'd swung back around, and with one hand on his chest I'd pushed him backward into the door and had a fist drawn back to hit him.

He threw an open hand up between us, "Whoa, Grif! Hold on, Big Guy, hold on."

I saw the fear in his eyes and immediately let him go, dropped my arm, and purposefully loosened my stance. What the fuck had I almost done? Jeez!

He suddenly threw both arms around me, locking his wrists behind my back, and trapping my arms to my sides in a tight hug. With his ear pressed against my collarbone, he said "Dude, okay...fuck. Just calm down...and don't fucking hit me, okay?"

I could hear the tremble in his voice, "Man, I'm so sorry, Tate. I'd never hit anyone, let alone you."

"Yeah, well you were doing a fine impression of a drunken, jealous redneck whose girlfriend had been hit on by Darrel and Darrel." His voice was still nervous, but I could hear his ever present sense of humor returning.

"Damn, I'm gonna miss you, Tate," I whispered.

He let go and pushed me back a bit to look at me. I couldn't hide the moisture in my eyes. He surprised me by firmly pushing me, and not expecting the movement, I fell backward onto my bed. I looked up, and he was clearly angry. What the fuck? What did he have to be angry about?

"Okay, we need to slow the fuck down here, Grif," and he stepped toward me. "Slow. The. Fuck. Down."

He rubbed his hands across his face and stared at me for a few beats. "Okay, let's, for a moment, forget about the sex and just talk. Wait! Fuck, not sex. We are not having sex…you're blowing me."

He spun around, took a few steps toward the door, and then turned back to face me again. "Okay, whatever it is, let's put it aside for a moment." He sighed, "Grif, you're my best friend and whatever just happened in the living room you are not moving out. Got it? You are not leaving simply because you've got…," he pinned me with a determined stare and continued, "…just because you've got a small dick and you feel like you fucked up by inadvertently telling me."

I started to push up from the bed and then stopped as he pulled his hand back and balled it into a fist, "Look, I don't want to fight…because there's no doubt in my mind you'd beat the living shit outta me. But I'm not above decking you to get your attention—consequences be damned."

I barked out a laugh. I couldn't help it.

His tension eased, and he let his arm fall out of its threatening position. "What the fuck are you laughing about? I wouldn't make it easy on you. I'm sure I could land a good punch or two before you took me down!" he said indignantly.

I grinned widely. "I just realized you're still naked."

"Oh," he said looking down over his body. "Well, I figured I'd fucked up pretty bad out there...and um, I thought I should use everything I had to try and fix it." He winked and took a step toward me, "Is it working at all?"

I winked back, "Maybe...," and chuckled a bit. "However, I'm probably still moving."

He stepped next to the bed and considered it, "Move over Big Guy," and then laid down next to me. "Um, Grif?"

"Yeah?"

"You get I'm not gay, right?"

I turned over so we were facing each other and said with an exasperated sigh, "Yes, Tate, I get it. Seriously."

"Okay. So, first, you're not moving. That discussion is o-v-e-r. Second, I'm sorry about calling you a fag. I sorta got carried away. I mean, the way you were looking at me...full of want and pure desire...fuck, dude, it was such a turn-on. Yeah, I definitely got carried away, and it just kinda popped out. But, if I'm being totally honest about it, well...it kinda made me hotter...but I'm sorry if I hurt your feelings. I won't do it again.

"Lastly—and I get this is the biggie—no pun intended...you're small. I can certainly understand being sensitive about...um, I mean, if you are, sensitive about it. But it doesn't make a fuck of a difference to me. It's not...like we're having sex and it's not like you're suddenly a different person 'cause you've got a small dick." He thought a moment and then asked, "How small is it anyway?"

I'd been silent since he'd begun talking and when I didn't offer any response at all, he sighed with resignation, "I'm making things worse, aren't I? I'm not gonna be able to fix this, am I?"

I raised my eyebrows and asked, "My turn now?"

He nodded wordlessly.

"First, you've gotta get over the whole 'I'm not gay' thing. I know you're not gay, Tate. And if you feel like hugging me, or lying next to me on a bed, or whatever, you don't have to feel like there needs to be a reminder or disclaimer spoken every time. I get it…fucking relax and be yourself. Two, surprisingly, I didn't get upset by you calling me a fag. I honestly never thought I'd say something like that, but I guess context is always important. And, in that context, I gotta say it made me even hotter too—for whatever reason. Maybe I'll think more on it later."

That earned me a big grin, "Well, that certainly opens up some interesting possibilities."

I reached over and halfheartedly punched him in the shoulder, "Still my turn to talk."

"Ouch! You do realize you're a big guy…in amazing shape, with freakish strength, right? No hitting, goddammit," he said laughing.

I pinned him with a stare.

"Okay, okay, still your turn to talk."

"Where was I?"

"Number two: 'fag,' makes us both hot, future possibilities."

I glared at him.

Giggling he said, "What? You asked."

"Three," and I took a much more serious tone, "Yes, I'm small, and the only person I've ever spoken to about it was my father. He's the only person, Tate—the only one. And I don't really want to talk about it now other than to say yes, I am sensitive, no it doesn't change who I am and there won't be a problem if it doesn't change the way you see me, because I'll never get naked during sex or any other time in front of you. Lastly, despite you being straight, and despite what you choose to call it, your dick in my mouth is sex, Tate."

He grinned, "You never actually said how small it is."

"Tate," I growled in warning.

He smiled so genuinely I couldn't help but smile back.

"So," he started jovially, "we okay, Big Guy?"

I looked down at his chest—so damn lickable. "Almost," I said.

"Almost?"

"Yeah," and I reached over and ran my thumb lightly over a nipple, "I seem to remember something about you promising to be splayed out on the bed and me getting to take my time with your body."

"Oh yeah," he said with a wicked grin, "I'm down with that...fag!" And with a waggle of his dark brows he flopped over onto his back laying himself out for me. "This," he said mischievously and gestured up and down his ripped brown body, like a *Price is Right* model showing off a new car, "is all yours to enjoy. Have fun, Grif...I know I'm gonna."

Oh, there was no doubt I was gonna have fun!

CHAPTER 7
MR. MATTHEW SMITHTON

Early Summer 2008

THE ANSWERING MACHINE was making that damn chirping noise again. I really needed to get rid of it now…well, now that I lived alone. Even though we both had cell phones, Tate had refused to budge on the point of getting rid of the landline. "Dude, I don't want every chick I bang to have my cell number," he'd reasoned the last time I'd brought the subject up. He'd then said, "You know, you can give it out to guys too."

Whatever. He'd known full well my dating pool had been limited to him. But now I was alone—with a fucking beeping answering machine that I was about ready to chuck against the wall.

I walked over to the kitchen counter and hit the play button.

I unpacked the groceries as the machine did its thing and played back the messages. The first three were all from girls wanting to hook up with Tate. Yeah, well that wasn't gonna happen, now was it?

The last was from the same guy who'd been calling since Tate's death. Over the first week or so his messages had been incredibly professional, but never really said exactly why he was calling. Recently, they'd begun to take on a more serious tone. This one was almost rude:

Mr. Griffin, this is Mr. Smithton calling again.

I could hear the exasperation in his voice.

Look, we really need to discuss matters of great importance...regarding Mr. Diaz.

There was a long pause, then he continued,

I'm currently in New York and I'd really rather not fly out to San Diego when this is something we should really get started over the phone. However, I will do exactly that, sir.

He was going to fly here to see me? What the fuck?

Unless I hear from you by the end of day tomorrow I'll be on a redeye flight tomorrow night.

He continued,

I hope I'm making myself clear, Mr. Griffin? Return my call, sir!

The unmistakable sound of him hanging up—quite loudly—filled the tiny kitchen.

The machine's disembodied, genderless voice spoke out, *Timestamp 8:37am*. The groceries temporarily forgotten, I glanced at the clock on the microwave and it read 5:16pm. That was 8:16pm Eastern Time. Well, not a lot of chance Mr. Smug Bastard Smithton was going to be in at this hour. I decided to call and leave my own pissy voicemail telling him to fuck off. God, I was so angry.

I picked up the cordless phone, punched in the number, and was surprised to hear it pick up after only the first ring.

"Mr. Griffin, good evening, sir," Mr. Smithton said pleasantly, devoid of all smugness.

"Um, hi," I said, caught off guard by the man actually answering at this hour…and knowing it was me calling. "I didn't expect…um, I assumed I'd be calling an office…and it'd be closed."

He ignored my comment and said, "I'm glad you returned my call, sir."

"Okay, first can we stop with the 'sir'…I'm only twenty-four, and it's making me feel a little creepy. Second, why on earth would you be flying cross-country to see me? I have no idea who you are or what you want…nor why you'd be leaving a fuck-load of messages on my and Tate's…on my machine!" My anger was building back up. Anger was good…it was oddly comforting.

"I do understand, sir…um, Mr. Griffin, I do understand." Man, the guy really was being polite in the face of my hostility. One point for Mr. Smithton. "But there are important matters to discuss regarding Mr. Diaz's estate. Matters which need to be settled and may no longer be put off, Mr. Griffin."

"Mr. Diaz's estate? Why would that have anything to do with me?"

Oh, maybe it was about the apartment. The lease had been in Tate's name and even though I'd spoken with the apartment's manager, perhaps this Mr. Smithton, represented the building's owner or something. And maybe simply putting my name on the lease wasn't going to be as easy as the elderly landlord had led me to believe. Dammit, I didn't want to even think about having to find a new place.

But that couldn't be it. Mr. Keeny, the manager, had sent over a copy of the new lease, and I'd even called and spoke with him after receiving it. I had several questions after reading it over. The least of which was the fact that it listed the monthly rent as $1,400—where Tate had told me it was $900—and that it showed the entire year had been paid in full. Granted, there was only a few months left on the lease, but it had been paid up to the point where Tate and I would have graduated and then given us a few months to finalize our plans before moving on with 'adult life.'

"Look!" I growled, "If this is about the lease on the apartment, I've already worked it out with the landlord, so—,"

"No, sir. This has nothing to do with the lease," he gently interrupted.

"Oh. Then what?" I asked, more confused than ever about what this guy wanted.

"Sir, you do know you're the sole beneficiary of Mr. Diaz's estate, correct?"

"Sole…. Wait, there has to be some misunderstanding. First, I don't think a laptop, some clothes, a car, and a totaled motorcycle quite constitute an estate. But, that aside, shouldn't you be talking to his extended family about this rather than me?" Shit, is that what this was about? Some distant cousin wanted Tate's stuff?

"Mr. Griffin," he said in a compassionate voice, and I wondered about the shift in tone. "I've already booked a flight to San Diego, because, well to be honest, I had no reason to expect a return call from you. I'll be arriving at 6pm Pacific Time tomorrow evening. Can we meet at your apartment on Albatross Street at 6:45? I assure you everything will be explained then. But, let me be clear, there's much more to Mr. Diaz's estate than the items you've listed, sir."

Wait, how did he know where we—where I lived? And who was he, really? And how did I even know he was who he said he was?

He must have sensed my hesitation. "Or, if you'd prefer, there's a quiet restaurant at the corner of 3rd and J streets, called Candelas, we could meet there."

I knew the place and it was kinda pricey on my college budget, but at least the guy wouldn't be knocking on my apartment door.

"Um, yeah, I guess that'd be okay." I answered.

I could've sworn I heard him exhale in relief. "Very good then, sir. Tomorrow evening at 6:45. Goodnight, Mr. Griffin," he said, and disconnected.

I made my way down to Candelas, in the Gaslamp district, and had a hell of a time finding parking, but that wasn't unusual. I'd briefly thought about riding my bike, to save the parking hassle, but it'd been a long day of classes, and I wasn't in the mood for physical exercise. That should have told me something right there—physical activity and I were normally joined at the hip.

I finally found an open parking space and squeezed in. Getting out, I locked the car and then made my way up 3rd Avenue to the restaurant. It was a pleasant evening and people were casually walking the street, dining at the sidewalk cafes, and generally enjoying the tropical, easy San Diego atmosphere.

But I didn't notice much of it at all; I still wondered what the fuck I was doing here. Parts of yesterday's conversation kept replaying over and over in my head and I kept trying to make sense of them. Mr. Matthew Smithton said he represented Tate's estate. What did that mean? And then there was the fact that Tate even had an estate.

I pulled open the door and made my way in. I'd only gotten as far as a few feet when I felt a light touch on my shoulder. I turned to see the distinguished man whom I assumed was Mr. Smithton. He was in his early 50's, and if the color of his salt & pepper eyebrows was any indication, his short hair had once been black. However, almost no trace of dark remained—he was prematurely silver.

He had friendly blue eyes, but they had a definite seriousness to them. He wore a simple button down light blue shirt, a navy blazer, jeans and loafers. He was definitely someone who wasn't a stranger to the gym and probably routinely turned more than a few heads. In his younger days, I'm sure he'd had to beat them off with a stick.

"Mr. Griffin, I'm glad you made it, I'm Matthew Smithton."

He extended a hand and I clasped it in a quick greeting.

"Mr. Smithton, it's nice to meet you. How did you know who I was?"

"It's all part of the job, Mr. Griffin. Please, I've taken the liberty of reserving us a quiet dinner table. I hope that wasn't too presumptuous, sir?"

I shook my head as he briefly placed one hand on the middle of my back and then gestured in the general vicinity of the dining area. I followed him to a quiet corner table where he waited for me to sit before taking the chair across from me.

Before either of us had the chance to say anything, a young waiter appeared and asked, "Mr. Smithton, may I bring you and your guest something to drink, sir?"

Um, okay, how did the waiter know his name? This was becoming more and more strange by the minute and I was beginning to feel as if I'd made a mistake by agreeing to meet someone I didn't know at all but who appeared to know quite a bit about me.

"Look, I'm not sure I should have come...," I said beginning to push my chair back.

He briefly stiffened, and his eyes seemed almost pleading, but, just as quickly, he appeared to make a conscious effort to relax.

After dismissing the waiter with a polite nod, he said, "Mr. Griffin, I've been representing the Diaz family, in one capacity or another, for over twenty years. I've known...," he stopped and cleared his throat, glanced down at the table and then back up at me, "I knew Mr. Diaz...Tate...almost from the time he was born. Believe me when I say I'm here because Tate wanted me to be here."

His voice had grown kind and somber as he spoke. I

could feel his loss even though he hid it well. He knew Tate's family. He knew Tate.

He reached into his jacket, pulled out a clean, pressed handkerchief and handed it to me. I was somewhat perplexed as I accepted it until I realized a tear had slid down my cheek. God, I missed Tate so much.

I cleared my throat, "Thank you. I'm sorry."

"Not at all, sir. You've suffered quite a loss. It's completely understandable."

The anger flared as I lay the handkerchief down on the table between us. My eyes caught his, and I held them firmly.

"Mr. Smithton, I don't know how you seem to know so much about me, but if you don't start explaining yourself, and pretty damn quick, I'm outta here. Do I make myself clear?"

The waiter had cleared the dessert plates and was serving coffee. I learned more about Tate's family, during the brief dinner, than I had the entire time I'd known and lived with him.

Tate's father, Juan, who eventually adopted the more American version of Jonathan, and his mother, Maria, had grown up in the same small Illinois farming community although neither family were farmers. They'd both been only children and had attended the same schools from elementary all the way through college. Once graduated from college, the two had gotten married. Maria's career was secondary to Jonathan's and the two moved from state to state following Jonathan's rise as a financial advisor initially and then eventually his tremendous success as an investment broker.

Focused on his career, the two had mutually decided to wait to start a family until they were financially secure and knew they'd be able to finally put roots down. Shortly after her forty-fourth birthday, Maria became pregnant with Tate. And although they tried to grow their family, after three miscarriages, they accepted Tate would be their only child and they devoted all their time, energy, and love to him.

The winter of Tate's senior high school year, the family had taken a ski vacation in Park City, Utah. Jonathan and Maria had gone to dinner leaving an ill Tate at home with enough cold medicine to fend off an epidemic and enough chicken soup to feed a third world county. They had ventured down the mountain to spend an evening at one of the family's favorite restaurants when their car hit a patch of black ice. Out of control, the car slid through the guardrail, down an embankment, and they were both killed instantly.

Tate, being of legal age—something he and I shared were late birthdays which saw us both turn eighteen during our senior year of High School—spent the next sixteen months in a haze before deciding to honor his father's wishes and enroll in college. He took his GED exam and was accepted to UCSD; as far away as he could get from cold, snow, and icy roads.

I knew the rest. Tate and I would meet on our first day of college.

"So, you see, Mr. Griffin, after Tate's parents passed, he was alone," he said sedately, as he looked at me. But a bit of warmth returned to his eyes as he continued, "Until he met you, that is. Oh, of course he had me, and we, most often, spoke at least once a week in the years since the accident. But, even though I've been a family friend, as well as an estate employee, for as long as Tate could probably remember, I was much closer in age to his parents than I was to him. And since the accident...well."

He looked out the window next to us for a moment before turning back toward me.

"Mr. Griffin...Grif. May I call you Grif?"

I nodded, "Yes, of course."

Odd how over the course of dinner, I'd gone from being completely suspect of the gentle man sitting across from me to feeling...a kinship with him; he'd lost both Tate's parents and Tate as well.

He smiled, "Good. And please, if you would, call me Matthew?"

I smiled back, "Okay, Matthew."

"I hope it's a bit clearer why, in part at least, I know so much about you. Tate spoke of you in every conversation we'd had up until his death."

He cleared his throat and, for the first time since we'd sat down, seemed uncomfortable.

"Grif, I'm completely aware of Tate's...um, well, let's just say we both know how much he enjoyed the fairer sex. Heaven knows I assisted in extracting, and then performing damage control, on more than one occasion when Tate's interest waned, but the young lady's hadn't." The small shake of his head and quick glance down at the table, told me he felt awkward talking about Tate's personal life—it was a feeling I understood well.

"However, that aside, I know the two of you shared something very special. Of course I'm not privy to any details, and I shouldn't be, it was...it is none of my business, but I know one thing beyond a shadow of a doubt; he frequently said you were the most important person in his life."

I reached out and picked up the handkerchief that had laid between us during dinner and hastily swiped at my eyes. Christ, the guy was going to think all I did was cry.

"He...," I stopped and swallowed. "He actually said that to you? Those were his words?"

Matthew nodded, "He did."

I briefly toyed with the handkerchief before placing it on the table, "I mean, we...I know we had something very special...but he would have never said that to me...," I shook my head, looked up and offered him a weak smile, before refocusing my attention on the handkerchief.

"No, he likely wouldn't, Grif. But you knew, right?"

I looked back up and nodded. "Yes, I knew. To use your words, Matthew, I knew beyond a shadow of a doubt how much he cared for me. It's not something he would have ever voiced aloud—at least not that succinctly anyway."

I reached out, took the cup of coffee and held it a bit before taking a sip.

"For Tate, well, being the uber-straight man he was...he was never going to tell me, a gay man, that he loved me. But, yes, I knew."

"Look, it's been a long evening, Grif," he said. "How about we call it a night and talk about the estate issues tomorrow? There's quite a lot to discuss and a few decisions need to be made, but putting those off another day isn't going to have irreparable consequences or anything."

I looked up from my coffee cup and into Mathew's kind face, "Sounds good to me. If you give me your number, I'll call you tomorrow?"

"Sure. Or, if it'd be okay with you, we can meet at Mike's Frozen Yogurt shop after your two o'clock class? I've always wanted to stop in but have never had the chance."

I looked at him in mock astonishment. I was no longer surprised by the depth of his knowledge regarding my personal life. "Okay, but only if you tell me exactly how you know I stop in there after my two o'clock class and you tell me exactly what else you know about me."

He laughed, "You've got yourself a deal."

CHAPTER 8
THE WORLD CHANGES

Early Summer 2008

TATE AND I had been coming to Mike's Frozen Yogurt since we'd run across it during our first semester. It was the kind of business that was definitely someone's afterthought. It was literally a hole cut into the side of what used to be a duplex apartment with a window counter inserted.

One ordered from the sidewalk counter, situated at a busy and noisy intersection, sometimes waiting in line for twenty minutes, and that was it; there was nothing more to the public aspect of the place. There was rarely any place to park, nowhere to sit, and absolutely nothing more than the window counter.

Fortunately, it bordered the Northwest end of Balboa Park, at Elm Street and 6th Avenue, and a short walk across the street offered large shade trees, comfortable benches, and endless people watching.

The day was typical for San Diego; bright blue sky and a warm, comfortable breeze. My tank top, shorts and tennis shoes were the perfect choice. As I rounded the corner, school backpack slung over one shoulder, I caught sight of Mr. Smithton—or, since we'd agreed the night before on using first names, Matthew.

He was much more casually dressed this afternoon and wore simple yet expensive looking jeans, a crisp t-shirt, which highlighted his well-defined arms and chest, and a pair of Nikes that looked like they'd come directly out of the box. No doubt about it, the man was striking.

He caught sight of me and offered a hearty greeting while extending his hand, "Grif, it's nice to see you again."

"You too, Matthew. You definitely have much more of a southern California vibe going today," I said lightly, gesturing toward his comfortable but handsome attire.

He looked surprised and then slightly flustered. What was that about?

"Oh. I was out walking downtown Coronado and then came straight here. I should have gone back to the hotel and changed. My apologizes, sir."

"Okay, first, why on earth would you need to apologize? You look great. And second, I thought we'd agreed to dispense with the 'sir' bullshit last night, hadn't we?"

He visibly relaxed and began walking backward making his way toward the counter, "We did indeed, Grif."

Surprisingly, there were only two people in line in front of us, and they'd just received their order as we stepped up to the window.

"If it's okay, I'll let you order for me...you're most certainly the connoisseur here."

"Sure, you got it. Would you prefer nonfat or full flavored?" I asked.

"Categorically nonfat!" he said with a hearty laugh. "You think it's easy keeping this body in shape? Every year it gets harder and harder. I need all the non-fat help I can get."

I skimmed a glance up and down his frame.

"You're not doing badly at all for an older...," I broke off for a moment. "Oh shit, that was downright rude and not at all the way I meant it."

Again, he smiled. Did anything ruffle this guy's feathers? Oh yeah, some young dumbass not returning his calls or that same dumbass commenting on his casual dress...those had certainly changed his tone. And now I go and pay him a sideways compliment? Fuck.

"Honestly, I didn't mean...I mean, dude, you're seriously, seriously hot. Not that I'm coming onto you or anything. But if I were...if someone my age were coming onto you, that'd be okay...I mean.... Well shit, you're just gonna let me babble on here and dig the hole deeper, aren't you?"

He chuckled while hooking his thumbs into his front pockets. "Why don't you order us the yogurt...and perhaps I can finagle us a senior citizen discount."

"Oh, jeez!" I groaned and tried to hide my face in my own shoulder. He rested a hand lightly on my upper back, still laughing.

"I said you were hot. Doesn't that count for anything?"

I looked up at the yogurt dude, "Two nonfat coconut mango sundaes with carob chips, please. Oh, in cups, not the wafer cones. Oh, and one more thing—my smoking hot friend here wants to know if you offer a senior citizen discount."

That earned me a perplexed look from yogurt dude and a playful whack to the back of the head, along with more laughing, from Matthew.

"Hey! I'm not too proud to hit an old man!" I snapped in mock irritation. "You'll love these...they're so good. They're nonfat and low in sugar. So, I'm doing my part to ensure you keep a banging, ripped, totally sick bod!"

Matthew grinned. "Okay, okay, you've made your point…you think I'm sexy and completely irresistible to folks of all ages. You're off the hook."

A few minutes later, the yogurt dude cleared his throat, "Um, sir? Your sundaes are ready."

Matthew barked out a laugh and moved several steps down the street. When I approached, he was grinning from ear to ear. "I guess it's all a matter of perspective, right, *sir?*"

We made our way across the street and sat on a bench, looking back toward the yogurt stand, when I noticed the silver Jaguar sedan—complete with driver and all. Matthew and I had been standing right in front of it, but with all the bantering back and forth, I'd completely missed it.

"Wow, really nice car," I said, after swallowing a scoop of sundae. "Aren't the coconut and mango together amazing?"

"It is indeed, Grif. It's part of what we need to talk about."

"Huh? What is? The yogurt or the car?" I asked, while pointing my spoon at the Jaguar.

Matthew rested his sundae on a knee and took on a much more serious tone.

"The car, Grif. And the driver. And my services. And a lot more. Much, much more in fact."

He suddenly sounded like Mr. Smithton from the answering machine and not the jovial Matthew of a few minutes earlier.

"As I informed you, you are the sole heir to Mr. Diaz's…Tate's…estate. The car and driver across the street are only a minuscule part of that."

I don't know why, but my stomach suddenly dropped.

"What kind of…," I cleared my throat and turned to look him in the eye. "Matthew, what size estate are we talking about here?"

"Well, sir, it's comprised of homes and condos, stocks, bonds, cars, a large boat, a medium sized aircraft, and cash...a substantial amount of cash. And, of course, there's support staff for all of these. In total, I believe you directly employ about sixty people in various states, sir."

I definitely felt sick. My heart was pounding so intensely I could hear it in my ears. A dog flew by chasing a tennis ball, and I barely even registered it.

"Ballpark worth, Matthew," I said as I stared, unseeingly, down at the ground.

"Roughly four hundred million in cash, sir, and...."

I didn't hear anything more except my stomach wrenching as I threw up into the trash can next to the bench. I heaved until there was nothing left in my stomach. I felt Matthew's hand at the middle of my back.

"Sir?"

I swung around and out of his reach...angry, and confused, and missing Tate more than ever.

"Fuck you!" I screamed at him. "Just fuck you!"

I backed away from him as I ran the back of my hand across my mouth.

"You think you can come here and...he's not even been gone two weeks...and on top of losing him, you wanna lay this shit on me too? Fuck you!"

I stood glaring at him—I was so incredibly angry. "I can barely eat," I shouted, "I can't remember the last time I slept more than a few hours, I've lost the only...the only man I've ever lov...." No, I couldn't do this! Not here, not now, and definitely not with a stranger.

I turned and ran across the park. I had no idea where I was going. In fact, I had ceased to have any conscious thought at all. But I knew I needed to get far, far away from him...from all of it...right the fuck now.

CHAPTER 9
PENANCE PART TWO

Summer 2014

"LET'S GO INSIDE, love," Wes said as he stood from the lounger and stretched his arms over his head. After re-buttoning his shirt and pants, he reached for my hand.

I placed mine in his. Now that the mood had settled down a bit, I was more keenly aware than ever of him being clothed and me being completely naked.

I squeezed his hand, "Let me just grab my clothes," I tried with a false air of nonchalance.

He squeezed back, "It really bothers you when I'm clothed and you're not, doesn't it?"

I wanted to lie. I wanted to tell him it didn't bother me at all, because I knew if I revealed the extent of my discomfort he'd certainly exploit it. But there were reasons I didn't go with the overwhelming impulse to mislead him; for one, we'd long ago agreed never to lie to one another—about anything—ever. And, for another, every time I revealed more, made myself more vulnerable, there was every possibility that he'd use it against me in the most painful, and thus pleasurable, ways imaginable. No, I wouldn't lie.

"Yes, Wes, it really does."

I squirmed a bit. I knew the questions were coming and, therefore, I knew I had to put thoughts and feelings into words. And the very words I was about to put out there would, at some point, surely be used to hurt or humiliate me. The knowledge that I'd enjoy whatever he might do with the information did little to ease my apprehension.

We hadn't made it very far toward the house when he stopped our progression and warmly—expectantly—looked down into my eyes. Jeez, how could I not tell the man absolutely anything he wanted to know?

I started to look down when he caught my chin in his thumb and forefinger. He had a thing about us looking each other in the eye when speaking. Especially when the topic was one such as this: an important one.

"When I'm naked, and you're not...when we're in Chocolate...I feel there's no chance for me to hide. I mean, when you're naked, I can do things to you to distract you, things I know will take your mind and eyes off me. Off of Junior. But, times like these...there's no place for me to hide, Wes, and it scares me."

"Scares you?" he repeated with brows furrowed.

"No, poor choice of words," I corrected. "You know I'm never frightened by you. You'd never harm me. What I should have said was, 'It puts me on edge, makes me feel incredibly vulnerable, and makes my heart beat like crazy.'"

He pulled me into his arms, kissed me, and slid his hands up and down my bare back saying, "But I've got plans for your pint-sized dick this evening, and they don't include the little guy being covered up."

A small gasp escaped my lips—both from the anticipation of what he might have planned, but also from the look in his eyes. "God, Wes, the way you look at me sometimes...like I'm the most important person. I hope I never get used to it."

He broke one side of our embrace as we walked back into the house, my arm around his waist and his around my shoulder.

Once inside, he said, "You are the most important person, Grif," and resumed his place near the middle of the sofa.

"Would you like another scotch?" I asked.

"Sure. I didn't really get more than a taste of the first one," he said with a waggle of his eyebrows.

Laughing, I made my way over to the bar, passing Tate's urn and the smiling photograph sitting on the mantle of the rarely used fireplace.

The picture had been taken on a sunny afternoon at the beach. I was trying out the camera on my new iPhone and had been snapping pics of everything. He wore a pair of red boardshorts, his pendant, and a smile. He looked young, healthy, and full of life; the exact way I always remembered him.

Not for the first time, I thought that he'd be happy for me; happy I'd found someone to love and who loved me as much in return. And he'd no doubt be thrilled with Tate's Place.

At the bar, I poured a double over ice and sipped from it as I made my way over to Wes. As I stood in front of him, he made no move to take the glass. Instead, he simply looked me up and down.

"Damn, Grif. Just damn!" He said with obvious appreciation of my fit body.

I let my hand drop, positioning it to shield my surging dick from view, and continued to hold the glass out to him. He finally accepted it and took a slow drink.

"Lie down here, across my lap, face up with your head resting on the arm of the sofa, please."

He spread his knees, and I lay down across him, my ass on the sofa cushion between his thighs, my head resting on one sofa arm, and my feet on the other. God, I felt so utterly exposed, so completely naked except for Tate's pendant around my neck and Wes' leather band around Junior.

"Please, love, make yourself comfortable, you're gonna be here quite a while."

He took another sip of his drink and looked down at my naked body. "Grif...fuck...so goddamned sexy."

I sighed in embarrassment and whispered, "Wes...."

"Put your arms back, head resting on your hands, please."

I complied, and he moaned a little. "Yes, just like that. But you don't believe you're sexy, huh? You don't see the perfectly shaped biceps?" He ran a hand over each. "The incredible chest—with these flawlessly shaped pecs?" He rested a hand on my left one, and I knew he could feel my heart beating beneath it. "The ridiculously flat abs?" He ran a finger over each one of the six-pack. "And this perfect package?" He palmed my inflexible dick and aching balls.

"Wes," I sighed again and looked away. "Come on. Okay, maybe the gym work pays off, but you completely lost me at *perfect package*." I was silent for a moment, and quietly added, "We both know that's not true."

"Grif, look at me."

I turned and met his intent eyes.

"Your cock is small, yes. But it's perfect, not only because it's beautifully shaped and so pretty to look at, but mostly because it's part of you—of who you are."

He shifted a bit, and his thumb drew light strokes on my dick's most sensitive spot under the head, filling me with both pleasure and longing.

"If you weren't the size you are, and you didn't need the things you need...then you wouldn't need me the same way...and I wouldn't need you in the same way. I love you, every single part of you."

I listened to him talk about me as if I were the most flawless thing on the planet and wondered, not for the first time, how the fuck I got so lucky.

"Wes, the way you make me feel...sometimes...."

He bent over and gave me a deep kiss. As he pulled away, he grinned, "Okay, lie back and relax. It's time for the *fun* to begin."

He started by alternating between light strokes across my hard dick, gently massaging my bound balls, and tweaking my peaked nipples. The touch was so gentle and soft, and it felt so damn good.

Grasping my dick, he pulled it down, away from my body, only to release it and have it slap back against my stomach with a sting. After giving my dick a few small, pleasant strokes, he pulled down again and released. The pain of the *pull and slap* mixed with the delicious, soft strokes, was driving me crazy. But he simply continued, completely focused on what he was doing, over and over: slap, stroke, pull away, and then slap again.

My balls received his attention next. They were tight and bound and he gently rubbed the flat of his palm over them. The delicate touch had me wanting to arch up and feel more—get more friction. It felt so nice until he gently took hold of them and tugged, extending my sac as far away from my body as possible and just held them there. The continuous stretch became uncomfortable and the pressure was just shy of pain. I squirmed slightly and the pressure instantly became pain—not unbearable but most certainly distressing.

With my nuts in his vice-like grip, he calmly, but with a definite sharpness in tone, asked, "How do I feel about wriggling, fag?"

I gasped out an answer between breaths, "You don't approve of it, Wes."

And he didn't. There'd been rules agreed upon for these particular types of torment sessions. I was rarely restrained, but I was to remain absolutely still. I was to keep my arms and legs where he'd placed them, or where I'd laid them when the session began.

My being unrestrained offered him the unparalleled pleasure of watching the conflicting desires as they coursed through me. His torments gave rise to an internal struggle; listen to my intellectual need to obey him and remain still, versus following my body's inherent desire to pull away and protect itself.

I could move my fingers and toes and most reasonable movement of my head was acceptable. And, of course, I could beg, and plead, and cry out—oh he thoroughly enjoyed hearing my pleas and moans of pleasure and pain. But above all else, I was to remain still and accept the pleasure or pain that delivered him the most gratification or amusement at the time.

He squeezed slightly tighter, and I let out a high-pitched yelp.

"And why is that?"

"Because I should eagerly accept any attention you give my midget toy."

I was straining against moving and doing all I could to be still, breathe and coherently provide the verbal answers he wanted—the spoken answers we both needed. But I thought I was going to lose my fucking mind if he didn't let up soon.

"And if it's pain I decide I'd like to offer your meager prick? If it's seeing you hurt that makes me hard, that gives me pleasure?"

And there it was, the key combination. Sure, I enjoyed the submission, the pain, and the denigration. But it was the combination—the indubitable knowledge—that he enjoyed my submission, inflicting the pain, and delivering the denigration, as much as I enjoyed receiving it. That's where the complete bliss lay.

Instead of offering the rote answers, the ones I both liked saying, and he thrived on hearing, I looked up into his intent, heated gaze and said through my pain, "I'm grateful, Wes. I'm grateful our paths crossed, grateful for every day we spend together and grateful we're a part of each other's lives. I love you and what you bring to my life so completely that I'll never be able to put into words how much. I give you my body to torment or pleasure, whichever you desire, freely and eagerly."

Shocked at my rather raw and unexpected answer, I heard his breath catch. The pressure on my nuts ceased, and he leaned sideways resting his arm on the sofa above my head. His face was mere inches away from mine as unseen fingers found the piece of skin right below the head of my dick and took hold of it. Gently kneading and pulling—fuck, that felt so good!

Ducking his head down, his tongue found the hollow of my throat and traced up, catching on the whiskers, as it made its way up to my bottom lip. I moaned against his lips, and his eyes met mine.

"Grif...never doubt how much I need you or how deep my love and my desire and my commitment to you are."

I smiled warmly up at him, "I won't, Wes. I promise."

Lightening the mood momentarily, he said with a mischievous grin, "Smiling, at least on your part, isn't generally supposed to be part of these sessions. Let's see what we can do about that, shall we?"

He winked and straightened, and I felt one of his hands digging around in his pants pocket. Then a muffled tinkling sound as he pulled something free.

"Watch," he said, and I caught sight of the velvet pouch from Bertrand's being emptied and the contents falling onto my stomach.

There, against my hot skin, lay the cold, metal clothespins. He fingered them, moving them about a bit, while staring down at them. Smiling, he picked one up, squeezed it open, and then slowly allowed it to close, testing and enjoying its resistance.

Nervous, I pulled my bottom lip between my teeth. It caught his attention. He glanced over to the side table, laid the clothespin back on my stomach, and picked up a cigar tube. The case was designed to hold a single cigar, and it was a gift I'd given him just days before. The black carbon fiber exterior had a distinctly masculine feel, and it was just his style.

He unscrewed the cap, slid the cigar within out and set it aside. Slowly, he recapped the tube, and said, "Open."

I obeyed and opened my mouth while completely unsure of what he was going to do. My dick twitched and bobbed slightly, straining forward, and that didn't go unnoticed either.

Glancing from my dick to my eyes and then my open mouth, he groaned, "Oh, you're such a fucking slut."

He slid the tube a few inches into my open mouth and said, "Hold it right there."

I closed my mouth around it, loving the slightly rough texture and roundness as my tongue played across the rounded tip. I let out a muffled moan.

I felt him snug down the leather wrist band around my straining toy. Wow, that was tight.

He reached up and took hold of the tube, "Let loose and stick out your fucking tongue."

I eagerly followed his instructions. He slid the tube across the slick, wet surface of my outstretched tongue—back and forth, up and down.

"Yeah, that's it. You like that, don't you, fag?"

"Uh huh," I enthusiastically moaned.

He fiercely watched his ministrations, and I could feel his cock twitching under his pants.

"You want the real thing, don't you? You want to feel my cock head sliding across your slutty tongue, don't you?"

Without moving my tongue, I managed to moan out, "Yes please." I wanted it badly.

He shook his head with a depraved smirk, "As much as I'd love to hold you down and use you, to fuck your mouth and shoot my load all over your face, it's so not happening, cocksucker."

I whimpered in disappointment and in anticipation. He was feeling brutal tonight, and I was going to be the recipient of that brutality—fuck, I couldn't wait!

He slowed the tube's movement, and said, "Close your lips around it." I did and felt him push it deeper inside and then inch it almost all the way out again. His other hand found a hard nipple and he steadily rolled it between his fingers. Fuck, so good. So fucking good.

"Of course there's punishment for your lack of a real, man-sized dick, but, thankfully, there'll always be that to penalize you for. No, this particular session is about your disobedience; for you blatantly failing to obey a single hard and fast rule we have whether we're in Chocolate or Vanilla."

He slid the tube all the way out and shifted his fiery eyes from my lips up to meet mine.

"Isn't it, Grif?"

Confidently I answered, "Yes, it is, Wes."

Without warning, the strokes on my nipple went from oh so pleasurable to downright painful.

"They are my fucking orgasms to give out. Mine, and mine alone. I decide when your little dick can squirt. Me. And, before this Chocolate session is over, you'll wish you'd practiced a bit more self-control and remembered that fact. Remembered that you gave me something and it's not only something I cherish, but it's also something I'm not willing to share. It's fucking mine, Grif!"

The twisting on my nipple grew more severe, and I bit my lip in a sharp cry.

Swallowing, I said, "I apologize, Wes. I'll try to do better, I promise."

"Oh, I have no doubt about your willingness or your sincerity. In fact, as I'm sure you guessed, I knew I was pushing you too far to expect control. But...," and he grinned wickedly, "...you still broke the rules, took something that didn't belong to you, and now I get the supreme pleasure of punishing you for it. It seems like I win twice; once when I got to delight in the horror on your face as your fucking little dick squirted without permission, and now when I get to discipline you."

Fuck, he was being cruel tonight, more than he'd ever been before, and both Junior and I appreciated it.

"And tell me, Grif, why do I get enjoyment, and you don't, huh?"

"Because you've got a big cock that deserves feeling good, and I have a Junior dick that deserves abuse. And because you enjoy hurting me—it makes your cock hard, and it's always about your cock, not my toy."

"Right you are, fag. So let's make my dick feel good, and yours hurt, shall we?"

He leaned down and brought his lips to mine. They moved in hard, and delivered a brutal kiss. His teeth caught my lower lip and clamped down. I groaned at the sting. He took advantage of my open mouth and sunk his tongue deep inside. Heat fueled my response, and I kissed back just as ferociously; briefly pushing my tongue along his before clamping my lips around it and sucking. He finally pulled back, panting against my ear, "God, you make me so fucking hot, Grif."

He sat up, and with a quick flick of his strong wrist, brought the cigar tube down sharp and flat across my balls. My body reflexively took in a harsh breath, which instantly stuck in my throat. My ass pulled downward into the cushions, and my hands flew to cover and guard my crotch against another blow.

"Hands fucking down, Grif! It's mine to hurt," he said without a hint of compassion or understanding. And when I didn't immediately comply he snapped, "*Now!*"

The ability to breathe again finally beginning to return, I removed my hands and placed them at my sides.

"Oh my God," I breathlessly murmured. "That hurt so much, Wes."

"I'm so glad. Do I have your attention now?"

He moved the hollow tube in light, methodical circles across the top of my prominently displayed, bound, nuts and my body shook in excitement and fear.

"Yes, Wes."

With the index finger of his free hand, he drew a light path from my breastbone down to the clothespins at my navel.

"You're shaking."

"I'm…scared," I managed to squeak out.

"Oh, love, we've only begun," he said with a gleeful grin.

He smacked me with the tube again—less harshly this time though. It caused fire to shoot through my crotch but, unlike the initial blow, I was still in control of my body—not the other way around. He smacked one nut, then the other, and then both, top, bottom, sides—*smack, smack, smack.*

I don't even know how many times he hit me. I remained silent, but my entire body broke out in a sweat as I rocked my head from side to side.

Fuck, it hurt so goddamn much, but that only added to the stiffness of my dick—it felt so good. Eventually, there was nothing else…just an overwhelming euphoria so strong I couldn't even think.

While he was striking me, I heard his deep voice speaking to me, feeling like soft caresses, "You're so amazing, Grif. I can see you're in enormous pain," *smack, smack, smack,* "but the way you give this to me—the way you take this" *smack, smack, smack,* "you're so strong—it's such a gift."

The blows slowed. *Smack. Smack..., smack.* Then, mercifully, they stopped altogether.

Loving touches brushed the damp hair from my forehead as I slowly caught my breath. "Shh, easy now. That's it...relax into it for a bit before I start again."

I opened my eyes and looked up at him to see not only the clear heat and undisguised cruelty, but also the enormous love I knew he felt for me.

I became aware of a cool wet feeling on my stomach and glanced down to see the clothespins were nearly floating. Panic overtook me and I immediately sought out Wes' eyes.

My thought must have been clear because he calmly answered, "No. No you didn't. Don't worry, love, it's pre-cum, a fuck load of it, but it's only pre-cum and not jizz."

Relief flooded my entire being, and I brought my arm up to cover my eyes.

After a moment or two, he reached up and took my hand. Pulling it gently away from my face and toward his, he pressed my palm to his lips and showered it with kisses.

He spoke into my hand, "You pay me enormous compliments without uttering a single word. It fills me with such joy to know how desperately you want to comply, Grif...and the pain makes it so much more difficult for you...I can't even tell you how fucking hot it gets me." Placing my hand back down at my side, he asked, "You ready, love?"

I took a deep breath and nodded, "Yes."

"Good," he replied. But the curtness of his response left me feeling anything but.

"Use your arms and legs to arch your back. Lift your ass up and bring your stomach up so I can reach it with my tongue. The sight of your pre-cum is driving me fucking crazy! I have to taste it."

He regarded my wet stomach ardently before cautioning, "And, fag? Do it carefully, you don't want to know what will happen if even one of those clothespins slides off your slippery belly. Understand?"

"Yes, I understand, Wes." I knew more pain was forthcoming, but there was little point in giving him any additional reason to punish me further.

Slowly, carefully, I brought my stomach up to meet his mouth. The awkward position, with its strain on my thighs and biceps, quickly became uncomfortable, and I trembled as I watched his tongue move in and around the pieces of black metal.

God, it was so hot watching his mouth on me. It was difficult to hold still, but I was managing until his evil tongue briefly swiped the head of my aching dick causing my thighs to violently shake and nearly give out. As I regained control, he whispered while grinning against my navel, "Careful."

"Fuck, Wes, watching you do that...," I gasped out.

He moved his head further down, past my nuts, and turned to look back up along my dick and into my eyes.

"Damn! Seeing you, there like that, looking at me...," I shook my head in wonderment. "I never in my life, Wes, thought I'd be in a position to experience such a thing." I swallowed and continued looking into his eyes, "You do get that, right?"

"I understand what you're saying, Grif. But honestly, you give me way too much credit. There are men, lots of men, good men, who would kill to be in the very position I'm in now."

Sticking out his tongue, he ran it along my balls, up my short shaft, and over my head, stopping at my navel.

"But they'd have to kill me first, because you're mine," he said with a growl.

Raising his hand, he swiped the clothespins into his large palm and set them on the side table. Leaning back into the sofa, he pulled his knees together.

"Straddle my knees, facing me, please," he ordered.

I rolled off the couch and onto the floor before swiftly getting up and sitting on his lap with my knees at his hips. He rested a hand on each of my thighs, leaned forward and licked my hard nipple. Kissing his way across my chest toward the other nipple, he stopped and leered up at me.

"I fucking love knowing tonight, when I feel like I've tortured you enough, that I'm going to shoot a nice big load—and it's going to feel so fucking good, Grif—and you won't. And when that time comes, I'm gonna have you so hot and so worked up you'll be fucking begging me to let you come. And I'll deny you, fag."

He flattened his tongue and licked the crevice between my pecs several times before continuing, "I told you you'd go to bed hurting, and you'd wake up hurting...that's a promise I'm going to enjoy keeping, Grif."

I moaned, knowing that Junior's current aching state was just the beginning and release was, at the very minimum, some ten hours away.

He found my other nipple, and lapped it, licking and worrying it with his teeth.

"Aw, feels so good, Wes. So good."

Ten minutes later my nipples were on fire. He had one in his mouth rolling it between his teeth while grinding the other between two evil fingers. As he let go of both to switch, I pleaded, "Wes, please. Please, no more."

He looked down at my crotch smugly, "See, my quandary is this: your handsome mouth is saying one thing, but your dripping toy is saying something completely different."

"I ache so badly, and I want you. Please, kiss me, let me take your cock out and touch you, please I need…something…I…I'm so hot…I feel like I'm going crazy."

I reached toward his crotch, and he very sternly said, "*No, Grif!*"

Dejectedly, I laid my hands back on my thighs, "Yes, Wes."

"This isn't about you. It's about penance and punishment. It's about me."

"Wes…," I pleaded.

"Yes, love?" He started gently rubbing his hands down the sides of my torso, up my back, over my shoulders, and then stopped on my pecs.

"Flex for me," he instructed.

I reluctantly brought my arms up and flexed my biceps and then my pecs while his hands appreciated the solid muscle beneath my tan skin.

"God, you're so fucking beautiful, Grif."

Reaching over to the side table, he gathered the

clothespins in his large hand and then, palm up, held them between us. He glanced up at me and then back down to his hand. "You said you needed something, and I have something right here for you."

He was speaking to me, but not taking his eyes off of his palm, "Oh, Grif, this is going to hurt, and I'm so looking forward to it."

Meticulously he placed the cold metal clothespins all over my body—selecting only the most painful areas. It was clear this wasn't his first experience with them.

He'd pull the skin up, place the pin and then sneer—almost scornfully—into my contorting face. No sensitive area escaped attention; my dick, my balls, my nipples, all along my torso, even under my arms. There was no discernible pattern to how they were removed—some stayed on much longer and were flicked back and forth—where others were placed and almost immediately removed.

But when any of them were snapped off, holy fuck, it sent blood rushing back to the area with intense pain. As he tortured me, he stroked Junior. Repeatedly bringing me right to the edge of orgasm and then stopping.

We'd been on the sofa for nearly two hours, and I had long surpassed being merely tearful; frequently I was a sobbing, begging mess. My nipples were burning, my dick was leaking a continual stream of pre-cum, and it felt like my balls would explode with a single touch. Through it all, he'd never touched himself. All of his attention was devoted to tormenting me.

"Please, Wes, please! I hurt so much. Babe, pleeease. I can't take anymore. Please stop!"

"Shh, fag. Hush now and tell me why it hurts."

"It hurts because...," and I broke off. I couldn't even

put coherent thoughts together I hurt so bad.

"Tell me why it hurts, Grif," he said patiently, but his fucking fingers didn't stop tormenting my dick.

I breathed in, "It hurts because I fucked up—I lost control and disobeyed. I shot without permission. I took something that didn't belong to me, Wes. But, above all, it hurts because it pleases you to hurt me."

"Very good, Grif. And, tell me again who decides when Stubby squirts?"

He was so calm—the pleasure on his face was clear, sure—but otherwise so calm as he pinched the head of my dick between his fingers and ground them together.

"Wes, oh my God, that hurts so much. Please stop, please."

"Tell me, Grif."

"You decide, Wes. Only you. Not me, but you. Please."

Grinding fingers...

"I know I pushed you too far, Grif. It's not your fault you failed. I did it intentionally so I could punish you, and I'm having a wonderful time doing it."

Grinding fingers...

"And make no mistake, I'll do it again—and again—and again."

Grinding fingers...

"Wes, please. Please...stop."

I shook, and I didn't know how much more I could endure.

Harshly he growled, "Be still, Grif!"

I bit my lip, closed my eyes, and willed my body into stillness.

Grinding fingers...

"But perhaps," he continued calmly, "next time I'll have to push you harder...your resolve may be strengthened by this evening...and won't that be fun for both of us?"

Grinding fingers...

I nodded my head, my eyes still screwed tightly shut, my lip still caught between my teeth.

Grinding fingers...

"Words, Grif."

"Yes...Wes...fun," I managed to blurt out before I pulled my lip back between my clenched teeth.

His evil ministrations finally stopped. He pulled me to his chest and held me in a tight hug as his strong hands made soothing circles on my back. I sobbed in earnest—intense, deep sobs.

"It's okay, Grif. You're doing so well. I love you, babe."

"Love...love you...sooo much...Wes."

After a few moments, when my sobs hadn't subsided, he asked, "Why are you crying so?"

I shook my head in a pointless and halfhearted refusal. I knew I'd tell him—he knew I'd tell him. I'd debase myself and ask.

"Tell me, babe."

"You...you...," I couldn't even get two words out coherently. I took a deep breath and started again, "My nuts hurt so bad...but I'm not going to be allowed to shoot, am I?"

He held me tight and spoke sedately into the side of my neck, "Love, I made it clear you wouldn't be allowed tonight, didn't I?"

I nodded, but everything in me screamed, beg him—

maybe, just maybe, he'll change his mind.

"How about a change of scenery? Let's take a shower, huh?"

I nodded again, swallowing back the hopeless plea.

He held me tighter and then, to my surprise, he lifted both of us off the sofa. His strength still amazed me. I'm not a small guy by any means; five foot eleven, one hundred eighty pounds. But, compared to his six foot four, two hundred forty pounds of muscle, I was like lifting a sack of potatoes to him and no more of an exercise. And, at the moment, I couldn't be more grateful—I honestly didn't think walking was an option. I wrapped my body around his massive frame, held on, and wallowed in his pure strength.

CHAPTER 10
PENANCE PART THREE

Summer 2014

THE BATHROOM WAS the one place in the house where I'd really splurged. The rest of the house was done nicely, but the bathroom was a work of art. Originally, the house had been five bedrooms and two baths.

I'd taken the master bed and bath and combined them with two other bedrooms to create a large master suite—complete with a seating area, walk-in his and his closets, and a master bathroom retreat. The entire bathroom was designed to give the feeling of being outdoors. There were four massive skylights and instead of going with tile on the floor, I opted for wide, distressed, teak wood planks that were reminiscent of standing on a deck.

Dual copper sinks were set into a rough stone counter top. I'd removed the entire outer wall and replaced it with full floor to ceiling clear glass that looked out onto the private backyard with its pond and pool. A third of the wall-of-windows was taken up by a large jetted tub—which could easily hold three men—and the other two-thirds were taken up by the shower room.

The room had no door, but rather walls positioned to offer a bit of privacy from the rest of the bathroom and to contain water. Its floor was tiled in small soft, natural stones which were heated and felt amazing on bare, wet feet. I'd gone with teak on the walls in there as well.

There were two rain showerheads, each with their own controls, and on demand hot water.

The ceiling-mounted heaters kept the entire space warm, a comfortable teak bench and chair, with a matching side table, positioned along the back wall, finished the room off. The shower room's overall feeling, considering its size, view, and furnishings felt like I was literally showering outside. It was bright, spacious, and designed for maximum comfort; a place you wanted to spend hours in, not just a few minutes.

Wes was carrying me down the hall, one arm around my back and the other under my ass with my legs wrapped around his waist.

"I love how strong you are, Wes," I said into his neck. "Outside the bedroom, it's so nice to know you've always got my back. But, in the bedroom, my God, it's such a fucking turn-on."

He chuckled, "Yes, I know exactly what you mean. I also like knowing I won't break you. And, as much as I'm always going to be there to back you up, it gives me tremendous peace of mind knowing I don't have to be— that if I'm not around, you can certainly take care of yourself." He passed us through the bedroom and directly into the bathroom where I dropped my feet to the floor, but didn't release my hold on him. In fact, if anything, my hold grew stronger.

He took my face in his hands, "I know, love. I know. You're hurting, really hurting, and probably hornier than you've been in quite a while. Perhaps hornier than you've ever been. But I'm not quite done with you yet, okay?"

Fuck, not done? Jesus, did he want my fucking nuts to explode?

Looking at his mouth—fuck, those irresistible full lips— I couldn't help but whine a little, "Wes…."

He didn't say anything, but simply stood there holding my face in his strong hands. I looked up into his dark eyes and got the clear message he was sending without him speaking a single word: 'Cowboy Up'!

I nodded, straightened my posture, and said with as much 'cowboy up' as I could muster, "Yes, Wes."

He smiled, "Ah, there's the man I love. And the man I love to hurt."

He bent down and placed a soft, chaste kiss on my lips and let go of my face. Taking a step back he ordered, "Undress me, please. Begin with my shirt."

I reached up and undid the buttons of his shirt. As each opened, more and more of his broad, furry, muscular chest was revealed. Fuck, his body was a work of art. It was so big and strong and powerful.

Somehow, after hours of play, his shirt tails were still tucked in. I reached for the belt to undo it when he caught my wrist, "On your knees for the pants, please."

I knelt down and noticed almost the entire front of his dark pants was wet. I groaned deeply with need. "Fuck, Wes," I said licking my lips and not taking my eyes off the massive bulge.

"Grif?" he said. And when I didn't hear anything else I

looked up and met his eyes.

"Yes?"

"You may look, but no touching, clear?"

I looked back down at the straining fabric and reluctantly nodded.

"Words, Grif."

I was horny as fuck and sorer than I'd ever been in my life. I'd been fucking tormented for hours, and I still couldn't touch? Beyond exasperated, I snapped, "Yeah, I got it, no fucking touching, okay?"

He grabbed the back of my hair so quickly that I hadn't even seen him move, and yanked my head back sharply so our eyes met.

He growled down at me with a harsh seriousness he'd never directed at me before, "When we're in Chocolate, you'll show me respect at all times. You'll respect my cock and understand it's a privilege for you to even look at it. You'll respect my orders, and you'll comply to the best of your ability. And if I don't like the result, you'll be punished. You'll do this because you've agreed to do this. At any time you're free to stop by uttering a single word. What is the word, Grif?"

I stared up at him defiantly, not responding.

He didn't waver, didn't flinch, didn't loosen his grip at all.

"The word is Vanilla, Wes." I finally hissed, staring directly into his eyes. "And the only reason your wrist isn't broken, the only reason I'm still on my knees, the only reason you're still painfully holding me by the hair is because I allow it! Is that fucking clear?"

His grip didn't vary, and he growled, "From the very first time we did Chocolate, I've understood that, Grif. It's not something I ever forget or take for granted. As I said, it's a gift I cherish. And I have no doubt you have the ability, and the physical strength, to extricate yourself from any situation I choose to put you in. But, this isn't about brawn, is it? This isn't about my big dick or your small one."

He released his hold, brought his hand around, and slid his fingers softly along my jaw. "This isn't about your worth as a human being or mine. And, this isn't about how much I love you—and I do, beyond description—or how much you love me—and I know in my heart that you do because I feel it every day that I'm with you."

More quietly he said, "This…," and he motioned back and forth between the two of us, "the occasional Chocolate, is about one thing and one thing only; my desire to physically and psychologically inflict pain and your desire to receive it. Nothing more. Of course it's better, stronger, infinitely more gratifying because we also love and respect each other."

His voice grew even softer, "I know you're struggling— you're in pain and I get that. I put you there. But, if you can't show me respect and willingly obey my orders then you will say the word…you have to say the word, Grif. You have to. We can't disrespect each other. But, more importantly, you can't disrespect what this means to both of us. Please, say the word if you need to, okay?"

I looked down briefly, then got to my feet and walked over to the bathroom counter. Resting my hands on either side of the sink, I took a deep breath, and I stared down into the copper bowl for a few moments. Turning around, I leaned back against the cool stone, unconsciously covering Junior with one hand, and looked over to him.

He was not only stunningly handsome, but also one of

the most honorable men I'd ever met—a good man. A good man, who knew me, really knew and understood me. And, most importantly, he loved me completely. And, I'd fucked up.

It was obviously time for me to really 'cowboy up'. I spoke clearly and with conviction, "I apologize, Wes. You're absolutely right; I disrespected this." It was my turn to motion back and forth between us. "Without a doubt, I am hurting. And yes, I am struggling. But I sincerely thank you for so succinctly putting into words what this means to both of us."

I sighed and looked toward the stretch of floor which separated us and then back at him. Shit, there was no holding back at this point; our entire relationship was based on being honest with each other—no matter how difficult, no matter what that honesty emotionally exposed either of us to.

I took a deep breath, ran a hand across the back of my neck, and continued, "Yes, I am struggling with the pain and the overwhelming need to shoot, but it's more than that. I get scared sometimes, Wes. This—the Chocolate—is part of me, but it's certainly not all of me. And, sometimes I get scared you'll love me less because I allow you to do this to me. Because I want you to do this to me. I get scared that you'll forget *me*, forget who I am."

He took a few steps backward, leaned against the teak wall, and slipped his hands into his pants pockets. He was silent for a few moments, and when he finally spoke, it was quietly, "I do understand, Grif. I do. I mean, think about it, I get scared too. I get scared that you'll forget me too, who I am. That you'll love me less because of what I do and want to do to you. I could live without the Chocolate. It'd be very difficult, but I could do it. What I can't do is live without you. There are times when I think, 'What if I go too far? What if his love for me turns because of something I've done, or something I've said, or something I've made him feel? What if I suggest something and he unexpectedly finds it repulsive? What if I lose him over that very small part of me that few other people would ever be able to understand—let alone desire.' Make no mistake, Grif, I'm scared sometimes, too."

I looked at him and with sincerity said, "I love you more now than I ever have, Wes. Thank you for that." Even from across the room, I could see him swallow in relief.

I continued on, "Wes, do I know you? Have you let me see all of you or is there something else? Some other desire you've not yet shared with me?"

He was momentarily surprised. Then shook his head and said seriously, "No, Grif, you know me. I mean there are things I'd like to try, a few things I fantasize about doing to you, but they are all within the sadomasochism realm. We focus on your dick and its size because that's where your desire for abuse and humiliation lie. And, again, for the record, I like your dick. I think it's quite handsome." He paused, smiled, and then continued, "But no, there aren't goats or feathers or any other weird fetishes I should be telling you about." He added with a grin, "Well, I take that back. Did you know feathers can be incredibly painful—with the proper administration?"

I chuckled. "Okay, then you've got nothing to worry about. You've never, ever, gone too far or suggested something I, or at the very least, Junior, didn't find appealing."

I pushed off the counter and walked over to him. Placing my free hand on his chest I said, "I'm sorry if I've spoiled or put a damper on the evening. That was never my intent, I hope you know that."

He covered my hand with one of his and kissed my forehead tenderly. "Grif, love, talking, especially about something this important, is never, and will never be, a damper."

He pulled back slightly and used his hand to tilt my chin up. Pinning me with affectionate, dark brown eyes, his hand slid along my jaw and cupped my face. "I love you so much, Grif."

"And I love you, Wes."

"Are we good?"

"We're so far past *good,* it's not even funny."

He glanced down between us, "May I see Stubby?"

I hesitated, and then slid my hand away.

He smiled as he studied my bound dick, "Thank you. I see he's still hard and weepy. And are your nuts still as painful as I hope they are?"

I grinned back, "Yes he is and, fuck ya, they are."

"Good to hear." Meeting my eyes once again—with so much love it almost hurt—he asked, "Shall we continue with Chocolate?"

I replied just as warmly, "Yes, Wes."

As quick as that, my kind, generous lover was replaced by my evil, and equally desired, tormenter.

Grabbing my hair at the back of my head—almost in the exact same spot, but much less tightly—he gritted his teeth and ordered, "Then get down on your goddamned knees and finish undressing me."

"Yes, Wes."

I dropped to my knees, and as I reached for his pants, he warned, "And, Grif? You may look, but you may not fucking touch my cock, are we clear?"

Sudden emotion overtook me. I felt so enormously grateful to the universe for delivering this blessing of a man to me. I looked up through glassy eyes and managed to say, "Yes, Wes. Absolutely clear. I may look at your beautiful, large cock, and be thankful, but I am not allowed to touch it."

He nodded down at me menacingly, yet obviously pleased with my respectful response.

I undid his pants and had to work at getting them off without even slightly brushing his returning erection. Once I'd gotten them down to his knees, his overpowering scent hit me. He smelled like Wes mixed with the undeniable spice of sex.

I moaned, "Wes, you smell so good. Fucking makes my mouth water."

Stepping out of his pants, and casually kicking them to the side, he stood there in bright white briefs, tented in the front with his gorgeous bulge.

"Now, the underwear, Grif. And, for your own sake, use care."

I swallowed, and said, "Yes, Wes." I told myself to be careful—I didn't think I could handle any further punishment.

I took hold of the waistband, on both sides, above his hipbones, and pulled outward, away from his body. I started bringing them down when they nearly slipped from my grasp. Alarmed, I gasped at the fumble and said, "They're so wet and slippery." And they were. The entire front was soaked with hours of pre-cum.

I finally got them past his cock and didn't realize I'd paused. I loved his dick. It was so big, so rigid, so straight, with that foreskin I loved to play with, all surrounded by thick, dark hair. Fucking wondrous.

I'd stopped to stare and my lips must have been slightly parted because a bit of saliva slid from the corner of my mouth. I reached up to swipe it away and caught Wes studying me.

"You are a true cocksucker," he sneered. "You're actually drooling."

I looked down at the floor fully embarrassed.

"Look at it," he demanded and reached down to glide his foreskin back, fully uncovering the head.

"You fucking want it, don't you?" Not waiting for an answer, "Oh, that feels real nice," he said lewdly and let go of his cock. I watched as the skin slowly came back over and partially recovered his head.

"Oh God, Wes. Can I please—,"

He cut me off with a sharp, "No, you can't." Then, continued more amiably, "Finish taking off my underwear, please."

I slid them the rest of the way down and watched as he stepped out of them. To my surprise, he knelt down along with me.

Looking me in the eye, he said, "Pick up the underwear, Grif."

Perplexed, I picked them up and held them between us.

"You know you're not going to be allowed an orgasm this evening, but I've also decided you won't have the pleasure of sucking my cock tonight either. I'm gonna shoot, but it won't be with your mouth."

He knew how much I loved sucking him. It was the thing I'd always choose, to be filled with his thickness, over any other choice offered. I loved that feeling of not being able to breathe as he pushed all the way into me and held my nose to his pubes. I truly was a cocksucker. I fucking loved it.

I nodded and looked down in disappointment.

He ran his fingers along the side of my head and through my hair. I leaned into his touch as I looked into his menacing eyes.

"Oh, God, that's incredible...you look so tremendously hurt." With a knowing grin he whispered, "Of everything I've done to you this evening, that was the most painful, wasn't it?"

"Yes, it hurts," I admitted, as a tear slid down my cheek. There was really no expounding upon it. I was crestfallen.

"Fuck, that makes me so hard. But, there's no reason you shouldn't have a taste of what you'll be missing, is there?"

Hope sparked.

"Take the front of the underwear, Grif, the wet part, and put it in your mouth."

What did he say?

I looked up at him in confusion, "Wes?"

Calmly he said, "You heard me, Grif."

Although my eyes didn't leave his, I slowly shook my head in refusal.

He reached between us and lightly tapped my nuts.

Tap, tap, tap...

Wow, it was amazing how rapidly it became impossible to think with the pain flaring in my balls.

"Wes, please...that's so...dirty. So...desperate."

Tap, tap, tap...

He grinned, and I found it almost obnoxious, "Yes, it is. Which is exactly why I'm making you do it—and why you want me to make you do it. And because I know you, Grif. If sucking on my shorts is the only chance you'll get to taste me, then you'll gladly take that over nothing at all, isn't that right?"

Tap, tap, tap...

My face was on fire and tears were streaming down my cheeks. I detested him in that moment. But I managed a defeated, "Y-yes, Wes. If that's all I can have then...."

"Then open your mouth, put my wet underwear in, and fucking suck like the nasty cockslut you are. Do. It. Now."

Fuck, I couldn't believe I was doing this—but it was either do as he ordered or say Vanilla and stop it. And, God help me, but I *so* didn't want it to stop.

Tap, tap, tap...

I raised the shorts, but when they'd made it as far as my chin, I knew I couldn't do it. I begged through the tears, "Wes, please don't make me do this. Pleeease."

Tap, tap, tap...

I took one look at his determined, spiteful, dark eyes, and I understood begging would be pointless. It would simply give him more pleasure and debase myself even further.

A loud sob caught in my chest as I acquiesced and brought the underwear to my face. As soon as they were close enough to smell, to breathe in his wonderful scent, I momentarily forgot about everything else entirely. I wanted to taste him more than anything. I eagerly stuffed the wet fabric in my mouth and, looking Wes in the eye, I bit down and started to suck with a needy whimper.

Tap, tap, tap...

Instantly I was filled with his scent and taste, and Junior grew even harder. I couldn't believe I was on my knees and allowing him to make me chew on his underwear—and I fucking loved it. Closing my eyes, trying unsuccessfully to stop the tears, I cried from humiliation and sucked harder.

"Jesus, *so* fucking stunning; you're beet red with shame…my dirty underwear are stuffed in your mouth…and you're desperately trying to taste me. Open your eyes and look at me you nasty pig."

I opened my eyes to find Wes caressing his cock, and I let out another whimper. He looked so good kneeling there, cock in hand, stroking back and forth.

"Yeah, I love the way you look right now…that longing for my cock in your eyes. And guess what? I'm gonna fucking shoot soon, and you're not."

Tap, tap, tap…

"Ohhh, yes…so good, Grif. My balls are so tight and tingling, and I have this fuzzy, electric buzzing all over. It's starting…I can feel the release coming…feels sooo fucking good!"

He was taunting me with his pending orgasm—he knew it, and I knew it. He closed his eyes, and I watched his entire body grow tense. His chest and arms tightened, the veins in his neck stood out, and I saw the pleasure written all over his face as his breathing became sporadic…he was close…God, it was spectacular.

"Oh, Grif…oh my God…feels sooo good…gonna…oh fuuuck!"

His eyes flew open, and we both looked down to watch as his thick cock spewed rope after white rope of warm cum over my chest and abdomen. Fuck, the sight of him coming was something I'd never tire of.

I was soaked with sweat, tears, and cum, kneeling with a man I loved more than anything, his underwear stuffed in my mouth, my balls aching with wonderful need, knowing he'd denied me any relief of my own, and I couldn't have imagined being more happy or satisfied.

I felt Wes take hold of the shorts, "May I have these, please?" His breathing had almost returned to normal, but his cock was still full, twitching, and standing at attention with a string of cum hanging from it.

But now that I had the underwear in my mouth, I was reluctant to let them go. With a wink, he brushed a sore nipple and took advantage of my pleasured moan, and slid them from my mouth. "I knew you'd fucking like it."

Running his index finger along my chest, he scooped up his jizz and said, "But I have something better for you. Open your mouth and stick out your tongue, Grif."

"Oh, please," I implored and immediately complied with a soft moan and an eager, quick nod of my head. I couldn't wait to taste.

He scooped finger-full after finger-full off of my chest and onto my waiting tongue until I was completely clean. I held it in my mouth until he said, *Yes*, then gradually swallowed his spicy seed—savoring every drop—and gratefully said, "Thank you!"

"You're welcome, Grif," he said with a smile.

I looked down at his still hard cock saying, with obvious desire and at a tilt of my head, "There's some hanging there, may I lick it off please?"

He chortled softly and said, "If you can manage to get it without breaking tonight's 'no touching' rule, you're welcome to it."

I hastily moved from my knees to my stomach,

momentarily forgetting my aching, bound-up cock and balls until they were painfully pressed between me and the unyielding floor, and propped myself up on my elbows so I was eye level with his cock.

Oh God, I wanted it so bad. Sticking out my tongue, I managed to snag the swaying string, pull it into my mouth, close my eyes, and enjoyed one last taste. Looking back to his dick, I noticed a bit had also slid down his shaft.

"Um, Wes?" I asked hesitantly, "There's some...on the underside...you think I might be allowed to lick it off?"

He beamed down at me and let out a bemused chuckle, "You, Grif, are incorrigible. Yes, *one*, single lick. No more, understand?"

I enthusiastically nodded, "Yes, Wes."

Shit, if all I was getting was a single lick, I was damn sure making it a good one. I leaned forward, stuck my tongue out as far as it would go and made it as flat as possible while pressing it as far back on his nuts as I could reach. Slowly dragging it across the still tight and wrinkled sack, I unhurriedly ran it along the veiny underside of his shaft feeling every single concave and convex ridge the thick veins made.

Finally reaching the tip, I dipped in between the fat head and foreskin and made a single pass around the crown before pulling my tongue out and finally, reluctantly, leaning back staring at his cock.

"Jesus Christ, Grif!" he husked with clear appreciation, "I've never in my life met anyone who either loves doing that as much as you do, or who is as good at it as you are. Ever!"

I looked up into his dark eyes. "Wes, there's nothing on earth I enjoy more, nothing," I said with complete and honest sincerity.

"Come up here."

Mindful of my nuts this time, I gingerly pulled myself to my knees. He took hold of the leather strap binding my dick and nuts and skillfully undid it.

Once he had it off, he handed it to me and held out his wrist. "Would you please put it back on for me."

As soon as I'd fastened it, he pulled me in for a kiss. His tongue immediately plunged in deep and swiped around mine, possessive, demanding, loving.

Leisurely breaking free, he looked into my eyes and said, "I love you. Thank you so much for this evening. Vanilla."

Instantaneously, I closed the distance that separated us and pressed our bodies together. Wrapping one arm tightly around his neck, I shoved my free hand in between us and grabbed his thick cock—I could touch again!

He laughed and I said into his strong neck, between kisses, "I love you too, Wes. So very much."

After a few moments he tenderly suggested, "How about we move into the shower and relax for a bit before bed…my knees hurt, so I know yours must be fucking killing you."

CHAPTER 11
HOUSE RULES

Winter 2004

THE BACON WAS was in the oven—damn, it smelled good—fresh coffee was in the pot, and the quiche was next. I woke up starving and decided to cook Tate and me breakfast.

Tate was still asleep. He'd come home late last night, but I wasn't sure how late, as I'd crashed by 10pm or so.

Standing at the sink, the first egg in hand, I heard a yawn from the doorway. I looked over my shoulder and dropped the egg I was holding into the sink; Tate stood there naked in all his glory. I hastily turned back to the sink. *Why was he naked? We were never naked around each other.*

"Morning," he said in a sleepy voice.

I dared a glance back and found him casually leaning against the door frame, arms crossed over his brown chest, hair sleep messed, and stubble covering his smiling face. He was wearing *that* smile.

"Uh, morning," I managed to croak.

I heard him pad toward me, "Smells good. Is there coffee?"

"Um, yeah. It's fresh, I just made it."

I tried to concentrate on cracking the eggs, and not simply smashing them, then getting them into the bowl without shells. I wasn't doing a very good job.

I tensed when I felt warm breath slide over my neck and shoulder as he peered over to take in the mess I was making. "You seem to be having a bit of trouble there, Grif," the amused smirk in his tone unmistakable, "Your hands are shaking."

I stopped, rested my hands in a wide stance on the counter and, with a bowed head, peered down into the sink.

Unsteadily, I finally asked, "Why are you naked, Tate?"

His reply came from farther away than I'd expected. He'd gone back to leaning against the door frame.

"Has something changed, Grif? Do you not like seeing me naked anymore?"

Was he serious? I turned around to respond but was once again struck speechless as I took in his fit body. God, he was ideal; textbook chest and arms, a flawless stomach, a thick patch of black hair right above a picture-perfect, uncut cock which lay heavily against one thigh.

I gulped with difficulty.

"From the expression on your face," he began easily, "I can see you do still like looking at me."

He unhurriedly uncoiled one arm and ran a hand lazily down his stomach. As it slid down past the top of his thigh, he extended his thumb, and it slid along his cock from base to tip as his hand continued its downward trek.

I gasped and whispered, "Tate."

"I'm naked because it's been three weeks. I understand you're new to all this, Grif, and I didn't want to push…but, three weeks, dude?"

"I know," I quietly sighed.

"Why haven't you asked? We have an understanding, right? *All you have to do is ask.*"

"Tate, I… I can't think with you standing there naked…I just can't."

I watched him straighten a bit and then calmly ask, "Would you do me a favor, Grif?"

Completely unsure of where this was going the only response I could manage was a slight, "Huh?"

"Just look at me."

"B-but I am looking at you, Tate."

He shook his head slightly. "No, I mean, look at me the way you'd look at me if I weren't watching you. Look at me the way you really want to, not the way you do when you know I can see you. Just let me see what you're feeling. Don't hide."

I nodded, tried to relax, and ran my eyes over his fit body—toes to face—and ended looking into his eyes.

He grinned broadly and whispered. "Ah, there it is…I see now."

I swallowed and asked, "You see what?"

Fire lit his eyes and he said firmly, "On your knees, Grif."

On my what?

It sounded suspiciously close to an order and I wasn't at all sure how I felt about that.

"Um, yeah...I don't think...."

Softer he said, "Grif, trust me, okay? Kneel down...please."

I nodded and, fucking inexplicably, went down.

"Does that feel better? Make you more at ease, maybe?"

"It makes me feel somewhat humiliated, Tate." I sucked in a deep breath, "And I'd really like to put a shirt on. But—oddly—I have to admit it does seem more relaxing."

"Good, I had a feeling it might." He paused and then continued, "And, to reassure you of something you already know, I can't see your dick just because you're shirtless, Grif. Now, will you please tell me why you haven't asked?"

I took my time to contemplate exactly how much I was willing to share with him.

"You know me, Grif. We know each other. Talk to me."

Glancing down to the floor, I caught sight of his thickening dick. I realized he liked me in this position—on my knees in front of him—it turned him on.

"The truth?" I took another deep, but shaky, breath, "I don't ask because I'm afraid you'll reject me."

And there it was—the truth—the whole of it. This situation made me feel things I hadn't felt since junior high school; the fear of being humiliated.

I had no idea where it came from, but from a very young age I possessed an amazing amount of confidence. However, on a day which had started out like any other, that confident teenager had entered a simple junior high school locker room and was shaken to the core.

The realization that I was permanently and forever different, and the resulting shock of understanding that no amount of dedication or work or study could rectify it, left me questioning nearly everything in my life; my future worth as a lover, my strength as a male, hell, I even began to question my intelligence. Abruptly, every single thought I had about my self-worth seemed to revolve around the size of my dick.

My father, with his uncanny ability to understand me, became my savior. He stood by me, encouraging me, supporting me, helping me grow, and all the while never bringing up the topic.

His favorite saying, *Responsibility breeds character and self-sufficiency breeds confidence!* were words I began to live by. In fact, they became my mantra. They offered me the ability to take something which made me feel uncomfortable and study it, analyze it, learn about it, and then go about mastering it.

I had become self-sufficient and wouldn't allow apprehension over something dictate my actions. I had grown from a scared, unsure teenager, after the locker room shock, into a strong—both physically and emotionally—confident man who didn't allow uncomfortable situations to remain uncomfortable very long.

Yet, here I was, kneeling in front of my best friend—a handsome, well-endowed, naked man—and surprisingly feeling much more comfortable on my knees than standing and looking him in the eye. Where was my self-sufficiency? Where was my confidence?

He was apparently pondering and then carefully decided on his next words, "How often do you want me?" he asked.

I swallowed and decided to continue with honesty, "All the fucking time, Tate. All the time."

His dick had grown completely hard. Unconsciously, I palmed the front of my shorts—my own dick had surged to its full length the moment my knees hit the floor—and I cut my eyes up to his in fear.

"I don't see the problem then. I want my dick sucked all the fucking time, Grif. You want to suck dick, and I have a dick that always wants sucking. There's not a problem."

Smiling, he added with a nod to my crotch, "And, in case you're worried, when you felt yourself up, I didn't see your dick. But the wet spot on the front of your shorts is kinda hard to miss."

He pushed himself away from the doorway and walked toward me, his thick cock bouncing and swaying, and my mouth watered. A small, involuntary whimper sounded from somewhere and it took me a few seconds to realize it'd come from me.

He stopped in front of me and looked down into my eyes. His voice was strong but kind and understanding, "I know, Grif. You're on your knees. There's a big dick right in front of you, and you're a cocksucker...you want it so bad you can taste it, can't you?"

I nodded, unabashedly displaying my desire.

"So, this is what we're gonna do...our new house rules, so to speak. If you agree, of course. And I really think we're both gonna like 'em, Grif. From now on, anytime we're home alone, I'll be naked."

A mewled sound of pleasure passed from my lips and playfulness danced in his eyes.

"Yeah, I was pretty sure you'd like that," he said with a wink. "I'll be naked, Grif, and you'll be free to touch all you want, any time you want. You'll be able to cop a feel while I'm bent over grabbing a beer out of the fridge, when I'm brushing my teeth, when I'm kickin' back watching the tube, while I'm at the desk studying. Any. Time. You. Want. Grif! And, of course it goes without saying, you can also blow me six times a day if you want. With absolutely no complaints on this end."

And there it was. Tate was offering me something I never thought possible; he was offering me a way to gain confidence in a sexual situation. He was giving it to me and all I had to do was what I always did: study it, analyze it, learn about it, and master it.

With a bit more self-assuredness, I looked up and found the biggest smile I'd ever seen on him. Glancing down, I noticed his dick had dripped pre-cum on his thigh and every-fucking-thing in me said, *lick him clean*.

"God, if you could see your face, Grif. The way you look at me with such open lust and need and desire. It's such a fucking high for me, and it makes my cock so stiff to know you want me so fucking badly."

One of his hands slid to the base of his cock, and barely stroked, while the other tweaked a hard, dark nipple.

"Tate, please."

"Oh, you're gonna get it…soon. But, before you do, tell me how much you want my big dick, Grif. I want to hear you say it, cocksucker."

I opened my mouth. I tried to form words, but they wouldn't come. I shook my head back and forth, disappointed I couldn't give him this and disappointed that I couldn't open myself up that much.

"It's okay," he said as he closed the last few feet separating us, "One step at a time. How about you show me how much you want it?"

He grabbed his cock at the base and held it firmly, "Stick

out your tongue, Grif. I'm gonna lay my fat head on it and then I want you to lick it clean."

I immediately stuck my tongue out and waited, but as soon as I felt his hot skin, tasted the sweet, salty pre-cum, I lost control and swallowed the entire fucking thing—buried it to the root—in my throat and held him there. Needy, desperate sounds erupted from someplace deep within me.

He let out a surprised chuckle, "Well, we can do it this way too. Damn, Grif, there's no fucking doubt how much you want it, is there?"

I shook my head in acknowledgement—completely unwilling to back off and speak.

I rubbed a palm over my straining crotch and then, realizing what I was doing, moved both around and placed them on his firm ass.

Ever perceptive, and not one to miss a thing, he said, "Grif, relax, dude. You know, honestly, I don't have x-ray vision—I really can't see through your shorts."

Completely focused on what I was doing, I heard but ignored Tate's ramblings. I concentrated on the feeling of his big cock buried deep in my throat, the feeling of being so completely full, the feeling of his soft, dark pubes rubbing against my nose, and the feeling of utter rightness.

This was only my third sexual experience, and yet, without question, being on my knees, with a fat dick stretching my mouth, giving pleasure to another man...felt like home.

I finally eased up, letting Tate's cock dislodge itself from my throat and slide out of my mouth. I gasped in deep breaths as I closed my eyes and ran my cheek over its length.

"God, Grif, you absolutely love it, don't you?"

I looked up and met his dark, sparkling eyes, "I do, Tate. I really, really do."

He reached down and wiped a tear off my cheek as I slid my tongue under the entire length of his shaft. The soft skin, only broken up by the occasional thick vein, gliding over my tongue sent electric sparks through my own dick. Jeez, I could do this for hours—days even!

"Do you mind if I ask why you're crying?" He questioned kindly.

Reaching a hand up, I gently took hold of his cock and stroked back and forth marveling at the sight of his head disappearing and reappearing through the foreskin. Damn, that had to be the sexiest fucking thing ever.

Not that my other hand was slacking at all. It was caressing the smooth, plump, well defined ass that I couldn't see but certainly felt amazing under my touch. I briefly wondered if Tate would let me lick him there.

"Huh? Crying? Um, no, I'm not crying. My eyes are just watering...f-from sucking, ya know?" I said, attempting to play off the emotion-filled tears. "I'm really enjoying this...it's all good, Tate, I promise."

"Oh, I know it's all good, dude...I think I even see a small tent in your shorts."

I blushed and turned—hiding my face in his crotch. *A jockstrap! From now on I'll always wear a jockstrap!* I hadn't worn underwear for years, but I'd start today. It was one thing for him to know, and, perhaps even to acknowledge my small dick, but it was quite another for him to actually see evidence of it. I would not allow it to happen again.

"Okay, that was a blush and not the flash of anger I somewhat expected. Interesting."

"Tate, please," I begged in between placing kisses to the

place where his upper leg joined his torso. God, I loved that spot.

"Ah, I think I get it; under these conditions, and perhaps only these very specific conditions, you might enjoy me talking about your small size. Am I right?"

That was it, I couldn't take anymore. I grabbed his cock and swallowed it whole while fire shot down my back and through my own dick. I stopped breathing, stopped thinking, and unleashed the biggest load of my life into my already wet shorts. My ears rang, my vision narrowed, and I gasped breath after breath around his thick cock. I had the brilliant feeling of flying... fucking amazing.

Once I'd come back to myself, I realized I still had Tate's hard cock in my mouth, and I was rubbing my tongue on the underside of his head. Although enjoyable, it wasn't distracting enough for him to lose his train of thought.

"Well, I'm not sure there could be a clearer answer." He was running his fingers gently through my hair as he spoke. "It's only the middle of your third blowjob, and I say middle, because I haven't shot yet. You are going to fix that, right Grif? And we've begun to compile quite the short-list, if you'll pardon the pun." He smiled widely down at me as I blushed again.

"One, you love sucking my cock; two, you like being called a fag and a cocksucker while you're doing it; and three, you've got a small dick and like having that fact mentioned in this context," I sucked harder and he moaned, "Oh, yeah, you definitely like that!"

His fingers tightened in my hair, and his hips bucked violently.

"Four, you're really, really fucking good at sucking my

big dick. In fact, you're one of only a handful of people who've been able to take me all the way down, and I've had more than my fair share of blowjobs, Grif!"

I was looking up at him and he was staring back down at me, trance-like, watching his dick slide in and out of my mouth over and over. Man, he was stunning. And if I wasn't mistaken, he was gonna shoot any second now.

"Oh fuck, oh fuuuck! Yeah, just like that…yessss…gonna fuckin' come, Grif!"

He started to pull out, but I grabbed his ass with both hands and pushed him deeper inside my mouth, sucking as hard as I could. Spurt after hot spurt gushed into my mouth, and I was filled with a spicy flavor I knew I could easily get addicted to.

Through deep breaths, he grinned and said, "And five, you'll eat my cum. Jesus. Fucking. Christ! Could it get any better for a sex crazed, big-dicked, straight guy; his own personal, fag cocksucker? Damn, Grif, this is gonna be a hell of a lot of fun!"

He pulled his softening dick from my mouth, "I gotta take a leak. You okay, dude?"

I smiled and nodded up at him, "Never better, Tate. But, I could use a hand up. I've been down here a while, and I'm pretty sure I stopped feeling my right leg about ten minutes ago."

He chuckled and helped me to my feet. I leaned back against the kitchen counter, while covering my crotch with one hand, and said, "Go pee. I'll change my shorts and then see what might be salvaged from breakfast. I don't know about you, but I could eat a horse."

Of course, as soon as the words left my mouth I knew he'd have something smart-assed to say.

"Well, you know, I've been told, on several occasions, that I do compare."

I snatched a towel from the kitchen counter and managed to land a solid snap on his retreating ass.

"Ouch!" He yelped.

"Oh, that's gonna leave a nice mark!" I laughed.

I heard him pad down the short hall. As he turned into the bathroom, he yelled out, with unmistakable cheerfulness in his voice, "Cocksucker! You're a fucking Cocksucker, Grif! My Cocksucker!"

CHAPTER 12
WATCHING FOOTBALL

Early Spring 2005

TATE RELAXED AT one end of the sofa, feet on the coffee table, Sunday Night Football on the tube, with snacks and beer on the end table within easy reach.

I rested my head on his thigh, and his fat, soft cock was nestled in my mouth. We'd been in this position for about the last hour and a half; him watching the game, occasionally talking to the TV, and his dick being bathed by my mouth and tongue.

About twenty minutes earlier, he'd made the comment that this was the best game watching experience of his life. I couldn't agree more.

In fact, I'm not sure I could come up with a better way to spend ninety minutes; lying here with a thick cock between my lips, mine to play with and do with as I pleased, and feeling oh so satisfied—yep, pretty perfect.

Tate had also been right about his new *house rules*. Over

the last two and a half months, we'd both been enjoying the hell out of them. With him constantly naked and me knowing any touch I made, any brush of my lips on his body, was not only welcomed, but thoroughly enjoyed.

Hell, I couldn't get enough. Thus, the reason, at the moment, I was enjoying a mostly soft dick. I'd already given him three blowjobs and had been rewarded with three massive loads to savor and swallow. "Fuck," he'd said after the last one, "I never thought I'd say this, but I think you might actually wear me out, Grif."

The head of his shaft was just inside my mouth. With my tongue wedged under his foreskin, I was sliding around the circumference slowly, over and over. When not distracted by the game, he was making appreciative sounds while absentmindedly running his fingers through my hair. It was all so easy and comfortable.

A commercial began playing, and I let him slip from my mouth. "Can I ask you something, Tate?"

Smiling, he reached for his beer and said, "No, I don't think I can shoot again, Grif," and then chuckled. Looking back down, he noticed the expression on my face and said more seriously, "Sure, you know you can ask me anything. What is it, Big Guy?"

"How do you know? I mean, how is it you seem to know, or at least easily figure out, what I want…what I need when sometimes I don't even know?" With my lips and tongue, I managed to grab hold of his cock and sucked and maneuvered until his foreskin was between my teeth. Once in my grasp, I gently nibbled—something I'd figured out he absolutely loved.

"Damn, I love it when you do that. Um, I don't know…I was pretty young when I realized I could read people easily."

He set his beer down and grabbed a couple of chips with one hand, and with the other he pushed his dick father into my mouth, "*Yeah, like that, Grif.* But I don't think it's some special ability or anything. I think it's more that I pay attention to the situation, to both what people are saying and not saying. Then there's the subtle body language and asking the right questions."

Washing the chips down he added conspiratorially, "And, of course, the psych classes don't hurt either."

He was majoring in psychology, but every time I asked what he planned on doing with his degree, he'd offer some sort of 'Sex Therapist' joke in lieu of a real answer.

I let him slip from me, "Damn, Tate, if you're this good with me…shit, with a chick, where you're having full-on sex…I bet you fuck really well. No wonder they don't wanna give up once they've had a taste."

He laughed, "Well, I don't often get complaints. And thank you for the compliment, Grif. But you know it's not just about fucking as many women as I can, not that that's not fun, but I really am looking for Mrs. Right. You know, someone to settle down with and build a life."

He grabbed his beer again and took several long swallows before putting it back down.

"And do you think about when this is over, Tate? I mean, I know it's only been a few weeks…and I know it's not really about me, well most of it isn't about me, but we will graduate…move on. I'm not the only one enjoying this, am I?"

"Of course I think about it. *Suck my balls, would ya? Yeah, damn that's nice.* And yeah, we'll move on…we'll have to. I mean, I want to find someone I connect with on an intimate level. I mean, don't get me wrong, you're my best

143

friend—you were before this, and I know, without a doubt, you will be after.

"We're friends for life, Grif. But I'm straight, and you're gay. I'm wired to want to fall in love with a chick the same way you're wired to want to fall in love with a dude. *A little more pressure, fag. Yeah, like that.*

"But that doesn't for one moment mean that I'm not gonna miss the hell outta having you absolutely fucking worship my body and dick. To feel the incredible high that comes from knowing you fucking want me all the time and expect nothing in return, particularly while I'm watching a game. *Oh, that feels so good, Grif.*"

He grinned and ruffled my hair.

I let his nuts pop out of my mouth, "But, Tate, you do understand how much you give me, right? That I do get something—a lot—in return. I mean, you realize that, don't you?"

He became more serious, "Of course I know. Every time I give you what you want—what you need—I see it in your eyes. It's not only unmistakable, but it's also hot as hell; a major ego boost." Then he grinned again, "I'm the one with super perceptive powers after all, right?"

I smiled and nodded into his nuts. God, they tasted so good, and I fucking loved the feel of them rolling around in my mouth. I sucked them back in and sedately moved my tongue back and forth over the soft skin.

"Damn," he gasped. "Speaking of asking the right questions, I have a few of my own. Do you mind?"

I let his nuts slip back out, "Sure, but then I won't be able to suck your balls…sure it's worth it to ya?"

He was all smiles. "I'll make the sacrifice. We've been together all day, right?"

"Yep, all day and," I stuck my tongue out and licked his balls again, "it's been great."

"Yeah, it has. But I've shot three loads—three pretty amazing loads, thank you very much—and, well, you haven't come even once today, have you?"

"Oh, so I'm expected to answer serious questions because I asked serious ones, is that the way it works?" Unfortunately, my humor was never enough to persuade him to forego answers. I knew the only way to do that was to flat out say I didn't want to answer. And, ninety-nine percent of the time, that was all it took; he'd not only drop it, but he'd be perfectly fine doing so.

"You know you don't have—,"

I sighed, "I know I don't, Tate. But other than exposing more of myself, there's really no reason not to, is there?"

I noticed a drop of pre-cum and swiped the prize with my tongue.

"How can you produce pre-cum when you're not hard? I don't understand how that even works."

I glanced up at him and was met with inquiring eyes.

"Okay, okay," I sighed. "No, I haven't come today. Satisfied? Now can we please go back to you watching the game, and me sucking your dick? Oh, and I've been wondering…um…how you might feel about maybe letting me eat your ass? Obviously it's not something I've ever done before, but I've been thinking about it a lot lately." That one was sure to distract him.

His mouth fell open in a gape and after a moment he swallowed and recovered. *Success!*

"I'd fucking love that, Grif! Seriously. I've only had one chick ever do that and she just sorta played at it more than anything. Seriously, I'd love it. I mean, anytime! Starting today I'll make sure I'm extra clean...just in case. Oh, dude!"

I grinned inwardly in triumph and assured him, "You're always clean, Tate."

"But, I mean, like extra, extra clean!" he promised and ran a finger down my cheek.

He got a strange look on his face and said, "Grif, you do know...I mean...shit. I'm so not good at this. I just want you to know I feel real lucky we're friends."

I stuck my tongue out and swiped it across his balls. "Yeah, I'll bet," I grinned.

His eyebrows shot up, and he quickly said, "No!" Then, much more calmly he continued, "No, not because of the sex—not that it isn't great...," He paused and looked into my eyes for a few moments before saying, "That's not right either; sure, the sex is part of it...how could it not be? It's back to what we were talking about before...no matter where our friendship goes—no matter what it grows into in the coming years—we'll always have this shared time. This amazing shared experience, right?"

The unexpected seriousness of his comments caught me by surprise. He rarely, if ever, talked about 'us' and what it meant to him. I was slightly overcome with emotion and managed to choke out, "Thanks, Tate. That means a lot to me. And yeah, we'll always have this."

He grinned broadly and ruffled my hair again. "So, if we're done with the gay shit, I think it's time you answered my question: How long has it been since you shot?"

He wasn't letting this one go. I turned my face into his crotch and resignedly mumbled, "Friday morning before class."

"Friday morning? Three days ago?" he asked, unable to

keep the shock out of his voice.

"Yep," I said simply.

"But…I've had like six orgasms since then."

"Seven, if you count the short shot last night in the kitchen before bed," I corrected with no small amount of pride.

"B-but doesn't that hurt? Aren't you in pain? I know what having blue balls feels like, Grif."

I nuzzled his nuts a bit before answering, "Yes, it hurts, and yes I'm in…I'm a little uncomfortable."

He sat looking at me for a bit, and I saw the comprehension dawn on his face, "But you like it, don't you? You like being in pain…being denied?"

A few moments of contemplation passed before he asked, "Do you correlate the pain with your size?"

I buried my face in his crotch and groaned in discomfiture, "Fuck, Tate, sometimes I really hate your 'non-super-powers' and those psych classes. How do you do that? How do you take seemingly unrelated things and connect them together?"

I looked up at him and continued, "To be honest, I don't know. Shit, this is all new to me…I'm still figuring it all out…maybe will be for years to come. You know I'm about a decade behind on my sexual growth. But yes…it makes me harder, hotter, knowing I'm not going to allow myself to come while giving you an incredible blowjob and watching you squirt…because—,"

"Because you're small?" he filled in.

I nodded in assent.

"Fuck, Grif! Just fuck!" He shook his head and grinned. "I'm not sure what it says about me—and I honestly don't care—but that's about too fucking hot for words. I get to come because I have a big dick, and you don't because you have a small one. We are so incorporating this into our blowjob sessions! I mean, if it's okay with you?"

And there was no doubt he thought it was hot; his thick cock was once again standing straight up. I hesitantly nodded, "Yeah, I guess that'd be okay."

His grin was massive. "Cool. Now fucking make me come, you little-dicked fag. And when I shoot I want you watching me and imagining how good I'm feeling!"

I whimpered and happily got to work.

CHAPTER 13
GRINDR

Fall 2013

I TOOK OUT my iPhone and decided to give Grindr another shot. The app must have been malfunctioning as I'd checked it about twice an hour for the last three hours, and it kept saying there was no one within twenty-five miles of me. How on earth was that possible—I was in Santa Barbara for Christ's sake, not on the moon. Something must be wrong with the app, there had to be.

Matthew and I had taken off this morning in the Gulfstream G450 from Montgomery Field, a small, private airport in Clairemont, where our hangar was located. Now I was in quaint Santa Barbara looking for fun before tomorrow's meetings.

We'd landed over four hours ago, and damn I was horny. It'd been several weeks since my last rather unfulfilling hookup, and I was ready to give Grindr another shot. The app was definitely a hit or miss thing, and the last several hookups had been much more miss than hit.

Sitting on the balcony of my hotel room, having a cigarette, I looked out over the lush, green landscaped grounds. The vanishing-edge pool appeared to blend into the shimmering ocean in the distance. Man, the place was stunning. The sun was still shining, but definitely beginning to make its descent as another picturesque southern California day was coming to a close.

It had been more than five years since Tate passed, and I was still no closer to finding a meaningful relationship than I was the day he died. Hell, no closer to just finding someone I could simply be comfortable with—to be me with. Not that I was looking for a meaningful relationship any longer—Grindr was about something else entirely— but that's exactly why it had become my sole means of sexual exploits. My confidence was bolstered by the years I'd spent with Tate. I'd gone out on a few dates in the months after his death—thinking I'd give it a shot. Truth was, once I revealed certain details of my anatomy, even the most promising looking guys suddenly weren't very interested anymore.

Then I'd discovered Grindr. Yeah, I wasn't going to find Mr. Forever, but at least it offered some limited intimacy. The app allowed me to explicitly spell out what I wanted— what I would and wouldn't do. I figured if I couldn't find true love—something I'd given up years before I'd even met Tate—then I could at least find hookups where I could dictate the parameters. Or at least try to anyway. There was always the occasional asshole who wanted more than what we'd agreed upon.

I picked up the phone lying in my lap and refreshed the app again. Bingo! Finally. It showed two guys less than three miles from me. I tapped on the first guy's picture and read the short description.

Name = No Hookups

Stats = Blank

Looking For = Friends, Serious Dating, Loving Relationship, NO SEX hookups.

Well, he was out. I hoped for better luck with the second guy.

Name = Nice But No Pushover

Stats = 30 yrs, 6'4", 240 lbs., Italian, Single

Looking For = Chat, Friends, Relationship, NSA

Comments = Conversation, dinner, or just dirty fun...it's all good.

Okay, this guy looked interesting and his picture—fuck, he was gorgeous; dark hair, strong jaw, and intense eyes that suggested tough guy. I clicked the chat button and started my standard spiel.

Me:
  Hey. Nice profile. Interested in a hookup?

Less than a minute ticked by before his reply came.

Him:
  Hi. Thanks. Yours is nice too. I haven't had dinner yet and was looking for a place to eat. You interested in food?

Me:
I've already eaten. Hungry for something else.

Him:
What's your name?

Me:
Profile says my name is Swallows Nine. I'd like to prove it.

Him:
LOL! Well, I've got a tad more than that. Wouldn't mind you trying to prove it though. But I really do need some food. Hit me back in about 90 mins if you're still 'hungry'?

Me:
Yep.

Damn, well ninety minutes would only make it 10:30pm. I could be back in my room by 11:30pm and be in bed by midnight…still plenty of time for seven hours sleep before my meetings tomorrow.

～

I got out my laptop and decided to do some work in preparation for tomorrow's interviews. Hanna, my secretary, had arranged each of the applicant's submissions in their own dossier. Each contained a detailed schematic of the proposed network security for Tate's Place, a recommended plan for vetting employees and volunteers—

background, credit checks, etc.—physical building security proposals, and pricing.

Each dossier also included information on the company and its current employees. She'd also taken the time to flag certain applicants whose proposal she felt showed promise. It was times like these I was reminded how much I depended on her.

I snagged my phone and dictated a reminder to bring her back something nice from Santa Barbara.

Some of the dossiers were so detailed I hadn't even gotten through half of them before boarding the plane for the trip. I grabbed the folders and went to work reading.

I'd gotten so involved in reviewing them that I completely lost track of time. It was only when my phone dinged with a new email notification that I remembered Grindr—and my potential hookup. I snatched up my phone and saw two hours had passed. *Shit, he's probably already hooked up or gone to bed. Dammit!*

I refreshed the app and, to my surprise, found he was still online.

Me:
  Hey.

Him:
  Hey, back atcha.

Me:
  Did you eat? I'm still hungry.

Him:

    I did. And I'm glad you're still hungry…I believe you promised to prove something to me, didn't you?

Me:

    I did. Ground rules. I've got some very specific ones. But, I'm sure you'll find accommodating me will be quite rewarding.

Him:

    Okay, you've got my attention.

Me:

    You freshly showered and naked. Me mostly clothed. You sitting. I service you. You DO NOT touch me.

There was a longish pause. But I wasn't particularly surprised. More often than not, my ground rules gave them pause. Actually, when they agreed too readily I became suspicious. It was the ones who agreed to do anything that wound up being the most unpredictable and problematic.

His reply came about a minute later.

Him:

    Are you suggesting restraints? If so, that's a deal-breaker. Not that restraints can't be fun sometimes, just not on me.

Me:

    No restraints. Just agree to ground rules. Sit back and enjoy.

Me:

    Enough talk? I'm ready.

Him:
    Sure, sounds like fun. Where would you like to meet?

I checked the app again to confirm he was still about three miles away. He wasn't; he was less than a thousand feet from me. *Shit.*

The last thing I wanted was to run into the guy at breakfast the next morning. I had a strict one-time-only rule. Anything more and they started to think the ground rules were negotiable—they were not. I checked for other guys online…nothing…he was the only option for tonight. Screw it, if I saw him later, I'd nod politely and keep moving.

Me:
    Your room. You're also at The Bacara, right? What's your room number?

Him:
    Yes. I'm in room 752.

Me:
    Fifteen minutes enough time for you to shower?

Him:
    Yes. Plenty of time. See you in fifteen, Swallows Nine =)

Did he seriously just use a smiley face in a hookup chat? I looked at the small picture on his profile again. Damn, the man was hot. I decided he could use all the smiley faces he wanted. I hoped, not for the first time with these hookups, his pronouncements of endowment weren't using Internet Measurements.

I took a quick shower myself, gargled and rinsed with Listerine, and donned my 'Grindr uniform.' From experience I'd learned exactly how to dress: a jockstrap, baggy shorts, t-shirt, and athletic shoes.

The resort was comprised of over twenty-five buildings. With its countless courtyards, swimming pools, and walking trails, getting turned around was actually quite simple. After calling the front desk and getting directions to room 752, I grabbed a bottle of water from the minibar and made my way out into the warm evening air. I noted the surf methodically crashing—a sound I never tire of—as meandering paths led me through a few different courtyards and made my way up the stairs of building seven.

Seventeen minutes from our last text, with slightly sweaty palms and my stomach doing its normal fluttering, I knocked loud enough to make sure I was heard on his door.

There was rustling noises and then the door slid open to reveal Nice But No Pushover. *Damn!* Not only was the guy hot as shit, but he was massive. I remembered his profile saying six foot four and two hundred-forty pounds, but the vast majority of the time, Grindr profiles were exaggerated—sometimes incredibly so.

I hesitated a moment. Big guys were certainly a major turn-on for me, but they could also be much more dangerous if things got out of control.

He looked me in the face, and then quickly gave me a once over from head to toe. His eyes widened as his gaze fell back to my arms and chest—lingering there for a moment—before offering a smile. Wow, what a smile.

"I may be a big dude," he said when he noticed my uneasiness, "but I'm not a Neanderthal or insane. I'm just looking for a good time—same as you."

"Cool. You remember the ground rules, right? There aren't going to be any problems, are there?" I tried to sound much more casual than I felt.

"I do remember. See? There's proof right there that I'm not a Neanderthal, right?"

He was still smiling, and I figured I'd come this far...and it'd been so damn long. Even though this had become my only form of sexual release, aside from jacking off, I still didn't do it that often. I enjoyed most all of the encounters as they were happening, but afterwards I still felt alone—sometimes more alone than before the hookup.

He'd stepped aside and was holding an arm out into the room with a slight bow.

"Okay, not a Neanderthal. Check. Now for the question of insanity," I said, moving past him and into the room.

It was slightly smaller than mine, and the view wasn't anything remotely close to mine, but it was still a very nice room. Since it sat at the corner of the building it actually had more windows than mine did and a large wrap-around balcony. It was decorated in dark greens and creams, and had a distinctly masculine feel to it.

I spotted the phone on top of the desk in the far corner—just beyond two club chairs and a round coffee table—and made my way to it, stepping around the pulled-out desk chair. The chair had a padded seat, but the rest of it was intricately carved wood and didn't look comfortable at all. But, I had to admit, it was attractive.

I set down my bottle of water and lifted the receiver.

Dialing zero, I waited for the operator to answer, and then asked for room service. Once I was connected, I ordered a bottle of dark beer and a plate of hot wings to be delivered in twenty minutes.

Picking up my water, I gave a casual glance at the desktop. It held a laptop, two cell phones, a neatly stacked pile of folders, a yellow pad with some notes—in appealing penmanship—and a well-worn, handsome, soft-sided leather briefcase.

I turned around and found him closing the room's door. Glancing toward the opposite side of the room, I noted the made bed, an open armoire holding a few suits, ties and dress shirts, jeans and polo pullovers, and several pairs of shoes lined up along the bottom shelf. The guy was certainly neat and well organized.

Through the open patio doors, I saw a nearly empty water bottle and a pack of cigarettes lying on one of the tables. I heard the minibar fridge open and turned to see him pulling another bottle of water out.

"You only ordered one beer; I'm assuming I don't get one, huh?" With a shrug and a glimmer in his eyes, he added, "I guess I'll have to make do with water."

He was leaning back against the fridge and offering me a playful grin.

"What?" I asked feeling defensive.

"The room service—which we both know isn't for either of us—the assessment of the entire suite, including my hand-written notes, and from the way you eyed the pack of cigarettes," tilting his head toward the balcony, "I'd say you'd like to have one."

I snorted, "You're a regular smart-ass, aren't you?"

How the fuck had he seen all that without me even

noticing him watching? Hell, I could've sworn he had his back to me most of the time I'd spent discreetly checking things out.

His tone changed immediately and became quite sincere, "No. I honestly wasn't trying to be. I only hoped, with your thorough scrutiny of the room, that I had passed the 'insanity check.'"

He flashed the smile again. Wow, it seemed so sincere. Dammit, he wasn't being a smart-ass. Turns out I was. I cleared my throat and tried to relax a bit.

"Look, sorry about that. You can't be too careful, ya know? And, like you said, you're one helluva big dude."

"Yeah, and like I mentioned in our brief chat, I'm big all over." He winked at me.

Just as playfully, I said, "Well it's nice to know some guys are honest in their profiles."

"Speaking of being honest...,"

Oh, here it came; the Buts, and the Why not just a small touch? and the How come you get to touch and I don't?

"...I had to take a call from an employee right after you and I finished our chat, so I haven't had a chance to shower yet. I can be quick...," then he added hastily, "thorough, but quick. I don't want you to get the wrong impression; I completely respect ground rules. Completely."

The dude was really trying without coming across as desperate. Perhaps it was time for me to be a bit friendlier.

"Hey, no worries. I completely understand duty calling at—literally—the most inopportune times. Go hop in and I'll make myself comfortable if that's cool. Or, if you'd prefer, I can wait out in the garden until you've finished."

He was still leaning against the fridge, and I was still

standing at the desk. Our entire conversation had taken place without either of us moving, and I found it odd. Guys always moved toward me. They were horny and wanted to touch. Hell, I was horny, and I wanted to touch. But the leering, and impending *don't touch* conversation, often left me feeling pretty uncomfortable. But this guy hadn't done any of those things.

He pushed himself off the fridge and started toward the bathroom, "Nah, you're cool here. I'll be only be a few minutes."

He walked into the bathroom, and I heard the shower being turned on. At the sound of running water, I realized I really had to pee. I tried to remember if I'd passed a public bathroom on the way here but didn't think I had. I could head back to my room. But maybe he hadn't gotten into the shower yet, and I could quickly pee and then leave him to do his thing.

I decided it was worth a shot and made my way to the open door. "Um…." Damn, I didn't know the guy's name. "Excuse me, but do you think I could use the bathroom before—,"

His response cut loudly over the noisy running water, "What was that? Sorry, I can't hear you."

I stepped in a bit farther and saw the large glass and tile shower was directly to my right, with the toilet in a separate water closet, just like in my room, at the far end. Thank God, because there was no way I could pee if there was even a chance he might be able to sneak a peek.

"Is it okay if I use the toilet?" I asked louder.

He hooked his thumb over his shoulder, "Oh sure. It's right back there."

After peeing, I stepped up to the sink to wash my hands

when our eyes met in the slightly fogged mirror.

"Sorry, but I haven't unpacked my toiletries yet. You mind handing me the bar of soap and shampoo from my kit?"

There, on the counter, was his kit. "Sure," I called back.

I slid the zipper open and rummaged around a bit. In doing so, I couldn't help but notice the condoms and lube—which caused me to sigh at my ever-present virginity. He mistook my pause for something entirely different.

"Unless you'd prefer I not use them? I mean, I assume you're sensitive to scents—the shower being part of the ground rules and all."

Man, I had to admit, he was being pretty damn considerate. "Nah, it's just…well, I don't really care for body odor and if I don't mention the shower some guys…."

He chuckled, "Isn't that the truth? I mean, come on, you wouldn't think it'd be too much to expect a guy to be clean when he's looking to get intimate. But, apparently, for some dudes showering is not a daily habit. I don't get it myself, but hey, to each his own."

"Yeah, I understand there are folks who really get off on body smells. I'm definitely not one of those guys."

I located the American Crew soap and shampoo, grabbed it, and turned around to face the shower and stopped mid-step. God, the man was absolutely unbelievable. Tall, broad, muscular, hairy, terrific olive skin, naked, wet, an impressive package—even while soft— topped off with an interesting tattoo on his lower abdomen.

He must have noticed me standing there staring. Smiling

broadly, he leaned forward a bit, grabbed hold of the top of the glass partition, and placed the sole of one foot on the top of the other foot. The casual stance showed off every bulging muscle in his body—from his arms, to his chest, to his stomach, to his legs. Fuck, he was amazing.

"Is it okay?" he asked innocently.

I was beyond keeping up the 'cool guy' routine and simply nodded and said, "You're beautiful...um...," I still didn't know his name. And even though everything was telling me not to do it, I did it anyway. "Um, can I ask your name?"

He blushed. I mean actually fucking blushed. Like he had no idea how impossibly gorgeous he was.

"Thanks for the compliment." And then with a wicked grin added, "But fair is fair, right? I tell you mine and you tell me yours, deal?"

I nodded, not taking my eyes off his handsome, wet face.

"I'm Weston, but everyone calls me Wes. And, by the way, I think you're plenty damn sexy yourself...um...?"

"Marcus," I blurted out.

I have no idea why I said Marcus and not Grif...but I did.

He smiled, "Cool. Nice to meet you Marcus. Would you like me to use those?" He was nodding at the toiletries I still held in my hand.

"Oh. Yeah. Um, that'd be great," I stammered like a damn schoolboy.

I reached up and handed him the items and then turned to head out to the main room.

"Stay? Keep me company, Marcus?"

"Oh...yeah, sure."

I stepped back and leaned up against the sink counter while he popped open the shampoo.

"What brings you to town?" he asked with closed eyes, as he lathered his short, chestnut colored hair.

"I'm here on business. And you?"

"Me too. But I hope to get out tomorrow and see some of the city. Not that the hotel isn't nice, it's great, but this is my first visit to Santa Barbara and I'd like to do some exploring before heading home, ya know?"

I heard him talking and had a vague feeling I should be responding in some way, but he'd finished with his hair and was moving the bar of soap over his furry, well defined chest and pert nipples. I couldn't think. I only looked up when his hand inexplicably stopped moving.

His knowing gaze met mine, "Generally, in conversation, one person talks and the other responds. Then the other person talks and gets a response."

I let out an embarrassed and hearty laugh. "God, I'm sorry. You'd think I'd never seen a naked man before...," I trailed off but my eyes didn't leave his as I shook my head, smiling. "But damn, Wes...you're just...."

"Yeah?" he said in a sexy tone.

Hand movement drew my eyes downward again. One soapy hand was rolling his fat, near tangerine sized nuts around and his cock was filling and lengthening.

"Some guys think I'm too big. I guess I intimidate them or something. I'm glad that doesn't seem to be the case with you."

His uncut dick was almost fully erect, and he hadn't misled me during our Grindr chat. He was sizable, and I wanted to do all sorts of things with it. I chuckled. "Are we talking about your overall size, or something," I nodded downward, "more specific?"

He laughed, "Both, I suppose. But, I get the feeling it's more about my overall body size. I think it frightens people."

"Well, since we seem to be having an honest, real conversation here, despite the difficulty I'm having concentrating with your hand doing what it is, I can understand being apprehensive, Wes, you're a huge guy. If you decided to hurt someone, well...most folks wouldn't be able to do much to stop you."

He waggled his eyebrows. "So, this is distracting you?" he asked, as he slowly pulled his foreskin back. "But you're not scared of me, right?"

My dick had skipped past being simply aroused and jumped straight to the painfully hard stage. I swallowed as I watched his soapy hand, and fuck, I wanted to jump into that shower with him.

"Yes, distracting. And, no, I wouldn't go so far as to call it fear, but certainly apprehension fits. I mean, I don't know you from Adam, Wes." I involuntarily licked my lips, "But we're gonna fix that, right?"

A knock at the door and a voice calling out interrupted his answer. "Room service!"

Wow, had twenty minutes passed already? I took one last look at his soapy hand and dick and reluctantly said, "I'll get that."

The room service attendant wheeled the cart in and, as I was signing the check for the charges to be billed to my room, I said, "There's an extra two hundred bucks in this for you if you can have another bottle of beer back here in under five minutes."

She smiled widely and said on her way out, not even

closing the door completely, "Not a problem, sir."

She was back with the second beer and two hundred and fifty dollars richer before I'd even popped the cap off the first bottle. She thanked me profusely—for both the two hundred and the extra fifty—and wished me a very good evening.

I had to admit, there were times when I allowed myself to frivolously enjoy Tate's money...but it was certainly much easier when I was helping someone else, like I'd just done, rather than spending it on myself.

Without a doubt, I enjoyed the Diaz Estate's toys, but every one of them, aside from the modest house I lived in, had been there before me, and I hadn't added to the collection. I didn't see the need, or have the desire, to spend much money on myself.

Wes had just finished brushing his teeth. He walked out wearing only a towel as I popped the cap off the second beer and snagged a hot wing. He spied the two beers immediately and grinned, "Hmm, I get one after all, huh?"

I handed him one, "Looks that way. I guess someone made a mistake." Me, I thought but wasn't gonna admit it to him.

He gave me an incredulous look and said, "Riiiight. The two hundred and fifty bucks didn't play any part in it, huh?"

I laughed. "How the fuck...? Is there anything that slips by you?"

He winked. "Not much."

Tilting his head toward the patio, "So, beer and a cigarette or beer and wings?"

I grabbed the wings and my beer and headed out.

"Who says we can't have all three?"

He grinned. "Ah, a man after my own heart."

We sat in companionable silence and enjoyed the small, unhealthy feast. It was still warm out and even though his balcony didn't offer the ocean view mine did, the sound of crashing waves was definitely louder here. It was soothing.

I looked up to find his hungry eyes locked on mine and felt the desire emanating from them.

"So, not to be too forward, but are we ready? 'Cause if I have to wait much longer for the proof you offered, I'm afraid I won't need it. Sitting here, looking at you, thinking about your handsome face in my crotch, I can barely contain myself."

Oh, if I wasn't ready before, I sure was now. But the only response I managed was a squeak—one I'm not sure I'd ever heard come from me before—and a jerky nod.

We both stood, but as I followed him inside, I couldn't help reiterating, "Um, y-you remember the ground rules, right?"

He didn't reply right away, but instead headed for the open armoire.

"I do."

He reached inside and pulled out two neckties and handed them to me as he stepped past and grabbed the desk chair. He placed the chair in the center of the room, pulled the towel from his waist, and took a seat.

Nodding to the ties, he said, "Ground rules are important. I want you to be comfortable, Marcus."

He placed his wrists on the arms of the chair, "I've rarely allowed anyone to use restraints on me, but I want you to. I want to know that you're comfortable. And I want you to know you can let go and enjoy yourself—here—with me."

Well if that didn't beat everything all to hell. No one in

the five years since Tate's death had ever taken my ground rules to heart like this—no one. And then, on top of it, to allow me to do something he apparently allowed few others to do—jeez!

"Fuck, Wes! I'm not sure which is hotter, you sitting there naked—just displaying yourself for me—or you allowing me to restrain you. Thanks for both."

I walked over and knelt between his spread knees and raised a silky, black tie to his wrist...but my body shook so badly I had to pause. I took in a deep breath and tried to relax.

"Are you okay?"

I could hear the concern in his tone.

I looked up and nodded. "These are shakes of serious anticipation—something I haven't experienced since my first time, by the way—and not anything related to being uncomfortable."

His sigh of relief was so strong it actually blew the hair across my forehead. It carried the scent of beer, toothpaste, and something else—something slightly spicy. The wings? Him? I couldn't be sure, but I found both appealing and arousing as hell.

"Good, I'm really glad."

While I bound his wrists, working around a leather band he wore, I felt nearly euphoric. I knew this was going to be good.

Placing my lips on the smooth skin of his collarbone, I breathed in his scent for the first time. He smelled manly with a slight hint of musk, but also like clean laundry—it was a heady mix. Slowly, I worked my way down his chest until I found a hard, peaked nipple. I took my time, rolling first one, and then the other, between my lips and then teeth. Running my nose through his soft hair as I worked my way down, I lathed his flat, furry stomach with my tongue—dipping in and out of his bellybutton. I payed a bit of extra attention to the intriguing tattoo there, and my chin rubbed against his thick cock as I traced the ink with my tongue. Softly he moaned, "Marcus, feels so good."

Only when his straining cock dripped with need, did I move on. Skipping down to his knees, I worked my way up each thigh, taking my time to find and lick and appreciate every inch of each. When I finally reached his balls, he was literally making soft begging noises. I had to work to get them into my mouth—they were pulled up so close to his body. Holding both between my lips, I slid my tongue across their firmness. I pushed my nose against his exquisite cock, and looked up at him.

"My God, Marcus, I don't think I've ever seen anything so fantastic in my entire life. And I know I've never met anyone who can do what you do or enjoy it as much. Jesus Christ!"

I let his balls slip out of my mouth and slid my chin up the ridge of his cock...never taking my eyes off of his, "So, it's okay then?" I asked with the most innocent expression I could manage. But before he could answer, I opened wide, swallowed him to the root, and managed to pull off and push down again only twice before his whole body stiffened and he started chanting, "Oh My God! Marcus, I'm gonna shoot. Marcus, Mar...I'm gonna...Jesus...Yesssss!"

Hot, salty jets filled my mouth, and I swallowed savoring the taste of him. Damn, that was so good. I plunged back down and held him there, feeling him jump and twitch as I managed to find a position which would allow me to keep him buried in my throat but yet still breathe too.

As he softened, I gently licked his shaft, nuzzled his balls, and nibbled at his foreskin while he made soft murmurs of appreciation.

I laid my head on his thigh and caught a glimpse of a necktie. Reaching up, without lifting my head from the comfortable spot, I undid one of his hands. He sighed contentedly and flexed his fingers back and forth.

"Marcus," he said sated, "that was absolutely fucking incredible," and his fingertips grazed the line of my jaw.

I reacted on instinct; before I realized it, I'd grabbed him by the wrist and held him tightly. He was alert in seconds and pushed the chair back—still seated in it—with a look of horror on his face.

"Oh my God, I'm so sorry. I...I just. Fuck! I can't believe I...that I forgot. I don't know what to say. You have my sincere apologies, Marcus."

Okay, clearly he was more upset than I was—which was certainly not anything I'd ever experienced before—and I found myself wanting to console him rather than deck him. Which, again, was way different.

"Wes. It's okay. Really," I tried.

But he wasn't having it. He shook his head adamantly, "Rules are rules—they're there for a reason."

I said more sternly, "It's my rule, and the rule really means no touching below the waist. I should have been far clearer about it in my text. It's completely my fault. People casually touch all the time—that's not the kind of touching I was talking about."

He shook his head. "Not how I understood it. And I broke—,"

"Okay, shut it!" I huffed.

Lifting myself off my knees, I walked over and pulled

the minibar open. They didn't stock them with beer, but thankfully hard liquor was another story altogether—go figure. I pulled out two mini bottles of scotch and poured each of us a drink. Handing him one, I set the other on the table while I bent down and untied his other wrist.

Looking back up at him I appealed, "This has been the best night I've spent in…well, a very, very long time—years, if I'm being completely honest." I took his hand in mine, "Please, don't do this."

I stood up, took my drink from the table, and with a frisky tilt of my head toward the balcony asked, "Would you be interested in having a post coital drink and cigarette with a master cocksucker?"

The comment earned me a genuine, if not still slightly sedate, smile. "It'd be my pleasure. Let me grab a pair of shorts or something."

"It'd be more of a pleasure, for me at least, if you joined me the way you are."

"Naked? On the balcony of a fancy hotel?" he grinned.

I laughed. "I'll tell you what, you do this for me and we'll call it even, deal?"

There was the real smile. "Sure, I can do that."

We'd finished most of our drinks and two cigarettes apiece when things suddenly became complicated. I was enjoying the evening so much I'd forgotten one important fact: if I spent enough time with the trick afterwards the questions always started—always.

I was admiring his wide chest when he said, "I've never

felt so appreciated, Marcus. The way you look at me, at my body, it's...it feels really good."

I felt myself blush. "You really are handsome, Wes."

"Thank you. I'm glad you think so."

He furrowed his brows a bit, "Is there something I can do for you? You know...you didn't get to...."

Fuck, fuck, fuck! Why did I wait so long to leave?

I glanced down at my watch. "Oh man, look at the time...I've got an early morning, Wes. I've really got to go."

"Whoa, what did I say?"

He was confused, and I knew it. Dammit, why had I allowed myself to hang around? Shit.

"Huh? Oh, no it's nothing. I just realized how late it is."

I walked to the door and turned around. "It was a real nice evening. I truly enjoyed it, Wes. Thank you."

I could see more questions forming behind his eyes— trying to figure out what the fuck was wrong—I extended my hand and he took it. "I hope you have a nice time seeing the sights of Santa Barbara. Take care."

I let go of his hand, opened the door, and slipped out closing it behind me. When I'd made my way down the stairs and around the building, I finally stopped. Leaning up against it, I took a deep breath. Fuck, I should have left earlier—before it could get awkward. Why hadn't I?

I knew why, because I hadn't felt anything close to what I was feeling with Wes since Tate. I had felt—hell, I still felt—like electric currents were running through my body. I was happy and, even though I'd stayed too long and almost ruined it, I felt alive.

Sure, the sex had been amazing, but it was more than

just that. It was the way he'd looked at me, the way he'd talked to me, the way he'd smiled at me—it left me feeling…. Damn, I wasn't sure what I was feeling exactly, but there was no doubt I was feeling something completely unexpected, and really good—for the first time in five years.

And even this had been different from what I'd had with Tate because Wes was gay. I could feel the way he wanted me. Rolling my head against the building, I sighed a little. It was over—but man, it had been amazing and I couldn't help but want more. However, I knew that was impossible. No, I'd have to settle for it being a lone, phenomenal evening…one to remember. One to replay over-and-over for months, if not years, to come.

CHAPTER 14
GRIF WEARS WES' RINGS

Fall 2014

"WES, I'M TRYING to get ready for work and you're making the mirror all foggy," I called out, as I wiped the glass down with a hand towel again.

"That's because I'm so hot, when the water hits me, it instantly turns to steam," he playfully retorted.

I barked out a laugh. "Yeah, and you're a damn fool, too!"

The noise of falling water stopped and was replaced moments later with the sound of wet feet padding up behind me.

"That may be, but I'm your damn fool," came his muffled reply, as he toweled his hair.

Damp forearms suddenly wound around my torso, and I was firmly pulled back against a strong, muscled, furry, moist chest.

"Um, and you're also wet," I said, smiling at his

refection.

An equally wet tongue darted out and licked a path from my collarbone up to the back of my ear sending shivers down my spine. Damn, even though he'd been joking, there was no denying the man was totally fucking hot! But I didn't have time for this. I really did need to get to work.

I turned in his embrace and immediately noticed his 'necklace.' He'd taken the stainless steel nipple rings from Bertrand's and threaded them through a simple leather cord saying, *I'll wear them until you decide if you want to.* That had been weeks ago and he hadn't brought the subject up again. I reached up and fingered them.

"Tell ya what, you forget whatever mischief you're thinking about making," I said, smiling up at him, "because I have to get to work on time this morning, and we'll go have these put in tonight. Deal?"

He grinned while letting his hands slide down my back and rest on my naked ass.

"Oh, that's definitely a deal I can live with."

His big hands softly kneaded each cheek. He leaned in and kissed me with such tenderness that I completely forgot about work.

"And how's this doing this morning? I wasn't too rough last night, was I?" he asked patting my naked butt.

His slightly raspy voice and mischievous hands on my ass brought back memories of last night. It all combined to immediately seize Junior's attention. I pushed out of his grasp and away from his reach.

With mock irritation, "Okay, that's not even remotely playing fair…you bringing up last night." With more sincerity, I added, "It was awesome. It's always fucking awesome, Wes."

I took a few more steps back, saying, "But I don't have time for this."

He eyed Junior and beamed. "Once again, your mouth is saying one thing, but your toy is saying something completely different."

Putting a safe distance between us, I said more earnestly, "Wes, it was incredible. Seriously and totally incredible. You were...amazing."

I turned my back and, while making a break from the bathroom, called over my shoulder, "Now get away from me—I *have* to be on-time this morning—you damn wicked, sexy fool, you!"

He didn't follow me but instead yelled out, "Okay, okay—I surrender in defeat. But only because you've made assuaging promises: tonight, you, me, rings. I can't wait!"

"And stop using such big words when I'm hard...you know I can't think like this!" I yelled back, while getting some clothes on my body, before he changed his mind and decided to pursue me.

He walked into the bedroom, took note of my nearly dressed body, and smirked.

"Can I help it if I learned more in the military than you did at that fancy college of yours? And, you do know that I can completely undress you in ninety seconds flat, right?"

I grabbed my shoes out of the closet and sat on one of the pair of side chairs I'd picked up at a flea market. Once my shoes were on, I was gonna be home free! I glanced out the French doors to see the back yard was drenched in brilliant sunlight...it was going to be another amazing San Diego day.

I bent down to tie my shoes, "Okay, one, it wasn't a fancy college, it was UCSD; and two, for the last time, I really have to be to work on time. Hanna took a couple days of vacation, and I have to open this morning. Pissy artists waiting to be let in is not my idea of a good way to start the day."

I made it; my shoes were on and tied. *I'm outta here!* I looked up triumphantly to find that he was standing across from me, beside the other chair, a hand resting on its back and one ankle crossed over the other. My God, he was stunning—damp, dark hair still towel-messed; a five o'clock shadow; thick chest and arms, flat stomach, a narrow waist, and a cock for days! I just sat and took the pleasure of him in. Wow.

I looked him in the eye and spoke from the heart, "God, Wes. You are so absolutely and phenomenally attractive that sometimes when I catch sight of you, like now, I honestly find it difficult to breathe. Jesus! I'm the luckiest guy on the planet."

He closed the few feet between us, and knelt down between my legs. With my face in his hands he spoke earnestly, "Nope. As we've already decided this morning, my education is far better than yours, and I say I'm the lucky one, Grif."

The kiss he gave me was warm and soft. I relaxed into it and simply enjoyed the taste of him. Then, distantly, I registered something else; fingers undoing my shirt collar. I broke the kiss, grabbed his wrist while turning it slightly, and pushed him backward.

He landed with a thud on his ass. I launched a hasty jump over his splayed body before he could recover and made it to the safety of the bedroom doorway before stopping to beam down at him.

"You may be hot, but your fancy military training can't measure up to my physical hand-to-hand combat superiority."

He let out a hearty laugh and then, in his toppy tone, said, "Oh, you're gonna pay for that one. You just wait."

"Ah, ah, ah, no Chocolate punishment for actions not to your liking during Vanilla," I said with a wicked smile of my own and threw in a wink just to goad him a bit more. "Them there are the rules," I called out merrily, making my way to the kitchen.

As I opened the back door, I heard him yell out, "Call me if you want to do lunch. I love you."

"Will do. Love you too," I called back.

～

With Hanna gone, I was so busy that we didn't end up seeing each other for lunch. In fact, I'm not sure choking down a steak salad at my desk would even be considered 'taking a lunch' by most folks. Wes called around what would normally have been close to the end of the day, and we set up at time to meet at Enigma Piercing Studio in Pacific Beach.

I pulled up to the Studio, at almost 7pm on the dot, parked in front, and started getting a bit nervous. I'd read up on the piercing procedure, so I knew what to expect. I really wanted to have this done...but still.

From everything I'd read, if you already had sensitive nipples this could immeasurably increase their sensitivity. There definitely would be some pain involved, but even that wasn't described as intolerable. I'd mostly talked myself back down when a tapping on my driver's window startled the shit out of me. It was Wes wearing a huge grin. I grabbed the keys and hopped out.

"Hey, handsome."

"Hey yourself," he said, and leaned in for a quick kiss.

"You got the rings?"

"Yep, still right here," and he pulled the leather cord out from under his t-shirt. "You ready?"

I took a deep breath and let it out, "As ready as I'm gonna get."

Grinning, he grabbed my hand and guided us to the front door. While holding it open for me, he said, "Then let's get this dog and pony show on the road."

Once inside, he led us to the front counter where a tattooed and heavily pierced blonde girl chirped. "Hi! I'm Amanda, can I help you?"

"Hi. Yeah, we have a seven thirty piercing appointment…the last name is De Luca."

She looked down at the appointment book, scanned the page, and then flipped a couple of pages in either direction.

"We're here to see Peter," Wes supplied when she seemed to be having trouble.

"Oh," she said brightly, "I'll let him know you're here."

She hopped up off the stool she'd been sitting on and made her way to the back of the store and through a curtain-covered doorway.

I looked over at Wes, "What was that all about?"

He shrugged, "Have no idea…too many piercings? Does copious amounts of metal affect brain activity?"

"Wes! That's not nice at all," I admonished with a grin.

He didn't have an opportunity to reply because a pale, rather short, young man approached extending his hand.

After getting a better look at him, I realized it was his demeanor and overall appearance which made him seem

178

younger than he probably was. His jet-black hair, which couldn't be natural; his rascally, moss-colored eyes; his bad boy, ripped-at-the-knees-jeans that hung so far down his thighs it looked like they might fall off at any moment; his slightly whiskered face, and fit body, all blended together forming a rather youthful, hoodlum-like rake. He was certainly a character.

With a friendly smile, he said, "You must be Wes and Grif. Hi, I'm Peter."

I noticed a small quirk of Wes' brow, before he responded, "Hi, Peter. Yep, I'm Wes, and this is Grif."

"Nice to meet you both." He jerked a thumb over his shoulder, and then quickly grabbed the front of his falling jeans. "My space is upstairs. You ready?"

Wes gave me a questioning look.

"Yep."

He smiled again, "Then right this way."

He led us up a set of steep, wooden stairs and down a narrow hallway with closed doors lining each side. The place had a worn feel to it, but was brightly lit and appeared clean enough. I heard what I assumed was a tattoo needle at work, and even though I wasn't getting tattooed, my stomach started doing that fluttery thing again. I reached down and took Wes' hand.

He squeezed back, "You okay, love?"

"Yeah, I'm good...just a little nervous, I guess."

Peter stopped at the next-to-last door on the left, opened it, and stood to one side to let us in. Wes stepped inside, and I followed.

The space looked surprisingly like an exam room with a table pushed up against one wall, bright overhead lights, a single white wooden chair in a corner, a short stool on wheels, and a tray attached to a rolling table filled with medical equipment wrapped in plastic.

It wasn't a large space by any means, and since Wes had walked in first and sat atop the exam table, I took the chair. Peter followed us in and closed the door behind him.

"So, who's getting the metal work done this evening?" he asked, looking back and forth between us.

"Well, perhaps both of us," Wes answered.

"Huh?" I asked.

Wes looked over at me and then said to Peter, "I'm thinking about a Prince Albert and Grif is going to have his nipples done."

"You're thinking about getting a PA?" I said. "Really?"

This was certainly news to me. Wes never mentioned wanting a piercing and certainly not a PA.

"Yeah, but I have a few questions for Peter before I decide." He turned to Peter, "Is that okay?"

Peter shrugged, "Sure, I have an hour before my next client so there's plenty of time to do both of you. What sort of questions do you have?"

"Well...," Wes started and then stopped. He seemed nervous—and it was rare that anything rattled him. But, then again, we were talking about someone sticking a needle through his dick, and the thought of even being in the same room when someone was having it done made me jumpy.

Peter, seeming to sense the tension said, "It's okay to be a bit nervous here guys. It's all cool."

"Well, I'm a bit on the large size, and I wanted to be sure there wouldn't be any complications because of it."

Peter looked at me and then back at Wes.

"I've never had any problems with larger men. Would you like me to take a look?"

Wes looked over at me, as if seeking my consent to flash his cock. Feeling lost as to exactly what was happening, I returned his look with a half-shrug.

"Sure, what do you want me to do?"

"Just slip your jeans down and I'll take a look."

Wes stood up, toed off his shoes, and let both his jeans and underwear fall around his ankles. The innate confidence having a normal sized dick offered, let alone an above average one, never ceased to astonish me. No matter how many times I'd seen a man unselfconsciously disrobe, I couldn't even begin to fathom what that security felt like. He stepped out of them completely and casually slipped back up onto the table with his legs spread wide. Peter, who'd taken a seat on the rolling stool, slid around in front of Wes.

"Oh," he said, when he got a look at Wes' dick. "Well, it is a bit on the larger side, isn't it?"

He looked at it for a moment or two longer, brows slightly pulled together, and then asked, "Is it okay if I have a closer look?"

"Sure, whatever you need to do."

I found it odd that Wes, now naked from the waist down, seemed much more comfortable than just a few moments ago when he was fully clothed. Why was that? He was talking about having his cock pierced. Shouldn't being naked, and closer to that actually happening, make him more nervous, not less?

Peter pulled over the table and removed the plastic wrap. He seemed to be looking for something but not finding it. Then, under a packet that held some kind of forceps, he pulled free a package containing several large, captive bead rings.

Tearing it open, he spread the contents out on the table next to Wes. He picked what looked like the largest ring from the pile and grasped Wes' cock, holding the ring next to the head.

Brows furrowed even further, Peter asked, "How much larger does it get when you're erect? I'm asking because we have to make sure the ring has adequate space to allow for full expansion without pinching and this is the largest ring we carry in the store. We can special order if necessary, but it's a bit more expensive...just so you're aware."

Wes lifted his shoulders, "I'm not really sure of the exact number." He looked at me.

"I'm not sure either," I said.

The longer Peter's hand stayed on my man's dick, the more I knew I didn't like it—and why was he still holding it as we talked?

Then I saw Peter's hand slide slightly back and forth on Wes' dick. *What. The. Fuck?*

"Well, if you keep that up, Peter, you'll see firsthand how much larger it gets," Wes said.

A wicked smile crossed Peter's face. "I got no problem with that, do you?"

Wes watched Peter's hand slowly move up and down his shaft and replied, "Nope, no problem at all."

I started to protest. I wasn't at all sure I agreed. But, I stopped short, having to admit, Junior seemed to be enjoying it just fine.

Wes' dick steadily thickened and lengthened, becoming more and more erect, as Peter continued his slow strokes. Wes spread his legs a bit more, and Peter took it as an invitation to use his other hand to grab Wes' low hanging balls.

As he gently kneaded them, Wes' head tilted back, and he let out a hiss of pleasure, as his dick swelled and stretched to its fully erect length. Peter dismissed any pretense about measurement concerns and stopped stroking Wes' cock. Instead, he used a thumb and forefinger to grab at the foreskin and tug gently.

"Ah, feels good."

"Damn, it really is big," Peter said. His voice had grown throaty, and he showed no signs of letting go of my man's dick.

I noticed a bead of pre-cum forming at the tip of Wes' cock and involuntarily licked my lips. Looking up, I saw Wes' dark, lust-filled eyes fixed on me.

"Grif, would you hand me a bottle of water, please? My mouth is kinda dry," Wes said, tilting his head in the direction of a glass-fronted mini fridge.

Glancing down at my crotch, I could see my small bulge was visible. I looked over at Peter, but he was far too engrossed with Wes' dick to pay me any attention, so I decided it was safe to stand up and snag the water.

I quickly grabbed a bottle from the fridge and took the few steps over to Wes. His eyes were closed again as Peter's thumb rubbed pre-cum over the head of his dick in steady, smooth circles. As much as Junior was enjoying this, I decided it had gone far enough.

I extended the bottle toward Wes and loudly cleared my throat. "Wes, here's your water. I think—," He opened his eyes, and the hunger in them stopped me short.

He didn't make the slightest move to take the bottle.

Instead, he husked, quite simply, "Chocolate?"

Instantly, my hand, still extended and holding the bottle out to him, shook.

"Wes?" I managed in a croaky whisper. My mind raced, thrown completely off-balance, trying to figure out exactly what Wes was doing...we'd been here to get my nipples pierced, but now....

"Chocolate?" he calmly repeated.

"Um, what did you have in mind?"

His mischievous, dark eyes met and held mine. At length, he finally said, "Ah, but you know it doesn't work that way, love."

And I did know. When we'd agreed on both the Vanilla and Chocolate terms we'd also agreed on a few ground rules: one, there were no conditions placed or details provided when he posed the question; two, I could stop anything at any time by uttering the single word *Vanilla*; three, replying with a *no* was just as welcome as a *yes* response was—this was about love and a different form of expressing that love, nothing more or less; four, my answer, to avoid any miscommunication, had to be verbal; and five, the Chocolate session would end when he said Vanilla— which meant it could last a few hours or a few days.

I swallowed and looked back up at him, sure the uncertainty and apprehension were clear on my face, and whispered the agreed upon affirmative response, "Yes, Wes. Chocolate."

He grinned widely, barely keeping his desire contained, his eyes never leaving mine, and said, "Excuse me, Peter."

He stood up, as Peter, still on his stool, rolled to one side to make room. Standing in front of me, blocking Peter's view of me but offering him a great view of Wes' muscular ass, he took me by the wrist, removed the unopened bottle of water—which he carelessly tossed on the exam table—and slid around behind me.

From over my shoulder, he said to Peter, "I've been getting all the attention here, and I seem to have forgotten my manners. I'm gonna make sure Grif feels like he's part of the fun, and then we can resume with you...worshiping my cock."

I croaked out an odd, surprised sound at his blatant and somewhat insulting comment toward Peter.

I felt him press the front of his body up against the back of mine and found it even more difficult to think. His nimble fingers slowly undoing the buttons of my shirt as he continued seemingly casual conversation.

"Grif's nipples are very sensitive—which is why we're interested in getting them pierced—right, love?"

I nodded.

"Use words, Grif," he whispered quietly against my ear in admonishment.

"Um, yes, they are...very sensitive."

His fingers, which had started at the top of my shirt, finished undoing the final, bottom button. He gently pulled the shirt tails from my waistband and parted the front—exposing my muscled, tanned chest for Peter.

"My god Grif, you have a brilliant chest," Peter said.

"He does, doesn't he?"

Wes' hands slid up my abdomen—sending shivers through my entire body—and moved across my pecs, where he stopped to squeeze, before landing on my nipples. Each was taken between his well practiced fingers, and he skillfully pulled, and tugged, and flicked.

I moaned in pleasure. I couldn't believe this was

happening in front of a complete stranger—but somehow it only made it that much more exciting.

"Yeah? Does it feel good, Grif?"

"Yes, Wes. It feels real good."

I leaned my head back against his shoulder and closed my eyes, sinking into the wonderful feelings; the intense burn when he twisted, the floaty feeling when he released them and used a thumb to ever-so-slightly brush over the tops, and the intense, 'can't think of anything else' feeling when he pinched them roughly—all of it shot bolts of electricity directly to my throbbing dick.

"Love, look at Peter. If the tent in his pants is any indication, he's enjoying this as much as you are."

I opened my eyes, lifted my head, and took in the huge bulge in Peter's lap. God, he had to be nearly as big as Wes…and the way he was looking at me…so fucking hot.

"Oh, without a doubt. You really are something, Grif."

"Thank you, Peter," I managed to moan out.

Wes pinched my nipples so hard I could barely think.

"Grif has quite a collection of jock straps…it's kind of a fetish. Why don't you show Peter the one you're wearing today, love?"

My body went instantly rigid and my mind began to swirl. What if Peter saw no evidence of my arousal? He'd put two and two together...he'd know.

"Hmmm, really?" Peter said. The heat apparent in his voice as well.

"Grif…?" Wes urged.

I turned my head and whispered into Wes' jaw, "Please, no."

I felt his arousal intensify as his cock jumped and pushed

harder into my lower back at the desperation in my pleading voice. Leaving not a single doubt in my mind about how much he was enjoying this.

Wes pinched my nipples even harder, and I cried out, "Oooowww!"

He growled in my ear, "Unbutton your fucking pants, fag, and show him your jock. Now!"

"I'm scared, Wes!" I whispered.

But, I knew my choices: obey or say *Vanilla*. I surrendered and moved my shaking hands reluctantly to the button of my jeans, popped it loose, and slowly slid the zipper down.

"I know you are. And you have every reason to be…wouldn't want him to realize he can't see your hard-on, would you?"

I shook my head.

Once the zipper was completely down, and I had spread the flaps of my undone pants open to reveal a pale yellow jock, Wes eased the pressure on my aching nipples and began a slow, gentle twisting.

"Oh hell yeah! That yellow against your tan skin...*fuck*."

Peter's voice suddenly seemed so loud compared to the intimate whispers Wes and I had been privately exchanging.

"I think he's got every color under the rainbow, and they all look amazing on him. They come in handy too, for practical reasons. I mean…,"

Oh God, what was he going to say? Please don't tell him why I wear them, I silently pleaded.

"…sometimes I ask him to keep them on while I'm fucking him doggy style…gives me something nice and tight to hold on to."

As if to emphasize the point, he thrust his cock harder into my back. God, he was as excited as I was.

"We've been thinking about Grif getting a PA too, but we have some concerns. Sorta along the same lines as with me...but, in reverse."

Oh God, oh God, oh God! No! Please, please, please no!

Unable to speak, I shook my head back and forth. I couldn't do this. I couldn't.

"You're gonna be fine, Grif, just breathe," Wes tried to quietly reassure me.

God no! I can't!

Tears pricked my eyes and I felt like I couldn't breathe.

"I'm not sure I understand," Peter was saying.

"Well," Wes hesitantly started, "Where I'm on the larger size, Grif's...hmm, it'd be easier if you take a look. If you don't mind that is?"

"Are you kidding me? I can't wait to see the rest of you, Grif!"

Again, in my ear, "Oh, I can't wait until he sees the rest of you either!" Then louder, "Take down your jock and let Peter see, Grif."

Wes must have realized my breath had become much too shallow. With authority I found impossible to ignore, he demanded, "Two deep breaths, Grif."

I did as he said—took two deep, long breaths—and then turned my face into his neck.

"Wes, I'm so sorry, I can't. I cannot do this. Please! If you want me to, I'll say the word, but I can't do this. I'm scared."

"Shh. Okay, I hear you...I'm right here, and I won't let anything happen to you. You hear me, love?"

I nodded, but a betraying tear ran down my face.

"Um, is everything okay? Should I leave you two alone for a few minutes?"

I felt one of my nipples being released, and Wes made a motion indicating that Peter should hold on.

"He's ready to leave. Do you want this to end?"

His breath was so warm on my ear and, despite being utterly terrified, it sent pleasure shooting down to my still yearning cock.

I only had to consider for a moment before saying, "No, I don't. But I can't. I just can't."

"Okay, what if I show him for you? All you have to do is revel in the fear and enjoy the fuck out of it while I expose your little dick to a total fucking stranger."

God help me, but that sounded like something I could actually do—and the thought made Junior strain even further—so I nodded.

"Words, Grif."

"Yes, Wes. But...please don't let me fall. I'm not sure I can feel my legs, and I'm...afraid."

"I've got you, love. I've always got you. Now tell Peter you'd like him to stay."

I turned to Peter and was surprised to see him still in place on the rolling stool.

"If you've got time...," I cleared my throat and swallowed loudly, "...I'd really like to see what you think."

The heat returned to his eyes, and he grinned. "Let's see what's hiding in that jock then."

"Cool," Wes said, and slipped his hands between my pants and jock and easily forced the jeans down to my knees.

His smooth hands reverently ran up and down my defined torso, "Isn't he beautiful, Peter?"

"Stunning." Then, to me, "You're incredible!"

Then Peter glanced down at his own crotch, "Do you mind if I stick my hand down and…?"

"Not at all. Help yourself," Wes said.

As Peter's hand disappeared beneath the waistband of his loose jeans, Wes' thumbs hooked in my jock's waistband, and I could feel the incredibly slow but steady slide across my hot skin as he began to expose me.

"Oh God!" I whispered in near terror.

Peter's hand had begun a slow rhythm, and his anticipation was palpable as he sighed, "Oh damn!"

Wes whispered stern orders in my ear. The closeness, the intimate brushing of his warm breath, so at odds with the harsh, depraved commands sliding past his lips.

"I want you to watch his face, do you hear me? From this point forward, I don't care what the fuck happens, don't you fucking dare take your eyes off of his face, you got me, fag?"

Wes had begun his own grinding rhythm, and his cock felt so good digging into my back.

"Yes, Wes," I managed.

Sliding. Slow sliding. Wes intentionally let the elastic waistband catch on my dick as he lagged the jock down. The painfully slow momentum pulled Junior straight down with it. Fuck, it hurt!

Peter's eyes were glued to my crotch.

Finally, Wes pulled the jock far enough down so my dick popped free and slapped back against my lower stomach.

Peter's hand immediately came to a stop.

"What the fu...," he started, but trailed off as he caught himself. "Um, I guess I understand your concern," and I couldn't miss the small snicker he barely tried to hide.

As Peter pulled his hand out from under his own waistband, Wes said, "I know it might be difficult to see from a few feet away...feel free to slide over and do a proper exam."

The sarcasm was clear in his degrading tone. Oh, he was fucking loving this.

As Peter slid over, he looked up and recognized the terror I knew I couldn't keep out of my eyes. His gaze shifted over my shoulder to Wes'.

He slid the rest of the way over, his face only a foot from my leaking dick as he looked up and said, "Ah, I think I understand. You, Wes, want him to show his...little dick. You get off on embarrassing him. And you," his eyes briefly met mine before going to my crotch, "you are understandably fucking embarrassed by this...this...tiny, fucking thing."

The grinding at my back grew stronger and more insistent. I watched Peter wedge his thumb and middle finger together and sharply flick the head of my dick.

I let out a cutting yelp. Instinctively, I pulled my ass backward and started to cross my legs to avoid Peter's flicking.

Wes reached up, twined his fingers in my hair, and yanked my head back. Holding me still, he ordered loudly, "No. Keep your goddamned legs spread, fag, and fucking take it. It's not like it can hurt all that much—there's really nothing down there to feel pain."

Releasing his grip of my hair, he said, "Look back down at him. I want you watching while he tortures your pint-sized dick."

I immediately followed Wes' instructions and looked back down. It wasn't so much the pain—although it hurt like a sonofabitch—but instead the sheer humiliation I felt at being so completely exposed and verbally assaulted. I'd never experienced that from anyone other than Wes—the person I loved and who I knew loved me in return.

With Peter, I couldn't feel anything remotely resembling kindness; nothing but disdain. The harsh way he was looking back and forth between my eyes—with something akin to loathing—and my crotch, with nothing but undisguised contempt.

The near gleeful way he watched my dick helplessly bounce around, sending pre-cum flying, and growing redder after each painful flick—he was clearly enjoying the torment he was inflicting. Over and over, flick after flick, only deepened his absolute scorn. I'd never been so fucking hot, or so fucking hard, or so fucking humiliated, in my life.

This was tripping all my triggers; the exposure, the humiliation, the pain. I knew I couldn't take much more. If this kept up much longer, I was going to shoot—without permission. I could already feel my balls tingle and burn with the unmistakable signal I was only moments from squirting. I turned my head and buried my face in Wes' neck and pled, "More please."

Wes, took a hand from one nipple and skillfully grabbed the base of my dick, halting my orgasm.

Peter understood and barked out a condescending laugh. "I'm not surprised you don't have any control either."

Flick, flick, flick...

With my face still in his neck, Wes released the tight hold on my dick and moved to cup my balls.

"I told you to fucking look at him—now do it!"

I fixed my gaze back on Peter's.

Flick, flick, flick...

"You got nerve, getting me all worked up, when you knew all you had to offer was this pathetic little wiener. What a goddamn, fucking disappointment!"

All at once, Peter's vulgar assault penetrated my resolve, and I lost the desperate fight I'd been waging against my unwanted tears. They broke free, streaming down my face, and only heightened my embarrassment—as well as my pleasure.

Watching Peter's enjoyment as he tormented my dick, and seeing Wes' big hand covering and squeezing my balls...I couldn't take it anymore.

"Goddammit, Wes...fucking more, please! *Please, more!*" I shouted.

Wes must've been completely supporting me because I couldn't feel my legs at all anymore. My chest burned as the tears took on a life of their own and matured into full-blown sobs. I couldn't make Peter's face out anymore either...everything was blurry.

"Wes. More. Please!"

Wes ground his dick into my back, and I felt his body stiffen behind mine. The hand gripping my balls tightened painfully as did his fingers clamping down on my nipple. I opened my neck up to him and felt his teeth bite into my tender flesh. He moaned as jet after jet of warm cum coated my back.

The tiny room was filled with scents of sweat and sex.

He paused only a second, before his strangled voice granted me permission. "Shoot, fag. Show Peter your little dick can at least come."

The fire in my balls as Wes' tight grip squeezed them, and Peter's insistent flicking, added to the one and only thing I needed—his permission. His consent allowed release, and set off an explosion that welled up from my core. Blooming outward, pulsing and contracting, it sent wave after wave of mind-altering pleasure coursing through my straining body. Complete and total darkness flowed over me, as I shot so long and so intensely, that I wondered if it would ever stop. I prayed it wouldn't.

"Christ!" I distantly heard Peter say.

Weightlessness and sleep simultaneously overtook me.

I awoke to kisses feathering my forehead, and Wes's brilliant smile beaming down at me.

"Hey," he grinned, as his fingers lightly made their way through my hair.

"Hey," I grinned back.

"Vanilla," he whispered against my lips, nipping the bottom one ever so gently.

He pulled back, and I looked around to find I was laying on the exam table with a cool sheet draped over me. I started as I remembered I'd been naked when I was last awake and reached for the sheet to check, when Wes' hand took mine.

"Your super powers are safe. I made sure your magic underwear are in place, Jockboy."

I laughed. "You take such good care of me, Alfred. I don't know what I'd do without your dedicated service."

His eyes became more serious, "God, you're so strong,

Grif. And you have such...impressive courage. I'm not embarrassed to admit I'm envious of it sometimes. But, never doubt I'll always be here for you to lean on—to take care of you in whatever way you need, I swear."

I raised my hand up and ran it along his strong jaw, "I love you so much, Wes."

We both turned at the soft knocking on the door, and I shot him a worried look.

"Don't worry, love. I promise you it's all right. Trust me, okay?"

I nodded, and Wes turned and opened the door.

"Hey. You asked me to check on you in about thirty minutes. You guys doing okay?"

"Yeah, great. Come on in."

Peter stepped in as I sat up. He gave me a cautious smile then turned his gaze to the floor.

Looking at Peter, Wes said, "I'd like to formally introduce you to my amazing boyfriend, Marcus Griffin. But if you ever call him by anything other than Grif, I can't guarantee your safety."

"Grif, this is my dear friend, Peter Walzac."

Peter looked up and extended his hand. I hesitantly I took it.

"It's really nice to finally meet you Grif!" he said sincerely, "Wes never shuts up about you and now I know why. Oh, and most folks call me Zac."

The shock must've been apparent on my face because both Wes and Zac chuckled in unison.

"Wait, you're Zac? The same Zac who was in the marines with Wes and who now works for De Luca Securities?"

He glanced back down and nodded.

"You're the *I can kill a guy a hundred different ways with a toothpick* Zac?" I asked, still unable to believe he was the person Wes had told me so much about.

Zac actually blushed and said, "So you've heard that story, huh? A hundred might be a slight exaggeration, but yeah, one and the same."

I covered my face with my hands, and groaned loudly. "Shit, I don't know whether to be relieved or even more embarrassed."

As I slid my hands back down, I saw the concerned look on Zac's face.

"Oh God, Grif, please don't be embarrassed. I...," He paused and looked at Wes and then down to the floor again. "I can't even put into words how honored I am. Honored to have been invited to participate in something...so beautiful...so deep. I mean, deep and totally fucking hot!"

Wes leaned in, mock whispering in my ear, "Fair warning, the *real* Zac is more of a happy, unpredictable ferret on crack—mixed with the twisted sadist of earlier."

When he finally looked back up at me, ignoring Wes altogether, I could read the sincerity and the excitement in his entire body.

"I mean, I'm not even gay—"

Wes snorted loudly and although Zac shot him a brief, cutting look, he continued without missing a beat, "...and that was fucking amazing! You saw my boner, right? Christ, when I left, I went right into the bathroom and jerked off—twice!"

I laughed, "Um, yeah—kinda hard to miss that monster!"

He blushed again. Seriously? This guy had actually killed a man with a toothpick, and he was blushing, and he was kind, and he was sweet? What the fuck? This wasn't at all what I expected from Wes' prior portrayal of him.

Wes frequently talked about how dependable and talented Peter was. And, then of course, there was the toothpick story—where he'd been downright ruthless. But, his *happy ferret on crack* description, with a healthy dose of shyness, seemed much more accurate at the moment.

"And if you ever want to do more. I mean, I can be even more cruel about your small…umm…if you want. Damn, that was so mind-blowingly hot!"

He was being completely earnest and had the look of a little kid asking for more candy when he knew he shouldn't be.

"And that's where we're gonna leave that, Zac," Wes said with a good-natured smirk and started guiding Zac out of the room with a none-too-gentle push to his back.

Zac's entire demeanor abruptly changed. He stood taller with his chest pushed out, his jaw set tight, his eyes took on a hard fierceness, and his tone of voice was nothing less than harsh. "Okay, okay…stop pushing me, you big fuckin' goon!"

Wow, now that was the guy from a half an hour ago— on Marine steroids. He was downright frightening.

He spun around, sincerity and kindness back. "Seriously, Grif, thank you for allowing…. Ouch! Fuck! You're hurting me, Wes. Let go of me! I'm warning you, I have fuckin' toothpicks…."

Wes was laughing as he shut the door on a still grumbling Zac.

He stepped back over to me, leaned down, and kissed

me.

Looking back toward the door, and with a shake of his head, he grinned, "I'd say the *straight boy* enjoyed himself." He used air quotes when he said, *straight boy.*

"Yeah, well he's definitely not the only one. It's gonna take me a while, but when I've had time to think and process, I want to sincerely thank you, both in words and deed, for this evening, Wes. It was…fucking indescribable."

He leaned in and stole another quick kiss. "I'm completely looking forward to that conversation—honestly, Grif. But for now, Mark, the actual, certified, piercing artist will be up in a few minutes…if you're still interested."

I grinned and fingered the rings hanging around his neck, "I'm not leaving here until these are in me."

CHAPTER 15
PAY THE PIPER

Fall 1998

ONE OF MY new favorite classes at Cheyenne Mountain Junior High School was Principles of Photography. I'd signed up for it not so much because I was interested in the subject, but because Mr. Harold, my guidance counselor, thought it would complement my other, more passionate interest in art.

I was skeptical—what did photography have to do with drawing and painting? Turns out, he couldn't have been more right. The two shared many commonalities such as balance, perspective and creativity. I found myself looking forward to this class nearly as much as my 'real' art classes.

I'd finished pulling the last print from the wash tray and hung it with the others to dry, when I heard the teacher's voice from the other side of the darkroom door, "Mr. Griffin, can you stop by my desk when you're finished, please?"

"Yes, ma'am. I'm cleaning up now, Mrs. Kelly. I'll be right out."

I was still drying my hands with a paper towel as I approached Mrs. Kelly's desk, "You wanted to see me, ma'am?"

She looked up, glanced at the wall clock, and then back at me.

"Ah, yes, Mr. Griffin. Coach Armstrong called and asked if he could see you the last fifteen minutes of this period."

Thankfully, she'd looked back down and resumed reviewing student photos—completely missing my terrified expression.

"If you leave now, you'll have plenty of time," she said pleasantly.

I swallowed deeply but managed an equally pleasant reply, "Yes, ma'am."

I stopped at my desk, grabbed my backpack, and made my way out into the hall before falling back against the wall for support. My hands and knees were shaking; I'd been caught. I knew it was going to happen sooner or later—I'd been expecting it. I mean, you can't skip class for three weeks and have it go unnoticed.

I took a deep breath, pushed myself off the wall, and decided to get it over with. It's not like I was going to get a beating or anything. Nope, the worst that could happen was my parents would be notified and I'd already decided, no matter what, I wasn't going back to gym class—ever.

By the time I'd reached Coach Armstrong's open office door, I'd stopped shaking and was breathing relatively normal again. I didn't know exactly how this was going to end, but I knew I was ready for it to be over. The constant worrying about when I'd finally be discovered was taking its toll on me.

I knocked. "Coach Armstrong?"

He was standing at the other side of the cluttered room, his back to the open door, at a filing cabinet. Looking over his shoulder, he asked, "Yes?"

"I'm Grif...err, Marcus Griffin, sir. You asked to see me."

He finished at the cabinet and took a seat behind his equally cluttered desk. He nodded at a chair which sat opposite.

"Have a seat, Mr. Griffin."

I nodded in return and sat stiffly while he rummaged around the desk before finally pulling a slim file folder from the disarray. Seriously, I wondered how he ever found anything. He read a bit and then looked up at me with a fatigued expression.

"You've not been to gym class since the first day of school, son. You mind telling me why?"

"No, sir," I replied respectfully.

"I'm sorry? I don't understand." His look had gone from weary to perplexed. "I'm asking why you haven't been in class."

"I understand, sir, but I'm not going to discuss it. And I'm not going back, sir."

He sat there for a moment and looked at me as if the answer I provided was the last one he'd expected. Then, resignedly, he laid the folder back on the desk, where it was immediately enveloped and lost again.

After a moment, he said, "Son, I don't think you understand. Physical Education isn't an elective class, it's mandatory. You must—you will—attend."

I replied with an evenness I didn't feel, "I do understand, sir. But I won't be back. Are we finished, sir?"

He briefly rested his forehead in his hand before looking back up. "Yes, you and I are. Please make your way to the administrative offices—I'll let Principal David know you're on your way."

I stood. "Yes, sir."

~

The student assistant looked up from her chemistry textbook and answered the phone, "Yes, sir. I'll send him in," and then placed the phone back in its cradle.

She looked over in the general direction I was sitting and said, "Principal David will see you now." Not waiting for an actual response from me, she retuned to her book and flipped to the next page.

I was back in the waiting area less than ten minutes after I'd left. The conversation with Principal David was so like the one with Coach Armstrong it could have been a playback from a tape recording. So, there I sat, waiting for one of my parents to come pick me up. Shit! Well, on the bright side, it was the end of the day so neither of them would have to leave work to come and get me.

~

In the school parking lot, after we'd gotten into the car, mom said Principal David had filled her and Dad in. Glancing over at me—with her intent *you're in serious trouble* look—she curtly informed me she and Dad had decided to wait until the three of us were together, at home, to discuss the subject any further.

Grateful for the brief reprieve, I leaned my forehead against the side window and zoned out, trying to pretend this awful mess wasn't happening, as Mom and I made our way home in silence.

I wasn't afraid of being in trouble. Because, to be honest, being in trouble wasn't the worst that could happen; forcing me back to gym class, with its mandatory shower policy, would be the worst. I was determined that wasn't going to happen—no matter what—but I didn't know how I was going to get them to see my side, to understand, without talking about *it*.

We parked in the garage and entered the house through the kitchen. I glanced around the room and noticed we were having lasagna tonight, mom had already set out the fixin's after breakfast. She always prepped for dinner after cleaning up from breakfast.

Without a doubt, the kitchen was her area of the house, and its starkness, reflected her well. She was a great mom; she made sure we were well-fed, that we had clean clothes, that we got to school on time, that sorta thing. And I knew she loved us, but she wasn't what I'd call warm.

I heard the TV in the living room shut off as soon as we walked in. A moment later, Dad joined us and sat down at the kitchen table.

Dad was pissed. He wasn't the kind of guy who jumped up and down or screamed and yelled. No, he got quiet— real quiet. And when he got quiet, you knew you were in trouble.

"Hi, Dad," I ventured.

"Marcus."

Oh shit, he was going with Marcus and not Grif. Everyone called me Grif—everyone. In fact, it was Dad who'd given me the nickname before I was even old enough to speak—it had been his grandfather's nickname, and he treasured it. He'd told me, when I asked how I'd gotten the name, that it reminded him of a person he loved very much, but it now reminded him of two people he loved very much.

"Where are the twins?"

I knew it was cheap, bringing up my younger siblings, Micah and Meaghan—cheap because he thought the sun rose and set with my kid brother and sister—but I felt like I needed to use every advantage I had available to put him in a better mood. It didn't work.

"Friend's house," he answered shortly. "We have things to discuss, don't we?"

I looked at Mom and then back at him and nodded, "Yes, sir. I guess we do."

I sat my backpack on the floor next to the table and asked, "Are we going to talk in here? Should I sit, sir?"

He eyed me with a bit of amusement and grunted, "Yes, please. And for Christ's sake, stop with the sir…it's not like you're on trial or something; we already know you're guilty."

It wasn't something I understood—at all—but for some reason Dad was never able to stay mad at me for long. Even when I'd seriously screwed up, I could usually snap him out of it rather quickly. I didn't take advantage of it, but I was thankful for it.

Mom, on the other hand, was a completely different story; she only came back around after she felt you'd either been punished appropriately, or you were sufficiently repentant.

I sat down across from him and gave him my best smile, "If you'll please call me Grif, Dad."

Mom snorted from the other side of the kitchen, "Hold on, let me uncork the wine…if we're having a party then libations should be served, shouldn't they?"

She walked over and pulled out a chair at the end of the table with more determination than was strictly necessary. The chair she chose placed Dad and me on either side of her and she sat down heavily. Oh, no doubt, she was pissed.

Looking at my father, she said, "Maddox, he's in trouble, big trouble."

Now she was using his given name rather than his nickname of Dex. Then she pinned me with her intent gaze, "You're in big trouble, Grif," she nearly hissed, as if I hadn't heard her saying the same thing to Dad.

"Yes, he is, Mia."

"I know I am, Mom," I quietly said to the table top.

"Grif, please help us understand. You had to know you couldn't keep skipping class a secret, right?"

"I did know, Dad, I did. It's just…."

I stopped because I didn't know what else to say. They sat there waiting for more—waited longer than I would have if the situation were reversed.

"Grif?"

"Mom, I'm not sure…I don't know what to say."

"Well, we can see something's on your mind, Grif.

Something you're not sure about sharing. Why don't we start there? What are you thinking right now, son?"

God, I knew he was still pissed, but he was really trying. I was so lucky; he really was an awesome dad. Then irrational fear gripped me again. Fear they'd make me go back no matter what.

I blurted, "I'm not going back to gym class—ever," and crossed my arms over my chest.

"You most certainly are young man!"

"Mia," Dad said, and put a hand over hers.

I looked up and saw apprehension and concern had replaced his anger. Well, at least he wasn't pissed anymore, that was something.

"Okay, it's obvious you feel strongly about this, Grif. And we both know you well enough to understand you must have a good reason to feel so…adamant about this."

He sat looking in my eyes, and I wanted nothing more than to bury my head in his chest and tell him everything, and I didn't have a single doubt he'd let me. I wanted him to make everything better like when I was a kid. But he couldn't, and I knew it. My throat tightened and my eyes burned and then a tear slid down my face. Great, I was crying. Could it get any worse?

"Grif, what is it? Have you done something? Are you in trouble?" Mom asked.

"It's already been determined he's in trouble, Mia," Dad said trying to lighten the mood.

"Grif, whatever it is, you can talk to us. We'll help you."

"I can't Dad…I can't go back…I won't go back."

The doorbell rang, and my parents exchanged a look. Then Mom said, "Oh, it's probably Ellen. She called earlier and wants to borrow a casserole dish. I've already put it next to the door. I'll be right back."

She pushed her chair out and I listened to her footsteps fade into the direction of the living room. I looked up at Dad.

"Grif?" Dad questioned with raised eyebrows.

Okay, maybe with Mom out of the room, I could somehow do this.

"Dad, you remember last year when we went to the ER for my appendix?"

He quirked an eyebrow, obviously a bit lost.

"Sure I do. But what does that have to do with—,"

I interrupted, "You remember the conversation you had with the doctor?"

"About you needing to have emergency surgery?" He still wasn't following.

"No. Not about the surgery. It was about...about my...size."

We were still looking at one another and long moments passed before I saw the sudden understanding in his eyes. Then he peered down at the table between us—had the table not been there he would have been looking directly at my crotch. *Christ.*

He nodded and looked back up at me, "I remember, Grif. But...."

Another tear slipped from the corner of my eye and slid down my face. I quietly said, "I can't go back, Dad. I just can't."

He reached across and took my hand in his and squeezed. With a short nod he said, "Don't worry son, you don't have to go back. I'll see to it."

Relief spread though me like nothing I'd ever felt before, and I was abruptly filled with happiness and gratitude.

I nodded my head and smiled through unshed tears, "Dad, I know I'm a bit old…b-but…I'm wondering if I could ask for a hug?"

Before I knew it, I was lifted out of my chair and tightly pulled into his chest. One strong hand wrapped around my back and the other rested on my neck and pulled the side of my head next to his. He held me and said, "Don't worry. I promise it's gonna be okay, Grif. I love you, son."

Nodding, I said, "I love you too, Dad. Thank you so much."

He pulled back a bit and said, "I do want to talk later, man-to-man. I have a few questions. I just want to make sure everything is working…," and he glanced down between our touching chests, "…down there."

I blushed ferociously, "Dad…I don't wanna—,"

He pulled me back in and hugged me tighter. "Tough! We are going to talk." Then, as abruptly, he let me go.

I heard Mom's footsteps stop at the kitchen doorway.

With a sturdy clap to my back, Dad said, "Go get cleaned up, Grif. And then maybe we can throw the ball out back or something until dinner time."

I nodded, briefly peeked at Mom, grabbed my backpack, and got the hell out of there.

∾

I was lying across my bed after dinner, trying not to fall asleep while studying art history minutiae about eclecticism, when I was thankfully saved by a knock on my door.

"Grif, can I come in?"

I sat up crossed legged on my bed, "Sure, Dad."

He peeked his head around the door. "I had a phone call with Principal David just now and wanted to chat with you about it."

"It's bad, isn't it?"

"Nah, it's all good," he said, as he closed the door behind him and made his way across the room to casually take my desk chair.

I noticed him looking around my walls, which were covered in posters. So much so, you could hardly tell the color of the paint. I was completely in love with Rob Thomas and the walls certainly reflected that.

There were posters of him solo, him with Matchbox Twenty, and the newest one was with him and Santana from the "Smooth" single. I'd been listening to the track nonstop for weeks—so much that one day Mom asked if I planned on auditioning for the band and, if I wasn't, could I please play something else on my stereo—or make use of the headphones she recently bought for me.

His gaze settled on my favorite poster; a reclined, shirtless Rob, which showed off the tattoo on his shoulder—a Japanese symbol meaning loyalty—and eyes so soft and brown I wanted to melt into them. Dad inclined his head and said, "You really got a thing for Mr. Thomas there, don't ya?"

I followed his line of sight and audibly sighed. I must have spaced-out a bit because I heard Dad chuckle and ask, "Grif? You still with me, son?"

I blushed a bit, "Sorry, Dad. He's just so…."

He laughed, "I know, I know. When I was about your age I had a poster of Farrah Fawcett in a red swimsuit. I'd sit in my room and stare at it for hours sometimes. She was so...."

It was my turn to laugh.

"Ah, so you do understand, huh?"

He looked at me more seriously, "Of course I do, Grif." He momentarily regarded the poster again before giving me his *dad look*. "Boys or girls, it doesn't matter. We want what we want...we love who we love, you know I get that, right? I have absolutely no problem with you being who you are."

I knew Uncle Jeff, my dad's older brother, was gay. But my grandparents never accepted it, and they'd made his high school years incredibly difficult.

He was so desperate to get away that he left home one night after everyone had gone to bed, a few months shy of his eighteenth birthday. He left everything he'd ever known; his friends, his family, and was completely alone while starting a new life. That was twenty years ago, and my grandparents hadn't seen him since.

He moved out, to San Francisco, and it took my dad ten years to track him down. When Dad finally made contact, Uncle Jeff said the only way he'd see Dad is if he agreed to never share his location with my grandparents.

Dad doubts they will ever have a real relationship again—too much took place during those high school years for Uncle Jeff to forgive.

Still pinned with Dad's gaze, I said just as earnestly in return, "I do, Dad. I absolutely know you love me, and I couldn't ask for more from either of you. I hear stories, read things, and of course there's Uncle Jeff...a day doesn't pass where I'm not thankful for you and Mom. You've been—you are—amazing parents."

His eyes became shiny as he studied some invisible spot

on the floor between us. His head nodded in silent assent before he cleared his throat and looked back up to me. He sat there for a few beats, silent, observing me.

"Dad, is everything okay? You're kinda…I don't know…worrying me a little."

"To be honest, Grif, I'm a little concerned. I mean, we've always been able to talk about anything. But you couldn't talk to me about something…about this gym class thing."

"Dad…I—,"

He interrupted me, pushed himself off the desk chair, and eventually made his way over and sat at the foot of my bed.

"Let me re-word that. I'm upset because something was deeply bothering you, and you didn't feel like you could talk to me about it…to come to me for help with it. And without coming to me, you were left to deal with it alone. To try to find the answers to a problem that, simply because of your age, there was no possible way of you solving."

I wished I'd had the courage to talk to him from the get-go. Hell, it's not like I had any doubts about how much he loved me. He wasn't one of those macho assholes who thought, *guys don't have feelings*. Not that he wasn't tough or masculine, he certainly was. But, he never thought twice about touching me, or hugging me, or telling me how much he loved me. And Lord knew he didn't have a problem with openly talking about feelings—which could be both good and bad sometimes.

"I know what you're saying, Dad. And I wish I could've figured out a way to deal with this in a more adult way…I kind of fucked things up, didn't I?"

He reflexively looked over his shoulder for Mom. Then he smiled and pointed at me.

"You are gonna get me in trouble. She'll kill me if she thinks I'm allowing you to speak like that—she might even think I taught you."

I laughed. "Learning to cuss isn't all that hard, Dad."

His eyes danced with familiar ease. "Okay. And no, you didn't fuck this up. One last thing on the topic and then I want to share my ideas about gym class."

He reached out, and thumped me with a knuckle, square in the forehead.

I laughed. "What the he—,"

"Grif, it doesn't matter what it is, I'm here. Talk to me, okay?"

He didn't wait for an answer, but got up and made his way back to the desk and leaned against its edge. His legs stretched out and crossed at the ankle with his arms lazily crossed over his large chest. I thought, not for the first time, he really was a handsome man, for an old guy, and everyone said I looked like him. Is he what I'd look like, I wondered, when I was older—when I was thirty-four?

"So, I located this business called Trail Blazers. It offers classes, for various age groups, on all sorts of physical activities; like mountain biking, canoeing, kickboxing, rappelling. All sorts of stuff, ya know?"

After speaking with the owner, and then with Principal David, as long as you're enrolled in one of these classes each semester, Principal David has agreed they would count toward your required gym class credits."

I sat there stunned—completely stunned. Could it be gym class was no longer a problem? Could something which had consumed nearly my every waking moment for the past three weeks be remedied so easily? It didn't seem possible.

"Grif? You don't like the idea?"

I looked up to see the concern clear on his face.

"Oh no, Dad. That's not it at all. It…. It sounds great. Perfect in fact. I can't believe you've done all this in only a few hours. I mean, I've been…for weeks I'd believed this was an unsolvable problem. I'm sort of blown away. Like, really blown away!"

I shook my head. "Wow. I don't know what to say. Except, thank you so much!"

Then it struck me, these classes wouldn't be free. "Dad, how much will these classes cost? I mean, next year I might be old enough to get a part-time job after school to help—"

"Nope. Your job is to focus on your studies. We, your mother and I, are responsible for your education—it comes with bringing you into this world and taking the duties of parenthood seriously. Understood?"

I nodded. "Yes, sir."

"Good. Monday afternoon you and I are gonna head over to the Trail Blazers office and take a look around. If we like what we see, we'll get you all set up. Sound okay?"

"Sounds fucking great!"

He glanced over at the door again. Then, with a wide grin and a conspiratorial whisper, he said, "Grif! Goddammit, keep your voice down. I swear, if you get me in trouble…."

I laughed with him. He made even the most serious conversations not so scary.

"So, one last thing and then I'll let you get back to

studying." He looked down at the books strewn across my bed, "Um, art history?"

I looked down as well and gave an exaggerated sigh, "Yep."

He pushed himself off the desk's edge and walked over to my open window and looked out. I could hear some of the neighborhood's younger kids playing an after dinner game of dodge ball or something. Our house was on a cul-de-sac and the area was a magnet for kids from blocks around.

"I wanna make sure...," he turned back and looked at me. "I need to ask if everything is in working order."

"Huh?"

"You know, everything down below," he said, with a quick nod to my crotch.

I followed his eyes down, and then whipped my head back up to look at him.

"Or should we make an appointment? You know, to get things checked out?"

"Dad!"

"What, Grif? What kind of father would I be if I didn't ask?"

Lord! I couldn't believe we were actually talking about my wiener! "Everything—and I mean everything—works exactly like it should, believe me. It's just...not as...large. Not that its tiny or anything. Christ, it can't have been that long since you've seen it."

"Well, not since you hit puberty. It's been a few years, but no, I don't recall being concerned."

I shot up off the bed. "You're not gonna ask to see it, are you?"

He laughed and shook his head. "Ah, that would be a *no*. How about I take your word for it?"

I sighed loudly in relief.

"But, Grif? I have your word you'll come to me if—,"

"Dad, seriously, it's…smaller…not broken. Fuck!"

He held his hands up in surrender, but his amusement with my continued profanity use was clear. "Okay, okay. So, we're almost done here then. But we do have to talk about your mother's expectation; she rightly assumes I'll be doling out punishment for you ditching three weeks of classes."

He walked across the room and stopped once he reached my bedroom door. Turning back to face me, he said, "I've never lied to your mother, Grif—ever. But the reason you were skipping class…well I thought it was probably something you'd prefer we kept just between us. And so long as it's not something medical related—health related—I'm okay with that."

I nodded my head, perhaps a bit too vehemently, but I nodded in agreement nonetheless.

"I thought so. So I asked her to trust me on this and allow me to handle the situation. I told her I understood why you did what you did and that you would not be returning to gym class. Mind you, this took a fair bit of talking on my part, but I thought it was worth it."

He gave a brief smile before continuing, "And, I also assured her the punishment would fit the crime. Therefore, as your punishment, you are prohibited from cleaning the garage until further notice, is that understood?"

Since cleaning the garage was the twin's chore, I grinned and said, "Yes, sir. You've made yourself very clear. Thanks again, Dad—for everything!"

"Anytime, Grif."

He opened the door, slipped from my room, and left me with both my art history quiz, and also an enormous sense of relief and gratitude. No more communal showers, and my secret was still safe. Damn, I was so incredibly lucky to have him as my father!

CHAPTER 16
FACING CHANGE HEAD-ON

Early Summer 2008

I RAN FOR an hour at top speed, trying to force all thoughts of Matthew and the Diaz estate from my head. By the time I'd crossed over the Cabrillo Bridge, the runner's high had done just that. But the moment I stopped to rest at the Botanical Building's lily pond, they flooded my brain again.

Cash.

I tried to hold them off with the distraction of pulling off my tank top and mopping my dripping head and face, but it only lasted a few moments.

Cars.

Next, I remembered I'd left my backpack sitting next to the bench back at the park with Matthew. It had everything in it; my apartment keys, my cell phone, all my school work. Everything. Well, everything except my wallet which I'd pulled out to pay for the frozen yogurt and then slipped into my back pocket. If I didn't feel like walking all the way back to the apartment at least I could pay for a cab.

Boats and planes.

I looked back out over the glittering pond and watched people milling about admiring its quiet beauty. I'd passed by the pond many times over the years but I'd never stopped, sat, and simply admired it.

Employees.

I gave up. Fuck! What did I know about responsibility? Sure, I was an organized person, and I was intelligent, but the only two things I'd ever truly been responsible for were my body and my education. Matthew was talking about more responsibility than I had ever imagined for my life. Hell, graduation was only two months away and I hadn't even decided what I was going to do then. In two months!

I knew I was passionate about art—shit, I loved art— but I wasn't an artist. Yeah, I could draw and paint, but only because I'd studied for so many years and understood the principals, but I knew I didn't have real talent—and I could never make a living creating it.

Not that I apparently had to worry about making a living anymore. But I was smart enough to understand the kind of estate Matthew was talking about was a full time job in and of itself. *Shit.*

I thought back over four years of conversations with Tate and realized he had never once spoken of money.

We'd worked part-time together at Starbucks last summer, but he'd never mentioned how nice it was to have the extra money. Whenever I paid my portion of the monthly bills, Tate had asked that I simply leave the check on the kitchen table—like he really didn't want to have much to do with it. I thought it was strange at first, but after a while, I'd stopped giving it any thought and just laid the check on the table at the end of every month.

When we went out to dinner, or a movie, or anything, I'd pay my part, and he'd pay his—we'd never discussed it. The only time I'd ever gotten him to speak about money was rather recently when we were talking about what we were going to do after graduation.

He didn't seem concerned with graduating and beginning real life, with all its financial obligations, and I'd asked him why. He was evasive at first, but then finally said his parents had left him some money when they'd died. I didn't want to be the cause of him dwelling on his lost parents, so I changed the subject.

But now I understood his lack of concern regarding money, and I wondered how involved he'd been with running a vast estate. Surely I would've noticed him spending time on something like that. Which only left Matthew—and God knew how many others—who probably did the majority of the work.

Matthew. I looked out over the pond again. A pair of ducks were clamoring for bits of bread being tossed in by a mother and her young daughter, and I thought of the way I'd left him; fuck, I'd been such a dick.

I sighed and ran my hands through my drying hair. Grabbing my damp tank, I slipped it on deciding to walk up toward Park Boulevard to see if I could catch a cab, and then I needed to try and find Matthew. I had an apology to make.

≈

As the cab approached my apartment building, I noticed

the silver Jaguar parked right out front, and I briefly wondered how the driver had scored the premium spot.

In the four years Tate and I had lived there, I'd never been so lucky; even for a quick run inside, I always had to pull around to the back security gate and park in our designated spot.

I paid the driver and got out of the cab. As I walked across the street, the Jag's door opened and out stepped a mountain of a man. I hesitated simply because of his sheer size and mass and realized I'd paused in the middle of the street. He had closed the door and stood in an almost military stance next to the car.

"Good evening, Mr. Griffin, sir," he said in a heavy accent I couldn't quite place—German maybe? No, not German, but most certainly an Eastern Bloc country.

"I'm your driver, sir, Pavel Alexandr," he continued, as I made my way up to him.

"Hello Pavel. It's nice to meet you. And please call me Grif," I said, extending my hand.

He looked down at me and accepted my hand, "Sir? You'd like me to call you Grif, sir?"

I smiled up at him, "If you don't mind, Pavel."

He shook his head in slight confusion and then composed himself. "That would be most unusual, sir."

Wow, my small request really put him off balance. So much so, he hadn't released my hand.

"Um, Pavel?"

"Yes, sir?"

"May I have my hand back, please?"

He quickly released my hand and tried to take a step back but the car was directly behind him. He was big, but not big enough to move an eighteen hundred pound car.

"Yes, sir. My apologies, sir."

I grinned even wider.

"Do you happen to know where Matthew is, Pavel?"

He cleared his throat.

"Mr. Smithton is at the condo, sir. He requested I escort you there if you wished. Or, if you'd prefer, I'm to go retrieve him for you, sir. But, Mr. Smithton also said if you'd like the evening alone, I'm to remain here, in the car, until you've dismissed me. Not that I expect to be dismissed this evening, sir. I'll stay here with the car until morning if you'd prefer...sir."

"Pavel!" I said with some irritation and perhaps a bit too abruptly. He startled slightly and, once again, tried to step back. Shit, I'd yelled at the guy for being too respectful. But damn, he was treating me like some fucking prince or something rather than the college kid I was. If he really was going to be around me with any frequency, I had to get this bullshit under control.

"Did Matthew happen to leave my backpack, or at least my keys, with you?"

"Yes, sir. Your backpack is in the trunk."

He walked around to the back, popped the trunk with a fob, retrieved the pack, and held it out to me.

I took it, dug around in the front zipper pocket and pulled my keys out.

"Would you please accompany me upstairs, Pavel?" I tried, in a more friendly tone.

He snapped to attention, "Absolutely, sir."

The car chirped as he used the fob to lock it, and we made our way through the apartment's front courtyard. He followed me up the two flights of stairs, and when we arrived at my door, he asked in a serious tone, "Would you like me to check the interior first, sir?"

I grunted at the humorous absurdity of someone waiting inside for me, "No, that won't be necessary, Pavel."

I unlocked and opened the door, tossed my keys on the hall table, and went directly into the kitchen with Pavel close on my heels. Pulling two glasses from the cabinet and opening the freezer, I asked, "May I ask where you're originally from?"

"I'm from Ukraine, sir."

"And they drink vodka in the Ukraine, right?"

"Absolutely, sir."

I gestured to a kitchen chair, as I brought the glasses and vodka to the table. "Please, sit."

He eyed the bottle suspiciously, then me, and sat with barely hidden apprehension.

I poured two fingers in each glass and handed him one. He raised an eyebrow but accepted the drink.

Doing my best to be friendly, yet firm, I said, "Please stop with the overboard respectfulness and the 'sir'...I'll never be able to handle that, okay?"

Not waiting for a response, I raised my glass and asked, "Did you know Tate?"

He looked me in the eye for the first time and answered solemnly, "Yes, si...Yes, I knew Mr. Diaz. He was a good man."

"Yes. Yes, he was. Then we drink to Tate, Pavel."

After showing Pavel the bathroom, I picked up my cell phone and walked over to the sliding glass doors which led out to a small balcony. On it we'd managed to squeeze in two chairs and a tiny table sat wedged between them. What it lacked in size it certainly made up for in views.

Tate and I would sit here for hours some nights after doing homework and watch the planes land at Lindbergh Field. Beyond the airport, the Bay and Coronado Island were visible in the distance. I took a seat, admired the view for the thousandth time, and dialed Matthew's number.

"Good evening, Grif," he answered amenably.

I felt better already. If I had to do this, I'm glad Matthew was going to be here to guide me.

"Would you mind if I came over? Or do you have plans for the evening?" I hesitantly asked.

"Um, no I don't have plans, per se. But there are a few rather pressing items I really should tie up this evening—and they involve you directly, Grif; decisions about projects, your signature on some important documents, that sort of thing."

I sighed and the anxious feeling started to return. I really wanted to see him. I wanted him to reassure me everything was going to be okay. I had so many questions and without someone providing reasonable answers, I was forced to come up with my own—and my answers were, for some reason, all completely unreasonable and they all ended with me totally fucking things up.

I knew I could call my parents, and I would, but I wanted a better understanding of what was going on before I dropped the same sort of bomb on them that Matthew had dropped on me.

He seemed to sense my anxiety. "Grif, is Pavel still there? I specifically requested that he remain with you this evening, and bring you here if it was something you decided to do."

"No. I mean, yeah, he's here. I just didn't know what your plans were...I don't want to intrude. But, I want to...I need to apologize. And I'd also like to talk with someone; I need to talk to you. I'm feeling so lost."

His voice was as confident and reassuring as always, "Grif, I understand. Believe me, I do. But I promise you, this is all going to be fine."

I stepped out onto the balcony, grabbed my pack of smokes off the small table, shook out a cigarette and lit it. Taking a deep drag, I breathed the smoke in and exhaled some of the building tension. Man, I needed that. I couldn't explain it in any logical way, but I knew I could trust Matthew.

"Have Pavel drive you over. We can talk, make some decisions, and get the paperwork I mentioned signed. Is that agreeable?"

Looking out across the Bay, I said with no small amount of relief, "It sounds great. I'll see you soon."

I stubbed out the cigarette, and as I grabbed a windbreaker from the closet, I noticed Pavel was tidying up the kitchen.

"You up for a drive, Pavel?"

I locked up, and we made our way downstairs. As I slid into the back seat, I patiently waited for Pavel to ease himself behind the wheel and deliver me to Matthew— patiently waited for my life to be forever changed.

CHAPTER 17
FIRST DAY OF COLLEGE

Fall 2004

I WAS SITTING in front of the Geisel Library and getting used to the idea of being a college student. It was the first day of my new life at college, and it felt like a milestone.

Actually, I'd gotten into town a few days earlier but ended up flopping at some cheesy motel because there was a small problem with the dorm I had been assigned: there was no water. It seems there was a water main break and the entire building was dry. I'd spent the few days excitedly exploring the grounds, and since I had the entire morning free, I'd decided to hang out at the coolest building on campus—the Geisel Library. The building itself was a stunning piece of art all on its own.

I was sitting on a low wall admiring the unique structure and enjoying the warm September day when I saw him from a distance. He looked lost and completely gorgeous. People were coming and going in a continual stream but

Mr. Hot-and-Sexy-Latin walked right up to me.

Smiling broadly he said, "Hey, dude. I could use some help. You don't happen to know where the campus bookstore is, do you? I feel like I've been walking around for hours, and I really need to pick up my textbooks today."

"Um, yeah," I stammered. God, he was beautiful. "I'm headed the same way, I'll show you." The truth of the matter was I had no intention of heading that way—but.

"Cool. I've got this map, but I can't make heads nor tails of it." Grinning, he waved it around, acting as if it held some sort of personal conspiracy against him, then crumpled it into a ball and comically stuffed it into his nearly empty backpack.

I barked out a laugh, "I think you may need that again at some point today and angering the map gods is nothing to be toyed with!"

Stopping dead in his tracks, he pulled the ball out of his bag with a distressed look, "You're absolutely right." He eyed the very same map I had sticking out from between the pages of my Eighteenth-Century European Art and Architecture text and casually snagged it.

"Hey!" I said in mock irritation, "What am I gonna do for a map?" Being ever prepared, I had actually grabbed several of them at the Student Services Center and they were stored safely in my pack.

"Oh, I wouldn't leave a Good Samaritan high and dry; I'm not that kinda dude." He retrieved the balled-up, mangled map and stuffed it into a back pocket of my jeans with a shit-eating grin. He paused, the sun in his eyes was causing him to squint a bit, but I could tell he was still looking at my ass, and said, "Damn, you've got quite the muscular butt there."

I coughed, "Um, huh?"

He laughed. "Relax, I'm not that kinda dude either. Not that I have anything against gays—to each their own I always say—but I know a firm ass when it's under my palm and, dude, you've got one solid behind goin' on there."

He slung his pack back over his shoulder and grinned at me, "So, are we gonna stand around talking gay about your ass, or are you showing me to the bookstore?"

I shook my head with another laugh, "Um, it's this direction," and started walking down a path leading to Library Way, which ran right next to the bookstore.

"You weren't far off, the bookstore is pretty close. But, I gotta say, I'm a bit surprised you're only now picking up your books…it's a little last minute, isn't it?"

"Yeah, well, there was some sort of screw up with my dorm…kinda threw everything off kilter."

I laughed, "Yeah, mine too."

He turned back around and looked in the direction we'd come from—like he was trying to get his bearings.

"Wow, that really is an unusual building, isn't it?"

I stopped as well and looked back at the library. "Yeah, pretty cool, isn't it? You know it's named after Dr. Seuss?"

He turned and smiled at me—God, he had amazingly white teeth.

"Like, Green Eggs & Ham, Dr. Seuss?"

"Yep, one and the same," I answered as I turned back around and headed toward the bookstore again.

Quirking an eyebrow he asked "And you know this how?" Then, grabbing my upper arm he said seriously, in what I supposed was intended to be a Sherlock Holmes accent, "Wait! Don't tell me. You know where the bookstore is, you have maps, you know who the library is named after...." He'd stopped us and stared down at the ground tapping his chin with a very long index finger. Then shot his head back up and snapped his fingers, "I've got it! You're a campus tour guide, aren't you?"

I barked out a genuine, amused laugh this time. "Yep, you're onto me. You're also an idiot!" I started walking again, "A humorous idiot, but an idiot nonetheless," I said smiling.

"Hey, you just met me...the insults don't usually start until the second date."

I grinned, "Yeah, well I've been told I'm a quick learner...guess they were right, huh?"

I glanced up and realized we'd made it to the bookstore.

"Here we are." Then I pointed off to the left, "Oh, and by the way, the Triton...," I said indicating the statue fountain, "...is the University's mascot. The piece is bronze and weighs 750 pounds. It was championed by the senior classes of 1998 and 1999 and designed by artist and alumna Manuelita Brown. And you wanna talk about a firm ass— he's got me beat all to hell."

He stood staring at me in shock.

I laughed and then held up my Art and Architecture textbook. "Art geek here." I turned, and as I walked away, called over my shoulder, "Later."

"Later," he called back, "And thanks!"

"Yep," I nodded.

∾

It was way past lunch time, and my stomach was beginning to protest in earnest. Following my map, and thinking of the handsome Latin dude once again, I finally located The Che Cafe near the Center for Neural Circuits and Behavior Building.

It was a cool, non-traditional place I'd read about. Curious, I wanted to check it out. From a distance, it looked like the building was a shack covered with graffiti. But up close, what had appeared to be graffiti was actually well-done murals in a street-art style. The cafe was completely staffed by volunteers and hosted some great alternative rock bands.

I made my way up to the takeout window and grabbed a tofu wrap and a bottle of green tea. Finding an old chair at one of the industrial-electrical-cable-spool tables under a large shade tree, I took a seat. I was digging into my lunch with hunger inspired determination when a familiar voice called out, "Hey, dude. I could use some help. You don't know where the takeout window is, do you?"

I offered a faux groan, and without looking up, answered, "If this is gonna end with you feeling-up my ass again, I'm not sure I wanna help."

He let out a howl of a laugh. "You fucking loved it, and you know it."

"I'm not sure about that," I said with a big grin. "Besides, you're the one who's stalking me. Do you have any idea how large this campus is? You may say you're not gay, but I think you felt something this morning you can't stop thinking about."

"Ha! But, I will give you points for quickness…not many folks come up with such snappy comebacks. Touché."

I pointed toward the take-out window, and he padded off to get some food. A few minutes later, he flopped down in the chair across the spool from me.

Looking over his salad he smirked, "So, what's the story with this place, Tour Guide?"

I'd finished eating and snagged the cigarettes from my front pocket. I raised a questioning eyebrow to him.

He didn't stop eating and answered through half eaten salad, "Doesn't bother me," before swallowing.

I tapped a cig out of the pack, lit it, and blew the stream of smoke away from him.

"Well, I wish I could say the same about seeing a mouthful of half chewed food. Yuck, dude. That's just gross!"

"Oh, it's one of my most endearing habits. But wait until you get a load of me trimming my toenails; I chew 'em off. I'm very flexible."

I snorted, "Well I can see my first impression wasn't far off the mark; an amusing idiot! And, since this is technically our second date, I can toss the insults out freely."

He laughed, "You really are quick! I like it."

I grabbed my trash and tossed it into a nearby bin.

"As much as I'd like to hang out and watch you massacre the rest of your salad, I really have to get to class."

"Oh come on, I'm not that bad," he said as he stuffed another mouthful in.

"Right, and I've got a flabby ass too."

I started up a set of wooden stairs which looked as if they'd seen better days, but fit right in with the character of the place.

"The name's Tate Diaz," he called out.

"Grif," I said walking backward up the stairs. "And if you wanna know more about the cafe, I guess you'll have to continue your non-stalking stalking."

"Is that your first name or last?"

"Yep."

He grinned, "Okay, later, Grif."

"Yep, later, Tate."

I stood in front of The Village: Torrey Pines West and studied the building. It would be my home for the next four years and it didn't look too bad. However, it wasn't anything to write home about either; it was sort of a big, beige rectangle.

Holding the paperwork I'd received from the Housing Administration's overtaxed student secretary, 1 found my unit number listed as #903 and decided to head in. As soon as I pushed through the front door, I smelled it. I didn't know what *it* was—other than it was damn unpleasant.

Making my way over to the elevator I noticed, with disbelief, the Out Of Order sign. Looking back at my paperwork, I confirmed my room was 903—on the ninth floor. You've got to be kidding me! Nine floors up the stairs?

Looking over to one corner of the lobby, I saw the stairwell with a stream of people both coming and going. I was glad I hadn't gone back to the hotel and brought all my things with me to move in.

With a sigh, I squared my shoulders and joined the

swarm of bodies going up. Once inside the stairwell the smell worsened—I shouldn't have been surprised, but I was. God, what was it? After nine floors, which gave my ass a workout that would have made Sexy-Latin-Tate proud, I thankfully exited into a crowded hallway.

Number 903 ended up being at the far end of the hall. Swinging my pack to the other shoulder, I dug around my jeans pocket, retrieved the key, shoved it in the lock and tried to turn it.

Nothing happened—absolutely nothing. I knocked several times, but the hollow, reverberant sound came without an answer. You're fucking shitting me! I turned around, leaned against the door, and slid down to the floor.

Fuck, fuck, fuck!

Suddenly, the door directly across from me, #902, opened and, unbelievably, Tate stood in the doorway.

"If I wasn't in such a foul mood, I'd make some crack about how I'm now positive you're stalking me. I'd also tell you I'm in no mood to offer a history on The Che Cafe at the moment either," I said with little humor.

Behind Tate, I noticed two things; a guy, completely naked, walking around the dorm room; and the smell in the hall had become noticeably worse with the open door. A new, strong scent mingled with the already horrid smell seeming to permeate the entire building. It wasn't the same sewer smell—but something much more organic; body odor perhaps?

Tate stepped into the hall and shut the door—rather firmly—behind him.

He snorted and then, jerking a thumb over his shoulder, snarled, "My assigned roommate has informed me he's a naturalist. Meaning, he not only doesn't wear clothing—

whenever possible—but he also doesn't believe in 'applying artificial cleaning chemicals' to his body. To put it bluntly, he's bare-assed naked, and he smells! I'm cool with the naked part but not the fucking odor!"

I looked down at the floor smiling and shaking my head. How on earth could moving into a dorm be so difficult?

"And why are you sitting out in the hall?"

"My fucking key doesn't work, and I was trying to muster the will to make the hike back down the stairs, over to the Housing Administration office, hassle with them about another key—which I'm sure they'll try to charge me twenty-five bucks for—and then back up here again. If I didn't have a scholarship I'd seriously be looking for another college to attend," I sighed.

He got this odd expression on his face and stared at me a moment.

"I'm kidding about finding another college to—,"

"No, wait. Do you routinely use soap and shampoo?" he asked excitedly.

"Um, yeah," I answered somewhat confused.

"And what about chicks? Would you be dragging them back to your dorm all the time?"

"Uh, no."

Nodding his head in approval—of what I wasn't sure— he said, "Last question: on a scale of one to ten, how neat or tidy would you say you are?"

"Oh, that's the easiest one of all; a twelve. Definitely a twelve. But as much as I'm enjoying the distraction of twenty questions…,"

He dug out his cell phone and said, "Give me a second."

I watched as he paced to the short end of the hallway

and was standing back in front of me in less than five minutes.

"Come on, let's go," he said and started walking toward the stairwell.

"Huh? Where are we going?" I asked while pushing myself off the floor to follow.

"Home."

"What? Wait."

But we were already in the stairwell fighting our way down through the throngs of bodies and conversation was next to impossible.

Once we'd made it outside I asked again, "Where are we going?"

He beamed but didn't slow his pace, "I've got us a place to live. It's furnished and off-campus. We're gonna go check it out and if we like it, then it'll be home for the next four years."

Hesitantly I said, "Um, but I don't even know you. I can't...."

He stopped and looked at me thoughtfully and then started walking again, "Do you know whoever is waiting for you on the other side of that locked door up there?"

"Well, no," I answered honestly, "But that's not the point...."

"Look, if this is about my eating habits, I promise I generally display far better manners—I was just really hungry this afternoon."

"Huh?" Man, following this conversation was becoming more and more challenging.

He grinned over at me, "Hmm, you didn't seem learning disabled during our first two meetings...is there something

I should know about?"

I gave him an incredulous look and snorted, "I don't know if I can afford to live off-campus. My scholarship...."

"I was assured it's comparable to dorm rates."

We arrived at a rather angry looking black motorcycle, and he dug two helmets out of its topcase.

Warily eyeing the bike I said, "I've never driven one of these before."

"Well, it's a good thing you're only riding, and I'm doing the driving then, huh?" With a wink, he handed me one of the helmets. "Here, put this on."

God only knew why, but I put it on. I watched him mount the bike and then pat the space behind him, "Climb on."

"The seat really doesn't look big enough for two. I mean, my crotch is gonna be pushed—,"

He barked out a laugh. "Now, now. You're the one with the muscular, fuckable ass, not me, so don't go getting any ideas."

Before I could answer—and I don't even know what I would have said—the powerful machine roared to life, and I climbed on. Sure enough, I felt his ass pressed up against my crotch. Wow that felt nice! He pointed to either side, indicating where I should put my feet, and then grabbed both my hands and brought them around to hold onto his sides. After giving me a thumbs-up, we were off like a shot.

~

He apparently located the address and pulled up in front of the building. Not waiting for the engine to be killed, I jumped off the back, ripped the helmet off, and was so angry I nearly screamed at him.

"Never! I will never do that again—*ever!* Do you fucking understand me?"

Completely and totally oblivious, he held his hands up in surrender then removed his own helmet. "No worries, dude. Riding isn't for everyone."

I was about ready to crack him over the head with my helmet when the building's front gate opened and a kind-looking older gentleman stepped out.

"Are either you of Mr. Diaz, perhaps?" he asked, glancing back and forth between us.

He looked to be in his mid-sixties with snow white hair that had been slicked back with pomade or something. And although he looked every bit of six-foot tall, he couldn't have weighed more than one hundred fifty pounds. His bright brown eyes scrutinized us as a half smoked, unlit cigar hung between his smiling lips.

Tate hopped of the deathtrap and extended his hand, "Hello. I'm Tate Diaz, and you must be Mr. Keeny."

"Harold. Please call me Harold. I'm heading out to an early dinner with the missus...," he waved toward a powder blue Chevy Bel Air parked in a single spot marked by a sign reading: *Building Manager. Park here and you will be towed.*

The car was immaculate and looked like he very well could have purchased it new in the mid-fifties. "She's waiting for me, but she's not the most patient woman in world," he said, with a good-natured wink.

Digging in his pocket, he pulled out a set of keys held together with a twist-tie. Handing them to Tate he said, "It's unit 304. If you like it, we'll sign the lease tomorrow.

If you don't, then drop the keys through the slot in my door. I'm in 117."

Tate took the keys, gave them a cursory glance, and then passed them to me.

"Thanks, Mr. Keeny. We appreciate you waiting for us to arrive. Please extend our sincere gratitude to your lovely lady as well. Have a wonderful evening, and we'll see you tomorrow to sign the paperwork, sir."

Okay, so he did have manners—that was nice to know.

Moving slowly toward his waiting wife, he called back over his shoulder as we were entering the gate, "The place has been closed up for a few weeks with the air conditioning shut off. In fact, all the power is off in the apartment. The breaker box is in the front bedroom's closet…flip the main one, and you'll be good to go."

We made our way through the small, quiet, lushly planted courtyard and up the stairs. The building was older but pristinely maintained. The apartment in question was an end unit at the southwest corner. I slipped the key in, relieved to find it actually turned, pushed the door open, and the heat came rolling out; it was like opening an oven.

"Jeez! I'll get the power," Tate said, moving past me and toward the hallway.

I made a beeline for the sliding door at the far end of the living room and stepped out onto the small balcony. The view outside was amazing.

I finally heard the central air kick on—after some banging and muffled swearing—and Tate, also seeking relief from the sweltering apartment, appeared next to me on the cramped patio. My pulse quickened when I noticed he'd removed his t-shirt and was using it to mop his sweating face.

While he was preoccupied, I used the opportunity to do a quick, furtive glance of his half naked form. Damn, his compact, smooth torso was even better than I'd imagined. Defined pecs flexed under caramel skin. Flat abdominal muscles led down to his navel. And, just below that, a narrow line of black hair disappeared beneath the waist of his low-rise jeans. *Christ!*

"Great view, isn't it?" he asked, talking about the San Diego Bay, as he ran the crumpled t-shirt over his chest.

I noticed the unique pendant he wore as I tore my gaze away and answered, "Yes, it certainly is." But, I was talking about both the man standing next to me, and the Bay. Nope, I didn't need to see the rest of the apartment—my decision was made.

CHAPTER 18
SEE YOU LATER

Early Summer 2008

MY JEANS WERE only half way pulled up, I was late—so late—and now my cell phone was ringing. It was Tate's ringtone; *I'm Too Sexy.* My choice had made him grin. Dammit, I wasn't even sure where I'd left it. I was hopping down the hall trying to reach it before it went to voicemail without killing myself in the process. I glanced into the kitchen, saw it lying on the counter just as I hopped past the doorway, and then had to backtrack. I reached it in the nick of time.

"Hey," I said, out of breath.

"Um, what are you doing, Grif?" the sexual innuendo in his voice clear.

"I'm trying not to kill myself, and I'm late. What's up?" I snipped back.

"Well, don't do that, Big Guy, I don't know what I'd do without you."

His unexpected seriousness caught me off-guard. But he was like that; laughing one minute and totally pensive the next. It was something quite unique to him, and I appreciated how it kept me on my mental toes.

"I love you too, dude," I said with a small chuckle. I'd begun telling him I loved him more than a year ago, but he'd never said it back to me—and likely never would. And I was completely cool with that.

The first time I'd said it, he freaked out a bit and I had to clarify it wasn't romantic love, but rather a love for our friendship and what it meant to me. Over time he not only got used to it—though he'd never admit it—but he'd also come to appreciate it.

"I…you're a pretty good guy yourself, Grif," he delivered in his best *bro-tone*. And I knew it was as close to him saying he loved me as he'd probably ever get.

"Okay, now that we've got the 'gay shit,' as you're so fond of calling it, out of the way, what the hell do you want? I'm late!" My words were harsh, but he knew me well enough to know I wasn't serious.

He laughed and said, "I wanted to remind you the air conditioner is getting fixed today. You remember what happened last time we let those assholes in our apartment without one of us being there, right?"

How could I forget—for weeks we'd found shit missing.

"I gotcha. I'll check around and make sure nothing's out. Anything I don't feel comfortable leaving here, I'll bring with me."

"Cool. Thanks! And I know it's not worth any cash, but can you grab my pendant? I left it on the bathroom counter this morning."

I knew how important it was to him—his mother had

given it to him, and the only time he took it off was to shower.

"You got it. Dinner and a bad movie tonight after classes?"

"Sounds great. See you later."

"Yep. Later, Tate."

I went around the apartment picking up anything valuable and stuffing it into my backpack—there wasn't much. I popped into Tate's room and took a quick glance around. I noticed a small wad of bills on his dresser and I pocketed those, but there was really nothing else.

Sure enough, Tate's pendant was sitting on the bathroom counter. I started to throw it in the backpack with everything else but then stopped. This was something important to Tate, and I didn't want it accidentally getting damaged. It was sturdy enough looking; a leather cord holding a weighty, but simple, sterling silver Celtic knot which signified love. Thinking my neck would be the safest place to keep it, I slipped the pendant on.

Classes were uneventful. It was only weeks before graduation and most of my professors had designed their courses to be light for seniors who stopped paying attention to anything about a month before classes officially ended.

In fact, I'd finished all of my assignments and was only

showing up for classes because it was expected, and I generally did what was expected of me. Tate, on the other hand, had no such qualms and consequently was spending most of his days at the beach.

Since Tate had taken his motorcycle this morning, I opted to drive his car. Most of the time I rode my bike down to Old Town and caught the number thirty bus out to campus, but since I was late—and since it was hot as shit outside—I went with the easy option. Also, if we were eating in tonight, I needed to grab a few things from the grocery store.

Traffic wasn't bad and I made it to school on time. After my last class, I headed to the Whole Foods on Villa La Jolla Drive. In the four years Tate and I had lived together, I'd become quite the cook. Tate staunchly refused to learn, but he more than made up for it by buying nearly all the groceries.

I'd managed to snag a spot in the crowed parking lot when I heard Tate's ringtone. I dug my phone out of my backpack and saw Tate's image grinning at me.

It was an iPhone 3G and way out of my budget. A fact lost on Tate when he decided we should both have one. Once I'd finally convinced him I simply couldn't afford one, a gift-wrapped 'early birthday present,' appeared on the kitchen table one evening.

I swiped the on-screen answer button and said, "Perfect timing. I just pulled into Whole Foods—anything special you'd like for dinner?"

"Um, Mr. Griffin? This is Detective Pine with the San Diego Police Department Northern Division. Do you have a moment, sir?"

Shit, I knew Tate wasn't paying those traffic tickets and

I'd jokingly told him he'd wind up sharing a cell with Bubba if he didn't stop collecting them like souvenirs.

"Look, Detective, if this is about the mountain of traffic violations sitting on our kitchen table, I really think you should talk to Tate."

"No, Mr. Griffin, this isn't…. Sir, I'm afraid Mr. Diaz was involved in a single vehicle accident this afternoon."

"What? Where? Is he okay?"

When he didn't answer right away, a sick feeling began to creep up. Was he hurt—in a hospital somewhere?

"Detective, where's Tate?" I asked, with a calm I wasn't feeling.

"Mr. Griffin, would it be possible for me to stop by your apartment and talk in person?"

Panic. Sheer, unadulterated panic hit me—I had to know where Tate was.

"No!" I shouted unable to hold back the fear bubbling up and then quickly apologized. "I'm sorry. Please, tell me where Tate is. If he's hurt and alone—,"

"Mr. Griffin, I'm very sorry…."

"No!" I whispered.

"Please, no," I pleaded.

"Mr. Griffin, where are you?"

I heard the question, heard the words, but they sounded distant and weirdly distorted—like someone talking from the other side of a closed window. Nothing seemed to be registering in my brain quite the way it should.

"Whole Foods. La Jolla. I'm making dinner," I heard myself mumble.

What was happening?

How could this be happening? My mind started jumping

around and grabbing random reasons why this couldn't be possible:

I'm cooking dinner for us...

He was picking up a movie...

He said he'd see me later...

"Mr. Griffin, please stay there. A car and officer will be by in a few minutes. Just stay there, okay?"

I dropped the phone and rested my hands and forehead against the steering wheel and let out a silent scream; mouth open, body shaking. No, I couldn't do this. Tate was the only person I'd ever let know me. He was my best friend, he was my companion, he was my lover; he was my *everything.* I couldn't do this. *"Nooooo,"* I screamed again before howling sobs overtook me.

CHAPTER 19
MIRÓ RESTAURANT

Fall 2013

"GRIF?"

"Um, yeah?" I asked, and looked over to find Matthew's bewildered expression. Now there was something I didn't see too often. He'd obviously been talking to me, and I'd been spacing out again.

With the proper look of contrition, I slid the dinner menu aside, and asked, "I'm sorry, were you saying something, Matthew?"

He studied me a bit before asking, "Is something wrong? You've not been yourself all day. Does Santa Barbara not agree with you? Is there a problem with your room?"

"No, no, nothing's wrong. I've just been...a bit preoccupied"

If that wasn't the understatement of the year, I don't know what was. I hadn't been able to stop thinking about last night—and Mr. Nice But No Pushover—all day. There was something about the man that sped my heart rate up every time I thought about him. The way he looked at me, the way he spoke to me, and his body—damn!

"I apologize," I said, "you have my full attention," and offered him what I hoped was a dazzling smile. "What were you saying?"

He gave me a curious look, almost as if he were deciding if he should press the issue, but then returned my smile, and said, "It's okay. But, you know if there's anything I can help with…," and then briefly laid a hand on my shoulder before continuing on, "I was saying, I hope this final bid interview works out. I mean, I wouldn't call today a bust, there were some promising candidates, but there also was an aspect of each which made them less than optimal, wouldn't you agree?"

I nodded, "I know exactly what you mean. I have high hopes for De Luca Securities as well." With a tilt of my head, I motioned to the file laying on the table between us and picked up my glass of Glenlivet on the rocks—I honestly preferred the blended Dewars, but, not surprisingly, the upscale hotel restaurant only offered a single malt selection to choose from. "Their file looks promising. Is that why you originally scheduled them for the end of the day?"

"Honestly, no. It just worked out that way. But after today's interviews, and the resulting lack of any particularly promising candidates, I'm certainly glad Mr. De Luca was accommodating with rescheduling our afternoon meeting to this evening."

"As am I. Would you make a note to include a little something extra in our standard 'thank you packet'…you know, for his willingness and flexibility in rescheduling, please?"

Once again pointing to the folder, I asked, "His company's file looks good. Did you happen to notice he's ex-military—along with nearly every one of his employees?"

"Yeah, I did. Couldn't ask for better qualifications from a securities firm, could you?"

Matthew continued talking, but I'd stopped registering almost everything around me; as I'd set my glass down, I glanced up toward the front of the restaurant and watched Wes being escorted through the dining room.

Once again I was struck by his sheer size. He was huge. But, despite his massive size, he moved with an easy, distinguished confidence. I took in his finely tailored suit, it was dashing. My mind briefly flashed back to him naked, and bound in a chair, as I noticed his suit's finer details; it was monochromatic, with a dark grey jacket, a light grey shirt, and a thin black tie. Was it the same *tie*?

I watched as the maître d' guided him between tables and my mind raced with thoughts. What was he doing here? I hoped he didn't look my way. Would I be able to hold a meeting without him noticing me, and also be able to slip out afterwards unseen?

I was once again struck by how incredibly handsome the man was without an ounce of cockiness.

Abruptly, the maitre d' turned, took a few steps in our direction, and stopped in front of our table. I sucked in a deep breath. Part of what had been distracting me throughout the day was I could still taste him; every time I took a deep breath or swallowed I was treated with his scent all over again. It had not only kept me on edge, but it had also kept me aroused most of the day. Distracting indeed. As I sat looking up at Wes, his *taste* filled my senses once again.

With a crisp introduction, the maitre d' said, "Mr. Griffin, Mr. Smithton—Mr. De Luca." Then, with a slight bow, "Good evening, gentlemen," and he departed.

Matthew had already stood and was shaking hands with Wes.

"Mr. De Luca. Again, may I offer our sincere gratitude for your flexibility and willingness to accommodate our rather chaotic schedule. I assure you, we are generally quite proficient at keeping on task but, inexplicably, things got away from us today."

Wes smiled—that smile—and said, "Not a problem at all, sir. The way I see it, I now have the privilege of unparalleled dinner company as well as an interview."

"Well, again, our sincere thanks. And please, if you don't mind, we much prefer the use of less formal address; I'm Matthew Smithton, but please call me Matthew and this is...,"

Matthew had turned to introduce me but stopped when he saw I was still seated. When I self-consciously cleared my throat and stood, he continued with a somewhat wary quirk of his eyebrows, "And this is Marcus Griffin, but I've never heard him called by anything other than Grif."

As he released Matthew's hand, he said, "Please, call me Wes."

His bright eyes took in mine—God, he was stunning. His thick brown hair shined and my fingers twitched; his strong, freshly shaved jaw beckoned my tongue; and as he extended his hand, offering, "It's very nice to meet you, Grif," I caught the slightest glimpse of the leather wrist cuff he wore—and my mind momentarily dwelled on the possibilities it held. Jeez!

He briefly looked around the room, "This really is a

lovely restaurant, and I'm looking forward to this evening."

My eyes, once more, fell to tie he wore. This close up, there was no doubt it was one and the same. I thought it would've been beyond salvaging, but it looked as crisp and pressed as the rest of what he wore. As my neck heated, I looked back up to find his bold, playful eyes fixed on mine.

"Wonderful. Shall we sit?" Matthew offered.

Oh God.

Dinner went surprisingly well. Thankfully I was able to keep control of myself and act like the professional adult I was. However, that didn't keep the internal cocksucker in me from trying his damnedest to break free.

Fuck, the more the three of us talked about Wes' proposal, the more I actually liked the guy—in addition to the unquestionable lust I'd felt since I first laid eyes on him. He was intelligent, referring to state of the art technology and methods; funny, with a dry and rather wicked sense of humor; and an engaging conversationalist. To top it off, his company was qualified for the contract.

We'd finished eating and were discussing 80s hair bands, of all things, when Wes said, "Gentlemen, if you'll excuse me a moment."

As I watched him cross the dining room, making his way toward the men's room, Matthew said triumphantly, "Well, I think we've got our man, don't you?"

I shook my head slightly, "I'm not sure yet."

Obviously surprised, Matthew's reply came quickly, "What? His company seems excellent for our needs and—

,"
,

I interrupted and said kindly, "I know it's late Matthew, but I'd like a full background report tomorrow by...is noon too early?"

He stared at me blankly. Okay, I think Matthew being speechless was another first. So I took the silent moment to push forward, "Not only of De Luca Securities, but of Wes as well. I'd like the report to be comprehensive and contain everything possible—no detail should be considered too small or insignificant."

He snapped into *estate mode*, "Absolutely, Grif. I'll get someone on it immediately."

A few minutes later Wes returned and Matthew stood.

Looking from me to Wes he said, "Gentlemen, if you'll excuse me, I'm afraid I must request my leave. It's getting late, and I have a few things to attend to this evening," he delivered this with a slightly embarrassed chagrin. "Grif?"

I stood, "Absolutely, Matthew." I took his hand in mine, "Goodnight," I said, and pulled him into one of those guy-half-hug things.

He turned to Wes, "Goodnight, Wes. I had a very pleasant evening...I hope you did as well."

Wes took his extended hand, "I did indeed. Thank you, Matthew. Goodnight."

Matthew's departure left Wes and me standing alone at the table.

I glanced out the window, stalling at meeting Wes' gaze, and I saw a well dressed, middle-aged couple making their way down the path toward the restaurant. Her arm was wrapped in his and the way they looked at one another— sometimes seeing people in love made me feel wistful. I was happy for them and all, but occasionally, it reminded me how lonely and lost I was without Tate.

They reached the front of the restaurant as Matthew was making his way out. The woman stepped up first. She and Matthew shook hands briefly and then embraced—her hand traveling a bit too far down the small of his back to be strictly friendly.

When she pulled away and stepped back her companion stepped in. Again there was a handshake, and then the gentleman reached up, cupped the back of Matthew's neck, and gave him a quick kiss on the cheek. Wow, Matthew did indeed have a few things to attend to—good for him.

I looked over and Wes was smiling at me. I knew I shouldn't, but I couldn't help myself, "Would you care for dessert, Wes? I hear the crème brûlée is quite good."

"I'd love dessert. However, I have an idea…something a bit less formal…do you like ice cream?"

I grinned widely, "Do I like ice cream? Does a duck like water?"

He laughed softly, "I'm taking that as a 'yes' then." He tilted his head toward the exit, "You game?"

Christ! What the hell was I doing? But, rather than going with the logical thing and heading back to my room—alone—I instead found myself agreeing with only a mildly restrained, "Yep!"

He led us out of the dining room, and we stopped at the coat check counter. After handing them over, we both loosened our shirt collars and ties. He pocketed our claim tickets and placed a hand gently on the small of my back to guide me through the door he held open. Once out in the warm night air, we headed up a paved path which took us toward the front of the property.

It was only a little after 9:30pm but the resort seemed

devoid of people aside from the two of us. A light, welcome breeze carried the soft smell of the ocean as we made our way to the resort's main lobby.

Once inside, Wes steered us toward the Suite Shop. It was like a high-end mini-mart with expensive chocolates, cookies, and even a few selections of wine. Following Wes' lead, I found myself standing at a glass-fronted freezer. The case contained so many different ice cream choices Baskin Robbins would have been envious.

"Wow, they have it!" I exclaimed. Reaching in, I snagged a pint of *Ben & Jerry's New York Super Fudge Chunk*. "I can't believe it."

I looked up to find Wes, a single eyebrow raised, grinning at me.

"Okay then."

I laughed, "It's my all-time favorite. I mean, my single most all-time favorite—of all-time!"

It was his turn to laugh.

"So, I'll have to remember that."

He opened another door to pull out a carton of frozen bon-bons.

I eyed them with open contempt. "Seriously," I asked?

"What?" he grinned and asked defensively. "They're good."

"Uh-huh," I replied—clearly conveying my disagreement with the ridiculous claim.

On the way out, we picked up a plastic spoon for me and a handful of napkins for us to share. We worked our way through the lobby and out onto the terrace where, scattered around, were lounges and chairs, all pointing toward a built-in fireplace. Despite the warm evening, a low fire was burning, and it bathed the entire terrace in a flickering yellow glow.

Aside from the two of us, the terrace was empty, but Wes nodded toward a couple of chairs off to one corner. In place of a response, I headed in their direction and took a seat in one. He sat down next to me and fiddled with his box of bon-bons.

Dinner had been nice, and even the short walk to get the ice cream had been enjoyable, but suddenly I felt uneasy; what did he expect? Did he want a repeat of last night? Because, if he did, he was in for a disappointment; I'd all but decided to hire his company which meant sex was removed from the table—not that I did repeat sex anyhow.

Looking into his open box, he quietly said, "You seem anxious, Grif." Then, looking over and considering me, he asked, "Or would you prefer Marcus?"

I looked down and shook my head, "No, not Marcus. No one calls me that—in fact, I really sort of dislike it—a lot," and then, still speaking toward the ground, I offered weakly, "I'm not even sure why I gave it to you last night; I never give my name to anyone I...meet under those conditions. But I had to offer something. The deal was you'd tell me your name and I'd tell you mine, and I couldn't lie. But I also couldn't bring myself to say Grif either."

I shrugged self-consciously and looked over into the fireplace.

"And, yes, I'm slightly uncomfortable; I've never had a conversation with anyone after I've had sex with them."

When he didn't respond, I looked over at him. He wore a strange, perplexed expression.

He finally asked, "Never?"

Looking away again, I answered honestly, "No, never."

"Grif, we don't have to talk. Honestly. I wanted to...I just didn't want the evening to end." Then, much more jovially, "Our ice cream is going to melt and I don't know about you, but I really did want ice cream. What's say we eat in silence and just enjoy the fire and our ice cream?"

I glanced back over at him and saw the warmth had returned to his handsome, dark eyes and felt myself relax.

I nodded my consent and went to work removing the lid from my pint of Ben & Jerry's with gusto.

After a few minutes, I noticed him looking into his box and then eyeing my pint, he said, "You know, these really aren't very good...you think you might wanna sha—,"

"What?" I said in mock shocked, indignation. "Last night it was my name you wanted, and tonight it's my ice cream? What next?"

I looked down into my half eaten carton, scooped out a spoonful and held it up to him. He ducked in, opened wide, and took the spoon in his mouth. The simple act of spooning ice cream into his mouth had me on edge again. I was quickly brought back by Wes moaning loudly and rolling his eyes into the back of his head—both with serious exaggeration—then exclaimed loudly, "Oh. My. God. That is fantastic!"

Without even thinking twice, I raised the empty spoon and conked him in the center of his forehead with it. "You, sir, are an ungrateful...,"

He'd leaned back in his chair and laughed so hard his body was shaking. I soon joined in. It was nice, easy, comfortable.

We finished sharing my ice cream, and he took both of our containers and tossed them into a trash can set in one corner.

"You interested in a walk on the way back?"

"Sure."

He nodded and smiled. God, he was so handsome and even though I knew I should be trying to put an end to the evening, I really was enjoying his company. Hanging out with him, being with him, glancing over and admiring him, and, when the breeze was just right, taking in the scent of him was so enjoyable I didn't want it to end.

He walked us back down the path toward the restaurant and skirted around to its backside where we picked up a gravel path. It wasn't lit, but the moonlight was bright and lent the path plenty of light.

"This, according to the map in our rooms, is called Cliff Path," he said, motioning to the split-rail fence to our left which separated the path from what looked like a pretty significant drop over the edge.

We walked in companionable quiet while simply appreciating the salt-tinged breeze and the soothing sound of the surf below. The path narrowed and widened occasionally and during a particularly narrow piece our hands brushed—and I'd have sworn I'd felt electricity flow from his hand into mine.

Damn, the man made me feel things I'd never felt before. His warm palm found mine as he tentatively and gently grasped my hand. My heart thudded and I had dual, overwhelming and conflicting desires simultaneously; squeeze his hand a little tighter to let him know it was okay, coupled with run—fast, very fast—away. Much to my complete surprise, I finally decided on the first and squeezed his hand gently.

I'd never held hands before and damn it was nice. We

still walked in silence, but now with a strange and welcomed sense of unity. My hand felt dwarfed by his larger one, and I had the odd feeling of being protected. Of being safe.

We'd come to a fork in the path with signs indicating one led back to the resort proper, while the other led down to a beach house. Wes turned us slightly, stopped at the split-rail fence, and pointed with his free hand off-shore, "Wow, that's a pretty big cruise ship, huh?"

I nodded wordlessly as my body began to shake—slowly at first, but steadily growing in intensity. I was okay when we were walking, but having stopped, I was suddenly afraid. Over the past five years, I'd become accustomed to a certain level—a certain type of intimacy—with ground rules I'd set; for the most part, I knew what to expect, and I knew there was no chance of Junior becoming a topic of conversation. But in this situation, I was incredibly uncertain of everything.

He turned to face me, not letting go of my hand, and leaned a hip against the fence. Quietly he asked, "Apprehension or anticipation?"

I turned and mirrored his stance. With my hip also leaning against the fence, we were less than a foot apart as I looked into his eyes and considered my options: honestly answer or get the fuck away from him—now!

I swallowed and opened my mouth to answer but my teeth chattered against each other. He raised a hand and slid a finger along my jaw before resting his hand back on the fence. He was looking at me with such sincerity and warmth I nearly lost my nerve—but I tried again and managed to work out, "Apprehension."

Concern briefly shadowed his expression before it was gone again.

"Are you frightened by me, personally, Grif? Because I would never…."

I shook my head and he trailed off.

"Good. Because…. Look, I know we've only met, and there's the whole business thing to consider, but I feel…unusually comfortable and drawn to you."

Hoarsely I said, "Me too, but…."

He placed a strong hand on the side of my neck. I felt his fingers reach around back and graze my shirt collar, while his thumb caressed my cheek. He started to lean in, and I knew he was going to kiss me—but I couldn't. I raised my free hand and placed it on his wide chest—clearly saying *stop*.

"Wes, I've never…," I broke off; I couldn't tell him—I just couldn't. What would he think of a twenty-eight-year old man who was still, essentially, a virgin? Like he'd said, we'd only known each other for less than twenty-four hours, but it was undeniable that I felt a strong, intense attraction to him—and I really liked the way he looked at me. I wouldn't see that change into something less.

We stood there, his thumb caressing my cheek and my hand on his chest—I could actually feel the beating of his heart beneath my palm—looking into each other's eyes.

"Grif, I think you're the most handsome man I've ever had the pleasure of knowing. I'd love to be your first kiss." He paused and flashed a smile I could easily get used to seeing, "And I've been told I'm a pretty good kisser." Then, more seriously, "But I'll never ask you to do anything you don't want to do. Never. You have my word."

I nodded.

"Now, unless that hand of yours does something more to stop me—which I have no doubt you could do—we're gonna share your first kiss."

I stared up into his genuine eyes and had trouble believing I was actually going to be kissed by this truly stunning and majestic man. I'd dreamed of this moment for years—and it was about to happen. My mouth was suddenly dry, the hand atop his chest was damp, and I felt like I'd started panting.

"Grif, listen," he said softly. "Do you hear the waves below?"

I nodded.

"Can you feel the breeze on your skin and smell the salt water of the ocean?"

I nodded again and whispered, "I feel it, Wes." Glancing upwards, "And the stars and the moon—it's all so...perfect."

"Can you see this as the place—this as the moment—you experience your first kiss?"

His kindness—his absolute thoughtfulness—caused a knot in my throat, and my eyes blurred with unshed tears—but I nodded my head in consent.

He noticed and released my hand so he could bring his up to the other side of my face. "Hey," he kissed my forehead and looked back into my eyes, "not that I don't appreciate tears, but this is supposed to be romantic and sexy...I must be doing something wrong," he said with a wry grin.

A tear finally escaped and slid from the corner of my eye as I shook my head, "You're doing everything perfectly, Wes."

A thumb slid over my cheek and caught the tear. He surprised me by bringing it to his lips and licking it off. "There's nothing I find more sexy—more incredibly hot—

than a strong, masculine man with tears in his eyes. You've no idea what you're doing to me, Grif."

His voice had a definite rough purr to it and the sound shot straight to my dick. I looked at his lips, so full, so manly, with a hint of dark stubble above the top one, and I longed to feel them pressed against mine. I longed to have his tongue meet mine—and I burned with the desire to know his taste.

"Ah," he sighed, "There it is. I can see it in your eyes; you want me to kiss you." His voice held nothing but kindness and sincerity.

I nodded.

"Words, Grif. I need words. Tell me, babe."

With the fear momentarily banished, to exactly where I wasn't sure, I looked him directly in the eye and breathed, "Yes Wes. Please, kiss me."

And there it was, my first real kiss. His lips softly brushed against mine. I could smell his spicy, woodsy scent as he took my top lip between his and lightly sucked while his fingers explored the hair behind my ears.

I moaned and relaxed into his touch as his tongue smoothly swiped across my bottom lip. I did the same, sliding my tongue over his bottom lip.

As I brought my tongue back into my mouth, I felt the brief but unmistakable touch of his tongue on mine. It was enough to taste the flavor of him; the ice cream we'd shared earlier mingled with scotch and something distinctly male. It sent me over the edge and leveled all the reservations and restraint I'd desperately been holding onto. I slid my tongue back out, seeking permission to enter—it was granted, and his lips gently parted.

Wrapping my arms around his waist, I stepped in closer

while our tongues touched, and danced, and pleasantly dueled. His fingertips moved to my back and drew circles through the light fabric of my dress shirt.

God, it all felt so incredible. I pushed our bodies closer and felt the ridge of his fat dick press into the side of my hip. The kissing, the petting, the feel of his arousal—I'd never experienced anything so pleasurable in my life.

Finally, out of sheer desperation for air, I pulled back, panting, and dizzily lay my head on his strong shoulder, watching his Adam's apple move up and down as he swallowed.

"Jesus!" I exclaimed breathlessly, "I seriously had no fucking idea."

He chuckled and agreed, "Yeah, real damn good."

He pushed his nose into the top of my head, his breath blowing my hair saying, "Are you sure you've never done this before? 'Cause seriously—damn!"

I raised my head and looked at him—yep, he was serious and knowing he enjoyed it as well…I mean, it couldn't get any better.

"I'm sure," I responded. "And, Wes, this…this is something I'll always remember. Thank you."

"Wait, does that mean we're done? Because, I could go on like this for at least another couple of hours," he said with a broad, easygoing smile. I felt his hands relax and slide from my hips down ever-so slightly to the tops of my outer thighs. I froze and time seemed to stand still.

Everything in me said, *move away*. I grabbed his wrists and took a step back. I knew it. He'd want more; he'd want to touch me. And why wouldn't he—I sure the fuck wanted to touch him. But of the two of us, only I knew why that couldn't happen. I needed to leave—now—but I didn't want to spoil the best evening of my life either.

Releasing his wrists, I said softly, "Honestly, Wes, this has been…completely amazing…I can't even put it into words. But I really do have to get back." I stepped in and laid my hands on his broad shoulders, brushed my lips across his cheek, and whispered, "Goodnight."

He'd placed his hands at my elbows and as I stepped back they slid along the undersides of my arms and eventually my hands were in his. He gently grasped them and prevented my full retreat.

His face, which had been so heated and untroubled moments ago, took on a somber quality, "This is because my hands slipped…below your waist, isn't it? I apologize, Grif. I honestly didn't mean to…."

I squeezed his hands and released them. "It's okay. It's just late, and I have a mid-morning flight I haven't completely prepared for yet. I had a wonderful time, Wes. Thank you."

I stepped away, turned, and started my way back.

"Will I see you again?" he asked.

"Matthew will be in touch regarding the bid within the next few days," I said over my shoulder, but I didn't slow my pace.

"Grif?" was his only reply.

CHAPTER 20
COMING CLEAN

Fall 2013

I OPENED MY eyes and stared at the ceiling for a while before yawning and stretching myself fully awake. My thoughts instantly turned to last night, and Wes, and that kiss. Damn, I'd actually had my first kiss and it was fucking amazing. So much better than I'd ever imagined. I wasn't even going to think about how there wasn't a chance in hell of it happening again. I was floating, and I was determined to enjoy it.

Grabbing the pillow next to me, I rolled on my side and snuggled it up next to me while closing my eyes. God, what I wouldn't give for the cool pillow to be replaced by Wes' warm body. Breathing in deeply, I could still taste his scent—spicy and woodsy. God!

I lazily opened my eyes and something across the room caught my attention. It was my jacket from the night before—the one I'd left at the restaurant's coat check—and on top of it was draped a black tie. The tie Wes was wearing last night. The same tie I'd used to bind him two nights ago. How the fuck?

Immediately awake, I crawled across the bed and made my way over to the desk chair where the coat and tie hung. Atop both sat a notecard sized envelope with my name in penmanship I recognized; Wes' writing.

I snatched up the envelope, tore it open, and pulled out the enclosed card. It was cream colored with a thin, elegant line border and had the initials WDL printed on the front. I flipped it open:

Most Handsome Grif,

I'm not a wordsmith, not by any stretch of the imagination, but the thought of last night possibly being the last time we saw one another is nearly more than I can contemplate. Thus, I've no option but to expose my epistolary inadequacy (I do remember some 'fancy' words from high school writing courses, though) and try my hand at heartfelt prose.

I need to see you again, Grif. I need to know that last night, that amazing night, was a beginning and not an ending. I need to know the things I feel when we're together, the way my heart beats differently, the way I can't think of anything but seeing you again, and the way I can't seem to stop smiling (even though I'm certain it makes me look like the Neanderthal I keep swearing to you I'm not)...I need to know it's okay to feel these things. And, that maybe, you feel some of the same things too.

Since my hands seem to keep causing rather abrupt endings to our otherwise perfectly exquisite encounters, I'm placing the tie in your safekeeping. If need be, you're free to use it to bind me anytime we're together.

So, if this hasn't completely freaked you out, and you're not calling the cops yet, could you please consider letting me inside—the balcony is chilly.

Yours,

~Wes

I slowly turned around and saw him on my balcony. He was mist-covered, shivering, and offering a pleading, crooked smile. Good Christ, the man was insane!

I threw the card on the desk. How the fuck dare he come into my room—while I was sleeping no less! Who the hell did he think he was, and who the fuck did he think he was dealing with?

I marched over to the door, grabbed the handle and I flung it open. He took several steps back, held his hands up, palms out, and evenly said, "Whoa, Grif. Calm down, man."

I pinned him with an angry stare and damn near shouted, "Look asshole, I'm an advanced-level kickboxer as well as a brown belt in karate. I can maim you without a single fucking weapon! Do you get me?"

He swallowed and nodded, "I understand." Then he added, "I guess you didn't like the card, huh?"

I stared at him in utter disbelief and then, much to my chagrin, I burst out laughing. "You fucking...," I gasped out before more laughing overtook me entirely, and I eventually had to lean my head against the doorjamb.

He was grinning at me like a schoolboy—a very wet schoolboy.

With his hands still up, he hesitantly said through

chattering teeth, "Um, Grif? I don't mean to push—honest—but I really am quite cold. I think I stopped feeling my fingers about twenty minutes ago. I had no idea you'd sleep this late and I'd be out here this long. Do you think I might be able to come in?"

Damn, seeing him close up, he really did look miserable; cold, soaked through, and teeth definitely chattering. Served his ass right. I half contemplated closing the door and being done with the whole fucking thing. Instead, I threw my arms in the air as I walked over to the nightstand. Grabbing the phone, I dialed room service.

"Good morning, Juan. Service for two please. A pot of coffee, hot cereal—oatmeal, cream of wheat, whatever you have—whole grain toast and fresh fruit…as quickly as possible, please. Thank you."

I turned back around and found Wes standing half in and half out of the door. Obviously overhearing my order, he started, "I really prefer—,"

I cut him off with a stern glare and a quick, "You really prefer what? That I call the police instead of ordering you hot food, perhaps?" I snapped.

"No, I…," He glanced down at his feet and back up at me, "I was gonna say of the limited outfits I've seen you wear, up to this point, this is by far my favorite." He waved his hand and openly admired my body from head to toe.

I looked down and realized I was still only wearing my jockstrap.

"I mean, *damn*, Grif!"

"Fuck you. You can't go making leering eyes a-and comments at me when I'm pissed off—there are certain rules one follows when someone's pissed off at you," I said harshly, but my eyes must have revealed my true emotions.

Jesus, the way he was looking at me—like I was all that and a fucking bag of chips. Shit!

"Thank you for the breakfast, it was overly considerate and very kind."

And there was that smile—that amazing smile—and the last of my anger faded.

"Well come the fuck in already and shut the damn door—it's cold. And get out of those wet clothes before you catch a chill. I'm going to turn up the heat and get dressed."

I turned and started for the thermostat when I heard a very low wolf whistle. I didn't stop but instead called out, "Okay, now you're really fucking pushing it. There's another robe in the bathroom; get out of those wet clothes and use the robe after you've had a hot shower, you damn fool, you!"

I went into the adjoining sitting room, turned the heat up, and as I passed by the desk, on the way to grab my jeans, I noticed the large manila envelope with my name printed on it in Matthew's unmistakable neat cursive. *Where did this come from?*

The envelope was lying next to my phone which said I had a text. I grabbed the phone and opened the text. It had been sent last night and was from Matthew:

Grif, I've left the report you requested on Mr. De Luca with the front desk.

I glanced back down at the envelope and picked it up. It was only then I saw it was actually two separate envelopes held together with a rubber band. Along with my name, Matthew had written across the front of the top envelope 'Report: Mr. De Luca.' And most disturbing was the top envelope's seal had been broken.

I was about to open it myself when the room service knock sounded at the door. I grabbed my robe off the side chair, made my way to the door, and allowed the waiter in. With practiced ease, he maneuvered the cart into the sitting room and rearranged the two chairs so they were on either side of the tablecloth-clad cart. "Will there be anything else, Mr. Griffin?"

I took the check, signed it, and returned it along with a twenty I'd grabbed off the side table "No. Everything looks great. Thank you."

"Thank you, sir," he said, with a slight bow as he left and pulled the door closed behind him.

It was only when the shower shut off that I even realized it had been running. I went back into the bedroom and was standing by the desk when Wes walked in wearing one of the robes and looking much warmer.

He followed my gaze and said, "Oh yeah, I brought those up for you," as he passed by me moving into the sitting room.

I grabbed the envelopes and followed him in. He stood looking at the breakfast table and then up at me, "Thanks again for this, Grif."

I smiled tightly back, "So, you're feeling better...warmed up, are you?"

"Oh, yeah. Much warmer."

"Great, then maybe you'll feel like explaining how this *opened* envelope made its way to my desk?"

He looked at the envelope, then back up at me and winked, "Um...can I eat first...before you get angry with me again?"

"Wes...," I sighed and shook my head.

Again, he flashed that fucking smile, "Come on, Grif, let

me catch a break here, huh?" He took one of the chairs and went about the busy work of pouring two cups of coffee.

Offering one to me with a grin, he said, "I mean, can't we talk about our completely amazing kiss last night, or...maybe what you thought of the card I wrote...or maybe how smoking hot you look in a jock! Damn, I'm not sure I've ever—in my entire life—seen anybody wear a jock the way you do." He let out another slow whistle.

I accepted the cup he held out and took a sip—stalling. I eyed him over the brim as he dug into his cream of wheat with eager enthusiasm. Okay, the man was obviously hungry and...shit he looked so good in that robe with his furry chest exposed. When he moved just right, I could catch a glimpse of a sexy brown nipple.

I took the other chair, cleared my throat, and asked hesitantly, "Um, so you...um...the kiss was all right then? I mean, I don't really have anything to compare it to, but you on the other hand...." Okay, what the hell was I saying? I needed this guy out of my room like ten minutes ago. After all, it's not like it was gonna happen again. And he'd fucking broken into my room!

He set down his spoon with purpose, and looked up at me. "Grif, I've kissed quite a few men in my time and...last night was, by far, the best kiss of my life."

He reached across the small table and covered my hand with his much larger one. Gently, and with an almost reverence, he watched as his thumb caressed the top of mine. God, even his hands were attractive; strong and neat. I'd always had a thing for hands and his were sexy as fuck.

"I haven't been able to think of anything else since our kiss," he continued.

He was still looking down at our hands and smirked a

bit. "I know how that sounds—believe me I do." Then, looking back up at me, "But, to be honest, I don't give a shit if it sounds corny as hell—it's the truth." His tone turned more pensive, "Was it...," he started and looked back down at our hands. He turned mine over and slowly rubbed our palms together. Looking back into my eyes, he said, "I know how it was for me, Grif, but was it okay for you? I mean, it was your first and I wanted it to be special."

Damn, he was gonna kill me; here was this hulk of a man, who I had no doubt could kill a person with a single blow, and he was being something I'd only ever allowed myself to wish for in those twilight times of night before falling off to sleep.

"Wes...," I started and looked down at our hands—I couldn't bring myself to look in his eyes and say this, "...it was everything I'd ever dreamt my first kiss would be and so much more."

I cleared my throat and scanned the desk, "And the card...." My eyes were starting to glass over a bit, "It's the most romantic thing anyone has ever...." Nope, I couldn't go on because I'd be damned if I was going to break down and cry like a schoolboy—*again*; I was a grown man for fuck's sake.

He took our hands and twined our fingers together and squeezed, "So you don't think I'm a crazy stalker, and you're not still pissed at me?" he asked.

I squeezed his hand back and then released it. I pinned his eyes with mine and said earnestly, "You'd be wrong on both counts; I'm not completely convinced you're not a fucking lunatic, and I'm so incredibly pissed off that I...." I broke off—unsure of exactly what my next course would be. Finally I said, "How about we finish breakfast before I throw your ass out or call the cops—I haven't decided which I'm going to do yet. Maybe both."

He didn't back down—not one single bit, "Okay, fair enough. But let me just get this out of the way first: I'm not—I repeat—not a crazy stalker. In fact, I've never done anything even remotely like this before. I completely understand why you're upset—I do. Hell, I would be too. And damn, you're so hot when you're pissed off." He finished with another wink.

I don't know what came over me. Maybe I was tired, maybe it was being angry, or maybe it was just Wes himself, but something gave me the courage to stand up. Once on my feet, I walked around the small table, grabbed his chair twisting it around away from the table and, straddling him, sat down on his lap.

"Um, okay then," he chuckled. "I'm not sure what I did, but I'd like to know so I can get the same reaction in the future."

I pointed at him, "Shut up." Taking him by the head with both hands, I gently pushed his head back so we were eye to eye, "We'll talk—lots—in a second, but right now...," and then some of my bravado faded, and I knew I'd lose my nerve if I didn't continue right then, "...Wes, I'd really like to kiss you again...is that okay?" I asked rather softly.

He swallowed and grinned, "Yeah, I think I can find a way to be okay with that."

I ran my fingers through his short, curly hair and looked down into his dark eyes, "God, Wes, you're too handsome for words." I brought a hand down and held his chin between my thumb and forefinger, looked at his full lips, and then pressed mine to his.

I caught his scent, darted out my tongue, and dragged it

over his lips. The prickly whiskers above his top one made shivers crawl down my spine. I stood back up—making sure my robe came along with me.

"Wait, no fair; I didn't even get a chance to kiss back." He started to reach for me but then, suddenly remembering, brought his hands back down.

I saw his gaze fall along my body and realized although I'd brought my robe along with me, it had come untied.

With obvious appreciation he said, "And, Grif, although I appreciate the compliment, you've got it backward; you're the one who's too handsome for words. I can't even begin to tell you how much I want to be with you; to kiss you, to touch you, to make love to you."

Fuck, was this man for real?

"Wes...I don't even know what to say. No one has ever...," I broke off because I didn't want to venture into territory that would only prompt more questions; questions I didn't want asked.

"Yeah, I'm beginning to see that. But, if you'll give me a chance—,"

"I'd like to know a few things about this morning," I said interrupting him. I didn't let him finish—I couldn't. I really liked him, and fuck kissing him made me feel like I've never felt before. But I knew it wouldn't last. If I allowed him close to me, then I'd only end up sorry.

He looked slightly hurt by my abrupt change in the conversation and tone. I grabbed and tightened the belt of my robe and then reached over and picked up the envelopes. "I'd like to start with these, please."

He sighed and then looked up at me with what looked like resignation, "Sure, Grif," and then tried to smile, but it never reached his eyes.

"I got it from the desk clerk. I stopped by to get your room number and as part of my cover story, as your assistant, I thought it'd be more convincing if I asked if you had any mail to bring up with me; turned out you did. I had to go back to my room, to change out of my suit, so I grabbed the second envelope there and put them together."

He looked down at his half eaten breakfast and considered it before picking up a piece of toast and crunching into it. He watched me as I looked between the toast and his face. "What?" he asked with a wink. "I figure if you're gonna throw me out I may as well finish my breakfast, right?"

I shook my head in disbelief and, I had to admit, some amusement. It was just so damn difficult to stay angry with him.

"You kinda find me charming, dontcha? Come on, you can tell me...I see it in the way you look at me," he said quirking an eyebrow and smiling that smile.

"Wes," I said slightly exasperated, "I'm not even gonna get into you impersonating my assistant—I don't even have an assistant—but you opened something private, something clearly addressed to me. That's just...."

He speared a chunk of banana and popped it in his mouth.

"Okay, you do have an assistant, his name is Matthew, and he's probably one of the best paid assistants on the planet. And yes, I opened something I knew was likely confidential...but was clearly about me. And, I read it."

I was starting to get pissed off all over again. How the fuck dare he!

"And before you lose it—'cause it looks like you're getting ready to—I apologize. Honestly, it won't happen again, Grif."

He looked sincere and then continued as he speared a piece of cantaloupe, "And, to kinda make up for it, I brought you the second envelope." He tilted his head in the direction of the envelopes I was still holding.

I removed the rubber band, flipped over the second envelope and saw that it was open as well. Glancing up and eyeing him briefly. I pulled the contents out and instantly understood what it was: a report on me. And, quite a thick one at that; obviously much more comprehensive than the unread, at least by me, one I'd been given on him.

"I saw yours, so I thought it was only fair that you see mine." He waggled his eyebrows in what I assumed was supposed to be seductive.

I barked out a laugh, as much from the absurdity of the situation, as his silly eyebrow waggle.

"But, seriously, I'll tell you anything you want to know about me, Grif."

Lowering his tone, "I'll even tell you what I'm thinking right now." His eyes moved down my robe covered body again before saying, "I'm thinking you better get the tie again, Grif, 'cause it's taking everything I've got not to grab you and tear that robe off you…I want to spend hours looking at your fucking hot body."

I none-too-gently tossed the envelopes on the table, bouncing some of the silverware, and strode purposefully into the bedroom. Grabbing the tie he'd brought with him off the desk, I returned to find him wearing a worried expression—until he saw what I was carrying; the worry was quickly replaced by a wicked grin.

I stopped a few feet in front of him, "Arms behind your back."

"Gladly."

As his hands disappeared, I stepped around and wrapped the tie around his wrists. I took my time and ran my fingers along his strong forearms as I worked. Looking up, I was drawn the crook of his neck. It's an area of the body I've always found intensely attractive. I gently nuzzled my nose against it and breathed in his scent. Fuck, he smelled so good.

Unhurriedly, I placed my tongue to it and, flattening it out, swiped upward toward the back of his ear. He shook and I watched as goose bumps popped up along the moisture I'd left behind.

"God, Grif, you make me feel...."

"I know, Wes, you make me feel the same. I feel so, I don't know, free with you...something I've only felt with one other person in my life. And even then, it was so different from what I feel with you. But, at the same time, I'm also rather terrified."

Straightening up, I moved around to the front of him, and I let out a small, needy sigh. His thick, uncut dick was already half hard and poking out from between the folds of his robe. His eyes were dark with heat, and he must have licked his lips because they were visibly moist.

"Grif," he said hesitantly but never taking his eyes from mine, "at the risk of spoiling what is turning into a perfect moment, I have to ask...," he paused to swallow and take a deep breath, "...why can't I touch you? Is it me, something I've done? Or did someone hurt you once, babe?"

Babe, there's a term of endearment no one had ever used with me...and...it sounded so good coming from him.

I shook my head, "No. No one hurt me, Wes. Physically, I mean." I assured him.

275

I lowered myself onto his lap again, straddling his knees, and briefly slipped my hands around his neck, before gliding my fingers through his hair.

Watching the curls of his soft hair thread through my fingers, I said, "But, you have to know, the jock will never come off, Wes. Ever." I shifted my gaze down to his broad chest, "You have to know that up front. I mean that point has to be understood if we're going to continue to…do whatever it is we're doing here. It won't come off and you won't ever touch my…." I broke off, letting my fingers slide down his strong neck and land in the dark hair at the center of his chest, before continuing, "And, badgering about either of those things will only confirm the decision I made years ago to never do…umm…whatever it is we're doing here."

"Grif, look at me, please."

I looked up into his kind and tender face.

"I'll accept the jock won't come off—and there'll be no touching—until you're ready. Because I know in my heart there will be a day when you are ready. There will be a time when you trust me. When you trust what I think we both already know—there's something between us. And, I give you my word as a man, I'll never badger you about either. I promise. That said, I can't say that I'm not curious about the reason, or reasons, which led you to make this long ago decision. But, again, I will never hassle or hound you for something you're not ready to do or to share."

I could feel his mostly hard cock pressing against my thigh and, surprisingly, I was getting hard too. The very subject of this conversation had me scared shitless but something about him—who he seemed to be—how he looked at me—how he made me feel— got me so aroused. I made up my mind to 'tell' him.

"Wes, I can't say this aloud…," I stopped and started shaking a bit but pushed on, "…and I do not want to talk about it—please. I know you don't understand yet, but please promise me we won't talk about it, okay?"

"Grif, you're shaking…don't be nervous about whatever it is. And, yes, you have my word; we don't have to talk about it."

I nodded and lifted myself off his lap. Stepping back a few feet, and looking him in the eye, I nervously undid the belt of my robe. It parted slightly and I looked down. I could see the ridges of my well defined chest and abs. Turning around, with my back to him, I gradually let the top of the robe slide down my back but crooked my elbows to catch it and keep it from falling past my waist.

Nerves overtook me for a moment, but I eventually said, "I work to keep my body in shape, Wes. Granted, most of it comes from the physical activity I enjoy anyhow. But, I do pride myself in keeping fit. Please don't misunderstand, I don't do this out of vanity, but rather out of a desire to love myself and to take care of the one and only body I've been given."

I slowly turned in a circle, and for a brief moment I faced him—flexing both my pecs and abs—before my back was once again turned to him.

"My God, you're absolutely beautiful, Grif. Totally fucking beautiful."

I looked back over my shoulder and saw he was fully and fucking magnificently erect. I let the robe slide completely off and stood there naked, except for the jock, for him to freely admire—something I'd never done before. I felt utterly exposed. I stretched my arms up and laced my fingers together at the base of my neck, knowing my biceps were flexed and bulging. I actually heard the breath he took.

Huskily he said, "Your arms and back are stunning, but, Grif, your ass—fuck! I've never seen such an incredible ass—so strong, and muscular, and...it's got this amazing curve to it. Would you bend over and...maybe...touch your toes for me? I wanna see so badly."

How the fuck could I resist a request like that? I widened my stance a bit and bent over laying my palms flat on the floor.

"Jesus, Grif. I'm so fucking hard."

"I know, so am I, Wes."

Here goes nothing.

I straightened, put my hands on my hips, and turned around. I watched in terrified fear as his eyes dropped to my crotch. I was fully erect and the tight jock, hugging my hard dick, would deliver the point wordlessly. He may not be able to actually see it, but the lack of a man-sized bulge would be unmistakable.

He looked for a moment longer and then I saw comprehension and understanding come to him, and I waited. I waited for the inevitable look of scorn, or pity, or whatever would signify the end. The end of the best thing that had ever almost happened in my life.

He looked up with such seriousness that it practically bore a hole in me, "I understand, Grif, and I want you as much now as I did ten seconds ago. You, babe, are the most breathtaking person I've ever laid eyes on."

I stood there staring back at him. I understood the words he was saying, but my brain didn't seem to be able to make sense of them. How could he mean that? How could he still want me? Maybe he didn't really understand.

I shook my head, "I don't...I don't think you

understand—,"

He interrupted, "I don't want to break my promise of not having to talk about this, so let me just say that I understand you're smaller than some men, Grif. I do understand."

"Most men," I corrected.

"Okay, most men, if you like. But, the point is I understand and what I said holds true; I think you're the most incredible man I've ever had the pleasure of knowing."

Tears abruptly filled my eyes, and I had to fight to keep them from spilling over. How? How could this be? How could he still want me?

"Grif, come sit on my lap again, babe?"

I hesitantly closed the small distance separating us and sat back down on his lap.

"Look at my cock, babe."

I looked down, "Yep, it's big and impressive, Wes. I see it."

He chuckled deep in his chest, "Yeah, I guess it's bigger than some guys—,"

"Most guys," I interrupted again.

He chuckled briefly, before pinning me with a firm gaze, "Actually, I wasn't referring to my size but to the fact that I'm so fucking hard I hurt."

He was too. And there was a delicious looking bead of fluid sitting right at the tip—fuck, I wanted to lick it clean.

"Grif, you've shared something with me...," and he paused until I brought my eyes back up to met his, "Something you were anxious about sharing and I'm gonna do the same."

His seriousness had my attention. "Okay," I said matching his tone.

"There are two reasons I'm so turned on; one, because you're totally fucking sexy; and two, this is the more difficult part—I like tears. I mean, sometimes I really like them, Grif—in the proper context, of course. And...I like to be the cause of those tears. Your glassy eyes—and the emotion behind them—God, Grif, they're really doing a number on me."

I didn't comment right away. I needed to let that sink in a bit. Of course I'd heard the term sadist—and masochist, for that matter—but I'd never really given either much thought before. I remembered back to Tate and the very different, avant-garde relationship we'd shared. There were certainly times, looking back on it, that sadism and masochism played into it; I'd enjoyed him periodically calling me fag, had enjoyed it when he held my face down and fucked me like I was a toy for his pleasure, and I'd enjoyed it when I'd deny myself an orgasm.

Those were certainly attributes I'd associate with masochism. How had I not seen them before? Was it because these things weren't always a part of our sex and therefore I'd missed taking note of them? Because, we frequently—more often than not, actually—had sex where none of those things came into play. Or maybe it was simpler than that; maybe I never thought about it—allowed myself to think about it—because I found both labels distasteful—ugly even.

I looked down into his strong, understanding face. God, how was it I found him so completely and utterly irresistible? "So...you're saying you're a sadist?" I questioned cautiously. The last thing I wanted to do was offend him by using a term I myself found so unpleasant.

He sighed faintly and looked out somewhere beyond my shoulder before shaking his head slightly, "I really don't like that term."

Distractedly, he brought one of his hands from around his back to scratch his nose and then returned it without a thought.

Turning back to me, he continued, "And, I'll tell you why. Because it suggests that's all of me—that I'm nothing more than that term…that label. It also suggests I'm only able to receive pleasure from one thing—and without it I'm unable to derive satisfaction. Neither of those suggestions could be further from the truth, Grif."

I didn't say anything right away because I wasn't exactly sure what to say.

He let out a deep breath. "Look, we've both shared something pretty personal and scary—something we've both been rejected for in the past. But, I've already made my decision—from nearly the first moment we met, Grif. I'm drawn to you in a way I don't completely understand. I want to spend time with you. I want to get to know you…know everything about you. You'll have more questions, I'm sure of it, but I've given you enough to think about for a while. So, if you'll untie me, I'll leave you to think, okay?"

I nodded; I did have a lot to think about, and then said, "Before you go, I have one other question: how did you get into my room?"

He relaxed at the change in subject. "Oh, that was the easy part—getting your room number from the privacy conscious front desk clerk was the challenging part. I climbed up the balcony."

"But…I'm on the third floor."

He answered simply, "Yep." Then, with a questioning look, he asked, "Untie me?"

I squinted at him, "But you're already untied."

"I am?"

"Yep, you scratched your nose a little bit ago."

"I did?"

I got off his lap, and couldn't help but notice his still fully erect cock. Walking behind the chair, I was surprised to find his wrists retied—exactly the way I'd initially bound them.

"That's one hell of an impressive skill, Mr. De Luca," I noted without attempting to disguise my admiration.

He shrugged his shoulders and sheepishly said, "Sorry, it comes with the job. But, I wasn't trying to mislead you or anything; you wanted me tied and I had fully intended on staying tied."

Then he added, with a wiggle of his fingers, "Obviously I could get loose on my own, but it would take a tad bit longer than if you did it for me."

CHAPTER 21
THE CONDO

Early Summer 2008

I SAT IN the backseat of the car, being driven by Pavel, as we headed to Matthew's condo. We'd gone south on Interstate 5 and then took the Coronado Bridge exit. In the distance, from atop the bridge, off to the right, Point Loma and its tiny lights were beginning to flicker to life as the sun made its steady decent into the Pacific. A bit closer, I could see North Island where the Navy Seals trained. Beneath me, I could make out the sail boats whose permanent home was the San Diego Bay.

It hadn't been but a few weeks since my last visit to the island. Tate and I used to make the short drive pretty regularly to spend time on the immaculately maintained, pristine Coronado Beach. We'd throw towels, sunscreen, and a few beers in a grocery bag and go lay in the sand for a few hours.

It was never a fussy or big production; we'd be sitting on the sofa and fifteen minutes later we'd be lying on the beach. There was very little, aside from his neatfreakishness that was fussy about Tate; he'd been so easy to be around and spend time with.

Sometimes we'd talk, and others we'd simply lay and watch the beautiful people walk or jog by; me the Navy Seals and him the bikini-clad girls aiming to get the attention of the aforementioned Seals. And, occasionally we'd even get lucky and join in a pick-up game of volleyball. Once we'd had our fill of sun, we'd usually grab a quick bite to eat at one of the casual, sidewalk cafes before heading back to the apartment and the endless studying.

Pavel had taken a left onto Orange Avenue and as he followed its winding path through the quaint downtown and past the famed Hotel Del, the street's name changed to Silver Strand Boulevard. Just past the hotel we made a right into the Coronado Shores entrance. The beach-front community, which was built in the early 70s, was comprised of ten luxury high rise towers and, ever since I'd arrived in San Diego, I'd longed to see the inside of one. Somehow, these condos seemed to represent the pinnacle of a luxurious life to me; like all of its inhabitants could easily be on that show from when I was a kid, *The Lifestyles of the Rich and Famous.*

Matthew had a condo here? Wow, he must be paid well. Pavel pulled up to a building, whose entrance announced it as the El Camino Tower. As a smartly dressed doorman opened my door, I thanked Pavel and told him I'd let him know when I was ready to head back home.

Stretching out from the backseat, I turned to the doorman. "Hi, my name is Grif…um…Marcus Griffin. I'm here to see Matthew Smithton?"

The helpful young man, who was about my age, smiled and said, "Yes, sir. He's expecting you. Just inside the lobby you'll find the elevators. He's in unit 1600, sir. Or, if you prefer, I can escort you."

I smiled in return, "Thanks, it sounds easy enough to find."

I looked around the impeccably landscaped grounds as I made my way into the quiet lobby. The place lived up to—surpassed, in fact—my expectations; it was upscale. Plush, seafoam green rugs covered the light hardwood floors, contemporary art hung from the walls, and across from the elevators was a concierge desk. The overall feeling was like an expensive, beachside hotel. Making my way toward one of the open elevators, I stepped in, and hit button sixteen.

Matthew's unit sat at the very end of the corridor to the right, opposite a matching corridor to the left. However, unlike the rest of the units, whose doors were either on the left or right side of the hallway, Matthew's door sat at the end of the hallway and could be seen in the distance as soon as I got off the elevator.

I made my way to it and then turned around to peer down to the other end. Funny, there wasn't a matching door down there. Huh. I took a breath and knocked.

A second or two passed before Matthew pulled the door open. "Grif," he said with a welcoming smile. "Come in, come in," and stood back to allow me to pass into the entryway.

With the door closed behind us, we moved down the short hall and into the main living areas. To the left lay the living room and the Pacific Ocean, and to the right was the kitchen and the Bay.

"Oh. My. God!" I exclaimed, moving toward the living room's floor to ceiling windows. Looking out I could see the beach below, the hotel Del, North Island, and Point

Loma. I stood there in complete awe. "Jesus! I can't believe people live like this...," looking back at him, "...that I actually know someone who lives like this."

I looked around and took in the rest of the room. Soothing, masculine colors complimented modern, but comfortable looking, furnishings. "Matthew, your place is...amazing. And I haven't even seen most of it. Wow!"

He grinned widely and then chuckled, "This isn't my place, Grif, although I do own a smaller adjacent unit." He nodded to a discreetly placed door in the corner of the room, "In fact, that door leads to my place. This...," spreading his arms out, "...is yours. It's part of the Diaz estate. Which is now the Griffin estate."

Utter shock overwhelmed me, and I felt like I was going to be sick again. Next to me sat a leather chair, and I grabbed the back of it to steady myself. "What? You're fucking with me.... I think I'm gonna be sick again," placing a hand over my stomach.

"Whoa. Here now, you'll do no such thing. Do you have any idea how much this area rug is worth?" There was playfulness in his warm blue eyes.

He stepped over to me, wrapped an arm around my shoulder, and walked us toward the opposite end of the large room. "Come on, let's go into the kitchen—I think you could use a scotch. It is your drink of choice, isn't it? And, besides, the kitchen has tile floors. Tile specially ordered and shipped from Italy, but easy-to-clean tile nonetheless."

I swallowed, "Okay, you're really not helping, old man!"

"Hey! What's with the insults? Just because I'm taking a small amount of amusement in your discomfort isn't any reason...,"

I reached over and poked him, none-to-softly, in the ribs. "Ouch!" he yelped and started laughing. "I can see you're gonna keep me on my toes."

In the kitchen, he poured us both a drink and passed mine over the granite breakfast bar where I'd taken a seat on a comfortable stool.

"Thanks," I said as I took a sip of the smooth liquor. "I can't believe all this belonged to Tate, and he never said anything about it. Hell, he never even mentioned the estate at all."

I glanced back toward the living room and just out of my current view lay the beach where he and I had spent so many hours. "I mean, Matthew, we laid down on that beach—right out there—I can't even tell you how many times, and he never even mentioned this place. What the fuck was that about?" Looking down into my drink I asked, "Was it all a game to him? I'm beginning to feel like such a fool."

He moved around the bar and took the stool next to mine. Placing a hand on my shoulder, he tried to reassure me, "No, please don't ever think that, Grif." He sighed, and looking into his own drink, continued, "He had real problems with the money after the death of his parents. It wasn't logical, or reasonable, or even understandable. Lord knows I never stopped trying to understand it though. But, and this is the best I was able to glean from our few, brief conversations about it, he felt if they hadn't had the money they wouldn't have been in Park City; without the money his parents wouldn't have been on that particular icy road which took their lives."

He picked up his drink, swirled the ice around a bit, and then took a long swallow.

"He was the most kind, caring, thoughtful person I

knew, Grif. I'd known him his entire life, and he never changed—even as his parent's wealth grew at staggering rates—he was the same, genuinely nice guy."

I looked over and his eyes were full with unshed tears.

"You miss him too," I said quietly.

"Not a day passes that I don't think about picking up the phone to call him. I called him every day for years. Granted, most of the time I got his voicemail; seems, particularly in recent years, he somehow equated me with the money. But, occasionally, he'd take my call and even more rarely, he'd agree to meet for lunch or something. More recently, I'd assigned an assistant to place all calls regarding the estate to Tate. He and I would review what Tate needed to do, or sign, or whatever, and then he'd make the calls. I'd hoped it would help Tate separate me from the money…and slowly, very slowly, I think the strategy had begun to work; in the last year or so he'd finally started taking my calls more frequently. But then…."

A tear finally escaped and crept down his cheek—he ignored it. I got up and tore a paper towel from the holder and handed it to him.

"Thanks," he said. He snorted, "Look at me, I'm supposed to be here helping you feel more comfortable about your new life and responsibilities, of which I haven't even begun to explain, and instead I'm—,"

"No, please don't, Matthew." I grabbed our empty glasses and moved to refresh them and then stopped, "Oh, sorry, is it okay if I make us another one?"

Amused, he shook his head, "Grif, this is your house. You don't need my permission to do anything here."

"Well, in that case, I'm definitely fixing us another drink."

I moved to the freezer, dropped a few ice cubes in each glass, and then poured in the amber colored scotch.

"Do you think we could move to the balcony? I'd really like a cigarette with this, if you don't mind."

"Of course." He got up and took his glass, throwing the paper towel into the waste can as we moved outside.

The covered balcony was not only beautifully furnished—with a full-size, round table and chairs and two lounge chairs—but also surprisingly spacious. "Wow, this is amazing," I said taking a seat at the table and fishing my cigarettes out of my shirt pocket.

"You know, Matthew, Tate and I didn't have many friends in common. In fact, he had very few male friends at all; I may have been the only one. My point is I don't know anyone, really know anyone, who I can talk to about Tate. If you want to talk about him, ever, please know I'd appreciate it."

He reached over and covered my hand briefly with his before picking up his drink. "I know we don't really know each other, Grif—although, I undoubtedly know more about you than you do about me—but I do have a few questions if you wouldn't mind."

"Not at all. Shoot."

He looked out over the ocean and didn't speak for quite a long time. He was deep in thought and I certainly understood that feeling when it came to Tate. He finally, in a low voice asked, "Was he happy? I mean, I know losing his parents was not something he ever fully recovered from, but was he generally happy?"

I offered him a small smile. "Well, as we've discovered, there was a large piece of his life he didn't share with me, but yes, I believe he was happy. We spent an enormous amount of time together, and I can honestly say I never saw him down or depressed."

Tate really was a very upbeat person, and I could always count on him and his quick wittedness for a good time. Even in our quiet, intimate times, he had a great sense of humor.

"One night we were lying in bed…," I started and then realized what I had said.

Matthew waited a few beats before asking, without the slightest hint of judgment or surprise, "So, you were lovers then?"

It was my turn to look out over the darkening water and think. There was no way I was going to give out details of what Tate and I shared. But I could offer generalities.

I glanced over at Matthew and said, "Tate and I had a rather unconventional friendship...relationship, but he wasn't gay. I don't imagine there are very many people who would understand what, together, we grew over the years—and I'm not interested in boiling it down far enough to be explainable—to you or anyone else, Matthew. I'm not trying to be evasive or rude, but I care about his memory too much to demean it that way—or in any way. I loved him more than I have loved anyone in my life. I hope you can understand and respect that."

I pinched the bridge of my nose and then rubbed my watering eyes. "I will say we were intimate on many different levels; both emotionally and physically."

I reached down, shook out a cigarette, and lit it. Taking a sip of my drink and a deep drag from the cigarette, I hoped Matthew understood I wasn't going to share any more than that with him. And, on the off chance that Tate happened to be somewhere where he could hear my words, I hoped he understood why I'd just shared what I had with Matthew.

I tentatively looked back over at him and found him staring down at the table smiling.

He suddenly looked up at me and then clapped me warmly on the back. "I'm glad he had you, Grif; you're a man of character and one who understands the value of loyalty."

"Thank you, Matthew. But I count myself as the lucky one; he was a very special person."

We sat in silence for a bit and then I said, "And, speaking of special, do you mind if I ask if there's anyone special in your life?"

He barked out a laugh, "Okay, that wasn't nearly as smooth as I think you believe it was."

I joined his laughter. "What? It wasn't that obvious, was it?" Still smiling, "Um, okay, I guess it was. But I'm curious if a handsome man as yourself is spoken for—can't fault me for that, can you?"

"No, no I can't. And, no, there's no one special at the moment. And before you try to figure out something equally as smooth regarding your next question," he said grinning at me, "I'm an equal opportunity kinda guy; I've had lasting and meaningful relationships with both sexes."

I laughed and grinned back at him, "Fair enough."

I took a long, last drag from the cigarette and stubbed it out. "So, you said there were things you wanted to talk about and papers I needed to sign. But, before we do, would you mind showing me around the rest of this incredible apartment?"

∾

"You've seen the living room and kitchen, back this way, behind the kitchen is the dining room. Down this hall," he pointed, "is the spare room, the guest bath, an office, and the master bedroom and bathroom. In total, it's slightly under 5,000 square feet.

"The Diaz's bought three units and combined them into the space you see here. My unit, the fourth, is completely separate, aside from the connecting door, which can easily be removed and reverted back to a full wall. Without the furnishings, and considering it encompasses two end units, and the quality of workmanship, I'd place the value somewhere between six and eight million."

The entire place was stunning and exquisitely done without being over the top; dark hardwood floors, wide moldings, and floor to ceiling windows in every room with spectacular views. And, it was…mine? It was still unfathomable. I looked down at my feet and shook my head.

"Hey, it's only stuff, Grif…nothing more. There are other parts of the estate which, in my opinion, are more important; like people and small companies and charities we—you—support."

The doorbell rang, and I looked to Matthew.

"That'd be our dinner. I hope you don't mind, but considering the hour I took the liberty of ordering us something after you called me."

As he moved off in the direction of the front door, I searched the kitchen cabinets and found plates and silverware. Matthew appeared back in the kitchen holding boxes from Cap's Pizza—my all-time favorite.

He beamed at me, "I know it's your favorite."

"Okay, this is getting a little freaky…but, since it really is my favorite," I eyed the boxes hungrily, "I'll wait until after dinner to hear your explanation on how the hell you know so much about me."

He laughed and set the boxes down and said, "I'll be right back. Dig in."

I flipped opened the first box; it was vegetarian—wouldn't be my first choice, but any pizza from Cap's was amazing. I moved to the second box and flipped it open; it contained the Mediterranean pizza I always ordered for myself—how the fuck did he know?

Matthew returned and, with a sort of 'plunk', placed a three inch thick manila folder on the counter. "It's your file. It contains everything from your blood type; to details about your appendectomy; to every grade and report card since primary school; to your favorite ice cream—which is in one of the freezers, by the way, the one to the right there; to how well you play poker; to how you've voted in the last two elections—and don't ask how we obtained that particular piece of information. Our team—your team, Grif—is very good at what they do. This file was started the day you met Tate and the two of you moved in together. It's yours now to do with as you wish."

"I don't even know how to feel about that," I said honestly staring down at the folder, "but I suppose it was all about Tate and keeping him safe, wasn't it?"

He nodded, "That's all it was about, Grif—nothing more." Then he smiled and said amiably, "Let's eat, huh?"

~

We ate pizza and talked about nothing important;

movies—I'd recently been to the theatre to see Star Trek, and although I was too young to have seen the original series air, I'd still watched every episode in re-runs; music—he was currently listening to The Fray and recommended their self-titled album; and physical fitness— a few weeks ago I'd started a kickboxing class I was really enjoying; and Art—my passion.

"You're really into your body, aren't you Grif?" He asked as he took our plates into the kitchen.

"What do ya mean?"

"Oh, you're always taking a class—kickboxing, karate, something—you go to the gym, and you eat pretty healthily too, you know…you take care of yourself."

"Yeah, I guess so. It started way back in junior high school—well, actually even before that—but that's when I joined up with this company called Trail Blazers and it sort of grew from there. But…," and I looked between him and *my folder* sitting on the counter, and said, "you already know all this, right? Anyhow, the physical stuff is equal parts enjoyment and keeping my body in shape."

He nodded in understanding. Then took a moment before asking, "About art, what is it you wanted to do after college with it? Did you want to teach?"

I tilted my head again to the unopened folder, "It doesn't tell you in there?"

He chuckled. "No. That only contains facts, not thoughts or feelings—well, at least not your thoughts or feelings."

I nodded in understanding, "To be honest, I don't really know. Tate and I sometimes talked about what we'd do after school. Although it was more often me talking about my plans—he was disinclined to discuss his plans. Guess I know why now, huh?"

"I guess," he mused. "But I think his lack of sharing may have had less to do with the money and more to do with his uncertainty; he honestly had no idea what he was going to do, Grif. He'd only pursued psychology at my suggestion. I knew all too well how he liked figuring people out—how fascinating he found people and what made them tick. I thought it'd be a good fit for him."

"And you were right. He fucking loved piecing together why folks did what they did—and he was *very* good at it too."

Matthew nodded in agreement. "Yes, he was. But, back to you and your art."

"Yeah, I know I'm not an artist—at least not one who could make a living at it—and, up until this afternoon, graduation in a few weeks scared the hell out of me; I had no idea what I was going to do with my life." I offered an ironic smile, "But I have a feeling you have some ideas about how I'm going to spend my time, don't you?"

"Well, we do have a few things to talk about. However, the estate shouldn't dictate your entire life; it should offer you some freedom to pursue what you're passionate about—which may be art. No?"

"That'd be nice," I admitted. "But, if you don't mind, let's get down to the responsibilities, because without answers my imagination is truly running wild."

"Sure. Would you like to move to your study? There's more room there and it's where I've been working."

"Cool," I said, glancing around. But then turned to him when I realized I didn't know where it was exactly. "Um, but you'll have to show me where it is. I mean, I know it's down the hallway there somewhere...,"

He threw an arm around my shoulder, "Right this way, sir."

We took the hallway leading off the kitchen and stopped at the first door on the right, "It's right in here," he said holding the door open for me. I walked in and immediately noticed the room, like all the others, had floor-to-ceiling windows. These looked out onto Glorietta Bay and I could see all the boats, sails tucked in, moored for the night—it was incredible.

It also had the same dark wood floors as the rest of the rooms I'd seen, and covering a good portion of the expensive wood was a thick area rug decorated with circular shapes of tans and browns. In fact, the entire room was tans, browns, and creams—it was very relaxing. Taking up the entire left wall was built-in cabinetry. It held books, knickknacks, a large screen TV, a stereo, and a wet bar—complete with a small sink and mini fridge. I spotted the two, comfortable occasional chairs sitting in front of the desk and took a seat in one.

Behind me, Matthew cleared his throat. "Um, wouldn't you be more comfortable in the desk chair, Grif?"

"Everything in its time, Matthew. For now I'm comfortable right here." Then, glancing back at the bar with a grin, "Mr. Diaz keep that thing stocked? With scotch maybe, because a drink would certainly aid in my comfort."

That earned me a grin, "Yes, yes he does—did."

He fixed drinks while I idly regarded the desktop. It held a mountain of neatly stacked paperwork, a sophisticated but rugged looking desk set, a shinny laptop, and a photo of Tate with his mom and dad—smiling happily, in what looked to be a European city. Although he'd only been gone a few weeks, I felt the loss almost continually, and seeing the picture of him looking so alive and happy—it was like I just took a fist to my gut.

Matthew sat the scotch down in front of me on the desk and then made his way around to the other side and took a seat.

"Since it's getting rather late, what do you say about doing a high overview tonight, signing some papers, and then picking back up in the morning for the rest?" he asked.

"Sounds fine."

"How about we start with the tangible stuff first?"

I nodded.

"In total, counting this condo, there are nine homes, and an apartment building; five here in the US, one in Athens, Greece, one in Venice, Italy, and last one is in London, England. The apartment building is the one you currently live in and was purchased as soon as the two of you moved into it—although he initially wanted to live in the dorms so as to fully experience college life and not live alone.

"All of them have at least one permanent staff person, but some have two or more. The caretakers don't reside in the home, but live in either their own place or, as in a few instances, there are separate onsite residences. I either have an adjoining condo or a nearby home in every location as well. The Diaz's, for the most part, preferred city living so several of the homes are in fact condos. All of them are about the same standard as this home—but some are much nicer."

"You're shitting me! Nicer than this?" I looked around and shook my head, "Jeez!"

He smiled and continued, "Also, with the exception of Venice, there's at least one automobile at each residence. Pavel is licensed to drive in London and Athens and travels with you so he's always in the same city. I'm also usually in the same city."

"Um…," I started hesitantly and he paused and quirked an eyebrow, "What exactly is your job, Matthew?"

"That, Grif, is a very good question." He seemed forlorn as he briefly studied the now dark windows but the despondence vanished as he turned back to me, "I'm a licensed attorney, although I haven't actually practiced in over twenty years. I guess I was Mr. Diaz's personal assistant—for lack of a better term. I also oversee all the other staff and have an expert handle on the whereabouts of essentially every dollar of the estate. Which, by the way, has a total value of about 750 million.

"For the past four years, since Mr. Diaz passed, I've also taken over a fair bit of the daily financial responsibilities; like signing payroll checks for all the staff, paying the bills for each property—that sort of thing. Tate had absolutely no interest in the estate at all. In fact, I could barely get him to look at financial reports. He gave me full leeway with more or less everything—with precautions I put in place to protect both him and myself; me not being able to sign a check for more than fifty-thousand dollars, for example. I have two assistants and the three of us take care of roughly every daily task regarding the estate. Of course, the estate contracts the services of financial professionals as well as professionals in other areas. Does that answer your question, Grif?"

I took a long swallow of my drink and nodded my head, "Yes, but it only adds to the growing list of others I have."

Smiling he said, "To use your own phrase, *Everything in its time*, right? Okay, moving on, there's a Gulfstream G450 and flight crew, which is currently housed at a private hanger in Clairemont, and a Triple Seven yacht moored here in the Bay. We retain the captains for both the boat and plane and they select their own crew—vetted by us, of course. I moved both the plane and boat here when Tate elected to enroll at UCSD; he never used either though."

"I...I don't know what to say, Matthew." I stared down at my empty glass.

He looked at me with concern, "It'll be okay, Grif. I promise. You are going to do fine; Tate couldn't have left the estate in better hands. I firmly believe that. And speaking of leaving you things, when he changed his will and designated you as sole heir, he also set up a sizable trust fund in your name."

I stared at him in shock. Tate had set up a fund for me?

"I can see from your expression you weren't aware." With a small shake of his head and a frustrated sigh, he said, "I advised him, on multiple occasions, to tell you...and he always said he would, at some point. He just didn't know how to do that without explaining the entire estate."

"N-no, he never...."

"I warned him you'd have to be told before it matured, and you had to be made legally aware of its existence. I'd tried to reason with him...tried to tell him dropping ten million dollars on someone without—,"

"Ten *million* dollars?" I gasped.

He grinned at my bewilderment. "Yes. Set to mature on your thirtieth birthday. Kind of small potatoes when you compare it to what he ended up dropping on you, but...."

"But that he thought of me.... That he wanted me to have some money when he obviously didn't want to think about money at all. I don't know what to say."

Matthew had taken my glass, refilled it, and handed it to me as he sat back down behind the desk. "He, without a doubt, Grif, understood the good money could do. And, to be honest, he was getting better and better with the notion...the reality...that he was a very rich man. I think designating your thirtieth birthday had more to do with him than with you. I think he believed by then, six years from now, that *he'd* finally be okay with it and he'd finally be okay with discussing it with you."

I didn't know what to say, so I simply nodded and took a healthy pull of scotch.

He pulled files from the neat stack and arranged them in front of me.

"Okay. So we have some paperwork—documents which require your signature. Most of the staff hasn't been paid yet—today being payday Friday—since Tate passed two weeks ago and I hadn't been able to get in touch with you."

"Oh, shit! I'm so sorry."

"Not to worry. It's just without you taking 'ownership,' if you will, of the estate, there isn't anyone with the authority to sign payroll checks. I'm able to sign regular checks, but the US government frowns upon not following certain established protocol when it comes to dispensing employee salaries."

He pulled a large checkbook out of a side drawer, and placed it next to the stack of manila folders already there.

"Anyhow, we've got about twenty documents requiring your signature as soon as possible. I'll go over what each means and does. And then we'll call it a night, okay?"

He handed me a pen and rotated the checkbook so it was facing me. "The checks have already been made out, all you have to do is sign them," then he added, "With your full legal name."

I smiled. "So, no *Grif Griffin*, huh?"

With a tap of the file folders, he continued, "We can talk about the small businesses the estate owns and the various charities we've historically sponsored. But, what you do with these businesses and charities is entirely up to you.

"You can sell the small companies and select new organizations which have personal meaning to you to sponsor for charity purposes. But none of that has to be decided tonight, or even in the next few months."

He paused long enough to take a sip from his own glass, before saying, "This evening's focus is to get the staff paid and bring you up to speed with all the rest. Then, once that's done, we can discuss my future employment and if you'd like to keep me on, or find a replacement."

"What?" I asked shocked. "You're gonna leave me with this?" I squawked and stood up.

"No. No, that's not what I meant. I was only attempting to convey I don't take my employment for granted— nothing more."

I stood staring at him—unable to speak. He couldn't dump all this on me and then leave. I didn't know the slightest thing about running...something...an estate of this size.

With a soothingly tone, he said, "Grif, I'm not leaving you. Honest. Please sit back down, okay?"

I nodded and found my chair again. I pinned him with a serious gaze, "You are not going any-fucking-where for a long, long, time. Do you understand, Matthew?"

He chuckled and said, "Okay, Grif. I understand."

"Okay," I said, with what I hoped was finality on the subject and relaxed a bit again.

JOSEPH LANCE TONLET

CHAPTER 22
POST PENANCE

Summer 2014

I GRADUALLY AWOKE to tender kisses at the back of my neck. "Hmmm, feels so nice," I mumbled.

"Yes it does," was the reply whispered in my ear.

Waking a bit more, I realized I was lying on my side and Wes' large, solid body was spooned up against my back. Next, I became aware of the light and leisurely strokes gracing the top of my thigh and his nose brushing through the back of my hair.

God, how I loved some of the ways he chose to wake me up. Today's was a good choice. Others...well, waking up to pain is something completely different, and not unheard of in our bedroom.

"I love you so much, Grif."

And there it was again; the fluttering excitement in my stomach coupled with the overwhelming sense of happiness every time he said those words to me. But, right now, I also had the overwhelming need to pee.

"I love you too Wes. Gotta pee bad, babe."

I started to swing my legs from under the covers and had two simultaneous sensations; my balls ached like nobody's business, and Wes' grip tightening around my torso.

"Ouch," I squeaked.

"Did I hurt you, love?" I could hear the concern in his voice.

I craned my neck around and gave him a quick kiss—obviously having not brushed my teeth yet—and said, "Nah, it's my nuts…they hurt like crazy."

His arm gripped me more firmly and easily pulled my back against his chest again. Nuzzling my neck and shoulder with a bit more intent, he growled, "Stay here with me. I like it when your balls ache…it makes me happy."

"I know you do, babe. But I really gotta pee. I promise my nuts will still hurt when I get back."

"Stay? I'll make it worth your while," his tone was clearly suggestive.

Well, that certainly had Junior's attention.

His grip was suddenly gone from around my chest, and I felt his thick fingers softly stroking the crack of my ass. The insistent movement unmistakably saying, 'spread your legs.' All thoughts of leaving the bed were swept away and replaced with intense desire. I eagerly complied to his unspoken request by bringing a knee to my chest as he pulled the sheet and blanket back, fully exposing me. He slowly stroked from the back of my suffering balls right up to the small of my back. His touch sent wonderful sparks of pleasure through my entire body.

Bringing himself upright, and glancing back and forth between my eyes and my spread legs, he groaned, "Oh, God. Grif, your ass, babe...I'll never get tired of looking at it...so fucking irresistible."

I felt the mattress moving behind me and the distinctive sound of the bedside table drawer opening.

Yes! He's gonna fuck me. From the very first time we'd done this, I'd fallen in love with the feeling of being filled, of him taking me, of enjoying how much he loved being inside me. I loved the surprise too; I never knew if he was going to be soft, or gentle, or loving, or playful, or if he was going to be rough, or demanding, or possessive and fuck me into oblivion. I enjoyed all of them equally; he was amazing no matter what mood he was in.

I heard the snap of the lube and then felt cool, slick sliding between my cheeks as his fingers caressed the sensitive skin.

"Ahh, Wes," I moaned. "Feels so good."

"Yeah? You like that, love?" he questioned as he stretched his body back down next to mine and put his mouth to my ear again.

A thick finger glided its way into my body. The initial resistance and burn were quickly replaced by a lust for more—for him.

Nodding, "Yes, I really like it," pushing back against his hand.

"But, I should really stop; you gotta pee, don't you, babe?"

I could feel his lips pull into a devilish smile against my neck.

With a smile of my own, I said, "I really hope you don't; I'd hate to have to look for a new boyfriend today...my schedule's already jam-packed."

He let out a soft chuckle and methodically moved his long, thick finger over *that spot*. He'd found it the first time we'd made love and, apparently, had memorized its exact location down to the millimeter. Deliberate, repeated soft and teasing strokes fell over the bundle of nerves as his wet tongue dipped into my ear sending my entire body into shivers.

"Ahhh, damn, Wes."

"You were saying something about another man, love?"

I wordlessly shook my head and then managed to breathlessly squeeze out, "Never...all yours...babe."

I wanted more, needed more, so I pushed back firmly, "Please, Wes. Wanna feel you inside me."

"You ready for another finger?"

"No. Please. Stop teasing me...I wanna feel you...need to feel you inside me...so bad, Wes."

"Such a pushy bottom, you are," he scolded while continuing the feather light licks at my neck and ear, "This isn't my first barbecue, ya know."

Swallowing hard, "I know what you're doing too, you evil man, you."

I felt his finger slowly slide free and heard him slicking himself with lube.

Feeling completely wanton and not giving one shit, I moaned out, "Please, Wes. I need it—need you—so bad."

"I'm right here, love."

A wonderful and unmistakable push against my opening had me quivering with anticipation and excitement, "Yes, yes! Put it in, Wes. Fuck me. Please."

"I fucking love how needy you are after a few days

without orgasm. With a single touch you're ready…so fucking responsive."

Slowly, oh so slowly, I felt him slide into me with a heavenly feeling of fullness. With a tortoise-like pace he only stopped when he was fully seated inside me and his balls lay next to mine. I reached up and grabbed his hip and pulled him close to me.

Removing my hand, he brought it to his lips, and took my index finger inside his mouth's warm wetness.

"Babe, please move. Please."

Releasing my hand, he nipped my shoulder and then slowly dragged back out.

"I am moving, love. Can't you feel me?"

"Wes, my nuts hurt so bad."

"I know they do. You're doing so good, Grif…feel so fucking good."

Completely unthinking, I moved my hand down toward Junior and only managed to get as far as my navel before he snatched it and brought it up to my chest.

"Love, you know full well touching is no longer allowed, don't you?"

I nodded, "Yes, Wes. I'm sorry. I wasn't going to…I promise. I…fuck, I'm so horny, and I hurt sooo much."

His dick was almost fully out and then he started pushing back in.

"I know, love. But you're that way because I want you that way. Tell me, who does Junior belong to, Grif?"

"He's yours, Wes. I…I just wanna come so badly…God I feel like I'm gonna lose my mind. Please, *please* fuck me."

He pulled all the way out this time and slowly pushed all the way back in. Oh God!

"I am fucking you, love. And believe me, I know you want to come."

His teeth caught my ear as he pulled back out and slowly pushed deep inside again. He stilled and released my ear.

"What if I said you could shoot, but under one condition: Stubby would receive no external sensation. I'd allow you to come but only if you could do it from this alone? You'd have to come from this…only from getting fucked. What would you say to that?"

I pushed back harder onto his thick cock. Damn, it felt so fucking good.

"I'd say those aren't the rules; there's no restriction on how I can come, only *if* I can come."

He pulled back, slowly dragging across my sweet spot again, and leisurely pushed back in. Oh, he was gonna drive me fucking mad!

"But what if I asked for it—for the pleasure of prescribing conditions?"

I'd had enough. In one fluid, determined, movement I pulled off his cock, swung over the top of him, and straddled him with my knees landing on either side of his chest. Clearly surprised, he didn't initially react.

I took advantage of the rare moment, reached around, held his dick straight up, and impaled myself down onto it in one swift motion. Once I was fully seated, I grabbed his wrists and pinned them above his head.

Staring down into his handsome face I said, "My reply would be an emphatic *no*. It'd be too much like blurring the line between Chocolate and Vanilla."

I began moving up and down—slowly but with resolute force. Ah, fuck yeah, this was more like it!

"I need definite and clear distinctions between the two. I

gave you—do give you—control over both my Chocolate and my Vanilla orgasms. I've even handed over when I can touch my dick, because it makes us both happy…brings us both pleasure. But those are the only 'cross-overs,' Wes. The only ones."

Still holding his wrists firmly in place, I quickened my pace and saw the resulting pleasure on his face; his brow crinkling and his lips parting in ecstasy.

Up, down. Up, down.

"Now tell me, do I get to come this morning?"

Coherent thoughts and speaking clearly were becoming more and more difficult for him. But then his determination won out and he looked up at me with a sexy, playful grin. "But I really like making you wait until the last possible moment to know. I like you being unsure…like seeing the hopefulness and uncertainty in your eyes…even when I've decided long beforehand. And, I like being able to change my mind…," he paused and licked his lips, "…oh God, feels good, Grif."

Up, down. Up, down.

"And…if I don't tell you right away…then I also have the freedom of changing my mind whenever I want. *Jesus, that feels good!*"

I'd begun squeezing tight, determined to make him lose the tenuous grasp he held on his orgasm.

Up, down. Up, down.

"Sometimes it's seriously difficult; I love seeing the extreme pleasure on your face when you come—and knowing I'm solely responsible for that. Me, Grif—no one else. But, nearly equal, is the indescribable pleasure I get from the immense disappointment—often accompanied by pain-filled tears—when I deny you."

Up, down. Up, down.

Fuck, I didn't know how much more of this I could take—the over-and-over friction on my sweet spot; the slamming of my burning nuts into his abdomen; the way he was allowing me to keep him pinned down and not attempting to break free; the talk—God, the hot conversation we were having about Junior, and orgasm control, and the amazing, complicated dynamics that made up our relationship—all of it combined had me dangerously close to the point of no return.

And I wouldn't allow that to happen. Fuck, not after last night's marathon torment session where I seriously thought I'd lose my mind. I wanted to come, badly, but it wasn't worth going through anything that intense again. Or was it? Last night had been incredible—the best yet.

Wes turned into someone completely different in our Chocolate sessions, someone I, on rare occasions, despised. But more often—much more often—he became the one person on the planet I knew, beyond a shadow of a doubt, who could fulfill my darkest desires and, in return, I could do the same for him.

"And have you made your decision about this morning yet?" I panted.

Up, down. Up, down.

He nodded, "Before I even woke you up, love."

"Tell me, Wes. Please tell me."

Oh God, I was so close…I either had to have permission, or I had to stop.

Using our words, I panted, "Wes, more please."

I saw his head begin to shake 'no' and felt my stomach and chest tighten with disappointment—and excitement too; if he didn't let me come this morning when would I?

Would it be today sometime? Tomorrow? I might be able to hold out for a few more days but, undoubtedly, it was gonna fucking hurt. But oh God, I wanted to come—really fucking needed it. Then, still shaking his head he smiled and said, "Yes, love, I'm going to allow Stubby to have a squirt this morning."

My eyes suddenly teared up, and even though I was still holding his wrists down, he easily brought a hand up to my cheek.

"I love you so much, Grif."

"I love you too, Wes. More than anything."

Up, down. Up, down.

"Love?"

"Yeah?"

"Hold on."

Before I even had a chance to process what he meant, he flipped us over and I landed flat on my back. His cock remained buried deep in me but stilled as our chests pressed firmly together. Fuck, my throbbing nuts were trapped between us and the pain had an immediate, subsiding effect on my bubbling orgasm.

He started again, and I wrapped my legs around his pumping ass and wound my fingers in his hair as he kissed me deeply.

"Feels so good, Grif. Love you so much, babe," he mumbled between kisses.

His furry, muscled chest pressed against my tender nipples, his lower body ground painfully against my nuts, his stomach rubbed against Junior, his tongue buried as deeply in my mouth as his huge cock was in my ass…it was all too much, and I felt the tingling sensation in my crotch once again signaling the wonderful orgasm I so desperately sought was within reach.

His body stiffened and he raised up off me, pulled his dick free—leaving an aching void—and fisted his swollen dick. His sheer beauty and maleness, this stunningly handsome man stroking himself while I looked on with pleasure, more than made up for my brief feeling of being unfulfilled.

I watched, like he knew I loved doing, as his entire body stiffened, as his chest went from sporadically heaving to completely still, as his eyes locked on mine and stream after stream of white cum jetted out of his thick cock and landed on my chest, abdomen, and crotch.

"Grif!" he groaned.

He stayed there, kneeling and stroking, as I stared at his slowly moving hand gently working his foreskin back and forth—milking every last bit of pleasure from of his orgasm.

When he finally came to a stop, I whispered, "Fuck, Wes! You are amazing. Absolutely amazing." I felt an overwhelming mix of admiration, and gratitude, and love, and desire.

He quirked a playful grin saying, "I bet you say that to all the guys who fuck you senseless and then come all over you. And, speaking of cum…," he said running a thick, long finger through the mess he'd made on my torso, "…it looks like I've got a little bit of cleanup to do, huh?"

Pushing my knees down, so my legs lay flat on the bed and then straddling them, he ran a palm down my body and scraped his cum onto my crotch. "But, I have a better idea."

With my dick nice and slick, he started slowly stroking Junior. I tilted my head back, and arching my back, let out a strangled moan. This wasn't going to take long.

As if reading my mind he stopped. My eyes flew open in time to catch a glimpse of his wet hand sliding between his legs and then, to my shock, he quickly spread his legs and sat down atop my dick.

I cried out in pure surprise and pleasure, "Oh my God...ah...fuck...yes...Wes!"

He grinned down at me and quirked an eyebrow, "Yes? You like?"

Straining for breath and words I nodded, "Yes. Oh my God, yes. So tight and hot and smooth."

I looked down at our joined bodies in disbelief, and stating the very obvious, breathed, "I'm inside you, Wes."

He didn't move up and down, he couldn't really without Junior slipping from his body, so instead he ground his hips down and worked them in a circular motion on my lap. The result was amazing.

I never thought I'd experience this mind-blowing sensation; the feeling of being inside another man—let alone a man I loved nearly more than life itself. He'd brought so much to me, to my life, and he constantly surprised me by bringing more and more.

"Wes, I love you so much...I can't even tell you...."

He put both hands on my chest and his fingers easily found my sore nipples. Softly, methodically, he plucked the sensitive nubs. Fire raced up and down my body as my hands grasped his strong forearms.

"Wes, I can't...not gonna last."

"Love, you don't have to last...just feel...that's all, just feel."

He fingers became more insistent and grinding—

matching the same rhythm as his hips—and I lost the ability to think. I had the overwhelming, innate need to thrust my hips but his weight made movement of any sort impossible.

My own fingers found the sheet beneath me, desperately twisting the fabric, as I cried out, "Wes, Wes, Wes…feels so good…can't…gonna…may I please…come?"

Faintly I heard permission granted and then speech and thought were completely gone and I could only feel bright, white lightness and an utter sense of calm—which was so totally at odds with my body's strangling spasms and convulsions. Bliss—total, absolute, fucking bliss.

A long while later, I refocused and found him looking down at me with so much love and happiness that my heart hurt. Throwing my forearm over my eyes, I felt a huge grin spread across my face.

He slid off me, leaned against the headboard, and easily brought me onto his lap.

"That was amazing, Grif. *You* are amazing," he said into the top of my head while running a hand up and down my back.

"Fuck. I…I don't even have words to describe it, Wes."

I ran my fingers through the hair on his chest—God, I loved his chest hair. Then I let out a small laugh and turned to grin at him.

"I'm completely serious when I say I can't even imagine someone being better at making love than you. You've taken me to places I've never even allowed myself to dream possible. I love you so much. So much!" I shook my head knowing I could never put into words what I felt for him.

He grabbed me tight and held on—and for a moment it felt so good. But I soon realized I couldn't breathe and the pressure on my neck was downright painful.

"Um, Wes, you're seriously hurting me here."

He immediately let go. "Oh my God. I'm sorry, babe," and then offered a goofy grin.

I laughed and smiled up at him, "It's okay, you damn fool, you."

I hopped off the bed and sharply pinched one of his nipples as I moved away.

"Ouch," he yelped with a chuckle.

I looked down at the messy sheets and said with a tone of mock authority, "I really think you should clean this up while I fucking go pee!"

He raised a playful dark eyebrow, "Oh, you do, do you?" and then he was up and chasing me into the bathroom before I could safely get behind the door and lock it. I laughed loudly as he grabbed me.

"Gotta peeeee!" I whined between laughs.

"Should'a thought about that before you poked a sleeping bear with a sharp stick."

I'd almost wrenched free when he'd distracted me by biting down on my shoulder—and I was firmly in his grasp again.

"Ow, no biting! You crazy fuck!" I laughed out. "Junior's small, but I didn't think he was sharp....," I couldn't continue and breathing normally had become difficult— he'd begun lightly running his tickling fingers over my abdomen and I could think of little else besides getting away.

"We-Wessss, if you fucking m-m-make me p-p-pee on myself...."

His evil fingers stopped, and he seductively whispered,

"Ohhh, there's an idea."

I took advantage of his distraction and pulled free. Ducking into the water closet, I slammed the door and locked it with mere seconds to spare.

"Grif?" came his playful voice, "You're a tease!"

I laughed as my stream found the bowl. Ah, relief—finally. "Yeah, and I've never heard of a better example of the pot calling the kettle black, you twisted, sadistic horn-dog!"

He barked out a laugh, "Ah, but you love that about me, right?"

"Hmm," I said loudly...seeming to ponder his question as I continued to find sweet relief. I finally answered, "Yeah, I suppose I do. But *only* because you're a twisted, sadistic horn-dog in the most lovable of ways. Now go change the damn sheets—I wanna spend the day with your cock in my mouth, and I don't wanna do it while laying in a wet spot."

I heard the heated growl I loved so much followed by the unmistakable sound of him padding off toward the linen closet. Damn, I loved Sundays!

CHAPTER 23
A PLAN

Fall 2013

"OKAY, SO JEANS, shirt, underwear, socks and shoes...anything else?" I asked. I was getting ready to head over to Wes' room and fetch him some dry clothing. 1 should just make him wear the wet stuff he'd hung to dry in my shower. What kind of person stands on someone's balcony, in the mist, for hours anyway?

I slipped off my robe and quickly snagged my jeans off the bedroom chair I had tossed them on. Of course, I was still wearing my jock, but the same fears of being seen resurfaced as I hurriedly bent over to pull my pants on. I heard Wes growl behind me. His attention gave me an unexpected heady feeling—but it also unnerved me; I'd never had someone look at me, or pay as much attention to my every movement, the way he did.

As casually as I could, I chuckled, and said, "Down boy."

"If I'd thought this through, I wouldn't have agreed."

I looked over at him, eyebrows raised in question, and pulled a sweatshirt over my head.

"In order for you to go to my room, you have to get dressed. Poor planning on my part for sure."

"You're a damn fool, too." I quipped as I slipped into a pair of flip-flops, grabbed my keys, wallet, and cell phone and headed for the door.

Wes stepped up to walk me to the door and innocently laid a hand on the small of my back. I panicked…didn't even think…only reacted. I tensed, swung my arm up behind me, grabbed his wrist firmly, and spun around.

He froze and said, "Whoa."

I could see from the expression on his face he felt like he'd done something terribly wrong.

"Fuck," I sighed, releasing him. "No. I apologize. It's…no one has ever…I'm not used to people touching me the way you do, Wes."

He smiled. "Hmm, perhaps it may have something to do with your no touching rule, huh?"

"Yeah, it might," I admitted. "But it has more to do with you than the touch itself." I shook my head. I was feeling anxious again and really wanted to just leave.

Trying to get my thoughts straight, I said, "People touch me all the time…but with you I know it means something else. It's different."

He reached up to touch my shoulder, then stopped and pulled back.

"Look, if we're gonna do this, I can't keep worrying I'm gonna end up with broken bones because I enjoy being tactile. Touching is who I am, babe."

That term of endearment again. Why did he feel so free to use it? And why did it feel so comfortable and so damn good to hear it? We barely knew each other.

"Look, yourself," I flippantly shot back. "I'm not at all sure what we're doing here. Yeah, we've shared some secrets, had a few moments, but other than that...," I broke off because I couldn't continue spewing the fear-induced bullshit I wasn't sure I actually felt. I had to get out—away from him. I needed time to think.

Realizing I was being a total ass, I backed off a bit and checked my tone. "I'm gonna run and get your stuff...I'll be back in a few, okay?"

Outside, I felt like I could finally breathe again, although it did little to calm my addled mind. How could I, on the one hand, want to spend time with Wes so badly that I'd thought of little else for two days, but, on the other, have the overwhelming need to run every time I got anywhere near him? Something had to give.

The moment he'd said, "I want to get to know you...know everything about you," I'd gotten an idea. Making my mind up, I headed for Wes' room and pulled out my phone.

"Morning, Matthew."

"Good morning, Grif."

Belatedly remembering the couple he'd left the restaurant with the night before, and wincing as I glanced down at my watch to find it was only 7:40am, I said, "I hope I'm not calling too early."

"Not at all. Is anything wrong...you sound...different."

"Um, no. Nothing wrong. But I'm hoping you wouldn't mind making a few calls for me. Again, if it's not too early."

"Grif," he said and I heard the beginnings of exasperation start to find its way into his voice.

"Okay, okay. Excuse me for having manners, sheesh," I said lightly.

Although I couldn't make out the exact words, I heard the distinct tones of both a male and female voice in the background. Shit. I had called too early and woken everyone up.

"I've disturbed the three of you, haven't I?" I asked, with amusement.

The innuendo of my comment caught the normally imperturbable Mr. Matthew Smithton off guard. I loved it and tried not to ruin it by snickering.

"Three of…how did…? Ah, the restaurant last night."

He lowered his voice and quietly said, "Look, Mr. Griffin, if you must know, sir, I haven't been to bed…err, to sleep yet. But, I'd be happy to type up a detailed report for your perusal and approval after the morning activities conclude, sir."

I barked out a laugh, "And you'd shit a brick if I took you up on the offer, wouldn't you, Mr. Smithton?"

Silence from Matthew's end of the phone.

"What? No witty comeback, Matthew?" I giggled. "But, now that I think about it, I bet it would be a fascinating read."

"Ha! Not on your life. Not even you have enough money—,"

"Okay, okay," I interrupted, "Don't get your blood pressure up…at your age it could be—,"

"You, sir, had better tread very carefully and choose your next words with tremendous care," he warned, "and it'd benefit you to remember who prevailed the last time we met in the ring."

It was true; he'd beaten my ass—and I wasn't too proud to admit a fifty-something year old man had surprised me—hell, shocked the fuck out of me—and taken me down.

"You have to bring that up, don't you? When you know full well it gives me a chubby every time I think about it."

"Again, sir, you don't have enough money—,"

"If you call me sir one more time old man!"

"Did you want something, because, unlike some folks, I do occasionally have bedroom company."

"Oh, now look who's treading dangerous ground. And yes, my call did have a specific purpose."

Although he was trying to hide it, I heard him laugh; he thoroughly enjoyed our good-natured banter as much as I did, if not more. His demeanor lost the snarky cleverness and returned to that of someone I considered a true friend.

"What can I help with, Grif?"

"I was hoping you wouldn't mind taking the plane back to San Diego today, whenever you're ready to head home?"

"Not at all. But how will you be getting home?"

"Oh, that's where the phone calls come in; I'd really like to take the boat back. If you could ask Captain D. to be here by 1pm, perhaps? I know it's very short notice, Matthew, so please let him know there'll be something extra in his, and the crew's, checks this week, would you?"

"I'd be happy to, Grif. And as far as provisions aboard, will you be coming directly home?"

"I might take as many as four days—for two passengers—or I might be home by this evening. I'll have to wait and see how it goes."

"Huh. For two people you say?" and I could hear the smile in his voice, "We may have to trade reports after all—seeing you have something infinitely more interesting than money to barter with."

"Ha! Now who's indulging in wishful thinking?" There was more good natured laughter from his end.

"Thank you, Matthew, I really do appreciate it. And, honestly, I hope I didn't interrupt your morning too badly."

"Honestly, Grif, it's no bother at all—I'm happy to be of assistance, you know that."

"I do. And, Matthew?"

"Yes, Grif?"

"Have fun."

Over the past five years, Matthew and I had become far more than business associates. Tate and the Diaz estate had been our initial tie, but we quickly found we had far more in common than simply managing my inheritance—and all that came along with it. He was funny, honest, wicked smart, generous, and I knew—beyond a shadow of a doubt—I could trust him.

He was my closest confidant, and we'd adopted the *Have Fun* as our own catchphrase—using it for everything from *I Love You, Man* to *Piss Off*.

"*Have fun*, Grif. And, please, enjoy yourself, will ya? I can't think of anyone who deserves it more."

"I'll do my best. You do the same."

"Well, then, I've got to go; there are two fascinating people waiting in my bed," and he disconnected.

I grinned broadly as I pocketed my phone. The only thing left was to see if Wes was even remotely interested in accompanying a shit-fuck crazy person like me back to San Diego on a boat.

Making my way through the multiple courtyards, I headed for building seven and Wes' room—and his dry change of clothes. The ground was still wet from the rare early morning rain, but the sky was already a bright blue with the promise of a beautiful, typical southern California day ahead. I bound up the steps with a lightness I hadn't felt since waking up this morning; making a decision and putting a plan in place always eased my mind. I hoped I knew what the hell I was doing.

Arriving at Wes' room, I let myself in and found the same neat organization I'd seen the first night; everything was in its place and tidy—a character trait I could certainly appreciate. But what I noticed even before that was his scent. I wondered how the fuck I could pick out his smell already...and find the aroma so incredibly pleasing.

Deciding it was best if I didn't dwell on that particular thought at the moment, I snagged up the backpack—right where Wes said it'd be—and opened drawers, selected items, and folded them inside.

At the armoire, I knelt down to grab his sneakers and couldn't help but notice the pair of sky blue designer, Todd Sanfield briefs lying atop his other dirty laundry. Given my fetish for underwear, I recognized the signature logo immediately. They weren't fancy or frilly, but they were leaps and bounds—not even remotely in the same category—from any run-of-the-mill JC Penney brand.

Long ago, I'd decided to wear a jockstrap for practical purposes—but donning one daily didn't lessen my aesthetic appreciation of them; I still found jocks incredibly attractive. However, I found most underwear and swimwear sexy and often longed to wear something...different. It's probably one of the reasons I loved underwear catalogs so much; admiring the male body in formfitting briefs I'd never allow myself to wear.

I tentatively ran a finger across the incredibly soft fabric of Wes' briefs, and wondered how much stronger his scent would be if I lifted them to my nose.

I withdrew my hand, and nervously inspected the room as if there might be someone here to catch me, and thus, realize my private thoughts. Then I wondered which had Junior more excited; the thought of being caught or actually smelling Wes' unwashed underwear. Again, best not to dwell.

Satisfied I'd collected all the items on my list, I closed the door to Wes' room, made sure it was locked behind me, and headed back down the stairs when my phone buzzed with a text from Captain Dalton.

Crew contacted. Should be docked in Santa Barbara by noon.

I replied:

Realize it's very short notice. I REALLY appreciate it. See you this afternoon.

Passing back through the courtyard, I noticed several couples heading toward the restaurant, to enjoy breakfast I assumed, and was struck again by my seemingly inescapable uncertainty; what the hell was I doing?

All of these people had whole complete bodies to offer a partner—something I clearly lacked. How on earth could Wes possibly be interested in me when I wasn't able to bring to the table an essential element of any healthy relationship: a robust and satisfying scx life.

This—whatever Wes and I were doing—would be over as soon as he actually saw my entire body. And I fucking hated that I was asking myself these questions—that I'd allowed myself back into a situation where I'd begun questioning my self-worth again. I'd sworn years ago living in this space, a space where I couldn't be confident, would never happen again. I'd also sworn I'd never allow myself to believe, even for the briefest of moments, someone—anyone—could want me that way. Yet, here I was again, destined to be heartbroken. Fucking idiot!

By the time I reached my open room door, I'd come to my senses again and made a few decisions—revised my plan; I'd text Captain Dalton and cancel, I'd get on the plane with Matthew and head home alone, and I'd choose one of the other security companies I'd interviewed yesterday and offer them the contract. But first I needed to get rid of Wes—and brushing men from my life was something I certainly knew how to do.

Realization of my room's door being open came just before I heard the raised, angry voices.

"Who are you, and why are you here? And where's Mr. Griffin?"

There was no mistaking the accent; it was Pavel and he was pissed. In a panic, I glanced down at my watch and realized it was 8:04am.

Fuck!

"Who am I? Who the fuck are you?"

And that was Wes—using a low, menacing tone I'd not yet heard come from him; it was more than a little scary.

I pushed open the door and found a chair separating them. Both were in striking stances, Wes holding a butter knife and Pavel swaying back and forth with a dangerous looking chain.

Where the fuck did he get a chain?

Wes' position offered him a better view of the door so he noticed me first. Calmly he said, "Grif, back out of the room, close the door, and call the police." Then, sneering at Pavel, he added, "And an ambulance."

"Yes, Mr. Griffin, but there'll be no need for an ambulance. Save time and simply call a hearse."

Christ. Next they were gonna be whipping out their dicks and a tape measure.

"Okay, both of you...."

I walked in and dropped the backpack against the wall.

"I suppose introductions are in order. Wes, meet Pavel Alexandr, my driver and self-appointed bodyguard. Pavel, meet Weston De Luca, a...friend."

Pavel immediately responded to the introduction and assumed a normal posture and, somehow—somewhere—the chain had already disappeared.

"My sincere apologies, Mr. Griffin." Then, to Wes, "And to you as well, Mr. De Luca."

I looked over to Wes, who was still holding the knife rather defensively, but I addressed Pavel, "No, I'm the one who needs to apologize—it's after 8am and I didn't call. I know better. Thank you for checking on me." Then, to Wes, "Please put the knife down and say hello to one of the most valued members of Diaz, Inc.'s staff."

As if suddenly realizing he was still holding the knife, he placed it on the table and extended his hand, "Wes De Luca. It's nice to meet you, Pavel. And, um, sorry about plotting ways for you to die a few moments ago."

Pavel gave Wes a wide smile and took his hand, "Pavel

Alexandr. It's very nice to meet you as well, sir."

Turning to me, "Mr. Griffin, if everything is okay, I'll take my leave, sir?"

Smiling I said, "Yes, Pavel, everything is fine. Thank you. But—,"

"Yes, sir, I know. 'Cut the sir crap'...Yes sir, Grif," he interrupted respectfully, and stepped out of the room.

I looked up at Wes and said, "I can't leave you alone for a minute without you causing trouble, can I?"

"Me?" he started, but then stopped and followed my gaze. He'd popped a huge fucking bone and it was sneaking out of the folds of his robe.

He actually blushed, re-closed the robe, and then brought the belt down lower snugging it tightly and effectively pinning his stiff cock up against his abdomen.

"Sorry, that's just rude. Effects of adrenaline I'm afraid."

"No worries."

I leaned down and scooped up his backpack. "I generally go for a run or something in the mornings. Would you like to join me?"

I set the pack down on the small sofa and walked into the bedroom, not waiting for his answer. I'd only just returned to the room and already felt like I needed to get out again; I needed us both out of here and somewhere nudity wasn't an option. A run would get us out of my room, and when we'd finished we'd each go back to our own rooms. Once we were apart, a clean break would take nothing more than a simple phone call.

"Yeah, sounds great. You pick up that sort of stuff from my room?" he asked, as I heard the pack being unzipped.

I slid off my jeans and sweatshirt, grabbed a pair of

workout shorts and a tank top from the bureau, and slipped them on.

"Yeah, there was only one pair of clean jogging shorts…," sky blue underwear flashed in my mind. "Um…I threw them in there. As well as a few t-shirts, sneakers, jeans…the typical stuff."

I sat on the bed and pulled on socks and my own running shoes.

He appeared in the doorway peering into the pack, "You trying to tell me something?" he said looking up at me.

"Huh?" I asked somewhat confused.

He smiled, "Well, there's no underwear in here." Lifting an eyebrow, "I'm wondering if there's a message there?"

So, I have no problem focusing on his dirty underwear, but remembering to pick up clean ones was apparently a different matter all together. Shit.

"Damn, I'm sorry."

"It's cool. I can borrow one of your jocks if you don't mind. It'll be a bit stretched out after, but…," he paused and then tentatively started again, "…I mean…I only meant I have about four inches more on my waist than you do. But, running without support isn't really a comfortable option for me."

When I didn't answer right away he continued, "Or, I can throw these shorts on and run back over to my room and grab some…no biggie."

He was floundering—actually becoming tongue-tied over my little dick. *Shit, shit, shit!* Say something, I thought to myself.

When I didn't, he sighed and apparent resignation was written all over his handsome face, "Help me out here, Grif, would ya?"

I hopped off the bed and pulled a jock from the still open drawer. I handed it to him with a forced smile, "It's all good. I'm gonna hit the head while you get dressed. I gotta pee."

He stepped between me and the bathroom and gave me a serious look. We were only feet apart and he started to bring his hands up but then stopped.

His dark, questioning eyes met mine. "May I touch your shoulders?"

I nodded.

He immediately, but gently, rested his hands on my bare skin, "I said it didn't matter, and it doesn't, Grif." Reaching up he cupped the side of my face with one large hand, "I'll never lie to you—ever, about anything. Even if it would be easier to. And even if it means telling you the truth will hurt your feelings; honesty is one of the traits I value the most from the folks in my life. You will always get that from me—count on it."

I nodded and swallowed wordlessly. Pulling my head away and clearing my throat I said, "I really feel the need to run, Wes. You gonna be long?"

"No, it'll take me two minutes," he said stepping back and letting his robe slip off.

It was a small gesture, but I didn't miss how he casually turned his back to me while stepping into the jock. Damn, if the back didn't look as good as I imagined the front would framed in the army-green support straps and black waistband.

As he pulled the t-shirt over his head, I heard a muffled, "I thought you had to pee?"

Fuck it. If it was honesty he wanted, I may as well start now.

"No, that was a lie; I went while I was in your room. I felt a rather desperate need to stop the conversation."

He pulled up his shorts and turned to face me. He was smiling and his eyes were kind...not exactly the reaction I was expecting.

"Thank you. That couldn't have been easy to say."

I went for nonchalance and shrugged. "Okay, okay...can we please run already?"

We ran northwest through the courtyard, followed the winding blacktop parking lot, and headed for Hollister Road. I was grateful we didn't talk. I wanted the endorphin high I knew would come. I wanted to stop thinking for a bit and feel the burn in my muscles, feel the air moving in and out of my body. I wanted to feel and not think.

Turning south onto Hollister, the run became easier with the road's slight downhill grade. Wordlessly, we picked up the pace and ran side-by-side in an easy silence. I glanced over at him, and he smiled back.

We tuned west onto a gravel road and wound our way around the tennis courts. Eventually the road turned into a path that led down to the beach. Turning north, we headed back toward the resort through the soft sand.

We were both sweating and breathing heavily. He knocked his hand against my shoulder to get my attention and gestured toward the water as he changed course in that direction. I followed his lead and as we reached the surf's edge he put us on a course parallel to it.

"More compact, slightly easier."

"Wait, you're not being a pussy, are you? 'Cause, to be honest, I'd be a bit surprised if you were," I goaded through paced breaths.

He laughed, "Look, one of us got sleep last night and one of us didn't. One of us spent hours sitting in the cold rain this morning while the other was snuggled between warm sheets—looking completely irresistible, by the way— and, finally, one of us had a pretty serious adrenaline rush less than thirty minutes ago with a rather scary Russian dude and one of us didn't."

He took a couple of paces before grinning and continuing, "So, yeah, I'm being a pussy. Get the fuck over it. But, tomorrow morning, watch out."

I looked over to see him sticking his tongue out at me…damn, he even made childish petulance sexy. I smiled despite myself.

"He's Ukrainian. I'll consider myself duly warned, and you *are* being a pussy!" I laughed and picked up my pace slightly.

Once we'd run a while, I steered us toward a steep path which led upward from the beach to the cliff-side resort— it was the only way back up.

At the top, I had to jog-in-place for a minute or two for him to catch up. As he crested the path he stopped, bent at the waist, and placed one palm on a knee while holding up the other one in the universal gesture for 'hold on.'

After a few moments, but still bent and breathing heavily, he said, "Yep, just wait until tomorrow morning. You think that little sprint toward the end was cute, don't you?"

"Oh, but we haven't finished yet," I said with a wicked grin, "depending on the route we take, there's still another fourth of a mile at least."

He didn't say anything, but silently flipped me the bird; the message clear—and funny as hell.

I stopped my jog-in-place and grinned as I waited for him to recover. Casually looking around, I realized we were only feet away from where we'd stood last night; the spot where I'd received my first real kiss. And Jesus, what an experience that had been.

When he spoke it startled me a bit, "I really hope it was okay, Grif."

I turned to find him, still bent at the waist, looking at me with—affection? He knew about Junior, at least in theory, and yeah, the way he looked at me now was different; it had knowing behind it, familiarity, understanding, but nothing more. None of the things I'd feared would be there.

"Wes, it's exactly as it was last night; the single most memorable experience of my life," and then, trying to lighten the comment a bit, I added, "Not to place too much importance on it, mind you," and chuckled.

Reaching out, he plucked a leaf off the ground before finally straightening back up. He twirled it a few moments, absently between his fingers, before letting it glide back to the ground.

He rested his hands on his hips and studied me briefly before saying, "Grif, I can't even tell you what hearing you say that means to me. Last night changed my life," then he grinned at me and parroted back, "not to place too much importance on it, mind you."

I shook my head in slightly irritated confusion. "I'm having difficulty understanding how you can be so sure. How do you know it was life changing and not just a kiss?

A really good kiss—again, I have nothing to gauge it against, and I admittedly have a difficult time imagining a better one—but maybe it was just a really good kiss?"

"Grif—," he started, but I interrupted.

"Wes, I have a proposal of sorts."

He arched an eyebrow and then surveyed the area, "Grif, out here? In broad daylight? What if someone—."

"Again, you're a damn fool," I said with a genuine laugh. "No. Depending on how you look at it, a less 'fun' proposal, perhaps."

I took in his abruptly changed expression and plunged forward.

"I'm wondering how you might feel about taking a boat ride back to San Diego—on my boat—rather than flying back. If you have time that is. We could be back by tonight, or take a few days; it'd be up to you. I'd like to have a chance to talk—just talk, Wes. Nothing more. I mean, if you're busy, or you have other—,"

"Grif. Stop talking already. Yes. The answer is yes. There's nothing I'd like more than to spend time talking with you."

I smiled, "But, seriously, talk, Wes. I honestly don't know exactly what we're doing here. And, as you said, I have questions, as I'm sure you do too, about…the secrets we've shared with one another."

He was grinning so wide, I wasn't quite sure how it didn't hurt.

"Yes, Grif…to all of the above."

CHAPTER 24
GRIF'S TOY

Fall 2013

THE BOAT HAD docked, and Wes and I were on our way to meet it. It was a short fifteen minute drive down Highway 101 South. When we pulled into the Santa Barbara Harbor, I spotted *Grif's Toy* and Captain Dalton standing on her bow waiting to welcome us.

Wes glanced up at the boat and then to me with wide eyes, "Jesus, Grif, I'm not sure 'boat' is the term I would use to describe this particular vessel; it seems a tad inadequate," he said, looking out the window at *Grif's Toy*.

I had to admit, he was right. The Triple Seven, with its navy blue and white color scheme, and overall size made a striking first impression. It was three stories, could accommodate ten passengers comfortably, and another sixteen crew. It had formal living and dining rooms, a gourmet kitchen, a small swimming pool, a helipad, and a master suite that made one never want to leave.

And there was yet another topic I knew we needed to discuss; the money. Wes obviously knew I was okay financially, but I wondered exactly how thorough his research team had been. Did he know the extent of the Diaz estate? Matthew and I spoke in generalities in the initial interview process and would expound only during the upcoming second interviews. Well, if second interviews actually took place now.

Thankfully I could put off acknowledging his comment as we'd come to a stop and Pavel was holding the door open for me—something I'd repeatedly requested he not do and a request he just as resolutely insisted upon ignoring. "Stubborn, disrespectful, disobedient…weak…Ukrainian," I mumbled good-naturedly at him as I pushed myself out of the back of the black, rented town car.

His lips quirked in a partial smile, "I proudly own all of those things, sir, with the exception of 'weak.' I'll fetch your bags momentarily."

"You do and I'll break your arm. Now pop open the fucking trunk, or I'm gonna pop you in the nose."

He moved to stand directly in front of me and closed his eyes while pushing his chin out a bit so I'd have a good, easy shot—the message clear; he'd willingly allow me hit him, but he wouldn't think of allowing me to carry my own bags.

I reached back in and grabbed the leather satchel I used as a brief case and glanced at Wes. He'd listened with curiosity to the exchange. As I made my way past Pavel, I quipped, "One of these days I'm gonna fire you."

Clearly amused he quipped, "I'm sure you will, sir. And it'll be a sad day for us both, si—,"

"And if you call me 'sir' once more today I'm gonna have the captain leave your ass ashore and all of my problems will be solved."

He was following me around the back of the car—no doubt on his way to open the passenger door for Wes—when he said with cheer, "No, not all of your problems, but I do understand your point, sir…Grif."

"I'm having your pay cut tomorrow."

"If it will aid in your acceptance of my position—and allow me to do the job you pay me very well to do—I'll happily accept it. I'll alert Mr. Smithton you'd like a meeting to discuss it. I appreciate you're very busy and wouldn't want to forget something as important as discussing your driver's compensation package."

He'd reached the passenger door and pulled it open, "Mr. De Luca, sir."

Wes got out with a bemused nod, "Mr. Alexandr."

"Wes," I said patting down my pants pockets, "I don't seem to have any cash on me, would you mind tipping the *driver?*"

Pavel grinned at Wes, "I'll have your bags onboard shortly, sir."

"Thank you, Pavel," Wes said as if they, together, were mollifying an insolent teenager.

"Oh no," I protested, "You do not get to corrupt unwitting newcomers with your misleadingly innocent face and staged, charming accent."

He'd acted as if he'd stopped paying me any attention and was moving around to the driver's door. Once he was inside, I stepped up to the passenger window and lightly tapped. It slid down and I stuck my head in with a smile, "Is cabin six okay for you, Pavel? Its close, but it's also far enough away for you to have privacy."

"You know I don't require privacy; my one and only job aboard is to protect you, Grif. But yes, cabin six is fine. However…," he paused and looked over his shoulder gauging Wes' distance—satisfied he'd moved far enough away that we wouldn't be overheard, "should we talk about Mr. De Luca? Respectfully, sir, do we know…."

I undid the flap of my bag and passed Matthew's report on Wes to him. "Here's his folder. Look it over." Noting the time on my watch. "Make any calls you feel necessary. We have an hour and a half before we cast off, and get back with me before then, okay?"

"Will do, sir."

"And, Pavel?"

"Yes, sir?"

"Thank you…for taking care of me. I really do appreciate it."

"Grif, it's my honor and pleasure," he said sincerely.

I slapped the side of the car door with my palm and moved to join Wes.

He smiled as I stepped up, "You get Pavel all squared away?"

I laughed, "That's so far removed from the realm of possibility…." I tilted my head toward the boat, "You ready?"

He nodded, "Yep."

As we walked out onto the dock he said, "Grif, do you mind if I ask you a serious question even though it's probably none of my business?"

Trying to keep my tone light, I replied, "Nah, not at all. Questions, getting to know one another, is what the ride back is all about right? But, I had hoped to be laying relaxed on the sun deck with a cocktail in hand before we started with the real serious stuff."

"Ah, so the plan is to distract me with drinks and your bathing-suit-clad-body so I'll spill all my deepest held secrets, huh?"

With a mixture of mock resignation and irritation I looked down to the ground and spoke in my best villain accent, "You've uncovered my dastardly plot, HandsomeMan!" I brought my shaking fists to shoulder height and looked skyward, "All of humanity must now pay!"

He laughed. "And you call me a damn fool?"

I grinned over at him and continued walking, "Honestly, ask whatever you'd like."

His playful eyes took on a more thoughtful look and he asked, "Do you have a problem with your position—with your wealth? I've noticed…the whole 'sir' thing really does seem to bother you."

I looked out to the boat, to the crystal ocean beyond, and even farther out to where it met the gorgeous blue sky. There was no doubt, I was living the life—thanks to Tate and the Diaz estate. But I'd long since gotten over any guilt with regard to enjoying what Tate's death afforded me. Tate had been gone more than five years, but I'd gladly give up every penny of the money if it would bring him back.

Thoughtfully, I said, "No, I don't have a problem with either the position, or the wealth. Not any more. What I have a problem with, what I won't tolerate in those who comprise my family, is undue respect. I don't deserve any more or less respect than the deckhands who will be tending us do, or any more than Matthew and Pavel do.

"The money should be respected—by me, yes—but I shouldn't be respected by others because of it. It doesn't define me.

"The people I choose to employ are here because they want to be. Sure, don't get me wrong, I pay them very well. But I'd like to think it's more than that. If I don't feel I'll be able to make a unique, lasting connection with someone, then I don't invite them in."

"Now Pavel," I said with a chortle, "I inherited him—and his pigheadedness. But I have no doubt about his intentions or his loyalty."

"Grif!" Dalton called out as we drew closer and raised a hand in initial greeting.

"Wow," Wes said, "if that answer, and its obvious candor, is an example of the level of honesty I can expect on this trip...I couldn't want for anything more, Grif." Then, turning an appraising, if not slightly unfriendly, gaze on Dalton, "And who's the male model waving at us?"

I laughed and embraced Dalton when we got close enough. "Wes, this is Captain Dalton Jared. Dalton, this is my friend, Weston De Luca."

Dalton beamed at Wes and then extended his large weathered hand, "Pleased to meet you Mr. De Luca. Welcome aboard *Grif's Toy*."

Wes briefly lifted an amused eyebrow in my direction, apparently at the boat's name, and said to Dalton, "Thank you, Captain. The pleasure is mine. And please, it's Wes."

"Perfect, Wes. I'm Dalton." Then, turning to me, "I sent a few of the guys ashore to grab some last minute supplies. We should be ready in under ninety minutes, if that's okay?"

"Great. Again, thanks again for coming up on such short

notice; I really appreciate it."

"It wasn't the slightest concern," he said, and I knew it was a huge, and well meant, fabrication.

"There's a pitcher of margaritas in the refrigerator and a plate of fresh cheese and fruit if you'd like a snack before dinner. Or, if you'd like something more substantial...?"

"Sounds perfect, D. Thank you. I'm gonna show Wes around and then I suspect we'll be up on the pool deck."

"Very good," then with a smile at Wes, "Again, welcome aboard."

Dalton moved off and I gestured toward the interior. "Margaritas interest you at all?"

"Absolutely."

"Great," I said, as we walked past the living room, through the dining room, and into the kitchen. I grabbed two glasses, poured us each a drink, and handing one to him said, "The cabin I usually stay in is this way...," motioning down a hall off the kitchen, further toward the front of the boat. "Let me get changed, and I'll show you where Pavel's put your stuff?"

"Sounds good," he said taking a sip of the cold drink, "and this is one fine margarita."

We wandered down the hall, and I'd pushed the door open when a familiar voice called out from the master bathroom, "Is that you, Grif? I'll be right out. Just getting your jocks in order. Oh, my sister, Annie, got a new puppy. She named it Socks, because it's black with white fee...."

Lance appeared in the doorway and immediately changed his tone upon noticing Wes. "I apologize. I didn't realize you weren't alone," he said faintly, and cast his eyes downward.

Lance was an amazingly handsome young man. Looking

at him, I often had the image of an innocent farm boy riding shirtless atop a horse flash through my mind. He was twenty-two years old, stood about five foot eight; had crazy, curly, blond hair, an infectious white, genuine smile, and sported a year-round tan.

He was wearing a tight green, fish-net looking tank top and equally tight red nylon shorty-shorts—clearly sans underwear. Put simply, he was sexy as hell.

"Not at all, Lance," I said with a bright smile to put him at ease.

"Excuse me," he managed, before disappearing out one of the cabin's side doors.

Wes looked at me with both eyebrows raised, "And, what exactly is Lance's role aboard? And, why on earth aren't you paying him enough to buy clothes his size; he's obviously outgrown those years ago."

I laughed as I opened a dresser drawer holding my swim suits. Grabbing a royal blue pair which looked more like running shorts, I said, "His role, like all of the staff's, is strictly family-professional. He's my…cabin assistant, for lack of a better title.

"As for the way he dresses, I'm assuming he does so because he believes I like it." Grinning broadly, I admitted, "And, to be completely honest, I do.

"As you might have guessed, by his hasty departure," I continued more seriously, "he's very shy. Believe it or not, he's gotten better over the years; he'll actually sorta speak in front of strangers now—but then gets the hell out as quickly as possible. There's much more to his story, but very little of it is mine to tell."

I headed for the bathroom, grabbing a loose, light blue t-shirt along the way, "Only be a second."

I came back to an admiring regard, "Very handsome, Grif." Wes clearly approved of my choices. "However, I didn't pack a suit; I didn't think I'd be at the resort more than a day."

"Oh, I guess there's really no need to go downstairs—to your stuff—until later then. I've got tons of trunks to choose from in here. I…um…have sort of an underwear and swimsuit fetish."

He chuckled, "That's nice to know. And, in keeping with the honesty theme we've got going, I couldn't possibly find your embarrassed blush more attractive. Do you always turn this amazing shade of red when you're embarrassed?"

I looked up and the heat in his eyes was unmistakable.

"Yes, I suppose I do." Turning back to the bureau, I pulled open another drawer, "Any of the ones in here should fit you."

"Um, since it's your fetish, would you enjoy picking out a pair for me?"

I stared into the drawer and nodded.

He'd moved a few feet closer to me, "Grif, can I ask…I'd really like to ask for a long-term favor."

I looked up into his deep brown eyes, "You can always ask, Wes. Sure, what is it?"

He cleared his throat, "When we talk, about important things—like sex, fetishes, feelings, for example—I'd really like to hear your voice…to hear your words. Particularly when using words is difficult; either from apprehension, or embarrassment, or fear, or shame…whatever the reason…I'd really enjoy you expressing those emotions vocally."

He looked down into the drawer and fingered a pair of gray board-shorts and then looked back to me. "If this trip back to San Diego really is about getting to know one another better, then I've revealed yet another aspect of who I am—as well as one of the many things I enjoy in a partner. Please, make no mistake—the request is only a means to share another piece of me, nothing more. If it's not something you'd also appreciate, then it's certainly not an insurmountable obstacle by any means."

He smiled and shrugged.

Well, that was a real moment, wasn't it? He wants me to be real with him—to share what I'm feeling with words—and, most likely, I could expect the same from him. And what part, if any, did it play into his fetish I wondered.

Looking into his eyes I said earnestly, "Yes, I would definitely enjoy picking out a pair for you to wear. And, I have a few questions about the root of your request, but they can wait until we're soaking up the sun above deck. Cool?"

"Yep." Then, looking back down into the drawer with cautious amusement, and a glimmer in his eye, "Do I even want to know what you're gonna pick out for me?"

"Tell you what, I'll chose three pairs—then you pick the one you like best, deal?"

"Deal."

I happily pawed through the drawer, made my choices, and then set them all together in a pile on top of the dresser.

"When you're ready, head out that door, onto the private side deck, and then take the stairs up—that'll put you on the pool deck. I'm gonna grab the margarita pitcher, and I'll see you up there."

∾

I sat in one of the recliners, fresh drinks for us poured, and enjoyed only my second cigarette of the day.

"Think I could have one of those too?"

I turned to see Wes standing at the top of the stairs wearing, what I had assumed was the least likely of the three pair of trunks I'd picked out. They were white briefs—not quite bikini speedos—but briefs which left nothing to the imagination. The white was brilliant against his olive skin, and just above the waistband sat his intriguing tattoo.

"Wow. I can't believe you actually put those on. I'm totally glad you did—I mean, really, really glad. But, I am surprised."

He grinned, spread his arms out, and did a twirl. "They look okay then?" he asked with a shit-eating grin.

"Seriously better than I could ever have dreamed. Wow, you do realize you're a stunning man, right?"

He padded over to me, his thick cock pushed right out there for God and everyone to admire, and said, "I'll admit I've had my admirers in the past, but I'm really glad you find me attractive, Grif."

He tilted his head toward the pack of smokes.

"Oh, yeah, sure," I mumbled trying not to stare at his crotch but failing miserably.

Then, getting hold of myself, I looked up to his face, "Shit, I'm sorry. I'm acting like a sex-starved, hormonal teenager. It's rude; I apologize. It's just damn, Wes! You're simply...."

He chuckled as he lit his own cigarette. "No need to apologize. 'Cause if you're openly ogling, then I can too— and I'm looking forward to that myself." He waggled his eyebrows and sat down on the recliner next to me.

As he casually crossed his legs at the ankles I heard, "Grif? May I come up, sir?"

"Yep. We're up here, Pavel."

He appeared at the top of the stairs, gave a quick glance at the snake Wes was doing a poor job of concealing in his shorts and said, "Um, this all checks out, sir." He leaned over and handed me the envelope face down.

"Great, thank you, Pavel." I looked over at Wes, "Do you think you could do me a favor and throw this big Ukrainian's ass overboard? He fucking insists on insulting me."

Pavel was backing toward the stairs, "If there'll be nothing else, Grif, I'll take my leave. Please don't hesitate to call if you need me, sir," and then with a nod, "Mr. De Luca."

"Mr. Alexandr," Wes answered in return.

But, as he was about to take the first step down, he stopped and turned back, "Grif, there's one other thing," cutting a quick glance at Wes before looking back to me. "Mr. De Luca had some weaponry amongst his personal belongings. I've cataloged them on the first page," nodding toward the envelope, "and I took the liberty, to ensure their protection, of placing them in the ship's safe."

With a slight nod of his head he was gone.

I pulled the top sheet out and recognized Pavel's surprising elegant cursive.

2 Handguns

4 Knives

1 Mace Canister

1 Pair Handcuffs (law enforcement grade)

I passed the sheet to Wes, "Does this look accurate?"

He gave the list a glance and passed it back to me, "It's not everything I brought on board, but he's done an admirable job finding what he did. It's important that you know, I have another handgun, two more knives, and an electric stun gun that aren't listed. But, even if he'd known to look for them, I seriously doubt he would have been able to locate them."

I smiled and said, "It's not important. I realize it's not the answer you'd like to hear from me, but it's the truth."

"Would you like to talk business first, Grif? I mean, as much as I'd like to talk about more personal things, business might be not only easier, but it'll also give us some insight into one another as well."

"Sure."

He nodded his head at the folder lying on the small table between us. "First, I'm glad you had Pavel check out my file before we cast off. Next, I'm wondering if he is armed? And lastly, for now at least, I'd like to know your net worth. I ask this last question on a purely professional level; it'll give me an idea of how many man-hours we're talking about my company potentially taking on. As a credit to your financial folks, my staff wasn't able to pinpoint your exact net worth. I'll need to know that so I determine the scope of what I'm dealing with here."

I stubbed out my cigarette and lit another one—offering one to him, which he declined—and then took a long swallow of my drink.

"I tend to go with my gut when it comes to people. I understand that would make a lot of folks in your line of work uncomfortable—but it works for me. It's kept me safe and sane thus far. Pavel checking out your file, which isn't the same one you picked up from the desk clerk this morning—Matthew dropped a second copy by my room while you were packing—was to put Pavel at ease, not me. I don't allow Pavel to be armed. And, again, I'm guessing you'll likely have a differing opinion.

"Matthew and I have weekly meetings to discuss the estate's current financial standing—more frequently if necessary. Last week, everything combined—stocks, bonds, various companies, homes, vehicles, cash, etc.—we're at just over a billion. That number is up from the approximate figure of 750 million it was five years ago when I inherited the estate."

Wes looked out over ocean, let out a low whistle, and then picked up the pack of cigarettes.

The cell phone vibrated next to me.

"Excuse me, Wes."

I answered, "Yes, D? Yeah, that's fine. Um, northwest first, around the back of the Channel Islands before heading south...that look clear? Great. Thank you, Dalton."

As I laid the phone back down, the engines beneath us came to life with a quiet hum.

Wes was still looking out over the water and inhaled deeply from his cigarette before asking, "I know it's a bit early in the day, but what are the chances of getting some scotch?"

I chuckled, "No problem. Neat?"

"Rocks please."

I picked the phone back up, sent the text, and had no more than laid it back down when Lance appeared with a tray. It held a decanter of scotch, an ice bucket, two glasses, the fruit and cheese Dalton had mentioned, along with napkins and various utensils.

After setting it down, he nervously peered at Wes, and then to Wes' monster crotch, before settling his gaze more comfortably on my eyes, "Can I...can I...is there anything else I can get for you and your guest, Grif?"

"No. Thank you, Lance. I appreciate it," I said warmly, which elicited a very small smile in return, and he retreated.

As I reached for the decanter, I noticed Wes scornfully eyeing the empty space Lance had just created.

"Wes?"

"Yeah," he said turning toward me.

"I get he's attractive. And you get it. But he doesn't get it at all. Sure, I know he's not stupid and I know he understands, in theory, that people find him attractive, but I don't think he'll ever be in a place where he believes it himself...at least not for a very long time anyway."

He made a kind of snorting sound and then shook his head in disbelief.

I poured our drinks and handed one to him.

"I mentioned there was more to his story, more that wasn't mine to tell, but I'm gonna share a few words because it...well, I think it's important for you to have some understanding."

I briefly thought back to that chilly night when I'd found Lance and shuddered. No, I wasn't going into full details, but I could paint a decent picture with a few words.

"He was homeless, addicted to drugs, prostituting himself to simply survive, he's HIV positive—although undetectable for the last year—and has been diagnosed with social anxiety disorder—put simply, he's shy beyond reason. Needless to say, the prostitution wasn't going well for him, on several fronts.

"There's a therapist he sees twice a week, who travels with us if we're on extended trips, and he's come a long, long way since he allowed me in two years ago. He's a good person; he's kind, intelligent, wickedly funny, and despite everything he's been through, he's also incredibly compassionate."

I paused, as much to take a drag off my smoke, as to let what I'd said sink in. "Please don't scowl at him," I asked. "It could do him real harm. Please."

He sighed, drained his glass, and said quietly, "Well goddammit, don't I feel like a real fucktard. Sonofabitch."

"I didn't tell you so…. I don't want you to feel…."

"I know, Grif. I know."

"The very best thing you can do is simply offer a sincere smile. If you can't manage that, then please ignore him altogether. However, having been the recipient of your smile, I know first-hand it'd go infinitely farther than ignoring him."

"Grif, I don't normally go around ignoring people—or scowling at them, for that matter—but there's something about you. I mean, he's handsome, he clearly thinks the sun rises and sets with you, and this thing between us makes me feel…unusually possessive."

I sipped my drink and then refilled his. "Yes, he thinks a lot of me. We're close. I love him and I'm quite certain he loves me too—platonically."

I looked out over the ocean and saw, to the east; we were passing San Miguel, the most northern Channel Island.

"And the *possessive thing*…." I turned back and met his

eyes, and found I could do nothing more than smile.

Wes reached over and briefly ran a finger along my arm before resting it back in his lap. I found it incredibly intimate, and I longed for more of the light touch.

"I'm truly sorry about Lance. I'll make sure he never feels threatened by me. I promise."

"Thank you, Wes. Seriously."

I looked over at the pool and found the sparkling water irresistibly inviting. "Feel like a dip?" I asked, hoping the distraction would lighten the mood a little.

He glanced over at the water and then back to me, "Sure, but before we end the work topic, I want to say Pavel should always be carrying at least one weapon. Always. I'll have lots more to say about that—and other recommendations you should consider before making your final decision regarding a new securities firm. I mean, you do get you're a billionaire, right? There are some pretty scary people out there, Grif."

Yeah, I got it; I was rich, there were bad people out there, I needed protection. It was the single subject Matthew and I actually fought about. And if I were honest, Pavel and I, too. Hell, pretty much everyone and I had fought about it at one point or another.

I honestly didn't know what to do, and so, I chose to ignore the situation because it was working fine the way it was. It was so unlike everything else in my life; if I saw a challenge I did my best to overcome it—not hide from it.

"I understand, Wes. I really do. And you have some good ideas. I've been intentionally hiding my head in the sand on this one, and I don't know why."

I stood up, pulled my t-shirt over my head, and looked over to him. "Enough with the talk, at least for a bit, let's swim!"

I took a few steps, and at the pool's deep end, dove in. God, the water felt so good. I stayed submerged and swam toward the shallow end when I heard Wes dive in behind me. At the other end, I surfaced with both a splash and slightly burning lungs as I took in deep breaths. Moments later Wes popped up next to me.

Droplets ran from his nose and chin, his dark stubble glistened with water, and his chest hair was pressed flat against his body's sharply cut muscles. Damn, wet or dry, he was a sight.

"Man, the water feels really good. I guess I didn't realize how warm I was getting sitting up there," he said, as he shook his head, sending droplets flying everywhere.

I laughed, "Hey! No dogs allowed in the pool."

He grinned as my phone started buzzing on the table.

"I'll grab it for ya," he said, as he bound up out of the water.

"Thanks. Would you grab our drinks too?"

I watched him walk away and couldn't take my eyes off his firm, round ass. Damn, he looked so good in the suit. Then I remembered that particular pair; I'd ordered them from an adult catalog and once wet, they bordered on being see-through. Half way to the table, the phone stopped ringing but he grabbed it and the drinks and started his way back. When my eyes darted up from his crotch and met his, he gave me a perplexed look before glancing down to examine his suit.

He stopped and grinned at me, "Seriously? You've gotta be kidding; a see-through suit?"

I started laughing, "I swear to God I'd forgotten all about that—I swear."

He grabbed a towel off the nearest chair, dropped it near the edge, and then laid the phone and drinks down on it.

"Uh huh, right," he said, and winked at me.

In a surprisingly swift motion for someone his size, he pulled the trunks down to his ankles and then stepped out of them and splashed into the pool next to me.

With a teasing smile he said, "If you want to see me naked again, all you have to do is ask."

All you have to do is ask. How many times had Tate said those words to me before I finally believed them to be the simple truth. Initially, I'd expected every time I did ask, there'd be a rebuff waiting on the other end of my question. But it had never happened. Not once in four years had Tate ever said no to me—not once.

He'd done so much for me in those years and I missed him terribly. There were times when I felt his loss so completely it nearly consumed me. During those hopeless times, I was sure the overwhelming emptiness would always be part of me. I missed him every day, and there were times, when something reminded me of the intimacy we shared, that it felt like the air was literally being knocked out of me. But the man standing in the water next to me, he gave me a tiny bit of hope that maybe, just maybe, I wouldn't be alone forever.

Wes, mistaking my reminiscence for something else, said with a concerned tone, "Hey, I'll put them back on. I didn't mean to make you feel uncomfortable."

He reached for the suit and I caught his arm gently, "Nah, it's not that...I was just remembering. Someone else used to say the same thing to me and I was...fondly remembering him."

I reflexively reached up and fingered the pendant around

my neck. Wes saw the gesture and asked, "Tate?"

"Yeah," I smiled, "How much of my file mentioned him?"

Wes reached over and grabbed our glasses. He handed mine to me and then took a sip of his.

"Not much actually. I mean, I know very little about the two of you...um...as a couple. There was the usual stuff about the two of you independently. You were a couple, right? I mean, I got the distinct impression he was straight...but...," he let out a small sigh, "Look, Grif, I'll understand if there are things you'd rather not talk about. I don't have any right asking personal questions, and I certainly don't have any expectation you'll answer anything I may ask."

It was my turn to take a sip. As I brought the glass away from my lips, my free hand found his jaw and stroked the stubble there briefly. God, he was so handsome and so genuine. And every time I touched him, even for a moment, I felt tingly all over.

"Wes, there's not much of me I feel the need to hide. I've already shared the biggie," and then I gave a short laugh, "No pun intended."

I hopped out of the pool and said over my shoulder, "Gonna snag our smokes." I grabbed the pack, the ashtray, and then moved back and sat on the edge with my feet dangling in the water. Lighting up and taking a deep drag I said, "Yes, Tate was straight, and yes, we had sex."

"But I thought you said you were a virgin. Well, you didn't put it quite that succinctly, but I certainly got that impression."

"Perhaps it was a poor choice of words on my part; describing what Tate and I had as sex, I mean—not the me being a virgin part. I've never...been touched below the neck in a sexual way, Wes. And last night was honestly my first real kiss."

I averted my gaze to where my hands lay resting on the pool's edge between my spread knees and studied the burning cigarette stuck in my fingers. I simply didn't have the courage to look him in the eye. What if I saw something I didn't want to; pity, or God knows what. What must he think of me—a twenty-eight-year-old virgin? How could he want that? Fuck, what was I doing here? What was I doing with him?

Peripherally, I caught movement and then, with my eyes still down, his torso standing less than a foot away.

"Grif, I wanted your—our—first kiss to be special, something you'd always remember," he said softly. "And I want every one after to be just as special—just as memorable. I'm wondering if I might ask for one now?"

My eyes flew up in sudden anger, and I spat out, "Why? Because you feel pity? Or, because you're attracted to freaks?" Raising my voice even more, I continued. "Why, Wes? Why would you want to kiss me—to be here with me? Or is it the money? Is that it?"

Sudden footsteps pounded the stairs and Pavel burst onto the pool deck looking both alarmed and ready to fight, "Mr. Griffin, sir? Is everything...?"

Wes, quickly, but confidently, took the steps out of the water, two-at-a-time, and stopped at the edge—directly across the pool from Pavel—naked with his arms spread out, "I'll let Grif speak for himself, Pavel, but we're only talking. I assure you, he's completely safe."

Oh fuck! Great, just great! I'm yelling at the kindest man I've ever met, saying horrible things, and Pavel comes running because he think I'm being killed or something.

"Pavel, everything is fine, honest. As Wes said, we were talking and I got a bit overexcited. But thank you."

He looked between Wes and me once more and then respectfully tipped his head, "I sincerely apologize for the interruption, sir. I thought I heard...I wanted to be sure."

I nodded in understanding, "And I appreciate it, I really do."

He backed down the stairs with a *Yes, sir.*

Wes stepped back into the pool and took up residence at my knees, "Hey," he said softly.

I clucked in embarrassment, "Well, I bet you never thought asking for a kiss would be accompanied by me yelling at you, insulting you, and calling your good character into question."

I reached over stubbing out the cigarette and picked up my nearly empty scotch glass.

"I remember the asking for a kiss part," he said slowly, "but things get a bit blurry after that." He acted as if he were actually confused by a loss of memory.

I sheepishly smiled down at him, "Fuck, Wes, I'm categorically sorry. I—,"

"Grif...," he paused looking down at my knees and then back up at me, "can I place my hands on your knees?"

I nodded and then remembered his fondness for the spoken word and said simply, "Yes."

Without taking his eyes from mine he gently placed his palms on my knees.

"Can I ask you something?"

"Sure."

"Did you read my file, the one Matthew put together,

the one Pavel read?"

I shook my head, "No, I didn't. As I said, I generally go with my gut feeling about folks. Requesting the file was a knee-jerk reaction. And one I was pretty much over as soon as I made it."

He clucked, "Yeah, well, that's a topic for another conversation."

Although his hands never moved, his thumbs had begun slowly stroking the inside of my knees and the small movement—that small, gentle gesture felt so good. It felt loving, and kind, and it also had an immediate effect on Junior.

He continued, "If you had read it—and Matthew and his team did a rather comprehensive job, by the way—you'd know I don't need money. Granted, I'm not a billionaire, not even close, but I've done okay for myself."

I tried to interrupt. "Wes, I—,"

He took one hand from my knee—the feeling of loss was instantaneous—and held it up as if to say, *hold on, let me finish.*

"No, you said some things—and even though you may wish you'd phrased them differently, perhaps—they're clearly things you have concerns about nonetheless. And, thus, I need to address them, okay?"

"Sure," I conceded with a small nod.

"The kiss, and why I want to kiss you again, and why I accepted your invitation to get to know one another better? Well, that's easy; I like you, as a person, Marcus Griffin. I also find you handsome, and beautiful, and sexy."

I raised my arms up and flexed first my biceps, then chest, and lastly my abs with a grin. "Yep, sex on a stick," I laughed softly.

"Ooo, I like the whole flexing thing."

I was suddenly self conscious and brought my arms back down.

"And that caused a blush. I'll have to remember that," he said with a grin.

He reached up and playfully tweaked a nipple.

"Ohhh," I groaned involuntarily and momentarily closed my eyes—surprising us both.

He raised a sexy eyebrow and grinned, "Well, there's a little something I'll certainly keep in mind for later; Grif's nipples are a definite erogenous zone."

I blushed so intensely I felt I might spontaneously combust at any moment. Wes' gaze fell to my chest and back up again.

"And your chest gets so red too—so damn hot!"

He cleared his throat and swallowed.

"Now, the more serious topic; I don't have, as you so unflatteringly categorized yourself, a 'freak fetish.'"

He briefly looked down at his hands covering my knees and then back into my eyes, "Think about it, how could I have such a fetish—and, further, have it apply to you—when I honestly don't have any idea of your actual size?"

He looked down into the shimmering water and I followed his eyes; he was hard. Looking back up at me he said, "I like you, Grif—not your size."

I wanted to believe him, I really did, "But, Wes…," I started but then stopped and bit my lip. "I believe I believe that—I do. But you're a man—a gay man. And gay men like dicks—man-sized dicks." Turning my head to the side, "I can't offer you that."

I turned, reached down and took one of his hands from

my knee. Separating one of his fingers from the others, I held it up and said, "This, Wes. This is about what I can offer you. This…," I breathed in deeply and felt a sorrowful resignation, "this is about the size."

He took my hand, turned it over, and bringing it to his lips placed a tender kiss to my palm.

"But, Grif, that's not all you bring. Just like, hopefully, my dick isn't all I bring."

He released my hand and placed his back on my leg—a bit higher this time—and took a step closer, his sides actually touching my knees, and I felt my pulse quicken.

"You also bring the rest of you; you bring goodness, kindness, compassion, generosity, intelligence, passion, drive, humor, playfulness," he paused with a frisky smile, "should I continue? Because I could go on at least until sunset."

I blushed and glanced down, "Nah, I believe I've got the gist of it; you think I'm the bee's knees."

He chuckled, "Yep, I do." And then more huskily he said, "And then there's the blushing and something…more. Something I hope means you might possibly appreciate the kink I like to occasionally indulge in."

I brought my eyes to his. God, he had such soft, kind eyes.

"The tears?" I asked hesitantly.

He nodded and said, "But can I ask something first? Would you mind telling me more about what you and Tate did, sexually?"

"Well," I started carefully, "there's not really a lot to tell. Although, I honestly think people would believe it was—perverted."

I brought a hand up to brush the hair off my forehead

and realized I was shaking. Wes took it in his, "If you'd rather not tell me...,"

I shook my head, "No, it's just I've never told anyone. But...but, I'd like you to know what my experience is. But also, I'd like you to know what he did for me—what he gave me."

"Then I'd like to hear it."

"To boil it down to its most basic, I serviced him. He was always naked whenever we were home, and I was always clothed. I could ask for it, or just touch him, or look at him, or service him anytime I wanted—he never said no. He never turned me down—not once, Wes. And only a hand-full of times, in four years, did he ask for it; the *when* was always my choice. He wanted me to know it was my decision—gave me that authority—and he gave me the gift of knowing he'd never reject me. Some weeks it'd only be once or twice. Then there were other days—a football Sunday for instance—when the only time his cock would leave my mouth was when he went to take a leak. Of course he was only human; even a young twenty-something horny dude can only come so many times in a day. But, on those days, I didn't care if he came once or six times—I just wanted the feel of his dick in my mouth—I liked it, and Junior liked it too."

"Junior?" he asked.

I nodded to my crotch, "Junior. Tate and I had several names for him."

"Ah," he said. "Junior is...well, sort of derogatory, isn't it?"

I started to look down but his finger caught my chin and brought my eyes back to his.

"Yes, it is. I...well, I liked that he knew I was small and

sometimes when I was servicing him—and only then, Wes—it turned me on when he…made fun of it."

I heard his breath catch and decided at this point I had nothing to lose and went all in. "I liked when he called me things too—like…," I paused, unsure if I could actually vocalize the very private part of me that only Tate had known and accepted.

"Like?" Wes delicately prompted.

"Like fag and cocksucker," I nearly murmured in embarrassment.

I felt his hand begin to shake as he continued to hold my chin.

"Grif…I…," He swallowed visibly and loudly. "I can't even begin to tell you how turned on I am. To think—to hope—that maybe you'd allow me to do something similar. When we know each other better, of course. Having confirmation that what I felt from you…that it wasn't just my imagination or wishful thinking. Well, that's huge."

I had a sudden sense of clarity, and asked, "So when you said you like tears, that you even like to be the cause of those tears, you were speaking more about emotional pain; humiliation? Or were you talking about physically hurting someone—hurting me?"

"Well, not like *punching kind of hurting*, if that's what you're asking. Sexual discomfort—pain, if you will—is something I enjoy when it furthers the emotional stuff. But no, not like striking someone just to be striking them. I'd never…."

He looked down at my chest and then back up to my eyes. Then, ever so slowly, he took each of my nipples between his fingers and gently rubbed.

Faintly, I moaned "Oooo," and closed my eyes.

I could hear the closeness in his voice when he asked,

"You like that, Grif? Feel good?"

I mumbled, "Uh huh, feels…oh…feels really, really nice, Wes."

"How does it feel? Can you describe it for me?"

I swallowed, "Um, never felt…anything like it. Ahh…makes me want to arch my back…to lean into it…to get more. It's sending tingles of pleasure straight down to Junior…like he and my nipples are connected somehow."

I opened my eyes as I felt his touch glide away and the sensations sadly stopped.

He smiled wickedly, "Yeah, that feels good. But after, say fifteen minutes, where that may be the only stimulus involved, I promise you it'd become rather painful—hot, but painful—for both your nipples and for...Junior...as well; I imagine you'd be begging me to stop—and I likely wouldn't."

He dropped his hands into the water and brought them wet back to my chest. After briefly rubbing them over my nipples he rested them again on my thighs—even higher this time.

He became much more serious, but not the least bit unkind, and said, "I feel I need to be very clear on this, Grif; there are times, sexually, when I enjoy being downright cruel. Where doing so excites me like nothing else can. However, the overwhelming majority of the time I enjoy *normal* sex. But there are times when I exceedingly enjoy the other too."

He leaned in and brought his lips to mine. The kiss was tender, but as he pulled away, he briefly sucked my bottom lip between his—it left behind his spicy taste when we separated. My. Fucking. God!

"As for this very moment, I'm gonna do a few laps in

this pool and try to get myself under control. It's either that, or you're not gonna be a virgin much longer," he said with a sexy wink and pushed away from me.

The phone rang next to me. I picked it up as I watched Wes' strong strokes take him across the small pool and then begin back.

It took me a few more seconds, but I was finally able to hit the answer button and speak. "Hey Lance."

"Hi Grif. I'm calling to see how far away from dinner we are. Will you and your guest be ready in thirty minutes, or should I ask the kitchen to delay a bit?"

"Nah, a half-hour sounds good. Would it be too much trouble to set up the table on my cabin's starboard patio? I'd kinda like to watch the sunset over dinner."

"No, no trouble at all."

"Great. Thank you, Lance."

I watched Wes do a few more laps—with his lightly-furred ass sitting atop the water as he moved back and forth between the shallower end where I sat to the other side. As he neared, I asked, "Are you hungry? They tell me dinner's about thirty minutes away, but I can ask them to postpone it a bit if you'd rather wait."

"Sounds great," he said, as he stepped out of the pool.

I looked up and saw what I considered, and I'm sure many others would as well, perfection. He stood gloriously naked, save for the band around his left wrist, wet, and breathtaking.

"Um, Grif? You're doing that staring thing again."

I glanced up and saw his beaming face.

"Oh...um...sorry...it's just...."

He broke into a wide grin, "Oh, no, please don't

apologize."

❧

We'd both taken a quick shower and redressed in shorts and t-shirts. Lance had set a nice casual table with a few hurricane candles in the center and dinner consisted of whitefish with a mango-papaya chutney over wild rice and broccoli. For dessert there was of course my favorite: ice cream. We split a pint of Ben and Jerry's…much to my dismay.

"Hey, you're eating it all," I said in mock protest.

He laughed, "What are you talking about, I've barely had three or four bites."

"Seems like a lot more," I said through a mouthful of delicious *New York Super Fudge Chunk* but held the carton out to him so he could dig another spoonful out.

"Um, Wes? Can I ask you a personal question?"

He licked his spoon clean and set it down, "Sure. Anything you'd like."

I continued to eat, "Have you ever been in love?"

He looked away uncomfortably and stared out at the darkening ocean. He was quiet for so long I was about to say something—anything—to break the silence when he turned back and said, "Grif, I'll talk about anything you want, but I don't really want to talk about…."

Then he looked down at the table and shook his head.

"That's not fair," he mumbled to himself. "Yes. I…loved before. Depending on the depth we're talking about, I've loved a couple of times. In high school…well, I guess I'd classify that as great fondness, not the type of love you're asking about. At the beginning of my military career there was someone—very briefly. The last one was a few years back. We were at different places in our lives and…things were complicated. His name was Thomas and he…died."

He looked down at the table, grabbed the pack of cigarettes, and shook one out. Taking a deep draw after lighting it, he exhaled through his nose and said, "He'd been sick for a long time and I didn't even know until…."

I reached over and laid my hand on his. He looked down at them and continued, "Grif, you can ask me anything you want. But I can't…I'd really rather not talk about Thomas just yet, if that's okay?"

He looked up and I saw his eyes were glassy and he tried to quirk a grin at me but it failed miserably.

"I promise I'll talk about it. But, it's really something I'd rather do on my own time."

He got up from the table and leaned his back against the railing. The look on his face was clearly asking for understanding.

"If you feel you need me to, I can tell you now, but…."

I tried for a light tone—but not too light, I didn't want him to get the impression I was being flip, "Nah, Wes, it's all good. I'm interested, but I can wait—for as long as you need."

With the sun having set, the temperature dropped and I shivered a bit.

"Thank you for understanding. Are you getting cold? You wanna go inside?"

I nodded and stood up, "Yeah, if you don't mind?"

I slid the door open and headed straight for the dresser to find a pair of thick socks. Sitting on the bed, I was pulling the second one on when I realized Wes had shut the door but hadn't moved any further into the room. He glanced at the bed and then to me.

"Grif?" he asked hesitantly.

"Yeah?"

"Do you think we could lie on the bed together?"

I looked at the bed and then back to him with complete uncertainty.

"We can stay clothed. I'd just…like to lay with you."

I slowly nodded my head. "Yeah, sure. That'd be okay."

I swung my feet up while he walked around and got in the other side. We fumbled around a bit, laughing at the awkwardness, and finally settled on him spooned up against my back.

"Comfortable?" he asked into my hair.

"Yes."

And I was, it felt so nice to have his strong body against mine, and I could smell his scent so much stronger close up.

He repositioned himself and, in doing so, his hand lightly brushed my lower abdomen. My entire body stiffened, and I instantly froze.

Wes noticed and said softly, but with assurance, "Grif, I made you a promise. You can trust me, I won't touch you—I swear."

"Wes…," I started and then swallowed and waited for my brain to catch up with my mouth, "Please don't take it personally. I know you've promised. And, more importantly, I believe you. But this is so new to me…and as much as I'd like to, I can't just stop being scared because you've made a promise. And believe me, I'm terrified."

"I understand, I honestly do," he said, and placed a

quick kiss to the back of my neck. "If there's anything I can do or say to put you at ease?"

I shook my head, "I can't think of anything. But…um…I'd really like it if you held me tighter."

"That I can do with enormous pleasure, babe."

He snuggled in, and we both fell asleep.

∾

I awoke to three things I'd never awakened to before: a man placidly snoring next to me; an arm wrapped snugly around my chest; and what was unmistakably a huge erection sporadically grinding into my lower back. I wasn't sure which of the three I was enjoying more.

I rolled over in his arms, trying to move as little as possible, so I could see his face without waking him up. He seemed to be a pretty sound sleeper as I accomplished all this without him missing a single beat of his soft snoring. Laying there on my side, gazing into his handsome face, I couldn't help but think all of this was going to end badly, but I felt strangely helpless to stop the eventual train wreck ahead.

Resigned, I decided to get up and call Captain Dalton to see where we were. Once back in San Diego, I knew I'd be able to gain some perspective and think more clearly.

I took one last look at his relaxed, sleeping face—so rugged and masculine—and was about to get up when I noticed his t-shirt had ridden up to reveal both his furry, strong abs and about three inches of his stiff dick peeking out the top of his short's waistband.

I knew I shouldn't, but I couldn't help myself. I reached down and ran my index finger over the smooth skin and felt it surge under my touch. A quick glance up told me he was still sleeping and I decided on one more touch before making my call.

This time I pressed a bit more firmly, with a downward momentum, and the foreskin slid completely back to reveal the large, light brown head. I ran a finger over the top—feeling the moist slit—and had the overwhelming desire to taste it. I brought my finger to my tongue and was slightly disappointed when I wasn't able to taste anything.

I placed the wet finger back on his head and started gently rubbing the slick saliva around the top when a sleepy, sexy voice said, "Mr. Griffin, if this is what it's gonna be like waking up next to you every day, please count me in."

I blushed and glanced up into his smiling eyes and then focused on his lips, "I'm sorry...I just...it was just there looking so appealing and...needy. But, it was rude of me."

And as much as I meant what I was saying, I couldn't seem to make my slick finger stop its gentle caressing.

His arm was still draped over my side and his hand had begun tracing my spine—it felt so good. I'd never laid with a man like this, allowed someone, to touch me like this. So many pleasant, new sensations.

"Oh, make no mistake, I wasn't complaining," he said.

He took his hand from my back and ran strong fingers over my jaw.

"God, Grif. Looking at you makes me ache. I want so badly to make you feel good."

I grinned, "Well, I'm feeling pretty good right now."

He gave me a sardonic smile, "Believe me, babe, this is nothing. I can offer you so much more. I'm just not sure yet how to get there."

My fingers, still gently teasing his cock, had gone from wet with my saliva to dry and then back to wet with his pre-cum.

"I want that, too. I really do. But, like you, I don't know how to start."

He leaned in closer and brought his lips to mine.

"How about we start with this?"

His kiss was soft and tentative at first, but I wanted more; I wanted to taste and be filled by him. I brushed my tongue across his lips, and he eagerly opened up. His warm tongue swept over mine, and I breathed in deeply to take in his scent.

His hand moved up, past my shoulder blades, and cupped the back of my head. His fingers slid through my hair as my fingers went from rubbing the head of his cock to playing with his foreskin. Fuck, I loved the smoothness of it. The way I could gently tug and pull on it; it was like cock with a bonus!

I pulled back and gasped for air, "Jesus, Wes, does kissing always feel this good? If so, I've really been missing out."

He reached down between us, and with a gentle grip took my hand off his straining dick.

"Babe, I'm slightly embarrassed to admit this, but I can't take much more without coming. I'm usually good at maintaining control, but you fucking make me crazy hot."

I looked down at his straining cock and licked my lips.

"Wes, I wanna…,"

"I know you do, babe. It's practically written all over your face, and it looks so goddamn good on you. But I have an idea I'd like to explore, if you'll trust me."

I nodded. "Um, okay. I guess."

With a quick kiss he slid away from me and off the bed. Pulling the t-shirt off first and then dropping his shorts he stood resplendently nude. My breath caught as I stared at him.

He walked over to my side of the bed and held out a hand to me. I took it and was pulled to my feet.

With a quick, deep kiss he said, "Grif, just trust that I'll keep my promise, okay?"

I looked into his kind eyes and saw the small laugh lines around them, the sexy smile and nodded, "I promise to try and remember that, Wes."

"Then we're half way there."

He hooked the hem of my t-shirt in both hands and brought it over my head and off. Looking down at my chest, he mumbled *beautiful* before his fingers moved to the button of my shorts.

He paused and asked, "I assume you have a jock on?"

"Never leave home without it," I tried for nonchalance, but failed as my voice cracked.

He looked down and easily popped the button. I grabbed his wrist, but I didn't pull it away.

"Wes…," I felt my eyes beginning to tingle, and my throat growing tight, "I'm scared." My voice was so low and indistinct I was certain he hadn't even heard me.

He looked up and met my eyes, "Okay, two things, babe; one, fuck you're so beautiful right now, and that fear in your eyes does crazy things to me, and two, why are you frightened? I gave you my—,'

"I'm scared of losing you if you see," I blurted out.

"Hey…," he said, as he brushed my hair back from my

forehead, "You've got your jock on. There's no way I can see. So put that worry out of your head—and just feel the moment, okay? And, more importantly, you won't lose me when I do see. There'll come a time when you'll believe that too."

He moved his hands back down to my shorts, slid the zipper open with an amazingly, practiced adeptness, and my shorts fell to the carpet.

My yellow jock practically glowed in the cozily lit cabin as if a spot light was shining on it. I barely had time to notice though as Wes stepped around me, pulled back the duvet and piled the pillows up against the headboard.

Back in front of me he whispered in my ear, "Grif, please trust me. I'll take care of you. Climb up on the bed and lean back against the pillows with your legs crossed. Don't think about it, babe, just do it."

His tone was kind, yet firm. I did as he asked. But, as I sat there, both hands covering my crotch, I felt completely exposed. And something else; I felt excited beyond words.

He grabbed the duvet and pulled it up over my knees so it rested against my stomach, and climbed up on the bed. Kneeling in front of me, just out of reach, he gave me a caring look and asked, "You good?"

"Yep," I said with a smile.

He nodded his head and winked at me, "So, we've already established you...like to look...to watch, right?" Then, to bring the point home, he casually laced his fingers behind his head and gently flexed his furry chest and ripped abs.

I studied his torso, got lost in his beauty, and completely forgot there'd been a question posed.

Slowly, he slid one hand over his muscled chest. Once

his thick fingers found a nipple, they took hold. Twisting and plucking, he sighed in pleasure before asking, "You like to watch, don't you?"

I didn't look up at him but nodded my head—completely transfixed on his hard nipple being gently pinched and pulled.

"Words, Grif—use words, babe."

I tore my eyes from his hand and chest and looked up at him, "Yes, Wes. I really like to watch. God, your body is so...incredibly sexy. Your big arms, your fucking amazing chest—with the exact right amount of hair—your sculpted abs...."

"Grif, I can't see Junior at all. Right?"

I looked down, knowing full well I was not only covered by my jock, but the thick duvet as well.

"No, you can't see," I acknowledged.

He slid his hand down, over his abs, and let a thumb hook his cock—right at the base—and pushed down and let it back up. His dick bounced up and down. Wrapping his middle finger around the underside he pulled the foreskin back and then let it slide forward again. I whimpered.

"Feels so good, Grif."

God, he looked so good, and I was so hard. I wanted to touch him.

"Wes, move closer?"

He was gently stroking, pre-cum making the head shine.

He nodded, "I will. I'll move closer so you can touch but with one condition. You put a hand under the covers and touch yourself while you're touching me. Whatever you do to me you also do to yourself. Remember, Grif, I can't see you."

My eyes shot up to his.

"Trust?" he asked.

Hesitantly, I slid my hand under the covers and nodded up at him, "Trust, Wes."

I'd never—not the first time nor any time after—touched myself during sex. I always feared it would lead to the guy wanting more—if I didn't 'go there' then, more often than not, the thought never crossed the dude's mind. He inched closer on his knees until I could reach out and touch him. My hand circled around his thick hardness, and I began a slow stroke.

"Oh yeah, babe, feels good," he whispered, as he watched my hand slide on his big cock. After a few moments he said, "But, you're not playing fair; I don't see your other arm moving." Then with a mischievous grin he continued, "Or does that mean you're done with mine?" and started slowing pulling away from my touch.

My thumb and index finger managed to catch his foreskin, and I held it firmly preventing a full retreat.

"I'll play by the rules. Get back over here," I said with a determined smile.

Over the next fifteen minutes I stroked, pulled, pinched and rubbed both of our dicks. We were both breathing heavy and leaking like crazy when he moved a bit closer and said heatedly, "I think you'll enjoy this."

Slowly reaching over, he took each of my nipples in his fingers—stroking and caressing. Electricity shot through me, flowed over every nerve ending, and landed in one place; my dick. I'd never felt such pleasure.

I continued stroking us, at a much more frantic pace, and looked up at him, "Oh my God, Wes. Feels so good.

I'm gonna...."

"Oh, babe, you look so fucking good. Yeah, shoot for me. I wanna watch your face as you come."

That was all it took—hearing him say he wanted to see me come. I arched my back as my dick shot the first stream and thrust my chest forward. Whatever the hell he was doing to my nipples intensified and spurt after spurt of warm cum filled my jock. Moments later, long, white ropes of Wes' seed hit my chest, and the sound of his growling pleasure filled the cabin.

He flopped over on the bed next to me, and we both stretched our legs out with mutual groans.

"Please don't get the wrong idea; that was fucking amazing, and I do wanna kiss and cuddle and whisper words of affection and all that shit. But my legs! I can't remember when I've knelt that long, or even if I've ever knelt that long before," he said with a wry smile.

I grabbed a pillow, shoved it under his head, and stretched out sliding up next to him, his cum slick between our bodies. Laying my head on his firm chest, I breathed out contentedly, "I know what you mean—on both fronts. Both of my legs are trembling and, Wes, that was the best hands-down-nothing-even-comes-close orgasm of my life!"

His hand gently massaged my shoulder, "Um, you're all sticky and um...it's kinda hot," he said with a chuckle. "There are even better orgasms on the way, Grif. I promise you," he said into the top of my head and my hair ruffled. He seemed to do that a lot—and I liked it.

"Not that that wasn't amazing, babe—watching you come was about the most satisfying thing I've ever experienced—but I know we've barely touched upon what we'll eventually share. I feel it. I've never been more sure of anything."

To my surprise, I believed him.

≈

"Let's take a shower," Wes said after we'd laid there kissing for what seemed like hours. I never dreamt kissing could be so fucking awesome.

"Um, Wes," I said hesitantly. There was no way I was getting into a shower, or any other place which required I get naked with him.

"You can keep your jock on, babe, right? I mean, you went swimming in it today, didn't you?"

Another deep kiss—tongues gently stroking one another, lips nibbling, he even licked my closed eyelids at one point—which caused me to completely forget what we'd been talking about.

"Come on, Grif...I promise it'll be good," he said so sincerely I knew there wasn't a chance in hell I was going to say no.

"Okay, but you promise—,"

"The promise is in place until the day you ask me to either touch or to look...and that day will come. So, honestly, the only thing you have to ask yourself is if you trust me yet. And if today isn't the day—the day to trust me enough not to need a re-promise," he paused to rub a thumb over my eyebrow, "then ask away...as many times as you need to, I don't mind. I'll never intentionally mislead or lie to you."

The things he said to me sometimes—how he knew exactly what I needed to hear—it made me feel so special, so wanted.

I nodded. "Yes, okay. I'm still scared…but…I find myself so willing to take chances with you. Chances I've never taken—or even thought of taking—with anyone else, and it surprises me." Laughing at the irony of what I was about to say next, "And realizing I'm willing to take those chances also scares me."

As he looked into my eyes, his thumb left my brow and ran gently across my bottom lip, "And, tell me if I'm wrong, but the fear I might somehow see Junior makes you even harder, doesn't it?"

The mischievous thumb moved lower, hovered just above one of my nipples, and barely grazed it—over and over.

I moaned with the teasing.

I cautiously nodded my head. "I've never been able to admit that to anyone, but yes, it does. As much as I feared it—did everything in my power to ensure that it never happened—I desperately wanted to somehow be exposed to one of the Grindr dudes and have him…." I broke off. I only had so much courage…could only share so much.

He picked up my thought. "And have him humiliate you?"

I nodded, but didn't speak.

"Grif…," he mildly chastised.

I summoned up the courage to give him the words he wanted. "Yes, Wes. That's what I wanted. But there's no way I'd ever trust one of those strangers to…," I shook my head—a bit more vehemently than I had intended.

He flopped over on his back, looked up at the ceiling, and smiled as widely as I'd ever seen him smile.

Turning his head toward me with a naughty grin, "Grif, I

fucking promise you we're gonna have the best time—the fucking best. It may be weeks from now, or even months, but the day will come when we'll both be ready for me to give you something only someone you trust implicitly can. And please, understand that just knowing it will happen—eventually—is all I could've ever hoped for; love and the occasional darkness."

"Love?" I managed to eek out.

"Oh, without a doubt. I already know I'm gonna love you, and you're gonna love me. The question of 'darkness' was really the only thing I was a bit uncertain about. But now…" And he grinned like Charlie holding a fucking Golden Ticket.

"Can we please find a better word for it than *darkness*?" I asked, scrunching my nose. "It makes me think of Satanism or something. This is something…well…on those occasions when Tate and I had less than Vanilla sex, I really enjoyed. And yeah, in a crazy terrified way, I'm looking forward to perhaps doing something like that with you—someday. And if we do, I want to use a word I like saying. You know, something that makes me smile."

He looked at me quizzically for a moment, and then leaned over and gave me a quick smile and a kiss, "Come on, let's talk about it while I'm rubbing my soapy hands all over your hard…," My apprehensive gaze shot up to his to see an evil grin spread across his face. "…body…all over your hard body"

He walked toward the bathroom and said over his shoulder, "Yeah, this is gonna be fun; the shower tonight and the eventual *less than Vanilla* that'll blow both our socks off."

～

We didn't talk much in the shower. Wes washed me from head to toe, minus the front and back bits, so thoroughly and sensually I feared I was going to shoot on the spot, with no stimulation to Junior at all.

When he reached my backside, slick soapy hands moved up and down my crack, sliding between my cheeks, every so often grazing the sensitive skin of my entrance.

My arms were spread wide, palms against the cool tile, with my back arched and my legs spread even wider. I shook my head back and forth and didn't care that I probably looked like a wanton slut. God, it felt *so* good.

Surprising even myself, I hoarsely croaked out, "Chocolate."

"Chocolate?" he whispered, clearly distracted by what he was doing to my hole. He'd kneeled down, *for a better view*, he'd said. His palms held my cheeks firmly spread apart, and a slick finger ran over and over the soft skin, and occasionally dipped just inside.

"Jesus, Grif, your ass is...God...fuck!"

I swallowed loudly, "Yes. For...um...darkness...*ohmigod that feels good, Wes!* You know, chocolate is something I really enjoy and...*oh, yes, please do that again, please*...and we're all familiar with the term 'Vanilla' to describe a particular kind of sex, so...*Jesus, yes*...so Chocolate makes sense on several levels."

"Sounds good. Chocolate it is," he agreed distractedly. "Have you ever...played back here, Grif? You know, with a toy or anything?"

I nodded and had to concentrate on words, "Yes, I have a toy that gets quite a bit of use. I really enjoy it, but...well quite obviously, I haven't had the real thing."

I felt him rise behind me. "Stay there, babe."

Warm water spayed over my back and ass rinsed away the soapy suds. After a few moments, a slick, wet tongue on my hole not only signaled he was back, but also made me jump a bit.

I had always wondered when I did this to Tate, exactly how it would feel to be on the receiving end. Now I understood why he'd enjoyed it so much; it was fucking heaven! His long, slow laps, and occasional nips, had my legs shaking.

"Oh. My. God, Wes—jeez, that feels so good."

His muffled replied came, "I'm really glad because I'm certainly enjoying doing it." Then he asked between laps, "Grif, have you ever had occasion to be tested—for HIV—I mean?"

"Yeah," I breathed out, "three weeks ago…required for my life insurance. You know, billionaire and all that shit. It was negative…but with oral being the only thing…Jesus, Wes, fuck!"

He began mixing the long, slow laps with heavy sucking and chewing. I'd never felt anything so wonderful—or been so fucking hard—in my life!

"Spread your legs further, and bend your knees more…I want more, Grif!"

More? Jeez, how much more could he get? But, I complied.

"Oh, fuck yeah! You look fucking hot, babe." His finger stroked my slick hole.

I felt his knuckles briefly brush the back of my jock-clad nuts, and I tensed up. He noticed, placed his lips on my ass cheek and calmly said, "It was only a slip. I promise.

Nothing more than a slip, Grif," his fingers never missing a stroke over my slick opening.

I nodded, and whispered, "Okay."

"Arch your back further—yeah, that's it. Damn, Grif, so hot! And how long since you've had a Grindr hookup, before me?"

"Huh? Oh...um...it's getting really difficult to think, Wes."

I felt him grin against my ass, "Try, babe?"

"Um...about four months I think. On a business trip in New Orleans, during Mardi Gras."

Mercifully—and sadly—he stopped. Slow, wet kisses started at my lower back and eventually ended at the side of my neck. With his chest pressed up against my back, his cock pressing between my crack, and his tongue licking the back of my ear he said, "I get tested every three months—negative—and I haven't been with anyone in over two years."

"Two years?" I asked, not managing to keep the surprise out of my voice.

"We can talk about it later. Right now, I just need to know if we're gonna trust each other, Grif."

I grabbed the bottle of conditioner and handed it over my shoulder to him, "Yes, Wes."

Placing my forehead back to the tile, I pleaded, "Please!"

In a more serious tone, he said, "I guess it's a bit late to be asking about this, but, Grif, are you sure this is how you want your first time?" Placing more tender kisses to my neck, "Here? Now? In this shower, with me?"

Was he serious? What kind of man stopped to think about that sort of thing when another guy's ass was poised right in front of him—begging to get fucked? My heart swelled. God, I was beginning to wonder what it'd be like to keep him. He was amazingly strong and masculine, yet incredibly sensitive. But, Junior pushed to the forefront and vanquished those fanciful thoughts; I'd only end up broken if I let myself dream. I pushed from the wall, instinctively dropping a hand down to cover the front of my wet jock, and turned in his arms to face him.

His heated eyes held more than desire; I recognized concern, honesty, and affection. Every time I looked at him—everything I saw in him—kept reinforcing my nearly instant impression of him; he's being real—he's the embodiment of everything you ever dreamed of, but never let yourself believe was possible.

Placing a palm against his furry chest, I tamped down the desire to convey what my heart was feeling and instead said, "Wes, I love how you want me to be sure, but I've never been more sure of anything; I want you—right here, right now."

Reaching down, I took hold of one of his nipples and gently rolled it around between my fingers. The effect was immediately apparent, as his dick twitched with appreciation. I teased with a sly grin, "But, if you don't want to…well…I may just have to take Dalton up on one of his many offers. Because, unlike Lance, he's made it abundantly clear, I'm his for the asking."

He growled; a serious, low, intimidating sound. Grabbing an ass cheek in each hand, pulling our bodies tightly together, and pushing me back against the tile, he murmured, "Mine!"

I looked up at him with a smile. His eyes were seductive and intent. "Well, I'm not sure about all that. But I'm certainly interested in seeing what your intentions are," I stood up taller and seized his bottom lip between my teeth. I needed to get this back to *fucking* and not feeling. Holding his lip and taking hold of his nipples again, it only took a few seconds of worrying both before hearing a rumble to know I'd accomplished my goal.

"Wanna show me?" I asked.

With a bit more force than I'd expected, he spun me around and almost snarled into the side of my face, "Don't tease me if you're even the slightest bit unsure you'll be able to take what I can give." He bit into the back of my shoulder to drive the point home.

I arched my back and pushed my ass into his crotch in response to the slight pain and moaned, "Aw, fuck yeah!"

A soft tongue replaced the sharp teeth and soothed the burn. "I want you so bad, Grif—but I also want it to be good for you. Please promise me you'll say something if at any point you feel uncomfortable, or if you feel pain, okay?" he asked, as I heard the conditioner top pop and then felt strong, slick fingers brushing over my entrance.

I breathed with heavy anticipation, "Wes, I'm a man, not a boy. I can take it. I want it."

"I know you're a man, babe. If you were a boy, we wouldn't be here. But it's been a long time since…since I've had…Chocolate. And that's not what this is…not what I want this to be. So, I just don't want to get carried away and scare you or hurt you. That's all. This is your first time, and I want it to be perfect."

"Wes! Please! Stick your fucking cock in me—now!" I demanded.

My ability to speak vanished, as I felt the head of his cock push past my outer ring of muscles. It was uncomfortable and burned, but I knew from playing with the toy, the sensation would soon go from mild discomfort to astounding pleasure. What I hadn't counted on was how fucking big he was. "Jeez, Wes, *so* big," I managed to gasp out.

He stilled, reached around, and took hold of my nipples. "So tight, babe. So good. You okay?"

Fuck, when he did that to my nipples it just…just made me want to open up further. It felt so good; pleasure, mixed with a bit of pain, shooting straight down to Junior. I nodded and he started inching forward again. God, the sense of being filled, of being taken, increased with every inch he slid into me.

"Wes," I gasped, "Please don't stop what you're doing to my nipples…feels so fucking good. Makes my dick…kinda hurt a little. So amazing!"

"Yeah?" he husked at my ear. "You like it when your dick hurts?"

"Yes," I whined, "Ohmigod, Wes. How much more? I want it all but…."

"Almost there, love. You almost have all of me."

Love? My contemplation of the new endearment was interrupted as he let loose of my nipples and grasped my hips. Jolts of electricity shot through my body. I'd never felt anything like it before.

"Ah, there's the sweet spot. Right there. That's it, isn't it, Grif?" he asked as he pulled back and then inched forward again. And repeated, back and forth. Slowly, over and over, holding my hips tightly in place.

"Jesus, Wes. Fuck, I…God, I feel like I'm gonna lose my fucking mind if you keep doing that. It makes me wanna crawl out of my skin, but in the best possible way. Oh. My. God!"

I felt his hairy thighs finally press against mine—his naked balls rubbing against my jock-covered ones.

"All the way, Wes?"

One of his massive arms moved around my chest, and he pulled me off the tile, until we were both standing, pressing my back to his chest. Holding me to him, with one hand clasped to my hip, he ground in with a bit more intensity and grunted, "All the way, babe. You feel me inside you—my big dick buried in you? You like that?"

Unable to form words, I leaned my head back against his shoulder and offered a jerky nod in response.

I felt his other hand leave my hip and fingers twine around my hair at the top of my head. They tightened slightly, not painful—but with his cock buried in me, his arm wrapped around my chest, his fingers holding my head still—I certainly felt pinned.

"Words, Grif. Tell me how you're feeling."

I swallowed trying to force my throat to work.

"Free...I feel free, Wes. And so full. And wound tight...so tight...like a spring. And I feel you here with me. And yours...I feel like I'm yours, Wes."

And I did; I never felt closer to anyone, more joined with anyone, or more possessed by anyone. I fucking loved all of it!

His cock started moving with purpose—fucking me—impaling me—but his hips were the only part of either of us that moved.

"Wes, Wes, Wes," I chanted through strangled breaths.

Without lessening his grip around my chest, his fingers found a hard nipple and ground down with the same determination his thick cock was showing, and I shouted, "Wes! Ahhhh!"

"Stick a hand down your jock and bring yourself off, Grif," he instructed.

I didn't even think twice. Sliding my hand inside, I stroked Junior. It wasn't gonna take much because, at that very moment, Wes' thighs began slapping against my ass in a fucking I'd never even imagined.

"Wes!" I shouted. "I can't...gonna come...so...good. You feel so good."

His fingers pulled my head to one side and he bit down where my shoulder met my neck demanding, "Come, Grif. Squirt your load with my fat cock fucking you."

We both shuddered and grunted. Junior spurted, and I felt Wes' cock expand even more, as warmth filled my ass.

As we both regained control of our breathing, Wes' grip on my chest and head eased. His hands fluttered over my arms and chest, before coming to rest on my stomach.

I felt what I thought may be him starting to pull out and said, "Wes, please...not yet...can we...stay like this for a while? You, inside me. Is that okay?"

He pulled me in tight against him, and turned us slightly so that the cooling spray of water slid over us.

"Grif," he paused and placed a kiss on my neck, "There's no place I'd rather be. This is absolutely perfect." With another soft kiss, he finished, "And this is just the beginning."

～

FINAL THOUGHTS &
ABOUT THE AUTHOR

THANK YOU for purchasing *Grif's Toy*. If you enjoyed your time with the story, I would really appreciate if you took a few minutes to leave a review on Amazon, Smashwords, ARe, Goodreads, or your favorite platform. It is especially important for me as self-publishing author, who doesn't have the backing of an established press. It makes the book more appealing to potential readers and helps others make an informed decision when considering a purchase. Not to mention I simply love hearing from readers!

Peace,
JLT =)
#pleasurethroughdenial

JOSEPH LANCE TONLET is a born and raised Southern Californian—with a twenty-year stint of living in the Midwest. He loves the laid-back lifestyle of San Diego and considers himself lucky to live where people dream of vacationing.

A lifelong reader of m/m fiction, he began his writing career one night sitting at his MacBook and has never looked back. He writes to bring the characters he dreams about to life.

Find more of his work at: http://www.JosephLanceTonlet.com

ALSO BY JOSEPH LANCE TONLET

TEASE AND DENIAL SERIES
Grif's Toy
Wes' Denial

BROTHERS LAFON SERIES
Brothers LaFon: Crucial Lessons

QILLON'S COVERT
(With coauthor Louis Stevens)

www.Ingramcontent.com/pod-product-compliance
Lightning Source LLC
Chambersburg PA
CBHW020508260626
47156CB00006B/1921